W9-ATK-746

MY 25 '96	DATE DUE	
MY 27 '96		
JE 18 '96		
JY 06 '96		
AG 13 '96		
SE 24 '96		

Shards
of
Empire

SHARDS
OF
EMPIRE

SUSAN SHWARTZ

A TOM DOHERTY ASSOCIATES BOOK
NEW YORK

SHARDS OF EMPIRE

Copyright © 1996 by Susan Shwartz

A Tor Book
Published by Tom Doherty Associates, Inc.
175 Fifth Avenue
New York, NY 10010

Tor Books on the World Wide Web:
http://www.tor.com

Tor® is a registered trademark of Tom Doherty Associates, Inc.

Library of Congress Cataloging-in-Publication Data

Shwartz, Susan.
        Shards of empire / Susan Shwartz. —1st ed.
            p.   c.m.
        "A Tor book."
        ISBN 0-312-85716-0
        1. Byzantine Empire—History—1025-1081—Fiction.
        2. Malazgirt, Battle of, 1071—Fiction. I. Title.
        PS3569.H8S53   1996
        813'.54—dc20   95-41250

First edition: April 1996

Printed in the United States of America

0 9 8 7 6 5 4 3 2 1

To F. Sargent ("Sarge") Cheever, Jr.,
host, diplomat, speaker-to-restaurants, and good friend

Acknowledgments

I'd like to express my gratitude to Harvard University's Center for Byzantine Studies at Dumbarton Oaks not only for its hospitality, but for its forbearance: the sources and texts are all theirs, while any mistakes are mine. Special thanks go to Dr. Harry Turtledove for his generosity in allowing me to work from his unpublished (and handwritten) translation of Attaleiates' account of the battle of Manzikert. I am also indebted to Daniel W. Sifrit for his photographs of southeastern Turkey, taken during Desert Storm, and Lynne Luerding for her generosity in lending me her family's collection of pamphlets and books on Turkey, drawn from their time stationed there. And thanks, too, to Willow Zarlow for the image of the Goddess.

I'd also like to acknowledge the advice of Dr. Toni Cross, head of American Research in Turkey (ARIT), Ankara, Dr. Albert Aurelius Nofi, Professor William Graham, director of Harvard University's Center for Middle Eastern Studies, and Professor Cemal Cefadar, of Harvard University's History Department as well as the Center for Middle Eastern Studies. I would like to thank my guide through Cappadocia, Ali Mert Sunar, for his astonishing tolerance in helping me sketch out the siege of the underground city Derinkuyu.

Thanks too to the usual suspects, including Evangeline Morphos, who is still talking to me, Richard Curtis, who is godfather for Asherah, and Tom Doherty, who saw a book idea in my photos of Cappadocia. Thanks especially to the Geniefolk without whom this book would probably have gotten done sooner, but less enjoyably.

Special thanks to the late Otto Teitler, a builder of bridges between nations, who saw to it that I had a chance to express my gratitude to the (also, and also regrettably, late) President of Turkey, Türgut Ozal, for the hospitality of his country.

SHARDS
OF
EMPIRE

The August sun shot hot arrows, slanting with the lateness of the day. Even this late and this close to the pitiless worn hills of Vaspurakan—Armenia that was, before the Empire of the Romans had won it, lost it, and won it again—the sunlight pierced the Romans and Turks who fought in it, an enemy to both. There would be no moon tonight, and no battle, unless the dead fought those who would rob them.

Slanting rays kindled the dust that rose from the brown earth and stone parched from the long summer. The broad river that glinted the brown of long-tarnished silver as it flowed near Manzikert, with its sheltering black walls and leafy gardens, might have been as far off as the Jordan, or the Golden Horn. Emperor Romanus's loyal—and not so loyal—men would have to pray they would live to see the Horn again. The Jordan was past praying for.

The sun beat down on Leo Ducas's armor. It was as great a torment as the air itself, laden with dust, the reeks of horses, sweat, and blood, and the threat of treachery.

Far forward, the actual fighting was marked by clouds of dust and rising and falling waves of clamor. The cataphracts of Byzantium advanced, paused, thrust forward again. Although this was Leo's first war against the Seljuk Turks, he knew how the riders forced their horses over bodies pierced with arrows.

They had been friends, once, those bodies. Or enemies—demons, some said, although any student of the learned Psellus (even if he had been dismissed) was not foolish enough to call the Seljuks demons. After Romanus's army won the day, they might even be granted some sort of burial.

More arrows buzzed back and forth. Outnumbered the Turks might be, but the Byzantine auxiliaries were no match for archer-cavalry on their deadly little steppe ponies. Slingers and infantry reinforced the Roman army; but it was the heavy cavalry charge of his cataphracts on which the Emperor relied. Again, Romanus hurled his forces forward.

Leo peered through the dust. Surely, that bright glint was the *labarum*, the great banner bearing the *Chi* and the *Rho* with which the Creator of All had inspired Constantine to found a Christian empire. Where the banner flew, the Emperor made his stand, guarded by Varangians with their deadly axes.

Thanks be to God. Leo blessed himself. This army—large as it was, such as it was—was the Empire's best hope for recapturing its eastern provinces. Defeat it or even check it severely, and it was unlikely that this century would see Armenia returned to the orbit of Byzantium by this Emperor or any other.

Leo stirred in his saddle, trying to ease the weight of what felt like several inches of padding, mail, iron klibanion, vambraces, greaves, gauntlet, and mail hood. His cloak was rolled up behind him on his saddle. If he had to wear that, it would probably puff about him like a bellows, if it didn't stifle him: either way, he would melt. He bore the Christian name of an Emperor and great general and a family name that should still have been enriched by the Purple, but he would have traded both for a drink of water or a clean breeze.

Best not think of water. Best not think of his harness galls or how his horse must chafe beneath his weight. Not even to his mother would Leo dare admit it: he was a poor excuse for a cavalry officer. Better the families had let young Alexius come in Leo's place. The boy was some sort of cousin—the ladies of Byzantium kept track of such family intricacies—and he and Leo had been raised almost as brothers. Alexius was only fourteen, eager to fight, and expert past his years; but he had been denied because of the death of his brother Manuel and his mother Anna Dalassena's grief.

Or what passed for it: the noble lady who had married into the powerful Comnenus family was at least as skilled as Leo's own mother in combining family and politics.

Leo's father had protested that he had always found his son an apt pupil, but Psellus, friend to patriarchs, *proedrus* of the Senate, and intimate of Leo's entire family, was very much heeded. So Leo had been sent to carve out the best future available for him. He had no vocation for monastic life; his blood was too good for a youngster's position in the civil service. God forbid he should be a eunuch: he was too old, in any case, to be cut. So, Leo accepted the very generous family donation that paid his way into a most aristocratic regiment indeed.

Psellus was riding higher than ever before in his distinguished career. Though he was a scholar, not a soldier, he was an accepted friend of Leo's uncle the general. Andronicus Ducas hunted with him and always came back looking glassy-eyed: no doubt from the high plane of Psellus's discourse. Friend to Emperors Psellus was now: nevertheless, he had begun life as a man so poor that he had had to leave off scholarship to dower his sister. He liked to point out that there had been patricians in his line. It was not as if he were an upstart, like the Latin Cicero, who had probably been another impossible bore.

Brilliant, Psellus might be: Leo did not trust him. He was too brilliant and too old still to have the place-seeker's supple back. Psellus worshipped his position and things as they were, Leo suspected, more than he worshipped God. For all his vanity, Psellus had shifty eyes. And he hated the Emperor.

Think of the battle, Leo chided himself. The others in the rear guard studied it, rapt. Perhaps the problem was that Leo's gifts for war were as meager as for scholarship. That made him a family disgrace. The Ducas men were warrior-aristocrats: the songs of the *Akritai* always showed them as lords and fighters. There had been Emperors in their line recently, as they *never* wearied of remembering, Autocrators sealed to their Empire, peer of the apostles, vicegerent of Christ on Earth. Once your line was anointed, the chrism could not be washed off, even in blood. Leo was a good enough theologian to see the fallacy in that line of reasoning, but Ducas enough not to relish anyone pointing it out.

Leo had served his uncle at least adequately on this campaign. He thought he had even won himself some respect to match the status borrowed from his name. From the great *strategoi* on down, no one could forget that before Romanus had won the purple in aging Eudocia Dalassena's silken bed, a Ducas had ruled as Emperor of the Romans. Certainly, his uncle Andronicus never did.

What was that cheering? Leo stood in his stirrups. The center was advancing. Someone behind him in the ranks set up a shout. It died quickly, crushed against the immobile, waiting silence of Andronicus Ducas. The *strategos* shot a glare under his helm at Leo. Another reproof: *your cousin Nicholas does not crane forward, does not twitch, does not fret like a horse with a fly on its withers.* But his cousin Nicholas had been practically born to the Tagmata regiments and was in Andronicus's confidence as deep as any of the younger men could be allowed.

With his father, the Caesar John, in exile, Andronicus was not safe for Romanus to leave behind. In that, though perhaps in little else, Leo thought the Autocrator had shown good sense. *Disloyal, Leo; your uncle owes his service to the Emperor of the Romans.*

If only he had not grown up in Constantinople, with its twin obsessions: religion and politics. Surely, a man who had grown up quietly on a small estate might be content to see the Emperor—any Emperor—as worthy of loyalty . . . until the taxes or the levies came due. But families like Leo's made sure that their sons and daughters knew that any action provoked not just consequences, but political repercussions for at least three generations.

Now, at least, Empress Eudocia's chamber was not the only place Romanus Diogenes wielded his lance. Like silk lured by heated amber, the Emperor followed the retreating crescent formation of Seljuk cavalry back into the dusty hills. On his right flank fought an honor roll of the great Themes of the East.

Surrounding the Emperor were the Varangians, loyal to their oath, if not fond of this particular Autocrator; the men of the eastern Themes; and the Tagmata, those military aristocrats with whom Leo might have ridden had he not been Ducas and deemed naturally of his uncle's faction. Flanking them were Pecheneg mercenaries and any other auxiliaries who had not deserted yet. Nicephorus Bryennius had command of them, and he was welcome to it.

The Seljuk army was smaller than that of the Romans, and "they have a eunuch commanding them," muttered a heavy-armored Norman nearby. The *barbaroi* were squeamish that way. Astonishing all the Franks and Normans had not all vanished with Roussel of Bailleul to Khilat or wherever it was the mercenary warlord had gotten himself to.

"That sultan of theirs—Alp Arslan—he doesn't command?"

"He stays in the rear." Someone chuckled. "Dressed all in white for what they call their Sabbath, like a walking target, God grant it."

"Who leads them, then?"

"This one is named Tarang. They say he's a eunuch." Someone snickered. The laugh came out oddly distorted by the nasal of the man's crude helm.

"Eunuch or no, he has more . . ."

"At least ours leads from up front . . ."

All the books said that was bad strategy. Even Bryennius, who was a *strategos* as well as a writer on tactics, and his friend Attaleiates, who had ambitions to be both, frowned at the idea.

"At least, the Empress thinks so. . . ."

"You want the *strategos* to kill you before you get in range of the Turks? I swear, one glare from him would be enough to freeze yours off so you'd call that Turk your brother."

The man subsided into grumblings. Here, where the reserves waited, the battle's ebb and flow sounded like a bloody sea.

Andronicus Ducas did not move. He had been ordered to wait, and wait he would, never showing impatience, hunger, thirst, or much beyond some image of the ideal *strategos* from the works of Nicephorus Phocas or Leo's imperial namesake.

Never mind that he, like Leo and the rest of the army down to the laziest servant, had fasted before Mass and while the Cross was paraded through the camp, and it had been mid-day since they left the camp. Still, Andronicus Ducas, *protovestiarios* and *protoproedros* and a throng of other titles, waited, as still as a mosaic Saint Michael with bitter eyes.

He was an immensely tall and powerful man: son of a banished Caesar, nephew to an Emperor, and Leo's patron as well as his uncle.

Further and further the Seljuks withdrew. They were fast. Let a *strategos* get troops into an area, and they melted away, to turn lightning-fast on their fierce little ponies and strike viciously, with arrows, mace, and sword. That was how Basiliaces had gotten himself captured and why Tarchaniotes had disappeared. Terrible thing for a *strategos* to be taken.

But not as bad as desertion or treachery.

Now Leo could see the first wave of Romans hastening toward the brutal horizon of Vaspurakan's hills. A hot gust of wind teased more dust beneath his helmet and into his eyes: he could almost feel the grit scrape between his eyelids as he narrowed his eyes. Again, the waning sunlight glinted bloody off the *rhomphaia*, the great axes of the Varangians; again, he could see the *labarum*.

Romanus dreamed of making himself another Basil Bulgar-Slayer by recovering the Eastern Themes. Of course, Psellus disparaged Romanus's military skill. He would have found ways of mocking a total triumph, if that would let him arrange things as he wanted, with his choices on the throne and ruling the Senate. Romanus was no fool. He had been an effective *dux* of Sardica under the Emperor Constantine Ducas. Still, he had admitted to plotting to displace his Emperor. That was by no means an unusual sin in Byzantium. It had been his record—as well as his personal charms—that had saved his life and won him Eudocia's favor; and Leo would have wagered his nonexistent patrimony that the *proedros* of the Senate, that Michael Psellus lost sleep, hair, and a goodly portion of his immortal soul raging about it.

"Do they not advance too rapidly?" he ventured to ask his uncle.

Andronicus glared beneath his helmet. "The Autocrator is an experienced general," he said. Which meant everything and nothing. "We have no money to pay our troops. Is it a wonder that we have no scouts or spies worthy of the name, and our *barbaroi* fall away from us?"

That was not an answer.

Use your own judgment, Leo.

Attaleiates, far superior to anything Leo would ever be as a soldier, would have answered the question, "aye." Attaleiates swore—out of earshot of all but aristocratic nonentities such as Leo—that the campaign had a nemesis to face as well as Alp Arslan, the mountain lion of the steppes.

Under the heavy armor, Leo's sweat suddenly cooled, and he shuddered at a memory of his own—the wizened face of an old woman at whom one of the Hetaeria had shouted and urged his horse.

She struggled out of his path, agile, despite her age from years of scrambling on these hills. Even so, he was mounted, and she tired fast. When she saw she could not escape, she turned at bay. Leo had a glimpse of her face: sunken, sunbaked, toothless, but with remains of that cleverness and intensity with which his mother had invariably gained her victories in the maze of Constantinopolitan family life. Rage flickered across her face. Then her eyes went strange, and she shrilled out a curse at Romanus and all who rode with him as traitors and murderers. Leo had started forward.

Had she been seeress as well as refugee from some village plundered by the Franks? Just so Leo's nurse—who had been his mother's before she was his—had ranted when confronted by some domestic tragedy; and a devastated village was far more than broken glass, stolen food, or the death of distant cousins.

When he had seen the crone who resembled his nurse struck down, he had tried to raise her, trying to see how badly hurt she was: not broken too badly to walk, thank God. She had clutched at his arm, pulling him down until he had recoiled, disgusted at the thought that she might snatch a kiss from a fine young soldier—in front of the army, which made the humiliation worse. He had drawn back, but given her what coin he had about him. She babbled at him, drawing his face down to hers again.

"Going to kiss her? Back to your post!" At his uncle's orders, Leo withdrew.

To his surprise, his uncle had later appeared at his side. "Did she speak to you?" the *strategos* asked.

"She babbled something. To tell you the truth, sir, I was more concerned with her breath than her words."

"Forgotten your milk-speech, have you?" So what if he had had an Armenian nurse. So what if his mother had Armenian blood. Neither was reason to taunt him. Leo shrugged. The old woman had mumbled things about treachery, slaying of kin: nothing worthy of mention.

Silently, stirrup to stirrup with his uncle (a mark of favor that won him a glare from his cousin Nicholas), they had ridden back to camp. That night the chaplain had given the army curses, instead of comfort and sacraments.

The campaign was ill-fated. Leo did not need the crone's words or his friend's croaking to tell him that.

"Are you trying to break your neck before you get to fight?" A guardsman slapped Leo's horse. He reined it in, hating the guardsman for exposing him. It was his duty, and duty was all part of Imperial and family service: scorn either, and not only would he not be granted another chance, he would speedily lose his life.

As he might right now if he did not put his mind on his duties. *We are not the* rich *branch of the Ducas family,* he had been told since he was a child. Enough remained to procure him this place in the host: for the rest, he must set himself to imitate his uncle. He had the height. He had the somber, aquiline look of all his family. But there the resemblance ceased. Leo fretted: Andronicus sat like iron behind his kite-shaped shield, waiting for word from the Emperor.

Leo must only obey. He had profited from obedience before. Twice, he had ridden between the reserves and the Emperor himself—the last time when Romanus rejected Alp Arslan's request for a truce. The Seljuks had even been made to prostrate themselves. Granted, the Autocrator had been more arrogant than prudent in the manner of his rejection. Still, he was Emperor of the Romans, while Alp Arslan, this mountain lion, as his name ran, from the steppes of Asia was—what?

Overmatched by a greater force, for one thing, and with the wit to know it. But a lion, even outnumbered, still possessed fangs and claws. Who would have thought that the half-bestial Seljuks could fight so long and so craftily? Maybe it had been that Persian minister standing at Alp Arslan's back. Persians, as any Roman knew, were treacherous as well as fierce.

What was that wave of riders breaking from the Byzantine line? A shout, jeer and cheer mingled, went up from Romans and Turks alike. The half-wild Uz mercenaries broke from the battle lines and trotted over to join their distant kin. Barbarians and not of the Faith, of course: not to be trusted.

Andronicus Ducas' gloved hand gripped his saddle for only a moment. *Romanus hasn't paid them for months, boy*, he muttered. Then his Caesar-mask fell back in place.

Leo swallowed hard, his mouth dry. He longed for light or water. Don't think of the Golden Horn. Don't think of the river, or of Lake Van, or of the black walls and leafy gardens of Manzikert.

The world narrowed to the uplands on which the Emperor fought. With their twisty, dried-up riverbeds, their rocky outcroppings, and their hollow shadows, they were hell-made for ambushes. The hot wind blew up in the hills, drawing a cry like unearthly battle horns from the caves and deep recessed crags there. The sky was darkening. Leo raised an eyebrow. He knew what the authorities would say: the Emperor should not have been in the forefront. The battle should not be lasting this long.

"Prepare yourself, boy," muttered Andronicus Ducas. "I shall have use for you soon."

I am not "boy," Leo thought, swallowing his anger with a lifetime's practice. He could hear his mother's urgent whisper: *He kept you with him? He spoke to you about the campaign and made use of you? Good, good. When can you expect promotion?*

The armies of Rome paid their troops well—when they paid at all—and paid their officers in pounds of gold. But it was not the gold that Leo's family craved, but influence. *You set hand to a weak tool,* he thought. But it was unthinkable to turn in their hands and gash them.

Mists were drifting down now from the bare, rockstrewn hills. It was getting difficult to see as the sun sank lower. It cast long beams over the waiting soldiers, turning his uncle's boots red as if he had waded in blood—which Heaven avert—or traded his own footgear for that of the Basileus and Autocrator. Heaven avert that too, whatever Andronicus and his father, the banished Caesar John, thought.

If the Autocrator were going to summon the reserves, it was time and past time to do so. Even an officer as green as Leo could see that. But it was no part of his duty to urge his uncle forward. Look at how his cousin waited, motionless, as obedient to command as any Spartan. The thought of them and how they fell, obedient to command—another bad omen, which Heaven avert. Still, if the reserves were to be of help, they must be summoned soon.

God, he was thirsty.

"Nephew." Now came the summons he had been preparing for all this long campaign. Andronicus barely troubled to raise his voice. "Go, ask the Autocrator how we may serve him." The *strategos* pleased himself with his irony. It was his nature: iron and irony forged together.

The order came as almost as blessed a relief as the water Leo craved.

His uncle sent *him*, not cousin Nicholas for all his experience, he exulted. Then he set himself to reach the Autocrator with a whole skin and a live horse.

Leo dodged over bodies and through the lines until he reached the Emperor, flanked by dour Varangians. Even now, Romanus looked like a fine figure of a fighting man. He wore the dress of a common soldier—except for the crimson boots of the Basileus. Tired as he must be, he sat his horse as if the day—and he—were fresh. Basil Bulgar-Slayer must have looked like such a one.

Did he regret not accepting Alp Arslan's terms? Had the Seljuk submitted, the Emperor might thereby have secured the turbulent eastern boundary of the Empire—then withdrawn, however, and awaited future onslaughts with diminished troops and funds. But he had not; and now it was growing late.

Under his helm, the Emperor's eyes narrowed. He would signal a retreat—Leo would have wagered any patrimony he might ever have on that. Not a rout, of course: even stripped of the Uzes, even with the casualties it had taken, the army could withdraw to its camp, regroup, then return the next day to crush the Seljuks for once and for all. If his strokes were sure enough, Romanus could win back Vaspurakan and ride home to winter securely in Constantinople and groom one of his own two sons for the Purple.

Romanus signaled Leo forward. In this moment, the Emperor saw him not as the kin of his enemy, but as a tool to accomplish a task he badly needed done.

"Tell the *strategos* to bring his troops forward," he ordered. How Andronicus would glare to hear his dignities handled thus baldly.

The Varangians closed in to guard the Emperor. Not *their* emperor, perhaps, but they would be loyal to their oaths. Their faces were sweaty. Their axes shone. And Leo wondered, not for the first time, if it were really true that some of the northerners actually did turn into bears and wolves in the madness of battle.

A wave of Seljuks rode forward. Those little ponies that wouldn't have lasted a moment against a charge from cataphracts on level ground. One of the biggest, his harness brown with dried blood, barked an order. The men raised shields against a deadly, whistling storm of arrows, then braced for a second volley.

Retreat did not necessarily mean defeat, any more than a feint with a blade meant that your next strike might not draw blood.

The camp was unprotected. Every man who had not deserted—yet—was in the field, without provisions, and probably exhausted. It was already growing dark, and the Roman armies had found no core of resistance to overwhelm. Help must come swiftly if it were to be help at all and retreat were not to become rout.

"Ride!" Leo waved away offers of companion guards he could see his Emperor needed. Hunched beneath his shield, he rode back toward the reserves, and his uncle, masked in dust, his helm, and his hatreds.

He heard horns on the wind: the retreat already? Andronicus was an experienced *strategos;* he could anticipate his Emperor's will and need. *Faster, Leo. Perhaps you can snatch a remount before you ride into battle.* Fear and hope churned in his belly.

His uncle broke from his immobility. Whatever else today meant, it was victory for the Ducas. This was, Leo knew, the moment he had awaited, when the Emperor of the Romans must acknowledge that his enemy had saved the day. He even rode a space away from the carefully arrayed battle lines, as if honoring his nephew's return.

Then, even as Leo saluted, his uncle's face changed. His mouth went grim, and his eyes widened in horror.

Andronicus lunged forward in his saddle. He had his hands on Leo's shoulders, he was shaking him as if he had announced the coming of the Beast of the Apocalypse, and he was screaming, "Tell me it isn't so! He's dead, you say? You say the Emperor is dead?"

The sun struck Andronicus's helm, leaving half his face in ruddy shadow. Nevertheless, on it, Leo saw a small, quick smile of victory.

2

Leo reeled. He might have fallen himself had it not been for Andronicus Ducas' hands, which held him upright even as they shook him till his brains rattled.

Had the sunlight boiled Andronicus's brains under his helm? Or had Leo mistaken the smile he saw?

Again, the *strategos* was shouting. "You say, you saw him fall?"

"Sir . . . uncle, *no!*" Leo cried. "The Autocrator is well, unwounded, but he says . . ."

It was too late to tell his uncle what the Autocrator had said. They both knew it. Andronicus had always known it.

It wasn't whispers he heard now in the ranks, but dismayed shouts. The Emperor was dead. Leo flung a desperate glance over his shoulder. He could not see the *labarum*. Perhaps it already had been furled for retreat. *In this sign, you will conquer?* Not today.

Rage: the armies were still unpaid. With the Emperor dead, who knew whenever they might expect their coin? Still, they'd be expected to soldier on until the Turks built pillars out of their poor, bleeding skulls.

Demands: let them retreat the way the Normans and others had done—*they had some use for their skulls, which were still firmly attached to their necks!*—while they still could.

In a moment, there would be mutiny and panic. And the general's officers did nothing to quell it.

How many of them had already been bought?

Andronicus turned his horse to face his troops. He was a patrician, a general, the son of a Caesar of the Romans. Like the Emperor, Andronicus had arrived at the *kairos*, the critical moment when he *must* do something or lose all.

Leo had been his uncle's cat's-paw: the cousin too inexperienced, too foolish, to count as a player in this game of family treachery. The toothless, angry face of the old woman Leo had rescued flickered across his consciousness, then altered into the polished elegance of his mother's visage. *Sweet Bearer of God, had she known she sent him to betrayal? Not* her *too!*

This was double treachery: family as well as politics. Why had the family turned on him? Had Leo not been humble enough, malleable enough, apt enough? Had he not swallowed every snub, obedient to his family's commands?

No, Leo told himself, the treachery was now threefold, a damnable, veritable Trinity of betrayal upon the body of the man who had been *made* Emperor with prayers and chrism in the Church of the Holy Wisdom itself. What Andronicus did was not only betrayal but blasphemy; and now it grew worse. So far from advancing to let the Emperor's body be recovered and borne home in dignity—assuming he was dead, which Leo doubted—Andronicus was actually ordering his army to retire from the field.

The Emperor needed the reserves; the Turks were advancing, yelping in joy and shooting as they rode; and Andronicus Ducas snatched away the troops that might mean victory, or at least life, for Romans who had fought all day.

The reserves' horns wailed like the last trump of the damned before the gates of hell clang shut at the end of time.

The Armenian troops slipped away into the twilight. They would slink into the shadowy hills where they knew every cave, avoiding the Byzantines whom they hated almost as much as they hated the Seljuks who watched—oh God, there must be ten thousand of the deadly mounted archers watching from the heights.

A dark mass of troops broke from the Autocrator's depleted forces. The Cappadocians deserted, men, perhaps, from Romanus's own estates turning on a lord they had followed lifelong. Another betrayal. What was it that had snapped their loyalty? One tax or one troop levy too many—too late to ask that now. None of them would ever see their homes again.

Leo glared at his uncle. He had always feared Andronicus: feared his *well, he may not make* much *of a warrior, but I do my best with what I have to work with* to his mother as much as her elegant disappointment. To think, he had spent all those years fearing a traitor!

He had feared two traitors. Now he remembered where he had seen Andronicus's secretive, smug look before—on Psellus. Did the scholar play such a deep game that he used generals and Emperors as pieces on his board? Leo was, of course, no scholar, but he had ears: had heard Psellus murmur to himself. Declensions, he had thought when he was a boy; when he was a very young man, he had thought it was sermons. And the glazed eyes of his chosen students—was that boredom (to think that Psellus was reputed to be such a spellbinding orator!), or was it . . .

No time to wonder now. Leo realized he was fighting for not just his life, but his immortal soul.

"Are you a lovesick girl or a monk contemplating the True Cross?" His uncle's contempt had always compelled his obedience. Andronicus seized the bridle of Leo's horse and sawed its head around. "Move!"

"The Emperor . . ." Leo protested. "He needs our help."

Like the half-wit his family clearly thought him, Leo gestured toward the uplands. The army dwindled like a plague-ridden city, and the Seljuks began to descend to snatch this treasure of an unexpected victory that Andronicus had just tossed into their bloody hands.

"The Emperor is dead, boy. Did you take a blow on your head when he fell?"

Andronicus leaned forward, his dark eyes spearing at Leo's will.

Obey. Submit. After all, he had always done so before. He followed the orders of his uncle, who was also his *strategos*, he could say. It would be easy enough.

And what an opportunity for the family, if men of the Ducas line brought home the army even after the Emperor died. Even Leo would earn praise: a young man of unimpeachable honor, who brought back word of the Emperor's death, yet had to be compelled to retreat. Even his mother might be content with the reward from such a reputation.

But it would be a lie.

"You can't . . ." Leo gasped.

"Can't *what*, boy?" His new enemy whirled on him like a maddened wolf. He might die in the next moment, before ever he drew sword today against the Turks. Or he might be taken in charge by his uncle and forced to play another role: madman and coward, the family disgrace, to be blamed and locked away in some filthy island monastery or hermit's cave where his lungs or his mind would soon rot.

In either case, Psellus would glide through the corridors of power, even into the palace, sleek and satisfied. Things were as he would have them; and he would keep them that way.

For his country's sake, Leo must not be used. For his soul's sake, he dare not. *Guide me, command me!* he howled soundlessly upward. *I lift up mine eyes unto the hills, from whence cometh my help.* The hills were boiling with Turks on those disastrously sure-footed ponies, and they shot as they rode. The shadows were growing longer. And more and more men were slipping away from the Emperor—those who had not already died.

How could God permit this?

No help would come from the hills—just wave upon wave of enemies who probably would fall quarreling first about whether to spit the Rhomaioi or thank whatever vile gods they served. A storm of arrows whined overhead, and it was only by the mercy of the Theotokos, the blessed bearer of God, that he and his horse were not feathered.

Or had she, too, turned away her gaze in despair after a man had invoked her to beg the Emperor's mercy and been denied?

Tell me what to do, he prayed in desperation. *Tell me.*

A shaft of light pierced through the clouds shrouding the now-deadly horizon. It brightened as if sunset were becoming dawn. Leo stared at it. Time slowed as the shaft of light changed form: a *Chi* superimposed on the letter *Rho. Christ rules.*

Leo shut his eyes briefly in thanks. His course was clear, even if the time he could steer it would be only a few pain-filled hours.

"Judas!" he shouted at Andronicus Ducas. "You damned Judas in purple. I'm not your *'boy'!*"

He backed his horse away from his uncle. He was no match for the elder man in battle, unless heaven defended the right. But if Andronicus did not strike him down, he knew what he would do. Like Constantine, Leo would conquer, though his kingdom would not be of this earth. He hoped that the first Christian emperor would look down from bliss and see how one Leo Ducas had not abandoned this Autocrator.

Andronicus, his sword out, lunged at Leo. Just in time, he twisted his horse's head around. Anger and fear made him cruel to the poor beast, but probably saved their lives for a few ignoble moments more.

He pressed with his knees and shouted. His horse stretched out to run toward the comfort of a herd—the mounts of the Emperor and his officers. He knew he would not be followed. Why would Andronicus—may Leo's tongue wither if ever he called him "uncle" again—waste more time upon a family renegade when he had an emperor to betray and an empire to win?

Uphill he rode, past dark caves that yawned like entrances to the Pit or temptations to refuge, over so many bodies that his horse no longer shied at them. The darkening land seemed to tremble.

Retreat had turned into rout, each man seeking safety in flight as the enemy chased them. Leo rode past heaps of bodies, past dark clots of fleeing men who had been loyal soldiers of the Empire only that morning. Eyes and mouths and open wounds glistened, and winds and arrows whined in the hills. And above all other sounds rose the shouts of panicked men who knew that all Rome was lost and their lives with it.

One of the last Cappadocians rode at him. He was screaming, screaming, froth coming from his mouth as well as his horse's as they fled in panic. Seeing Leo, the fellow—an officer once and most likely accounted brave—struck with his mace as if he expected Leo single-handedly to arrest him. The blow cost Leo his helmet and might have cost him his brains had he not swerved in time. Damn. He would need a helmet where he was going.

Do you truly think you will live long enough to use it, fool?

Hunched beneath his shield, Leo rode on. The salt of his sweat stung where the mace had grazed his brow. He would have retched from the blow, let alone the stinks of blood and bowels on the field, but this was no time to be any weaker than he already was.

I'm coming! Over and over, he screamed it. Let the Turks hear. Let the others hear. One Ducas, at least, was no traitor.

Some trick of the wind and the light showed him the standard of the Emperor of the Romans. For a moment, it blew, tatters of gold and silk as brave and as foredoomed as the stand that the Emperor and his personal guard had made. The Varangians stood like cliffs around the Emperor's horse. They might neither like nor respect Romanus, but they had given their pledge, and they would die for him. Their faces were set, and their eyes wild. One hailed Leo with a swing of his axe, then, on the downswing, cut the arm from a rider who ventured too close.

The last shafts of light from the sunset splattered onto that axe and fragmented like light on the mosaics in Hagia Sophia where the Pantocrator sat in majesty. The Emperor ruled on earth, but there was One, Three in One, higher than he, Who watched over all and would punish treachery. After all, life was short and bitter. But judgment came quickly, and the hereafter stretched out for eternity.

Tears clouded Leo's sight, and he almost sagged with relief. He was no child to expect the Emperor's presence to save him, when Romanus could not save his own life or his Empire. But at least, Leo would die vindicated, revealed as no traitor before God.

That is, if he could reach the Emperor's side before Turks or traitors cut him down.

Leo's horse lowered his head. Poor beast was tired. Well enough: they would all be sleeping soon.

"Ducas, go back to your own!" a cavalry officer screamed at him. "Go back!"

"I *am* with my own," Leo shouted back.

His sword was out; he would cut a path with the flat of it if he had to.

"Came back to die with us? You ass . . ." the man's voice choked as an arrow took him in the throat. He gurgled; blood poured from his mouth; and he fell from his saddle.

Leo rode over him.

Up ahead, the Varangians had encircled the Emperor. Their axes rose and fell, almost as if they chopped wood in those faraway lands they would never see again now. Leo could even see the Emperor, no splendor, no panoply about him now, fighting as fiercely as any of the big, blond guards.

One of them saw him and pointed.

"*Nobiscum!*" he shouted. Would the man understand? "The Emperor! For Miklagard!" If he used their word for Constantine's jeopardized city, maybe they would . . .

His horse screamed and crashed down, an arrow in its chest. In time,

Leo kicked free of the stirrups and leapt free, almost into the arms of some of the guardsmen, who dashed out to draw him to—he could not call it safety.

Someone was swearing without cease or originality about the folly of unlicked cubs who rode *toward* danger and had not even the excuse of being Varangian. Leo felt the breath of the man who reached him first gust against his ear, felt himself steadied against the immense man. There was no safety, yet there was reassurance in being where he had fought to be, in the circle of loyal men defending their emperor.

To his astonishment, the man began to *sing*.

Leo struck out at a Turk who had aimed a swordslash at them.

"Good stroke, boy!"

Abruptly, he was furious. "I am not *boy!*"

"No," said the Varangian in guttural Greek, "you are a loyal man. Like those at Maldon, when Beorhtwald the faithful swore 'Let our spirits be higher, our hearts more keen; our courage the more as our might dwindles.'"

"Save your breath!" bellowed another Varangian. He sluiced blood off his axe. "Were you struck on your head at Hastings?"

The big man, Leo's rescuer, laughed. "*Ic sceal nat fleon fotes trym ac sceal furðyer gan.* I vow not to retreat the space of a foot, but to go on further. Like this, you sneaking bastards!"

He thrust himself forward, closer to the Emperor, taking Leo with him.

"Go to your own!" one of the nobles shouted at him. He was going to get mortally tired of that taunt, if he weren't mortally wounded first.

"I *am* with my own," he snapped, testing the muscles of his neck. He saluted the Emperor, then looked around, a worker awaiting the command to begin his bloody work.

A hand on his shoulder stopped him.

It was Romanus himself, leaning down from his horse.

"I shouldn't let you stay," said the Emperor. "I have a son with your name, a boy I won't see again. But your horse is down, and I've no way of getting you out safe."

"I," not the "We" of Empire.

"We all owe God a death, sir," Leo said. Greatly daring, he twisted his neck and tried to kiss the Autocrator's filthy glove.

"Don't be a fool, boy," said the Emperor. The word did not sting, coming from him.

A litany of defeats rang in Leo's head; Cannae; Carrhae; the legions in the West; Adrianople itself, when an Emperor was taken captive.

God grant that this one die before that happened again, and God forgive Leo for praying thus—when he knew he would not have the
courage to ensure it. Oh God, he was tired.

It would be better to die and abide Judgment than to live as what
his family would call him: fool, dreamer, too weak even for the politics
in a monastery. Compared with that, to be Romanus's "fool" was an accolade.

A Varangian howled, dropped his axe, and lunged forward, sometimes running on two legs, sometimes dropping to all fours. He hurled
himself at a mounted Turk whose splendid silk coat was scarcely
sweated and brought man and horse down. It took an entire band of
horsemen to pull him off his prey and cut his head off. When a man
held it up in triumph, its teeth were bloody.

"*Berserkrgang*," a man nearby said. And laughed.

"We have enough fools around here," said the Emperor. His face
was set with despair that had become a form of resolve. "And the
biggest one—well, there's no fool like the man who forgets what he's
learned."

"He is *Ducas!*" another officer put in.

"A Ducas' death answers for a Ducas' shame," said Romanus. "He
came back here to join us. That makes him my son or my brother—
like the rest of you. Now, do we fight, or gossip until they cut us down?"

Sweet Mother of God, Imperial favor here at the end of all things.
Leo could have laughed or wept, if either would not have spoiled his
sight of his Emperor, bloodied, filthy with a day's fighting, the knowledge of certain defeat hollowing his cheeks until he had the look of an
ancient tomb sculpture. But his hand was on Leo's shoulder, and
strength seemed to flow down into him and back up into the man he
served until his smile burst through the fear of impending death.

He was the Emperor's son. He even had the same name as the Emperor's son by birth. They were all the Emperor's sons or brothers.

Ah, *that* made the Varangians roar.

"Brave fellows!" cried Romanus. "Let's do it your way. Why wait
for the Turks to come to us? Let's take our war to them and make them
pay for it!"

Leo asked permission with a glance. Slinging his shield, he took
hold of the Emperor's bridle. His weight, added to the horse's, ought
to give them some advantage.

For a very little while.

The Emperor nodded. *Now!*

Leo grasped his sword more firmly. They pushed forward, testing the

Turks, attacking first with the deliberation of fighting professionals, and then with an abandoned glee.

"*NOBISCUM!*" they shouted. The air burned in Leo's lungs from the weight of his armor as he ran. His temples throbbed and a queer red mist seemed to haze the night, as if a ring shone around the moon. There *was* no moon. He must be seeing things. Well enough, as long as one of the things he saw was dead Turks.

Around them, the Varangians bellowed out their warcries, and even the Turks' black eyes filled with the light of battle against a foe that proved worthier than they had dreamed.

Shouts rose all over the field of Manzikert. Leo's heart rose and he begged for a miracle. Surely, this Emperor's fighting heart would put heart into what remained of the armies, and they would rally, rally and advance and drive the Turks back from Vaspurakan and the bounds of the Empire.

He screamed with a kind of mad delight and forced his now-wavering legs forward, his hand tugging at the bridle of the Emperor's mount.

The horse's head plunged down upon his shoulder. Romanus sprang free, the rags of the clothing he had put on that morning flying about him. Leo could see the knowledge in his Emperor's eyes. There would be no rally. No miracle. Hopes like that were for boys.

Romanus shouted for his guard and those of the *archontes* remaining loyal—and alive—to re-form. There were far fewer of both.

Hoofbeats raced across the uplands as the Turks broke into wings the size of hunting parties—parties, however, to hunt Romans, not wild beasts. More closed in on the center of what had once been the Army of the Romans. He could hear them gabbling, see them pointing behind their deadly bows.

They had recognized the Emperor.

Someone brought up the *labarum*. Romanus muttered what was probably a twin to the prayer on Leo's tongue. With one hand, he grasped the holy banner's tattered folds and brought it to his cracked and bleeding lips, then let it fall. Blood spurted across it from a terrible wound in Romanus's hand. His face whitened, and Leo darted in to support him.

"*Enough,*" said the Emperor. "Now we make an end."

There were more Seljuks on the field than there were demons in Hell. And they had all gathered round. The red mist shone in Leo's eyes; he could not see the full count of his enemies. But that was as well: the hosts of Hell were innumerable.

"Into thy hands . . ." he breathed.

He could hear a buzzing in his ears—not just his blood, but words, wishing him to falter, reminding him of his own unworthiness, his incapacity. He was incapable, all right—incapable of heeding the words of a man who had meant him no good, who had tested him and found him incapable of being twisted to his use. Traitors did that, aye, and mages. Hard to think of that prim old scholar as a mage, so like the Persians he detested, but Leo had indeed learned *some* logic; and when you eliminated all that was impossible, what you had left might well prove true.

An arrow stuck in the fleshy part of his arm where he had it around his Emperor. One less wound for Romanus: well enough. It was not as if he could feel it, or anything else, except overmastering weariness. Perhaps it would kill him before the Turks: his heart would just give out.

Another footstep. Forward. Damn you, forward! He met a Varangian's eyes, saw their bleak-sea color warm into praise and won strength enough for another step.

The haze was very bright now. If this were a harbor, they would be calling out to passing ships, lest they crash together and be overwhelmed. The trampled earth felt curiously insubstantial, as if it, too, could not be relied upon.

A mounted man tore through the mist that had so beclouded Leo's consciousness, his mace swinging down.

Not you again! Leo had time to think before the mace all but missed the side of his head. A glancing blow, or his brains would have bespattered his Emperor. Bad enough to have been hit once, let alone twice in what was close enough to the same spot to make no difference.

But no, that first blow had been Roman traitor striking at loyal man. This, however, was enemy against enemy . . .

He flung up his blade in hopeless defense. He could feel his eyes rolling back in his head, losing focus as he stared up at the sky, seeking—what? Hope? Consolation? An axe crashed down nearby upon metal, and sparks flew up. The light seemed to shift, to form the letters *Chi* and *Rho*. But Leo had not conquered. He had failed. The Emperor had failed. Their world was surely ending, and if the dead did not rise, it was only because there were so many slain that not even Christ the Redeemer Who would harry Hell could bring them back to life.

Leo cried out in despair. He reeled and staggered, lurching hard against Romanus. Wounded, the emperor could not sustain him: he *whined* as Leo fell—pain and shock and apology, even as he fought on.

That sound drained Leo of the last of his strength. He toppled at Romanus's crimson boots, a useless prostration before a doomed Emperor. The fog of battle wrapped him and swept him out into blackness.

*F*ace up, eyes open to the stars, Leo drifted through the long night of defeat like a sailor too newly dead to sink.

Not dead, then. Not yet. The Turks had won the day and the field. Whether or not he wore chains now or later, he and anyone left out here alive was a captive—for however long they lived. He flinched, remembering the last intolerable sight: Turks closing in on his Emperor. Romanus had fought until he could no longer hold a sword.

Leo had no feeling in one arm—where *was* his arm? Where were his legs? In a panic, he tried to kick to see if he could even move. Someone groaned. Leo was sorry he had tried.

He turned his head—a wave of dizzy nausea and a wet, hot rush he identified with appalled disgust as his own blood pouring across his brow overcame him.

Wait. Moving more cautiously, this time, he managed to shift his head. The dizziness returned, bearable this time. Now, he saw the cause of his arm's numbness: a trooper lay across it, a dead Varangian atop him.

Dear Bearer of God, which one of all those corpses might be the Emperor?

The knowledge that he lay in a tangle of flesh, unable to tell the quick from the dead, panicked him. Leo thrashed his other arm and both legs to free himself. The dizziness returned in a rush of blood and darkness.

After a long while, the stars came back. Careful even of so small a movement, Leo blinked his eyes clear of clotted blood. He lay still: too spent to move; too afraid.

At least I can say, I lie like an Emperor, he thought. He would be buried like one too—or left to lie unburied. And that would have to be glory enough.

Would anyone ever see or know? *Thou conquerest, Psellus!*

But Psellus was not Emperor, but the servant who manipulated their rise and fall, and who protected his position by . . . what *had* Psellus learned in those long years of scholarship; and why had he withdrawn from the monastery where he had enrolled?

Leo chuckled bitterly. It hurt his head and turned too quickly into a cackle too near hysteria for his liking. He had no desire for Turks or Armenians or other robbers to find him while he yet lived. A pity the night was no colder.

The Varangians, he knew from their songs, prized noble deaths. Surely, they were all dead. He would follow them.

A few weak tears coursed unwilled down his face. Certainly, he was dying. Would he weep, otherwise? It was proper to weep at the fall of Empire, more proper still to weep for his sins.

Since he was dying, perhaps he ought to pray.

Kyrie eleison. Christe Eleison.

Help.

But there was no mercy anywhere.

Faces floated across the moonless sky: Andronicus Ducas, that Judas, for all he looked like such a prince. The Emperor's face, trusting Leo, welcoming him, even, but regretting his presence on the field since that meant another death. The Varangians, laughing as they fought, grinning in the face of death.

He had better tend his soul.

"I am heartily sorry I have offended Thee . . ." Leo mumbled. Those were the right words, the abject words. But they were not the words that Leo wanted. More like: *Why have You turned against us? What have we done?*

Eloi, Eloi, lama sabachthani? Christ's lament on the cross: My father, why hast Thou forsaken me? See, he had an authority for his despair.

Curse God and die. Well, the Jews had not done that, and there were still Jews in Constantinople and scattered throughout the Empire, not that it made any sense to think about them right now. His head whirled, and then such sense as he had returned to him.

Oh, but it does, it does. It did make sense. Now, the Greeks would be strangers in a strange land that had once been their empire. Had they oppressed Vaspurakan? They had been punished. The Christians of Byzantium would face an even more cruel fate, a Babylonian captivity in their own land.

How shall we sing the Lord's song in a strange land?

Could they do less, at the last, than the Jews they were taught to scorn?

Pain tightened like a torturer's vise across Leo's temples. He turned his head and vomited.

If the *Rhomaioi* had won the day, after prayers, medical assistants and burial details would have emerged from the camp. In that case, Leo could have counted on being found. But here, the Turks had won the day. The riders of Alp Arslan would rove the battlefield. Perhaps they would give him the mercy-stroke.

Thieves would be slinking onto the field too. Robbers laired in the caves in these hills. The poor Armenians of the villages, poorer now that battles had floundered and bled back and forth across their fields, would come out looking for coin. Even a runaway troop or so might search for whatever they could bear away: horses not too badly wounded to save, usable harness; plundering from the dead and the not yet dead.

No matter how much blood and filth covered him, they would find the Emperor. They would find Leo, too. Hearing of how he fell and where he lay, his mother would finally have to admit that he had done something right. But she was no Spartan: she was a Greek of Constantinople. She was as likely to call him a traitor and a fool for going against Family.

He pressed his head against the mucky earth, which trembled beneath him as if it, too, had been assailed. The arch of sky shivered. *As above, so below*, he thought, wondering if fever had set in to teach him such words. They seemed right. The clouds seemed to shift, forming plumes of smoke rising above pallid mountains, and to shift again, shaping the very form of the land. Crafting an aspect of the Empire— as fragile as clouds, as swift now to pass away in the storms sure now to follow, sweeping its people before it into exile.

The sky held it all, from the weathered teeth of the hills of Vaspurakan to the sanctified caves of Cappadocia, where perhaps the monks praying within the living rock itself might pray for a lost emperor, to the ransacked fields of the Anatolikon theme. Under the skull-like gaze of ancient fortresses looming over them on cliffs, soldiers fought back and forth over the land, for it was an ancient one. Some survived to build, abandoning the others, bodies and blood, to lie in those fields, to become part of the land. Hittites, Midas, Alexander, Rome and Constantine's New Rome; and now, would the Turks replace them, only to have, in generations to come, their blood and bones overlay all the others in these ancient, battered fields?

Wave after wave of invaders had flowed over the land in a bloody tide. It was old in the time of Christ, older than Troy. It was even old when Byzantium rose upon the Golden Horn, long before Constantine left the West to found a City of God on Byzas's foundations. The land had survived, though people had come and gone, leaving their treasures, their ruined houses, their bones, and, for all Leo knew, all their false gods. Doubtless, the land would survive this new onslaught of victors;

and, in generations to come, farmers would lift from their fields hacked bones and battered weapons and wonder what manner of men left *these*. It was a land built as much *of* blood and bones as it was built *on* them.

A wail sounded across the battlefield. Leo twisted his head so quickly that blood welled anew. *Thy brother's blood calls out to heaven. . . .* Was that the cry, Abel's blood appealing to God? Hardly: there were no innocents here.

Again, that heart-stopping wail. Leo almost laughed. It was one of the cats, the countless thousand cats that prowled this land each night as the sun slept. Did they follow their masters out onto the field? They were sunlike themselves, the cats around Lake Van, white and gold, with golden eyes. They had no place on a field of battle.

No more than you. Or anyone else. Now, that thought really made Leo laugh. What choice had he? What choice had he ever had? The time was coming when no one—man, woman, child, or the smallest beast—would have such a choice. And he worried about a small and yowling cat? Absurd. Better it slink back to its back streets, or, if it were very fortunate, to a child that cherished it.

He would never have children now, Leo thought. The idea of fatherhood had never moved him: now, it drew tears from his eyes. But his sons and daughters would only have been pawns in the game, as he was.

With an effort, he thrust himself back into his unquiet dream, staring eyes open at the indigo sky in which the stars gleamed like the tesserae in a church's apse.

After awhile, the blue formed into folds, rustling across the maimed land as if they were the cloak of some searcher in no particular fear or hurry. Again, the cry of the hunting cat, louder now. Nearer.

The cat sounded disturbed; and that was not the only noise that troubled the field of dead and dying. Wheels, as of some chariot; and Leo didn't think that the Turks used such things. Who would drive in a chariot over a bloody field? Nothing from this time or place. He shuddered. Here, at a bloody crisis, the bones that underlay this field might well be feared; they might *rise* to inspect their new brethren.

And he had not strength now to raise his hand and ward himself against such restless, warring spirits.

The chariot wheels rumbled nearer and nearer. The cat's cry rang out again. In a human voice, that would be joy. Leo bit his lip until more blood ran against a scream.

Something wet touched his face. This time, he did scream, only to find himself soothed. He felt as if he lay in noon light. With a moan, he shut his eyes. He could not bear to look, not from the too-bright light, but at the eyes that saw him now, defeated and debased.

What felt like a gentle hand wiped the filth, the blood, and the tears of fury and defeat from his mouth, then lingered on his brow. He remembered such tending from his childhood, before he grew too old for a nurse and he had turned out such a disappointment that he had been sent away with an uncle who betrayed him.

The hand pressed on his brow as if it sensed the anguish of that thought. *Well, it was true!* he insisted. The pressure intensified. The hand warmed, easing some of the inner hurt.

Why did it comfort him and not the Emperor?

Perhaps Romanus, too, felt its compassion. Or perhaps it was a sign. A private sign from God, just for Leo Ducas? He managed a chuckle and sensed a pat, as if of approval, upon his brow, which no longer felt quite so fevered.

Show me your face, he begged silently. Show me. For an instant, the stars shivered and the sky seemed to *change*. He had an impression of compassionate dark eyes, a gentle mouth held taut by courage, and a veil the color of a moonless night being drawn across them.

Then fingers slipped down over his eyelids as if closing them before weighting them with coins.

Benediction.

Rest.

He heard chariot wheels he surely must have imagined rumble away into the distance.

Silence.

Leo woke to light prying at his eyes. Not noon, then. And the full heat of the day had not yet begun to beat down. He opened his eyes and came immediately under attack. His armor cut into him like daggers. He did not know how he would further disgrace himself first—by vomiting again or by soiling himself like an old man turned child a second time.

The battlefield came to obscene life—the hum and buzzing of fat-fed insects and the cries of the wounded, fevered, and dying. The land stank of blood and ordure and a more subtle fog of treachery and hate. A horse not yet fortunate enough to die whickered at a footstep, then screamed, or would have screamed if it had more sense. Leo's eyes filled with tears. *His* horse had died swiftly.

Pleas for water, for God, God's mother, or men's own mothers, mercifully unable to see the human tatters of the flesh they had borne and tended, went up, punctuated by the occasional scream as someone shifted, or a sobbing whimper. One hoarse, cracked voice sang a child-hood song with the simplicity of delirium. It started to tease Leo's consciousness away from the field with its intolerable freight of misery, but he reeled it back in.

No. You live. Yet. See what you can do for your Emperor. See if he lives. He cannot be far away.

Hesitantly, he attempted to rise.

Hoofbeats pounded through the earth, the vibration nearly piercing his temples. The dying singer's voice grew weaker: he too was afraid for such short life as might remain to him.

Leo froze where he lay. Those were not the hoofbeats of such a horse as he had ridden, but of the agile mounts of the steppe archers. The Turks surveyed the field of which they were masters, and they laughed and shouted as they rode.

God send that they did not take it into their heads to shoot a triumphant volley of arrows into their vanquished enemies.

So, you still wish to live, Leo?

Inconceivable as it seemed, he did. Surviving one battle, it also seemed, made him a wiser man than he had been just the day before, when he was still a Ducas, still his uncle's loyal man, and his uncle had not been a traitor.

The thin, delirious song started up again. Pity, as well as fear, made Leo's eyes run, and he fought it: dead men did not weep. He remembered that song from when he was a child playing in the inmost courtyards of their fortress of a house prestigiously close to the Imperial Palace for all its shabbiness, back when the world was innocent and no shadow of blame or fear touched him or anyone he knew.

The Turks turned. One of them pointed to the singing man and cried out something. All of the other men laughed. The first man gestured at the others, who spread their hands out or reached for bows. Except for one, who shook his head and turned away. The first man shrugged, then spoke. His words were scornful, but a definite command. Drawing his bow, he laid arrow to it and shot. The song ceased.

Bile filled Leo's mouth. All he would have to do was scream, and an arrow would find him. Like the arrows of Apollo, swift to their mark—though if a Turk resembled Apollo, Leo had yet to see it.

Wait, then. They will think you are dead. You bear no arms particularly worth the having, compared with what other pickings they can find here. Wait, and under cover of darkness, creep away.

For his life's sake, he listened. Gradually, he realized: he could pick out words from the Seljuk's conversation, enough like that of the mercenaries he had soldiered with . . . And what good was that? Should he try to bargain his way to freedom?

No, but he might learn something. Learn something and slip away until he found a general, Bryennius, perhaps, or an officer like Attaleiates, whom he still trusted, and tell them, for whatever good that would do a renegade Ducas. It might profit him not at all, but if it saved lives for the Empire, even at the cost of his, he would count it a job well done.

Back and forth across the field the Turks rode. Officers, mostly, though now Leo realized that the fourth man, the one who had shrugged as if reluctant to fire at the delirious soldier, was a different type of person altogether. For one thing, he was a *gulam*, one of the slave-soldiers who bore arms, yet held himself in subjection to a noble. Leo had heard of the mamluks, as had all the army; and he had a healthy fear of them. So, this was a slave-soldier: unusual, if he were capable of judgment and moderation, then?

But no, judging from the laughter. This man—Kemal—as his scoffing comrades called him, was a reluctant companion of theirs. His master had tried to give him to the vizier, but he had been such a wretched creature that the minister had refused.

"What good are you?" jeered one of the Turks. "What would you do? Would you bring us the Emperor of the Romans as prisoner?"

Another shout of laughter at what sounded like an old taunt. Even the wounded men who were almost maddened by thirst had fallen silent.

"If it is the will of Allah," said the mamluk. He smiled, as if scoffing at himself.

Leo held his breath, forced himself to lie still. Men stiffened after they were dead. How long after? Would the Turks know? No doubt, his uncle Andronicus would have sneered at him for a coward; but he had stayed here, while Andronicus Ducas had withdrawn. He would be sending fast riders to his father, the Caesar John, who had always opposed Romanus. His elder kinsman would return from banishment, celebrate Romanus' death with every evidence of piety—and every inward sign of joy—and settle down as soon as was decent, and probably before, to the choice of a new Basileus. A successor was obvious: Michael, Eudocia's son, born in the purple and, better yet, a Ducas on his father's side. His family would be ecstatic, and so would Psellus. It meant advancement and vengeance; and both were very sweet.

God, don't make me sneeze.

The riders had divided into several groups, trotting, occasionally slowing to a walk or even stopping, as man after man dismounted and roved the battlefield. Greatly daring, Leo allowed his eyes to fall open as if that was how he had lain all night. He saw the *gulam* called Kemal kneel swiftly and catch up a sword from the ground, examine it, and throw it down, unworthy of his attention with so much richer booty on the ground. Soon the Turks would be gone . . . wouldn't they?

And then he could move. Just not yet.

Aye, and he would make sure before he fled of the Emperor's fate.

A voice sang out over the battlefield. The Turks all dismounted. Facing sunward, they prostrated themselves as if before an Emperor. Shoulder to shoulder, they knelt—one man somewhat apart from the others—chanting prayers. These did not look to be pagan rites, but rituals, duly and carefully observed, with exultation underlying what sounded like set prayers.

Thank the Bearer of God for her mercy and intercession, the Seljuks were occupied by their air-scrubbings, bowings, and chantings. Leo sank back down, seeking, for the first time, a position that eased the weight of armor on his back. Though he had lost blood and most likely started a fever, he found himself able to push away just a trifle from the tangle of wounded, or dead, or dying men in which he had fallen. They were stained with muck and blood, but he could recognize red leather boots: the boots of an Emperor.

Romanus groaned. He stirred and tried to rise.

Dear God, no!

Leo summoned any strength he had and tried to hurl himself at the older man, force him back down onto the ground where he could hiss caution in his ear . . . as if Romanus had listened to counsels of prudence all this entire God-cursed campaign. But as Leo hurled himself at the Emperor, Romanus overbalanced, and they went over not in a neat pile, but in a tangle. A kicking tangle.

"Ho!"

Kemal again, damn him, scouring the battlefield for portable wealth.

Let him just see two men, bled out and dying, clinging together in their last moments. A babble of prayer ran through his thoughts and would have forced itself out his lips, had fear not locked them. Let him turn away.

Again, Romanus kicked. A clean patch on one boot—the crimson, finely made boot that only an emperor might wear and that had been a gift to him from his loving wife the Basilissa Eudocia—caught the light of the sun.

Kemal turned around. His eyes narrowed even more than by nature. Their cunning darkness lit with greed, hope, and a sudden astonished surmise. He raced over to where the Emperor lay, seized the boots, and tugged hard. The boot came off in his hand. Kemal spat on the filthy leather, rubbed it, and when he removed his hand, he stared at the Imperial color.

A rush of butterflies, incongruously gleaming, innocent on that field of death, made the *gulam* leap back. He recovered in an instant, delighted by his fortune.

"Allah be praised!" he shouted. "They shamed me, the men who would not have me as their servant. Would he, they asked, bring us the Byzantine Emperor as prisoner? Would he? I, I, Kemal the worthless, the fool—behold, I am justified, my brothers! For here *is* the Byzantine emperor. And he is my prisoner."

Then it really was the end of the world. Well, best to leave it swiftly and with whatever honor he might salvage.

Leo snarled and launched himself at the *gulam,* who whirled and struck him down.

F rom a distance, someone was calling Leo's name. Stubbornly, he refused to turn back, to turn around. Beneath him, the ground shivered. There had been no place to hide upon the earth, but there might be sanctuary in it; and he might see the faces he had dreamt of all the night he had believed he was the only man left with life enough in him to have to survive.

"Leo! Wake up, man! We need you!"

What need had anyone ever had of him? Poor relation, unsatisfactory son, cat's-paw nephew, inept defender: better to retreat below, into the darkness.

The voice grew louder, and Leo became aware once more of his own body, huddled, chin practically cupped against his knees like a newborn, cowering from the light.

"Leo!"

"Like Arslan . . . the Lion . . . *this?* This boy?" That was Greek, horribly, barbarously accented, in a voice Leo identified with loathing as Kemal's.

"Our khan is called Alp Arslan, a lion of the mountains." Pride and even delight quivered in his voice. "I have caught me an Emperor and a lion's cub."

"As well you were no better warrior, *gulam,* or it would be a dead man and his kitten you dragged back."

The clamor of armor, dropping from a man's grasp, the edged laughter of a scuffle that was only partly a jest, mutters of "he's luckier at finding than fighting. . . ."

Kemal's laughter brought Leo's aching head slowly around. The Turk who had captured an Emperor sounded more assured now: he could afford to be, for he had won himself such fame as the Turks might well celebrate for a thousand years.

Fabric billowed and sloped overhead: they must be in some sort of tent. Sheltered, then. Tended after a fashion. No, not after a fashion: well-tended. The army's own medical corps could have done no better. Perhaps it could not have done as well; the Turks might have with them Egyptian or Jewish or Persian physicians, and they were the finest in the world.

Outside, Leo heard shouts and whoops. There must be enough spoil from the camp—from the Emperor's own baggage train—to assuage the greed of a thousand such armies, let alone the folk of Manzikert and Khilat.

He opened his eyes. The light did not thrust in at them like a lance in the brain. He stared up at the billowing fabric until a tall figure blocked his view.

"Leo, you're alive! Thank the Bearer of God!" The sound of that voice, as much as the warmth and strength of the handclasp that accompanied it, teased Leo the rest of the way back from the darkness he had courted.

He glanced up at the Emperor. The arrogance was long gone from his face. He bowed his head and his lips moved in brief, fervent prayer.

"I was certain you were dead, boy. So were . . ." A jerk of the head meant the Turks. "Except for him. He insisted that his luck had turned from the time he too had been a captive so wretched that the vizier would not accept him."

"I heard," Leo muttered. He paused. Then he confessed what he believed to be the truth. "I should have died," he whispered.

"When I saw you fall," the Emperor said, "at first, I thought you had the luck. But now, I am glad that you did not."

Tears poured down Leo's cheeks. With his unbandaged hand, Romanus wiped them away. The Basileus, *kneeling* at his side.

"You don't kneel to me," Leo forced the words out. Scandalized, he tried with what little strength he could muster to force the Emperor back onto his feet. The older man moved his hand away. Leo heard the rattle of the chains they both wore.

"I used to tend *my* Leo when he was sick," said the Emperor. His Leo. The son he would most likely not see again. One hand was bandaged. Though Romanus still wore the dress of a common soldier: apart from that, he might have been the Emperor Leo had seen all that summer.

No, perhaps not: the anger, the strain, and the rising tide of rash-ness were gone, leaving a man with a grave, pale face. Certainly, he would be pale; he had lost blood enough. No doubt he knew he faced— along with any other survivors—losing the rest of it. Slowly, if what men said of the Seljuks could even be half believed, and in great torment.

Unless, of course, he could strike a bargain that could win them all their lives and a chance to regain what had been lost. In that case, where would Leo stand? At his Emperor's side, facing his kin? He hoped he would have the courage.

Shouting rose outside once more. This time it did not subside.

The Emperor pressed Leo's hand.

"Help me up," Leo begged. The Emperor moved to stand between Leo and the entrance to the tent, crowded now with Turks, heading toward them.

Leo began to struggle upward. Romanus turned swiftly, for all his wounds and the chains that burdened him, and helped pull him up. He staggered once as if he stood not upon his feet, but on the rocks of Mount Ararat, dizzy with the height. A huge, fair man with blood in his matted braids steadied him with a grunt of approval, then moved to stand before the Emperor.

"Better move aside," Romanus ordered under his breath.

Seljuks grasped the Autocrator's sacred person by the arms and dragged him, his chains clattering, from the tent. When Leo, the Varangian, and some of the others lunged to restrain the guards, they were themselves forced along in Romanus' wake, so much human booty in Alp Arslan's triumph.

Even the tent abandoned in the Byzantines' camp was not as splen-did as this council chamber—this *divan* of the Seljuks and their Persian ministers. Brighter than the mosaics of Constantinople, carpets covered the ground, one strewn on top of another in a rich display of patterns, wool and silk, in crimsons and rich blues. Cushions lay atop them.

Seated at the center of this presence chamber was Alp Arslan, his long beard and mustaches giving him somewhat of the look of a hunt-ing cat. He wore simple white, and he held a mace.

As a hand against the Emperor's back thrust him into Alp Arslan's presence, a cluster of men spoke up at once. Envoys. Leo recognized them. No one troubled to interpret; no one needed to interpret the look of amazement on the Seljuk ruler's face, replaced quickly enough by a fierce triumph.

"No!" From somewhere in the back, another man rushed forward and hurled himself at Romanus's feet, weeping, babbling out apologies and verses from the Book of Lamentations.

"Forgive me, forgive me. When we lost, I should have known it was an omen of defeat. I have been a fool . . ." The *strategos* Basiliacus, whose force had been cut down but whose body had never been found, had his face pressed against the Emperor's feet.

"In the name of God, sir, control yourself," Romanus said. "I am hardly in a position to punish you for losing."

Basiliacus kissed the Emperor's boots and sobbed once more. At least, this hothead had one redeeming point: he was far more loyal than Leo's kin.

Well, if there were any chance at all that Romanus might not be recognized . . . folly, folly even to assume it . . . Basiliacus had just given that away. No one betrays you as thoroughly as your dearest friends, Leo thought.

Leo was a fool to assume for an instant that the Emperor's face might pass unknown—even without Basiliacus's outburst. The Turks were not fools, infidels and killers though they were. And they had Persians among them, and Persians were known to be outstanding spies.

Alp Arslan leapt from his cushions.

He shouted like one possessed, and his eyes gleamed with what could be madness as easily as triumph. Foam sprayed from his mouth.

Beside Leo, the Varangian tensed; Turks at his side tightened their grips upon his arms and their weapons.

"Down!" commanded the Sultan of the Seljuks.

Leo felt himself forced to the ground, until he lay as low as Basiliacus. The Varangian toppled, brought down by the weight of guards. As two more Turks pulled at Romanus, though, he pulled away. His chains rattled. Then, as if he were subject, and not emperor, he went down on his knees before the victor: down upon his knees, then down onto his belly, kissing earth, or at least the carpets beneath his face. And Alp Arslan strode forward and placed his foot upon the neck of the Emperor of the Romans.

Basiliacus gave another wail, then fell silent. The Emperor himself, humble as any slave! Why did the sky not darken? Why did the world not cease in that very moment?

Leo closed his eyes and waited for the blade to seek his heart, or the axe to cleave his neck. The clamor of cheers, laments—and interpreters buzzing in their masters' ears—fell silent.

"Now," said the Sultan of the Seljuk Turks to the vanquished Emperor of New Rome, "let me help you rise."

With his own hands, Alp Arslan raised the Emperor and clasped his hand, not once, but three times.

An interpreter, a veritable gaggle of them, hovered nearby. No doubt the Sultan spoke some Greek; Leo had heard the Emperor speak to his Turkish mercenaries. But the interpreters translated, their voices buzzing all around the rich tent: regrets for the loss of a battle; promises that Romanus's person would be as sacred as Alp Arslan's own; assurances that Alp Arslan understood the dignity of princes and the waywardness of Fate.

"Strike off my *guest's* chains," he commanded. Men crowded around to obey.

"These shall be your guard," said Alp Arslan. "Now, who else do you choose to release from bondage? You have only to speak their names."

Romanus gestured. Basiliacus rose, dashing his hand across his face. One by one, the men herded into the Sultan's presence chamber clambered to their feet and were released.

"Leo Ducas," said the Emperor.

"He bears the name of a man who deserted you," said Alp Arslan. "Do you truly wish him free?"

Romanus nodded. "He bears my son's name as well. In the battle, when he might have fled with his kinsman, no son ever showed a father greater loyalty. It is not always," he remarked, "thus in Rome."

A man in rich Persian robes whispered into the Sultan's ears.

"The lad named after the mountain cats!" Alp Arslan said, the interpreter tumbling after his words. "As I am myself. Yes, release him, and he will sit at your feet as befits a lion's cub."

Leo swayed as the Turks unchained him and ushered him, behind the Emperor, to a tent nearby. Alp Arslan sank onto cushions of Persian brocade behind a low table, intricately wrought. At a gesture, Romanus joined him. Leo was waved to cushions nearby. Near him, with a grin, settled the *gulam* who had brought them in. Leo supposed he had earned the right. He took a deep breath. His head throbbed from the color and the clamor and the growing realization that he was not immediately to die.

Thou preparest a table before me in the presence of mine enemies. . . .

Hammered brass dishes appeared beside him, heavily laden with lamb and fragrant breads. "Use only your right hand," whispered Basiliacus, who had been a prisoner longer.

Perhaps only hunger that made Leo dizzy. Please God, he did not keel over in a fit.

"You are my guest," announced the Sultan, "and you must eat and grow strong again."

Romanus Diogenes inclined his head.

"What treatment do you expect to receive?" asked Alp Arslan.

"If you are cruel," said the Emperor, "you will take my life. If you listen to pride, you will drag me at your chariot wheels. If you consult your interest"—the Basileus' eyes narrowed—"you will accept a ransom and restore me to my country."

Leo sat up as straight as he might. Now, he must pay attention, very close attention, as the dance of kings, armies, ransoms, and treaties began. For begin it would: why else had Alp Arslan spared a conquered Emperor?

"I have promised you your life," Alp Arslan replied. "But had Fortune smiled upon you, not me, what would you have done?"

There was no gentleness in Romanus' smile. He took bread with his right hand and tore it across. "I would have beaten you to death," he said.

This time there was a lag in the translation. Several of the envoys supplied the missing words. The Turks milling around the tent muttered, some with anger, others—much to Leo's astonishment—with approval. The grins on their faces were even fiercer than the smile upon the Emperor's.

The Sultan's smile was mild, deliberately so. "I," said Alp Arslan, "will not imitate you. I have been told that your Christ teaches gentleness and forgiveness of wrong. That he resists the proud and gives grace to the humble."

"So He does," agreed the Emperor.

As if aware that he had won that point as well as the battle, Alp Arslan changed the topic like any noble host.

"You fought well," he told Romanus. "I myself would not have trusted so much to strangers, and I surely would have guarded my own camp. But I should hope that if Allah withheld his gift of victory I fought as bravely as you and that my son Malik-Shah would stand by me as your lion's cub defended you."

Wait for it, Leo told himself. Soon, the bargaining would begin in earnest and would last . . . he only hoped he could hold out.

The throbbing in his temples intensified. He longed for wine, but the Turks would serve no wine—whether it was true or not that it was forbidden them. He watched the scribes, attentively writing down every word spoken by his master and theirs. They knew both languages. The time would come when all would have to . . .

His attention drifted away, to be brought back with a jolt—

"Ten million gold pieces?" Romanus echoed the demand Alp Arslan had evidently just made, his voice incredulous. He laughed, as if the sum were an absurdity. Leo detected the shock in that carefully accomplished laughter. A bargain would be struck, a ransom set, and a treaty signed. It would simply—if the word could be said to apply—take longer than anyone anticipated.

 5

*W*ith *drums and horns and flourishes of banners, Alp Arslan* rode out with the Emperor of the Romans to set him on his way back to his throne—and their treaty.

The townspeople of Manzikert and Khilat, jaded with the rich spoil they had lugged off the battlefield, ceased their gleaning to watch Alp Arslan and the Emperor ride out. There *should* have been soldiers hereabouts—wounded men, traveling slowly; officers on weary horses; officers and soldiers and auxiliaries, willing to rejoin their Emperor now that Romanus was freed, and his surviving men with him. Most likely, those who were not dead had shed their armor or turned their coats.

Master of all he surveyed and puppetmaster of much that he did not, Alp Arslan grinned the predatory satisfaction of a full-fed hunting cat. His smile widened as he saw Leo, riding with the other Romans among his Turks.

"The lion shall lie down with the lamb," Leo had heard him say as he and Romanus wrangled over the treaty. But Romanus was no sheep, nor had he allowed himself to be led like a lamb to the slaughter. By now word of his capture, or his death, treason being what it was, must have reached the city.

"Well, Lion's Cub? Sorry to be leaving us?" Kemal rode up to him. "The Lion's Cub is my luck!" Kemal had announced to the other mamluks, who were less skeptical than they had been.

The man who had captured an Emperor hurt Leo's eyes with his splendor. For half a dinar, Kemal had acquired an undented helmet. For another, he had purchased three cuirasses—perhaps not mail of the best quality, but quite good enough for a mamluk who had scarcely a decent weapon to his name just days before.

Leo steeled himself not to flinch at the slap on his back. He thanked God for his own part in the treaty. He had his armor and weapons, enriched by gifts of "the mountain lion to the lion's cub." Alp Arslan had taken a liking to his captives. So the Emperor rode not as a client but as a prince, dressed in Persian silks rich enough to satisfy Alp Arslan's desire to honor the man he had embraced and signed a treaty with, the emperor who had brought him half a world in thrall.

Perhaps it was that liking—and Alp Arslan's plans—that stopped this escort from being the vanguard of an invading army. It was not the banner of their Allah that made Leo shudder; it was the wilder things that flew with it into his consciousness—the sense of a great wind sweeping down from the East across Anatolia, to New Rome itself, and even across the Middle Sea.

Surely, Romanus saw that, or he would not have insisted so on his release. No mean bargainer himself, he had not had to cede the ten million gold pieces of the sultan's first demand. The terms were still severe: one and a half million gold pieces, a staggering annual tribute and a supply of soldiers, and the loss of Manzikert itself, Antioch, Edessa, and Hierapolis. A daughter of Romanus would be packed off to marry the eldest son of Alp Arslan, God pity her.

Romanus was free to ride back to Constantinople and impose this treaty on his Senate. How could the Emperor ride at Alp Arslan's side, as easy in Seljuk dress as if he were born to it, laughing as if he had been the victor? Did he truly think he could simply ride through the Golden Gate into Constantinople, up the Mese, and into the palace?

Leo's Emperor tossed back his head and laughed on the road. His face caught the sunlight like a mask.

6

The fields beneath the unpromising hills turned gold and brown as the Emperor rode west toward Dokeia. The day was cool for autumn. Several storms marched across the horizon.

Leo's mouth was foul with the taste of hellebore, a safeguard against madness. His dreams had worsened. At first, men had kicked him awake. Now, *Ducas is going mad,* he could hear the other officers whisper.

For now, however, he could not be denied the duties that were his. Thus, he still could wait outside Romanus' quarters for his summons. The entrance was guarded by two of the few remaining Varangians. The nearer of the pair grinned at him.

"Bad night?" he asked in heavily accented Greek.

Leo shrugged.

"You dream? We heard shouting."

"The storm woke me," Leo muttered.

"You dreamed." The Varangian touched a piece of metal that gleamed at his throat.

The two Varangians chuckled.

"Dreams. A goose stepped on his grave, eh, Thorvaldr?" He chuckled. "Be grateful that's all the goose did, yes?"

The Northerner thus appealed to patted Leo on the shoulder with an immense hand. The other polished his axe.

"Tell us your dreams, young lord." Leo had the Emperor's favor, or the Varangian would not thus jest with him. Or make jest of him.

"You heard the storms last night," he began.

The Varangian nodded. "Only land storms. You ought to see them on the swan road, when the water spouts. . . . Once, I saw a waterspout punch through a *knarr* and suck it down without leaving as much as a rope or shield."

"Let the lad tell us. . . ." the one called Thorvaldr cut in.

"I was seeking shelter from the storms. I came to a house beneath a cliff. I looked through a window. Looked *down*." Leo shook his head as if to clear it.

"I saw a loom."

"On the floor? That is not where the women of my steading keep their looms."

"Nor women in the Empire either."

"Fine silk they weave," chuckled the guardsmen, with an appreciative glance at the crimson of his sleeve.

"But it was not silk that strung the loom. It was the Empire that was the loom, and the threads—riders, back and forth . . ." Leo put a hand to his head. In his dream, the riders had darted back and forth at horse-killing paces, the warp and weft of a terrible tapestry being woven.

"Did you see the weaver?" Now the blue eyes were intent on his.

The Varangian's hand had slipped off Leo's shoulder and again touched the silver at his throat.

"The weaver, lad. . . ." He had heard veterans urging recruits in just that way to speak, on nights when soldiers scarcely out of boyhood huddled head down, afraid or ashamed to talk.

"She had bloody hands," Leo breathed. "And her hair . . . it was serpents. . . ."

"That is *seithr*, power of the deepest black."

A man pushed past Leo, his leathers and armor reeking of dust and horse and sweat.

"Leo Ducas! Get in here!" The Emperor's shout from within his quarters made all three of them jump.

"In you go," said Thorvaldr.

He could have dispensed with the honor.

The battered table on which Leo usually wrote his emperor's letters had been overturned, and ink had splattered the rugs beneath it. Back and forth Romanus strode.

"Never mind all that bowing," ordered Romanus. "Did you note the last messenger?"

"Yes, sir." Leo bent to turn the writing table upright. A pity nothing could be done about the ink. He looked about for the pen and whatever document Romanus had not seen fit to trust him with . . . ah, there . . . crumpled beneath a chair lay a stained letter. Leo picked it up, read the name "Eudocia" on it, and handed it mutely to the Emperor, who burned it.

"He seemed frightened."

Romanus barked laughter that hurt to hear. "You think I'm a Persian, boy? You think I would kill the messenger who brings bad tiding?"

"Sir, you wouldn't ask a boy that question," Leo said. "You sent for me?"

"You *do* serve me, don't you—Ducas?"

Leo stood silent, allowing the Emperor to meet his eyes. Compelling it. *I called my uncle Judas. I fled his side, repudiating his treachery. I fought before you until I fell. Oh yes, I serve you.*

"Have you heard from the City?"

"You mean from any of my family, sir? They'd hardly write the family disgrace now, would you?"

Time to be greatly daring. "Have *you* heard from home, sir?"

Romanus had a son named Leo, other children. Still, it was his Empress-wife who counted now. He had written her as soon as he might, a letter in his own hand, carried by the fastest means, reassuring her as wife, asking counsel of her as Empress.

Now, again, he had been writing her—a letter so private he would not call in even a confidential and aristocratic secretary. Romanus stood over the fire, rubbing his hands together as if they would never be warm.

During her reign with her previous Emperor-husband, Eudocia had saved Romanus' life. That time, he had been *dux* of Sardica, a fighting general for whom an older woman, much mewed up, might easily develop a passion. Now, he was not her lover, but her husband; not a lucky general, but a defeated Emperor. How much was he relying on her this time?

"Sir . . ."

Romanus sank into the chair Leo had set back for him. He gestured toward a stool and at the wine.

"And I alone escaped . . ." he muttered.

"The news from Constantinople is that bad?" If Romanus quoted the Book of Job, it must be nothing short of calamity.

"Worse than I could have imagined. The entire city bubbles like fermenting tavern swill. The Emperor is dead . . . no, the Emperor is a prisoner . . . no, it doesn't matter *what* the Emperor is.

"I have written to Alp Arslan. He promised me troops, allies. Let's see how good the word of a Turk is. It can't help but be better than the word of a Roman these days."

"Not all Romans, sir."

Leo rescued the winecup and pitcher, poured, and served.

The Emperor drank. *And if my word were no good, you would not dare that without a taster!*

Romanus set down his cup, more carefully this time. "No sooner than the news of the defeat—and I wouldn't have *lost* if it weren't for that Caesar John's Judas of a son!—reached the City, those damned court officials called a council."

Another gulp of wine. The Emperor filled his cup, then filled Leo's. "Don't give me that look, boy. You have a better chance than I do of wearing the diadem now. Those stoneless wonders decided to ignore the Emperor's fate, whatever it might be, and Eudocia and her sons . . . that fool of a Michael . . . were to be invested with full imperial power."

Eudocia had to want him back, Leo thought. A less welcome thought hit him. His mother Maria had made the best of a scholar husband: but had her husband been a defeated general, would she want him back? Would she prefer that he be honorably dead—or see to it herself?

"Who rules, then, sir?"

"Messenger said that they almost stabbed each other to the hearts with their pens: should Michael and his brother rule with their mother or without her? Hell of a world when the most experienced ruler in Constantinople is a middle-aged woman, isn't it, Leo?"

Eudocia was tried, experienced. Romanus might be right to have placed his trust in her. And perhaps, just perhaps, she loved him. Leo thought his mother loved his father. Otherwise, wouldn't she have herself tonsured and retire to a convent? She had never even threatened that, not even when she had been angriest that his father had not accepted an official post.

"The decision came through—from that precious Psellus. What *is* it with the man? You'd have thought the old Basileus was his . . . never mind that; but he seems under a spell himself. So Psellus wrote and Psellus skulked in corners, and the logothetes crept out of their holes. With the upshot being this: Michael and Eudocia rule jointly."

"For you, sir, that is *good* news, isn't it?"

If my wife's loyalty holds. But, of course, no man and especially no emperor could say that.

Romanus leapt up and began again to pace. Outside, Leo could hear soldiers splashing toward them and the Varangians acknowledging them. "I think staff's outside, sir."

"Let them come in."

"We're moving out of here to the fortress at Dokeia. At dawn," the Emperor told them. He took another turn across the room. Then, as if imposing composure upon himself, he sat down.

"Now you can hear the bad news. Right after Eudocia was vested with co-rule, by design of Psellus, who hoped I was dead . . ."

The officers grumbled. One started to spit, then reconsidered.

"Can you imagine the effect when my letter arrived?" Romanus paused and grinned. "Psellus must have pissed himself.

"But you know Psellus, never at a loss for long. Straightaway, he hatched up the idea that I should be outlawed. That's my copy of the order."

God help us, he doesn't know. Leo could hardly blurt out his suspicions. He forced himself to shrug. "He's a clerk, sir. A brilliant one, but still a clerk. If the Basilissa holds firm, my cousin Michael will give in. He is an obedient son. And he always yields to the last speaker. All she has to do is keep him away from Psellus."

Romanus shook his head. "How I'd love to get my fingers around Psellus' scrawny throat! I'd squeeze the eloquence from it soon enough.

"We're going to have to fight to take the City," he added. "So I'll need an army. Right now, I need a good man willing to track down the Sultan in his camp. I think I'll send Scylitzes. Alp Arslan will listen to him. Holy Mother of God, I never thought I'd be grateful to a god-damned Turk."

"I thought you liked Alp Arslan, sir."

"Well enough; but he is still a *Turk!*"

The messengers continued to be Job's messengers. Once again, Romanus paced, today's bad news crumpled in his strong hand.

"Eudocia," Romanus said, "has recalled Caesar John from exile in Bithynia. I would have expected her to hold out longer. If she'd both-ered to think about it, she might have secured the Varangians. But *John* was the one who won them over. Here: read for yourself."

"She thought you were dead, sir," Leo looked up. "And she needed a strong arm."

He knew Varangians, had heard them beat shields with axes. He could imagine his mother if the likes of them had stormed her house; and Eudocia was not nearly as fierce.

"Her Majesty must have been terrified," he murmured.

Romanus turned, lowered his eyes. "I promised to keep her safe. I promised. *And I was not there.* But still . . ." he sighed, "when did an Empress of Byzantium ever *run?*"

The Empress Theodora, a woman of no birth at all, had declared the Purple to be the finest of winding sheets, had held firm, and had helped saved the Empire for her husband Justinian the Law-Giver. It diminished the Empress to imagine Eudocia, a veteran of a lifetime of Palace schemes, cowering, her face covered by her veils, her hidingplace in a deep crypt illuminated, perhaps, by one flickering torch because she didn't know which she feared worse: darkness or the Varangians.

"She's finished now," Romanus said.

Leo nodded.

"You're missing the best part," Romanus told him. His voice strained over the words as if each cut him as he uttered it. "Read what happened to Psellus. Can you see him scampering after my wife, prob-ably stumbling over his robes, nigh on to wetting them, muttering prayers and gasping for breath? It's almost worth losing an Empire for."

Psellus had fled to the crypt, cowering with Eudocia. And there, among the very bones of imperium, the Varangians had found him. *Bar-baroi* though they were, they were not stupid. *Barbaroi* that they were, they could still sniff out a magus, and they knew what to do with one who wished them ill.

"The writer here says that Michael—now the *Emperor* Michael—sent the guards looking for him . . . he always looked at the people he admired like a dog pleading for scraps, sir." Leo found himself laughing. It hurt.

Romanus joined in the laughter. "Eudocia is gone, gone with John; and meanwhile, Psellus hasn't figured out a flowery enough way to say, 'forgive me; I miscalculated; now I will be *your* lickspittle'—oh God, and he hears the Varangians shouting and lumbering down into the crypt and tries to scratch his way into the stone itself! I swear, if he could have moved the stones, he'd have clambered into a tomb!"

"So the Varangians find him and bring him to Michael. . . ."

"And instead of chopping Psellus's head off, your idiot cousin—my wife's mindless excuse for a son—all but places the diadem upon it."

"They've sent Eudocia to an island convent. She won't find it easy to escape from there." Romanus shrugged. "So I am no longer Emperor by marriage. Must I make myself Emperor by conquest?"

The older man's eyes blazed; his breath came faster; and then he subsided. Not enough fire remained.

Leo handed the closely written leaves back to the Emperor, who laid them gently aside.

"Leo," the Emperor asked, "would you go home?"

"As your emissary, sir? They would hardly welcome me, or believe me. Still, if you command . . ."

"No, it is not my will. You are useful here," Romanus said. "*Not* to keep my eyes on you; you think I can't tell the difference? But I would see you safe.

"Leo . . . if I come back into my own, it might be that two Caesars would bear the name Leo. You, and my son."

Become a piece in another man's game—to keep him and his dream of power alive a lifetime longer, a generation, a decade, even a day. He shook his head—the buzzing subsided to its prior level of disturbance—and flung out a hand.

Romanus smiled at what must appear to him to be admirable humility. *I will not play this game.*

"You have proved yourself a thousandfold."

The bridge before the fortress of Dokeia was a mongrel structure of wood and slapdash stone atop sturdy Roman columns sunk deeply into the swift Halys. This was the road of conquerors who had left their seed behind: not just Greeks, but the Romans before them; a few fair children, the far, far descendants of Macedonians on their way to Persia; and others, black-haired, black-eyed, the stamp of the most ancient times upon their features.

Capitals, their acanthus leaves battered yet still showing fragments of their original grace, upheld hovels that would not last a fraction of the old stonework's years.

Eyes upon Leo's back made him turn to look into the eyes of a woman, wrapped in black, perhaps a farmwife—or widow, the great woman of her family. Her daughters-in-law in subjection and hard at work, she had taken a few moments to hobble out from her house and watch the armed men pass. And, no doubt, to make certain that they stole nothing, from the scrawniest fowl to her most restless, army-mad grandson.

Light glinted on the road. Leo stooped, curious. A gem, perhaps, dropped by some mercenary or some refugee? He swung down to retrieve it: a blade flaked from black stone, shining in the buttery afternoon light. The old woman set up a clamor.

"Yours?" Leo asked. "Since it's on your land? Take it!"

He would have tossed it to her; but she reached his side and grasped the hand that held the tiny blade as if she would claim them both. The serrations of its flaked edge cut his palm.

"Found another sweetheart, Ducas?"

The old woman's head rose.

"You? You are Ducas?"

He spared her a nod.

Old as she was, she was still hale: one of the black-eyed round-faced people, the oldest dwellers in these parts. They were very black indeed, those eyes, and they drew him in.

"You're the one," she said. "You'll do."

"*What* will I do?" he whispered. Despite the heat of the sun, he had trembled at her touch, her words.

"Keep the knife, young prince," she told him.

"Ducas, how long do we have to wait for you to finish courting?"

The woman disappeared into her low door faster than he would have thought she could move.

7

I wish my mother had permitted me to ride with you against the Persians, but my brother's death was a wound in her heart, and I owe her a son's obedience. Now, however, that we have been exiled to this island, I think that she wishes she had permitted me to serve as befitted a man of conscience and a Roman."

You might not have survived, my friend.

By now, Alexius was getting on toward fifteen. Man enough to ride, he had insisted. Old enough to fight. It was no small achievement for a boy to smuggle a letter out of monastic imprisonment. It was an even larger achievement that it reached Leo with the Emperor's dispatches.

Alexius' neatly formed, indignant writing danced before Leo's eyes: Anna Dalassena, Alexius's mother, had been accused of sedition "by a snake, Leo, that I would not have bothered to bruise as we are commanded with my heel if I had seen it slither out across a garden walk."

Letters had been forged to prove she had been writing to Romanus. "Your cousin, though I am shamed to reproach you with that kinship," wrote Alexius, "thereupon called my mother, whom I know you esteem as her son, to a trial that he was too shamed to attend, perhaps because it was not of his instigation."

Not as discreet as you might be, lad, Leo thought. Anna Dalassena had been almost more of a mother to him than his own. Please the Bearer of God that Leo's own mother had had nothing to do with the Lady Anna's downfall.

"Whereupon, when ushered into the presence of the court, my mother drew an icon of the Savior from within her garments. 'Behold the Judge who will today decide between you and me. Observe Him well when you utter your sentence and try to ensure that it is not unworthy of the Judge who knows the secrets of the heart,' she declared.

"A woman of valor, who can find, for her worth is far above rubies: truly, I think that proverb can be applied to my mother, and I should have thought that all the world, or that piece of it that is Rome, would have agreed. But the judges were cowards and like the Sanhedrin of Caiphas, they have exiled her and her sons to Prinkipo, where we stare out over the sea and, like the scandalous old Roman poet, lament our city.

"I have been able to send no word to my friend the other Leo, though I remember him for his own sake and for the sake of his father, whom my brother served so nobly. My mother does not know that I write you, but I am certain she would want you to know that you are included in her prayers, as you are in mine. . . ."

Psellus again, Leo thought. Now, he moved to destroy the powerful Comnenus family, as he would move to thwart anyone who might influence his Emperor—or place another candidate on the throne. Psellus might even have written the letters purporting to be from Anna Dalassena rather than tossing the task to some cat's-paw: capturing, then perverting, the voice of a great lady celebrated for her wisdom might have been a task he would enjoy.

A shout brought Leo's head around. He thrust Alexius' compromising letter into his breast and ran back along the hollowed pavement.

"Is there not one fortress they would leave me? Not even one?" The Autocrator's voice almost cracked with fury.

They did not need Michael Psellus to tell him that that was a rhetorical question.

"Out!" Romanus shouted. He crumpled something in his hand, then hurled it to the stone floor. A military secretary deftly retrieved it and smoothed it, to preserve it for the interminable, inevitable records.

Three civilians bowed with the trained grace of Byzantium, exaggerated almost to the point of contempt. The odor of the court clung to these three, and Leo thought he heard the sinuous rush of silk along the passageway as they followed the officer, at a fastidious distance, out of Romanus' presence. Civil servants, ostensibly sent from Michael and his puppetmasters, Caesar John and the scholar Psellus.

Leo felt their eyes slice across him like an assassin's blade. Clever eyes, hooded eyes: the eyes not even of civil servants, but of scholars. Power quivered in them like a plucked string—to a tune struck in Byzantium by a man who had vowed as a poor boy that all the world would dance to his playing.

"Whom the gods wish to destroy, they first make mad!" Romanus exclaimed. He paced across the room even more vigorously than was his custom, as if spurred. A shadow lay on his face.

"Get over here!"

A table loaded with documents divided them: not enough, should Romanus run mad in truth. Leo had seen animals confined and baited past their control turn suddenly at bay and savage keeper and tormentor alike.

"I fight a war with rumor, rather than swords," he raged. "All rumors. Did you know I have renounced the throne, Leo, and that I shall become a monk—should they allow any monastery to accept the likes of me?"

Leo met the Emperor's eyes. "Would you indeed receive the tonsure, Majesty?" he asked.

"A forced vocation? To speak of such things, even as a ruse of war, is blasphemy," Romanus said. "I have letters . . . veritable epistles . . . from the august bishops of Coloneia, Heracleia, and Chalcedon. Surely, they would surely tell me so if I did not know it myself."

Not an answer. Leo glanced down at the table again. Alp Arslan fought far to the East.

"The boy in Constantinople leaves his wretched verses and his schoolmaster and orders—orders!—me to yield Dokeia to Constantine. Not one fortress shall be left to me, Autocrator of the Romans. This is civil war. . . ."

The Emperor's voice trailed off, then strengthened. "Well, if it is war they want, they should send the traitor Andronicus, not his little brother. I shall beat him like a child."

Kyrie eleison, Christe eleison flickered through the shadowed chambers of Leo's mind. If he were indeed mad, he might not be the only madman in this room. The Emperor turned, looking out over the sunset plain of Anatolia. His head was up, his eyes alight with eagerness and zest for battle as if, already, the sun had risen on a brighter day and he turned aside from the body of his enemy to see the sun flash off the shields of his cataphracts and the great axes of his northern guardsmen.

Whom the gods wish to destroy . . .

Leo withdrew to stand against the wall. It would be a very long evening, and a longer night.

Another Constantine had conquered at Dokeia. Even though this one was younger than Leo himself, the very name of Constantine was a powerful omen. What would the Emperor do now? And was he emperor of anything at all?

The surgeons had set up operations in half-makeshift quarters. Lit by torches, they cast long shadows like demons, tormenting the most recent harvest of damned souls, who writhed and cried out under knives only slightly more merciful than the ones that had brought them to this pass. Covered bodies lay nearby; more lay outside the fortress.

"Young Ducas?" Beneath the rasp of exhaustion, Leo heard the snap of a senior officer.

"Sir."

"The Emperor's in there. . . ." The man pointed with his chin.

"That's no place for me, sir," Leo ventured.

"Ducas, if it had been me, you'd have been long gone. But, for some reason, he likes you. If you can play David to the Autocrator's Saul, we'll all thank you. . . ."

"Is the Emperor badly hurt, sir?" A boy's question, asked with the disingenuous frankness that won results more often than it should.

"He couldn't shout like that if he'd been badly wounded. But the *strategos* Alyattes has gone missing, and the Emperor is taking the news badly. Now get in there. I've still got work to do. Christ, who was the fool that said if he'd been defeated, he wouldn't be this tired? Another madman."

He strode off in the direction of the stables.

It had been an Emperor who had said that. The full burden of the officer's words hit him. Theodore Alyattes, who had commanded the right wing of Romanus' troops at Manzikert, was missing. If he were slain or captured, Romanus had lost his right arm.

Surgeons had the armor half off Romanus, who was pushing them away as he tried to reach the table on which a map had been unrolled.

"Get those surgeons into the square, treating my men . . . they deserve the best. . . ." His voice cracked. "I want as many of them ready . . ."

"Damn you, then, yes, bring the crone in, if that will shut you up. All these grandmothers have some skill in herbs; how else do babies survive in these wretched towns?"

"Get her in here," someone gestured.

"But . . ."

"If her hearing's as bad as her breath, you think she'll understand a word we're saying? Besides, he wants it that way." Two officers had their heads together.

Leo saw their glances shift toward him, distrust and complicity combined. "We'll get *him* to keep an eye on her. That way, if anything goes wrong . . ."

The crone they had spoken of squatted outside, waiting with patience akin to the rock against which she hunched with her bundles of herbs and the blessed Virgin only knew what else. Under the swathings about her head, her eyes were dark, withdrawn into shadows of her own. He put a gentle hand on her shoulder, drawing her attention back.

"Will you aid us, old mother?" Leo asked gently.

She looked up, and he knew her then: the woman by whose hut he had found the tiny stone knife.

She smiled, those surprising teeth glinting in the torchlight.

He began to raise her as he might have aided a lady of his own kind in Constantinople, but she refused to move. Her hand clasped his: he felt the twists of its joints, its calluses, and its strength. "Have you still got the knife, young hero? Do you keep it safe?"

He nodded.

"Nah, there, nah . . . I will not say it is not so bad. You are a man, not a suckling, and so you know it is hard. A moment longer . . . there."

How he got there, he never knew. But he was kneeling at the woman's feet, his head down, almost buried in her lap, and those capable hands had cast his helm aside, had smoothed his matted hair, cupped his skull, and pressed over his closed eyes. *Bless me, mother.* The words faltered behind his lips.

His own mother had pecked him on both cheeks and prayed aloud. Anna Dalassena had secluded herself in mourning, and had had no blessing for him. Warmth from the gnarled fingers eased him, relaxing for a moment against her knees, in an aura of herbs and soil.

"Better so? Look up. Do you think we will not weather *this* storm? You ride out from the city with your power. But we remain, as we always have. Now, bring me to this great lord of men."

As if she were the Empress herself, Leo raised the farmwife to her feet. She shook out her skirts and nodded briskly at him; and he brought her through a press of crack troops and weary officers, to stand before the Emperor. Bobbing awkward obeisance to Romanus, she straightened and then knelt, sturdy as blocks of stone cut a thousand years ago from Dokeia's foundations.

Matter-of-factly, she began to unpack her herbs. Aristocratic nostrils, heedless of the stinks of wine, of blood, of mud, and sweat, wrinkled at their fragrances; but for the first time in a very long time, the tightness in Leo's skull eased.

Without being told, Leo fetched a bowl of warm water.

"Turning surgeon yourself, Ducas?" Romanus asked. "Get yourself looked to. I want you able to ride." He flinched, then eased under the old woman's ministrations. As his officers had foreseen, he paid no more attention to her than to any of his body servants.

"Ride, sir? Where?"

"My birth country. Cappadocia," the Emperor said, over the old woman's head. "We'll cut across the mountains and pass the Gates into Cilicia. They'll be waiting for us there, the men still loyal to me—Khatchadour and Alyattes."

The old woman shook her head, as if over the injuries she tended. She had washed the worst of his scratches and, from one of her bundles, had extracted a grayish strip of cloth to serve as a bandage.

A pause. Shadows danced in the brazier, leaping as more fuel was added. The air grew thick. Leo could imagine the shrugs as eyes met eyes in secret signals. Some trick of the air let him hear the whispers.

"We all know who is piping the tune in Constantinople. Psellus for the aristocrats; Caesar John for the army. He sent his younger son out to make his name: now he'll call him back. . . ."

"You think he'll send Andronicus? He's served under the Emperor in the South, he knows the land. . . ."

Muttered oaths.

"The chance to fight that one would overmaster our master's good sense, wouldn't it? If he has any left."

"Quiet!"

If Romanus' officers turned their coats and turned on their Emperor, Leo's Ducas connections might prove valuable. Still, he had turned on his uncle Andronicus. In either case, he remained what he had always been—profoundly suspect. He walked to the table and poured a cup of wine, then another. He brought the cup to Romanus and gave the other to the woman tending him. That caused some murmuring. She grinned and contrived to spill some of the dark-red wine upon the stone floor.

"What do you see?" Romanus' voice was a harsh whisper.

"Most Exalted?" A thread of fear underlay the country accent, thickened, Leo suspected, for the Emperor's benefit.

"Tell me what you see in the wine."

Let a priest hear the Emperor, and there would be, quite literally, hell to pay.

"This is a matter for women," the old one said, avoiding the glare that Romanus used to frighten his officers. "A game to awe the children or to ease the mind of a woman who bears a child." Her small, wicked smile implied that the Emperor was neither.

"So they say. Amuse me, then. Humor your Emperor."

The old woman bent to gaze into her cup.

"No," said the Emperor. "Take mine. Look into it and see."

Leo wanted to avert his eyes. Was he in truth to play David to Romanus' Saul? Saul had tried to *murder* David, after all.

The air prickled as power seemed to gather and concentrate in the body of the woman who knelt before a fearful Emperor.

They were fleeing, riding until their horses dropped, remounting, and riding, riding until exhaustion and fear forced them to sleep where they fell. A Gate, darker than the wine, loomed before them; but they left it unguarded; and, as they slept, their enemy came upon them, and they must flee again. . . .

"A poor omen," Romanus mused. "Try again. . . ."

"Great lord, I beg you," the old woman began. The suppliant's whine was a pose: there was no begging in this one—except perhaps for Romanus to turn aside from this desire to see his future.

"Again!"

She squared her shoulders. He had commanded her: he would see what there was to see. God might have mercy on his soul: she would have none. She bent over the Emperor's cup and breathed upon the wine.

Fumes rose from the cup. When they cleared, more fumes remained within, captured in the cup. No, Leo thought, not fumes: that was smoke, the smoke of a brazier in which the coals were burning down, and in it, tent stakes, glowing red hot.

Romanus' hand, holding the cup, shook, then steadied.

Soldiers led out a man whose mouth was pinched with the pain of old wounds and a dreadful, present fear. His eyes started in his head, as he scanned the faces—Roman, Norman, Armenian—of his enemies first, as if seeking the mercy he would not find.

"Alyattes," breathed the Emperor. "Has this happened or is it yet to be?"

Uunable to look at the brazier or, any longer, at the world that would so soon turn dark for him, Alyattes shut his eyes. They forced him down, to his knees, then onto his back, and pinned him. A man with wrapped hands extracted the irons from the fire. Alyattes screamed, and from his seared-out eyes, steam rose. The wine stank of cautery. . . .

The wine splashed up, destroying the hideous image within. Romanus dashed the cup to the floor. Its contents, steaming ever so slightly, spurted over his muddy crimson boots.

Romanus covered his face with his hands. "Get that old witch out of here, Leo," he whispered.

"Guard yourself, young lord," the woman said as Leo escorted her outside.

A tired surgeon searched his cuts and pointed him toward the nearest priest. Thus it was that he fell asleep in a state of grace, but he did not sleep in peace.

He lay out under the skies. An icy rain poured down. Lightning stalked the earth, bounded from point to point, spiking and fragmenting wherever it touched. And then They came. Male and female they were, taller than mortal men, wearing kilts and high diadems surmounted with horns. Their eyes were grey, and their mouths turned up in the mirthless smiles of ancient statues. Slowly, they advanced, as if in ceremony—yet wind rushed by them. The leader raised his hand. The lightning flew to it, like a well-schooled bird, and he hurled it across a landlocked sea to strike the cone of a mountain far away. The ground trembled like a woman in labor, groaned, and shuddered. . . .

Leo woke. Outside, the rain poured down, accompanied by rolling thunder.

9

As armies from the City pushed Romanus south, he claimed to have good hopes of recruiting an army in his native soil. For now, however, the Emperor's luck seemed to have turned. Did Constantine exult that a second army from Constantinople had arrived to augment his forces? It was his turn for chagrin as soldiers and a general in whom he had placed his hopes deserted.

Letters from Byzantium reached Romanus. Reached him, and enraged him.

"They offer me co-rule, then amnesty—for what? In the same breath, they demand that I abdicate, or moderate what I seek? How can a man be only moderately a Basileus?" Romanus shouted.

At Khatchadour's suggestion, they withdrew into Cilicia, shutting the Gates most firmly shut against Andronicus Ducas. They descended from winter into early spring. Southward they marched, into Adana.

Someone was weeping in the early dawn, deep, heartfelt sobs that brought Leo out of a dream of deep passages and flickering shadows. The camp should be stirring. Nothing. Even the cookfires had sunk into gray ash. Leo found the watchmen seated and staring out toward the mountains, their eyes vacant.

As Leo started to shake the nearest man awake, his gaze fell on what should have had the guard up and sounding the alarm. Unimpeded by any watchers or any traps, their enemy's army had passed the Gate by night and, like water seeping past the level in the hull where a ship can safely float, massed in formation beneath the hills.

Once again, Andronicus had proved too much for Romanus. Perhaps because Leo came of the blood he did, the bemusement that worked on the others did not seep into his consciousness and paralyze his will.

Leo shouted and shook the man awake. At the next guard post, a man stirred, spat out a prayer or a blasphemy at the sight of Andronicus' army, and sounded the alarm. Now the camp boiled as if one of the Emperor's zookeepers had thrown a chunk of meat into a cage of starving animals.

There would be no time, now, for Khatchadour to make good on his promises of more aid from Antioch, no time for Alp Arslan's reinforcements to arrive.

Men with the stolid, weathered faces of small farmers or tenants from Cappadocia stood with weapons shaking in their hands, their weathered, stolid faces unusually pallid. Soldiers with the clever, volatile features of city-dwellers or the intensity of Armenians, distant kin, perhaps to the governor of Antioch, tightened their harness.

The Emperor knelt before a priest, then prostrated himself before the signs of holiness. When he rose, he forced a smile onto his face as if it too could shield him. He wore his parade armor.

Had he some notion of challenging Andronicus hand to hand?

Even now, the last of the City's troops moved into formation. As the dawn haze faded, the last mists withdrew from the minds of the men around him, allowing them, in a final cruelty, to know how desperate their plight was.

In that moment came the cry, *Nobiscum!* And the forces of Byzantium rushed upon the Emperor's host like a bird of prey upon a helpless fowl.

A lull in the fighting allowed Leo to blink the dust from his eyes. Someone thundered by him on a lathered horse: Khatchadour. The governor's eyes were wilder than those of his mount, flaming as if he had seen the Furies and they had made him mad. Screaming oaths in Greek and Armenian, he and a few of his men charged. Then he disappeared from sight in a cloud of dust and a welter of soldiers.

"Ducas! Andronicus Ducas!" Leo could hear Romanus screaming his adversary's name.

Clean, safe, mounted on a fresh horse, and positioned where his troops could see him, Andronicus did not so much disdain the challenge as ignore it out of existence. He sat his horse while blood flowed over the flat land, aloof and terrible as image of Empire.

The surviving Varangians massed around Romanus and forced him away. Some men tossed their shields and weapons away to run the faster. Leo's horse screamed and fell. He kicked free of the stirrups and, for a miracle, landed on his feet. Then it was run, run in harness, run until he thought his heart would burst. At dawn, Adana's earth had been yellow-brown. Now it had been churned into a hideous red muck on which flies were already beginning to land.

The routed army reached the city, spreading panic in their wake. Shouting, they rushed past its guards, into the city, up into its acropolis. In that temporary safety, they cast themselves down, gasping, bleeding, retching over ancient, austere stone while the sky, which had seen such sights before, remained pitilessly bright.

 10

A gain, messengers brought the death of hope. Khatchadour, it was said, had been battered so disastrously outside Adana that he had taken refuge in the underbrush. Andronicus had received him as much as a host as a captor. Spies whispered of a great gem that he had presented to Andronicus—and that he had reserved, he said publicly, for the Empress. He could scarcely mean Eudocia.

With the loss of Khatchadour, Adana's suppliers grew restive, the soldiers more so. Andronicus tightened his nets around the city on the plain.

"Do you hear rustling?"

Leo started.

"Easy, easy . . ." To his surprise, Attaleiates grinned at him. Leo had not seen the older man for some time: trusted, responsible, he had been as often away from the Emperor's forces as riding with them.

"Rustling? As in men preparing to turn their coats upon their shoulders?"

Attaleiates leaned closer to Leo. "He knows we can't go on this way."

Leo shrugged.

The man he had counted a friend shrugged back. "We all want to survive through this, if we can. If only to write histories and bore our grandsons."

Attaleiates gestured at the next group of men awaiting their chance at the Emperor—priests, surrounded by soldiers.

"They could be bringing him guarantees of safety," he muttered.

Leo himself had written letters from the Emperor to the bishops of Coloneia, Heracleia, and Chalcedon.

"I've my own news from the Domestikos' camp," he said. "Truly, Andronicus does not want a massacre. You mark my words, Leo. We will have a treaty before long."

"And him?"

Attaleiates made a cutting gesture. "He won't be the first to turn to a life of prayer. He can always try again in a few years. Psellus did."

The Emperor rose.

The officers and priests fell back. He was still Basileus, still *isaposteles*, God's vicegerent on earth.

For a long moment, Romanus stood, staring at his hands as if surprised that, even now, they could not pull victory out of thin air. Then, he began to laugh.

"My beautiful, costly whore of an army. I can no longer feed you. Adana can no longer, it seems, feed you. And thus . . ."

He held up his empty hands and shrugged. Then the Emperor of the Romans seated himself on plain stone as if upon the Lion Throne in Byzantium.

"Bring the Domestikos' messengers before Us. We shall hear their terms."

Black-clad men led the way to Andronicus Ducas' camp. One upheld a large cross. The bishops of Coloneia, Heracleia, and Chalcedon marched behind it. One held a letter, the seals on it of the Basileus plainly visible. There was no doubt now who was meant when that term was used: Michael in Constantinople.

Clad in black, his hair shorn as befit a monk, Romanus followed the bishops toward the victor's camp.

Andronicus Ducas stood waiting. His armor glittered; his head was high; and his face gleamed with satisfaction. Hand outstretched, Andronicus strode forward to clasp his former master's hand, to bring him, as an honored guest into camp, and to invite him and . . . for the first time, his fine flow of speech hesitated. He wrung Romanus' hand again and invited him to a feast in his tent.

"So noble, it makes me sick," Attaleiates muttered rashly.

Leo kept his face carefully impassive. The bishops' guarantees had secured his life—perhaps. He was giddy with the odors wreathing up from the silver dishes generously arrayed upon a long table.

"Thou preparest a table before me in the presence of mine enemies." Romanus showed teeth in a feral smile.

"You have no enemies here today," Andronicus Ducas declared. There was no mention, of course, of anointing his guest's head with oil: that was for coronation, not deposition. He strode to the table, chose two goblets, and filled them to overflowing. Handing one to Romanus, he sipped from the other. Servants approached and began to pour wine for all those present.

Attaleiates grasped Leo's arm. "Get it over with," he recommended, but Leo needed no urging.

Let him see me as a proper officer. Leo stiffened to attention.

His uncle's eyes bored into Leo's as if he were a captured spy.

"Your mother asked me to tell you she and your father are well," he said.

"Sir, I could not have a more noble messenger," Leo replied. His eyes dazzled, and he covered the momentary lapse of control by sipping his wine. If some poison had been added, he could not taste it. He turned away to see Romanus watching them. The former Emperor shook his head.

"I beggared myself to provide you with a future," said Romanus. "I'd take it, if I were you."

"Why?" Leo asked his uncle.

"Let us say we do not cast men of honor from our family as quickly as you believe. Come, it is not quite a fatted calf that we have here on the table, but will you sit and eat something? Your mother would be distressed to see you so thin."

Romanus was eating as appreciatively as if he might never again have a meal this lavish. Leo seated himself. It was good to eat his fill. As they took the initial edge off their hunger, Leo found himself able to look about. The Emperor—he could not think of him as . . . as what? Brother Romanus? Or would they give him some name untainted by imperial dignities? Yet another messenger left Andronicus Ducas. This time, he leaned back from the table. It was not, Leo realized, the gesture of a man replete and expansive after a feast, but the movement of someone settling down to a tricky piece of business.

Air currents seemed to hiss and whisper in the great tent, stirred by the press of many bodies. When had all the guards entered?

Andronicus rose.

"I have," he began, "a most difficult duty to perform."

Romanus smiled without mirth. "Difficult? I renounced an empire and cut my hair. What is *your* difficulty, weighed against that?"

"I must take a former Emperor in charge and return you to Constantinople."

"Then I am under arrest?"

Andronicus inclined his head, a formal, gentlemanly gesture that, nevertheless, brought the guards forward in case Romanus harbored unmonastic thoughts of snapping his stiff neck for him.

"My life was guaranteed," he reminded his captor.

"Have I said otherwise?"

Romanus rose to his full height and straightened his shoulders. Unlike the robes of the bishops, his black was drab, bedraggled in token of humility.

"When do we leave?" he asked.

"At dawn."

The former Emperor and his enemy locked glances. Andronicus looked away. "I have my orders from Michael."

"Michael" was likelier to be Psellus than that fool whom Caesar John had lifted onto the throne the way a boy is lifted onto his first pony.

"Leo." Just a breath of sound from Romanus, but it stopped him before he could ask why Andronicus had not kissed Romanus' cheek before betraying him. Even that whisper drew the general's attention. Holding his uncle's gaze, Leo tipped over his goblet in repudiation. The last of his wine dripped off the table.

Andronicus' guards marched to Romanus' sides. He smiled.

"I am a humble monk now, remember? I must humbly offer this up."

"I think I can sneak you back to Adana," Attaleiates whispered quickly in Leo's ear. "From there, we can figure out a way . . . if you come now!"

If Attaleiates helped Leo escape, it could end his career. And, unlike Romanus, Attaleiates' life had not been promised him. The senior officer had given Leo a gift too precious to be accepted. Another of Andronicus' servants came to stand at Leo's shoulder. Oh, they were being very gracious, very familial. The errant nephew would be retrieved from his misadventures, nobly forgiven—no doubt, with the entire army (it always was a sentimental beast) beaming approval on Andronicus Ducas.

Leo turned his shoulder on the servant. "I remain with my Emperor's other officers," he told the man.

Let them see how the Ducas "prodigal" had returned to his husks.

In the grayness before dawn, guards brought them outside. Horses awaited them. Standing among them, swaybacked, as if abashed in such noble company, was a mule. To this, the guards led Romanus. They seized him and bound his hands before hoisting him into the mule's shabby saddle. One of them mounted and took the wretched creature's reins.

"I will say this for you," Romanus told Andronicus Ducas. "You—or your masters—do not miss a single detail."

Ducas thinned his lips. Almost, in the torchlight, it was as if he flushed. "I regret this."

"Do you? What have you left me now?"

The other man smiled, finally. "Your life, as we pledged to do. The opportunity, as a monk, to amend it and purify your immortal soul. Weighted against that, what are the vanities of your former rank and of this world?"

"Enough," said Romanus, "to make you jeopardize your own soul." He tried to lift his hand in the gesture a man sparring with another uses to acknowledge defeat, but his bonds did not permit it.

Andronicus turned in his saddle. Even as he oversaw the last details of departure, he nodded slightly at Leo. *Ride with me.* Was this, like the mule, another subtle vengeance on his enemy?

"Someone must stay with him," Leo said. "And he was ever kind to me."

"This one?" he took the reins from a groom and raised his brows. At the general's nod, he swung up into the saddle. He edged up as close behind Romanus as his guards allowed.

The Emperor's head was up, his eyes as distant as if he sat in the throne room he might never see again except as a prisoner, cast onto his belly before his successor. The mule shambled along in the dust of the cavalry.

Rumor outmarched the army. Along the roads and in villages and markets villages where Romanus had been hailed as godlike, farmers, merchants, and cautious minor nobles ventured out to see an Emperor in bonds.

At first Romanus had tried to ignore the staring, whispering crowds, the occasional jeer, the casual humiliations of imprisonment: of having to wait, for example, until it occurred to a guard that even a deposed Emperor might need to relieve himself. But that last downpour had accomplished what Andronicus and petty indignities could not. He had retched by the side of the highway. And he rode now with his head down, unsteady in what passed for a saddle on his mule.

Romanus' eyes were bright, too bright; his face was flushed, sweaty; and he was mumbling. Leo edged his mount nearer.

"They compass me about . . . they compass me about . . . out of the depths I cry . . ."

He stood in his stirrups, hoping to locate Attaleiates. The senior officer had taken one look at Romanus this morning, cursed under his breath, then jerked his horse's head around and set off to fetch a surgeon. Neither he nor any surgeon had returned, however.

Now, the older man rode up beside him. "They won't come," he said.

Leo spat.

"Softly," Attaleiates warned. "Someone said something about hemlock—I promised I wouldn't say who."

Fear gripped at Leo's bowels. Romanus's sickness, his too-bright eyes, his fever could all stem from despair or being drenched once too often by the rainstorms of late spring. But when a noble, publicly disgraced and under arrest, sickened this conveniently, that other possibility always lingered in people's thoughts. He himself had expected to be struck down before now.

The sky clouded again.

"Oh no," he whispered.

The raindrops were fat and heavy, making the ride a silent misery. As the rain lashed down, seeping through armor and garments, steaming with his body's heat, Leo allowed himself to weep.

At the next halt in a town before Iconium, the Emperor's keepers discovered he had fouled himself. By the side of the road, Leo performed the offices of a bodyservant. The Emperor, white-lipped with shame, permitted it.

The sun emerged, casting long beams onto the road, more cracked and scarred now than in the millennium since the Romans built it atop a path that had no doubt run along this way longer far than that.

A child emerged to stand by the side of the road. Leo would willingly have boxed his ears and packed him off away from Romanus.

"Is he sick, master?" asked the boy. To his credit, the child took pains to whisper.

Leo waved off the guard who looked ready to administer the blows that he had himself had thought of striking. He shook his head.

"I will fetch my mother, or grandmother," the child offered. Leo saw him running from the road across a field and into a house that could be said to be tumbling down as much as it was standing near a gently mounded hill far larger than the Hippodrome. From it emerged a woman, her head covered. A child clung to her skirts, and she had her arm around it, as if to console it for the presence of the army so close, so dangerously close to home. With her other arm, she restrained the boy who had spoken with Leo.

From his gestures and the shrillness of his voice, he knew that the child was pleading the case of the sick man by the road. "But he'll *die* if you don't go to him!"

Was there ever a time when Leo had thought his mother all-powerful? There must have been, or he would not have dreaded her judgment all the years of his youth.

The boy's mother shook her head vigorously, and began to drag her protesting son inside, when a much older woman pushed the sagging door aside. She was massive, sturdy. Still, there was nothing ponderous, nothing feeble about her. She shouted at the younger woman, who released her son's hand. Nodding approval, she handed the boy the bundle that she held, spoke quickly, urgently to him, and pushed him back toward the road.

Gasping for breath, the child tumbled to a stop. Despite the warmth of the day, he was shaking with fever. Leo had wrapped a blanket stolen from a pack animal about him. He looked down at the sick man, then at Leo. "My grandmother says that these, steeped in water, will help the poor sick man. Is he your father?"

To their horror, Romanus began to weep. Greatly daring even now, Leo laid a hand on his brow. It was fever-hot. "I told my mother and my grandmother that you were a good son. My grandmother says *hot* water, tell him *hot* water, and come back home."

"My thanks to you and her," said Leo. "You are a brave, good boy."

"I shall be a soldier when I am grown," the child declared.

"*No!*" So Romanus had retained some shreds of rationality. The child recoiled, his eyes open with terror.

"Be a farmer, a priest, be anything you like. But not a soldier." Romanus panted for breath.

"Go quickly," Leo said. He attempted to give the child a coin.

"My grandam says we do it for the blessing, not the coin."

As the child ran off, Leo rose to his feet, turned in the direction of his decrepit home, and bowed in deep respect.

"Can he ride? He'd better," said a trooper.

Leo sniffed at the cloth bundle the child had given him. At tonight's stop, he would boil the herbs and give them to Romanus. A pity he could not do so now. It was pointless to ask. Romanus had been granted his life. He would be given no more.

The Caesar must be enjoying every moment of this, Leo thought.

News that the army guarded no less than a former Emperor, now in chains and very probably poisoned, spread across the countryside more efficiently than if relays of messengers had borne news from the capital. Men and a few women watched crossings or at the edge of their fields as the army passed: frequently, at the sight of Romanus, swaying on his mule, they knelt. And it was a rare evening when the boldest boy in a village did not dash to the army's camp, at least trying to bring gifts to the "poor sick man."

"Not *their* Emp . . . Emp'ror," whispered Romanus as Leo bathed his face or attempted to spoon some herbal brew into him.

No, he had been an Emperor for soldiers. But the countryfolk made their own stubborn, silent judgments: he had lost all, and now he was suffering.

When a surgeon finally summoned up courage to appear, he stared at the former Emperor, blanched, and hastened away.

The roads wound past outcroppings of rock carved with figures of dragons and old pagans, hollowed out, in places, into caves. The sun waxed as the year neared midsummer. The fields became more richly green, the brilliant poppies marking them like splotches of blood.

And then, one evening, the army marched into Cotyaeum beneath rounded white hills and twisted pines.

eo let himself sag with relief. For at least a day or two, he could get Romanus off that wretched mule, safely inside perhaps, cleaned, and even onto a decent bed. Leo himself might have the luxury of a bath and at least a dry place to sleep. Romanus, tossing his head back and forward, saw Leo smile and smiled himself, as easily pleased by comfort to come as a sick child.

"I don't want to think how many horses they've killed going back and forth from the City," Attaleiates told Leo a day or so later.

Leo had lost track of time. He rarely left the Emperor's side. If a monk had not offered to help him, he might have had no rest at all.

"How is he?" Attaleiates asked.

"He was lucid this morning. I asked him if he wanted me to fetch someone from town. Trade's good here, and a lot of Jews have settled here. You can usually count on them to have a real physician, maybe someone trained in Egypt."

"That would be one in the bishops' eyes, wouldn't it? You'll lose your monkish assistant." Attaleiates' bark of laughter held no mirth at all.

Leo shrugged. "What, a monk not aid a brother monk? Rest assured, I shall complain. But I think it's a good idea. Every time an Emperor gets a stomach gripe in Constantinople, they send a summons to Pera or the Chalkoprateia and haul out the physicians there. Why not?"

Because we're no longer dealing with an Emperor. Neither he nor Attaleiates would say that.

Hoofbeats. He saw his friend raise an eyebrow and knew that he had tensed, listening for any word he could hear. Another messenger had arrived.

Just the idea of a physician such as Romanus had had in Constantinople might reassure him. The Empire's laws restraining Jews were strict: they could not intermarry, own Christian slaves, build synagogues, or plead cases against Christians in their own courts. Jews faced the occasional riot and constant abuse from the lower orders—not to mention times of unusually strict laws. Still, they managed to prosper, and their medical training was famous.

"I should go in and check on the Emp—check on his condition," Leo said. "And you?"

"The usual," Attaleiates said. "Waiting upon my betters. If nothing happens, perhaps I can steal some time to write. . . . Leo, they're coming out of the Domestikos' quarters. God help us, he's got on his Caesar mask!"

Andronicus did not look as much imperial and remote as he did resolved, a man who had come to a decision he would see through to its bitterest consequences.

At his orders, soldiers dashed to the left and to the right, even, in some cases, outside the camp. But his orders, spoken quietly enough, produced a buzz of comment and complaint.

Attaleiates signed himself, then grasped Leo's shoulder. "My God, look what they're setting up," he whispered.

Leo had seen such a sight only in a vision: stakes, ropes, a brazier, and in it, heating, iron tent stakes. A growl rose from his throat.

"Hold hard, Leo!" His friend's voice reached him from a distance. "I'll try to hold them off, while you—no, the monk may be too slow— you run and get those bishops. By Christ the Pantocrator, they promised him safe conduct!"

Leo ran. The high wind that seemed to drive him forward brought him snatches of rumor.

"They say the Emperor wept. . . ."

"He always weeps and swears his milk-white innocence, but in the end . . ."

"The Caesar calls the tune. He and that minister, that Psellus . . ."

"Quiet, for your life. You want to wind up like *him?*" An infantry officer gestured toward where Attaleiates stood blocking the entrance to the Emperor's quarters.

Outside the quarters reserved for the bishops of Coloneia, Heracleia, and Chalcedon, Leo stopped long enough to draw breath and compose himself.

Leo pushed past the monk at the door and hurled himself to his knees before the bishops. One rose as if to defend himself. Another knelt before an icon, while the third—he of Chalcedon—made no move whatsoever.

"Most blessed lords," Leo gasped. "I most humbly beg your pardons, but I must beg . . . entreat you . . . messengers have come from the City, and the orders are to blind the Emperor."

He hurled himself forward, onto his face.

The bishop of Chalcedon assisted him to his feet, a bleak compassion on his face.

"We had our own messengers at dawn, my son. And we have been praying . . ."

"Sirs, you guaranteed his life. I beg you, come . . . they will not do such a thing in the presence of men of God. . . ."

"It is the Emperor's will," said the bishop.

Leo shook his head. "I beseech you . . ." He was on his knees again, tears and sweat hot on his face.

Chalcedon's arm was about his shoulders. "Look at this good lad," he said. "Kin to the Basileus, yet he begs for mercy for his enemy. Faced with such a noble example, can we, my brothers, do any less than try?"

Leo sagged against the bishop's arm, waiting for the others to decide. The roaring in his ears subsided, to be replaced by the dangerous buzz of soldiers angered past silent obedience.

"This is not a popular decision," said his grace of Heracleia.

The bishop of Coloneia smiled a thin, ironic smile and rose.

"I will tell them you are coming." Pulling free of the bishop's arm, Leo ran back the way he had come.

"They're coming, the bishops are coming. . . ." he gasped as he ran.

Attaleiates blocked the way to the Emperor's bedside with both arms. For once, he had forgotten the discretion of a prudent man, a survivor in Byzantium, and was shouting at Andronicus, "He spent his life in the service of the Romans. Even the *Sultan* gave him honor, treated him as a companion—and you would deprive him of light?"

"Will you, as Christians, do less than the Turks?" To Leo's horror, his voice cracked into a sob. "I have been to beg the bishops to intercede. They are coming. . . ." He gestured. Like a wave, crested with black, not foam, the bishops and their entourage approached Andronicus Ducas. Most of the men crowding around went to their knees.

"What . . . what is it?"

The voice was parched, unsteady. Romanus appeared at the door, fighting to stay on his feet.

Attaleiates flung out an arm to brace the former Emperor.

"Sir, I have brought the bishops." Leo pushed through to the Emperor's side.

"The bishops, yes, but for what?" With every word, Romanus' voice grew more resonant.

Leo pointed. Leo felt the Emperor's shudder of revulsion in his own body.

Romanus bowed his head as the bishops approached. "Most blessed sirs," he raised his voice, trying to pitch it over the clamor, "I beg you to fulfill the promises you made to me."

"A fine monk," Andronicus Ducas snapped. "You speak of broken promises? You broke your own vow the first time you made it."

The Bishop of Chalcedon held up a hand as finely shaped as old carved ivory. "Our vow, not his, is under question. We guaranteed his life."

"He *has* his life."

"Men die when they are blinded. We implore your mercy. We cannot believe that the Emperor, who is a merciful young man, would not forgive even his greatest enemy. . . ."

Andronicus Ducas shook his head. "These young men . . . these young men. . . . His Most Sacred Majesty wept for pity. *This* young kinsman of mine looks likely to run mad. But older heads have ordered . . ."

"Then you yourself do not like this," Attaleiates snapped. "In the name of God, man, you are *Domestikos of the Scholae*; you can use your judgment."

"Sir, you forget yourself!" snarled Andronicus. "No, I do not like my orders. But I am a soldier, sir, as you are. And we would both do well to remember what we are—and obey when we are commanded.

"Now stand aside."

Romanus lurched forward to face his former subordinate. "I never gave you orders such as this," he said. "And the one order I most needed you to obey, you *betrayed.*"

Ducas drew himself up. Romanus swept a glance about the assembled soldiers. One or two men groaned. Several fell on their knees, their hands raised.

"What if they do refuse to obey you?" he asked his enemy. "Will you wield the iron yourself?"

Chalcedon sank to his knees. "I beg you, send again to the Emperor. What is a small wait, compared with a man's sight?"

The Domestikos gestured. His secretary left his side, knelt before the bishops, and presented a letter.

"My instructions come from the Autocrator," Andronicus Ducas repeated.

The bishops averted their faces.

"Harden your heart," Leo told his uncle. If Andronicus had not ordered him silenced or killed yet, there had to be words Leo could use to reach him. "Go ahead and try. You hate this as much as we do. Command, and see if they obey. Where is your precious army then?"

Again, Andronicus shook his head. "These young men," he said again. "I do not need to command then. Others have obeyed my commands already."

He turned and faced the gates of the camp. A file leader and his leader of ten headed the party that pushed toward him. Several of their sixteen men had weapons drawn, more to ward off attack than to protect the prisoners whom their fellows, two to each prisoner, brought before their commander and threw down before him.

They were civilians and, as their garments indicated, of some prosperity. One was a woman, young insofar as one could tell beneath her veils. But it was not their civilian status, or their fear, or the way they had been dragged into the camp, or even the presence of a young, modestly veiled woman in their midst that drew gasps of outrage from the bishops. It was that all of them were Jews.

"One of these Jews will blind the false monk," Andronicus declared. "We shall have them draw lots. The female is exempt, of course, from that, but not from punishment, should they fail at their task."

"At least," Leo pleaded, "summon a surgeon. Even one from town. Let him, even blinded, have a chance to fulfill his vows and serve God as a monk."

To think, earlier that day, he had planned to seek out a Jewish physician.

"My orders do not speak of surgeons."

Leo could taste blood, fire, and iron in the air around Andronicus Ducas. It was not his orders, then, but a desire to humiliate, to crush the life and pride from Romanus—and the last vestiges of resistance from his supporters.

Romanus laid a hand on his shoulder. "Let be, Leo. Save yourself. One last order. Try to obey it, son."

Tears blinded Leo, and he bowed his head. A soldier went among the Jews, holding out his helmet. In it were shards of pottery. The man who chose the one bearing a mark would be the one forced to blind the Emperor.

"Why should I not bear the same risk as the others?" the woman asked. Her cultured Greek bore a faint accent that might have been enchanting were it not so angry. A shaft of light showed her more clearly to the soldiers. She had pulled her veil from her face. She was indeed young, her skin the color of amber, her eyes dark, long, and filled with intelligence and anger. Beneath the veil, which was picked out with gold threads, her hair was dark, richly curling, and gleaming with highlights almost the color of wine.

"Girl, you would faint before you could do what is required," the dekarch said. "We are soldiers and even we do not willingly watch such a deed, let alone do it."

"No," retorted the woman. "You steal us from our lives and work to do it for you. I but seek to reduce my kinsmen's risk."

"Asherah, peace," called one of the older men, who tried to rise to his feet and go to her.

"The lady . . ." The Emperor's hand gave Leo a slight shove.

Leo knew what Romanus wanted. *Lead the maiden hence: do not permit her to see me abused.*

Leo steadied him, transferring the bulk of his weight to Attaleiates, then went to stand before the woman Asherah. "Let me take her out of here," he offered the Jewish men. "Surely, you would not wish her to watch . . ."

A tiny tremor shook the ground. Asherah swayed slightly, and Leo put out a hand to touch her arm.

"I thank you, sir." She spoke for herself. No downcast gaze for her; and her voice, once free of anger, was husky and sweet.

She followed Leo's gaze. Romanus looked about the camp as . . . *in Leo's dream, Alyattes had stared about him, cherishing the last sights he would ever see.* The former Emperor looked at the assembled soldiers and Jews before his glance lighted on Asherah.

"It is well," he said, "that the last lady I see is so fair."

Asherah inclined her head.

A wail went up from her kinsmen. One held up a shard with a black cross marked upon it.

"How," her whisper to Leo was almost a hiss, "dare you use the symbol of your faith for such a purpose?"

"Jesus wept, lady," Leo said. "I beg you, let me take you away."

Her hand toyed with her veil. Clearly, she wished to cover herself modestly and be conveyed safely away from soldiers who might turn upon her and her kinsmen. But she looked again at the Emperor, his face grey with illness and the mortal fear that had struck him in these last moments, and she straightened her shoulders.

"If he gains comfort from any sight of me," she said, "he shall have it."

"Take her from here," begged the man holding the marked shard.

"I do not think that they will harm me," she told him.

"Asherah, Joachim's daughter, this is no sight for a daughter of Israel!"

"Menachem, your task is no task for a son of Israel! Shall I do less than the women of Judaea when the Romans stormed their fortress?" she demanded.

"Lady," Leo ventured. "Maid, how can you say they will not harm you? They prepare to force your kinsman to blind an emperor!"

"You are here," she said. "And they . . ." She gestured with her chin at the bishops.

Again, Leo attempted to lead her away, though he hated the idea of using main force upon a woman.

"Let be," commanded Andronicus Ducas. "She is surety for the rest."

He turned back toward Romanus.

"Take him," he ordered.

The file leader pointed. Two of his men, clearly wishing themselves fighting the Turk or anywhere but here, hesitantly approached Romanus and grasped his arms.

"I can walk," he gasped, pulling free of them and Attaleiates. But his long sickness had weakened him. His knees gave out, and he would have fallen unless the soldiers caught and held him until he could steady himself.

"Go on," the Domestikos commanded. "And bring *her*. Perhaps her presence will give him more strength than he showed at Manzikert."

And so the Emperor of the Romans fought his last battle: not to

falter as he walked on his own to the place where he would face torture; not to humiliate himself by one last, futile appeal to the priests
who had shown themselves to be mere men, and cowards at that, rather
than servants of God; and to bear what he must now bear.

With almost appalled carefulness, they bore him down onto his
knees. His eyes closed, then fluttered open as if unwilling to lose the
last scraps of painless light that he would see. His lips moved. *Kyrie Eleison. Christe Eleison.*

At his side, Asherah whispered husky syllables in a language Leo
could not understand. Her perfume wreathed them both, incongruous
amid the stinks of sickness and betrayal.

When Romanus fell silent, they forced him onto his back, then tied
him, hands and feet.

"The Jew doesn't know what he's doing," said the file leader. "Better secure him."

At his gesture, soldiers piled shields upon Romanus' stomach and
chest.

"Now, Jew," said the dekarch. He wrapped a cloth about the
tentstake and seized Menachem's hand. He flinched from the iron as
if from something unclean.

"Your brothers' lives are forfeit," said the dekarch. "And hers. Now,
do it!"

Menachem grasped the iron. The tip of it was barely red.

"Lady," Leo implored her. "Look away."

Asherah was whispering those strange prayers again, her hand light
and steady upon his arm. To his astonishment, he drew strength from
the touch. Even when Romanus screamed, he did not flinch.

"Oh God, it's a botch!" the file leader spat his disgust.

Leo could have hated all Jews in that moment for the clumsiness
of one man—were it not for the woman standing at his side, as courageous as any soldier.

"Try again."

Menachem sobbed. His second blows went awry. Blood sizzled on
the iron. The smoke of burning flesh reeked in the air.

The youngest of the soldiers staggered aside, to vomit in a ditch.
The priests' prayers rose. Menachem begged in at least three languages,
to be let go. One of the soldiers drew his sword and held it near the
throat of the oldest Jew, obviously a well-to-do merchant.

Asherah gasped and clasped Leo's arm hard. Her father Joachim,
perhaps? Leo would return her to him if this horror ever ended.

"Harder, Jew."

As blind as Romanus now from tears and terror, Menachem struck, then struck again. The former Emperor screamed and spasmed, all but scattering the shields that weighted him down before he fainted.

Menachem fell to the earth himself, keening helplessly.

The old man stepped away from the sword and went to him, raising him, then holding his head as he retched himself dry.

"Will someone bring him water?" he asked. His eyes blazed, revealing his resemblance to his daughter. "Water," he repeated. "I can pay you gold for it."

A monk kneeling behind the bishop flushed and fetched a cup of water. He handed it to the file leader—even now, he would not willingly touch a Jew—who brought it to Asherah.

She took it and stepped away from Leo to give it to Menachem. Her arm went around him, and she crooned to him and dried his face with a corner of her veil, heedless of how she ruined its rich fabric.

Leo turned away from the sight, from the sound of the old man's voice, "Daughter, Asherah, in the name of God, let us go *now* before they change their minds; he knows you're grateful," to Romanus, who lay unmoving beneath the eyes of the guards, the shields that had been used to pin him scattered about.

"Pick those up!" Leo ordered and knelt at his emperor's side. He had no idea of how to tend a blinding, but Romanus must be tended, unless there was more mercy in the world than Leo had seen recently and the man had died from shock and agony. He turned him over, trying not to gag at what he saw, attempting to bandage the ruined face until a surgeon finally arrived.

By the time he was free to look around, Asherah, her father, and their kin were long gone. Safely, he hoped. Her discarded veil lay upon the fouled ground.

12

Had Fortune been kind, Romanus would not have survived the night. The iron had been scarcely hot enough to sear the bleeding sockets closed. So the surgeons muttered, prayed, and applied poultices and bandages, which Leo already knew would have to be soaked away. He forced himself to watch: unless Andronicus ordered him away, the task would fall to him.

Outside the tent in which the blinded man moaned and writhed, restrained lest he tear at his bandages, Leo heard the orderly tumult of breaking camp. At dawn, guards approached, leading the weary mule that had carried Romanus from Cotyaeum. One of Andronicus' officers stood waiting, armed and inexorable.

"The Emp—how can you even think of making him travel?" Leo demanded. "The Emperor is barely conscious."

It was provocation to refer to the blinded man as Emperor, and Leo took a risky satisfaction in doing so.

"Then he won't know what's happening to him, now, will he?" asked the officer. "We but take the good monk to his monastery on Prote. He can offer up his pain there."

"Man, that's days away in the summer dust! Do you want to kill him?" Leo started forward.

"Quiet! Let the surgeons handle this." Attaleiates strode forward and caught Leo's shoulder, pressed it hard. If Leo's immunity had a limit, Attaleiates had no desire to find it out.

Leo snorted his contempt for surgeons who had abandoned a sick man to suffer all the way from Adana to Cotyaeum when he should not have had to travel at all.

"Quiet, I said," the older officer repeated. "You have already pushed the Domestikos harder than anyone I have ever seen and lived to tell of it. But even blood kin can push a man too far. Make trouble now, and who knows? He might start with the tongue. . . ."

"They mean to kill him. They guaranteed his life, and now . . . even the bishops are foresworn."

"Leo, that's close to heresy!" Attaleiates whispered, honestly appalled.

"The Holy Fathers do not lie," said Andronicus' man. "They serve the Empire as *he* failed to do. The strong do as they will. The weak . . . well, at any rate, I've got a horse for you, so he'll have at least you to care for him along the road. Do you want to risk losing him that?"

Leo turned slightly aside. Inside the tent, he heard one surgeon, braver than all the others and more competent than most, losing the same argument he had just lost about rest and quiet and time to heal.

Well, he had expected that. But then the surgeon lost a second argument, this one a plea for, at the very least, a covered cart to convey Romanus to the monastery he had built on the isle of Prote, within sight of Constantinople. Surprisingly enough, however, the surgeon won permission for himself and a monk to accompany the dying man.

Romanus had been Emperor and friend. Now he was "the dying

man"—soon to be less than that, assuming God mercifully took him to Himself.

Soldiers carried him from his temporary quarters. He was a big man, and now his limbs sagged. They tied him to the saddle, binding his legs and hands. Leo and the surgeon mounted up beside him.

"Try," Leo ordered the man who led Romanus' mule, "to pick the cleanest road."

"You should have been a nursemaid, young lord," the groom replied with a mirthless grin.

Leo shut his eyes. The sun was pale on a cloudless horizon. The day would be hot. Most likely, all the dust of Anatolia would stick to the stained bandages that swathed Romanus' head. If he had to support him all the way to Prote and keep off flies, he would do so, he vowed.

By noon, Romanus' body seemed to shed heat like wildfire. He and the surgeon had given up trying to plead for stops by the roadside. Now, they simply packed cloths between him and the saddle, as if he had reverted to infancy or fallen into the most squalid old age.

The stink grew hideous. Now, Leo longed for Romanus to remain unconscious: no use for him to awake to this humiliation.

He wetted the Emperor's lips—or whatever he could reach of them through the discolored folds of bandage. The bandages were hot with more than the fever Romanus had had since leaving Adana. Already, the poison in his body had reached the sockets of his eyes. The dust would filter through, and everyone knew that dust bred maggots in fresh meat. What would it do to wounds?

Lord have mercy. Christ have mercy. God send a miracle or a quick end to the Emperor's pain.

"I am . . . a brother to owls . . ." Romanus' voice was hoarse. Leo's eyes filled with tears.

Curse God and die. Romanus would not do so, any more than Job. He would have made a monk of outstanding steadfastness.

"Try to drink this," Leo whispered and gestured—carefully, lest he jostle the man he supported—to the surgeon.

"Time," muttered Romanus. "Time to serve God . . . oh my God, I am heartily sorry. . . ." A dry sob forced itself from his throat. "No tears now . . . will God understand?"

"He must," Leo told him. "He surely must."

"Praise Him." Romanus fell silent. The mule jogged along. It placed a forehoof wrong and stumbled. The Emperor flinched.

"Can't you lead a mule better than that?" Leo shouted at the man holding its reins.

"Offer . . . it up."

"No reason, sir. None at all. They take you to Prote. . . ."

"Ah. Built well there . . ." he sighed in what Leo was astonished to realize was relief. "Home."

Mercifully, he fell into a kind of doze. The surgeon appeared at Leo's side, driving him away until they halted for the night. To protect him from contagion, he said.

But it was not *his* eyes that had been gouged out, not *he* who had been poisoned. But "Go," whispered his Emperor, and Leo went.

He was shadowed as he rode, he knew, watched as men might watch a prodigy. *There goes the man who defied the Domestikos.* Kinsman or not, Leo knew he flirted with disaster. They would be taking bets, he thought, on how long he could go before he too was forcibly shorn and consigned to a monastery—if he did not succumb to Romanus' fate.

What of it? Ever since Manzikert, he had considered his life forfeit. Now, he rode along as if balanced upon a knife's edge in the dark. He had never felt so free.

That night, Romanus refused all food. Only the reproof, "Are you trying to kill yourself?" made him try to drink. He had bitten through his lip rather than cry out. Leo held the cup carefully, lest he subject Romanus to more suffering. He was painfully thin, dried out by fever and the poison that coursed through him.

"Lion . . . lion's cub."

The cracked whisper brought Leo up out of sleep. Leo rose from his pallet, his bones aching. He could hear the surgeon stirring on the other side of the man they served.

"Raving," said the surgeon. "The end is near. Shall I fetch the priest?"

Leo shook his head. "He is not raving, but remembering. The Turks called me 'lion's cub.' " The surgeon's face showed clearly what he thought of any Byzantine who jested with Turks.

He knelt by Romanus' side and took his hand. It was hot enough, however, to belie his words about the Emperor's fever.

"I will get the priest."

Glad to escape the stinks of fever and corruption, the surgeon pushed out of the tent.

"Leo . . . they hunt lions, you know," Romanus whispered. "Do not try . . ."

To avenge him? What could one man do, except remain blindly loyal to a blind man? *Why do you do this, Leo?* He could hear his mother asking that. In point of fact, he had asked himself the same question a thousand times. *Because it's right. Because it's all I have.* He took a deep breath to ensure that his voice would not break like a sad boy's.

"Rest, sir. Do you want more water?"

He laughed, like wind whistling through bone. "I will rest . . . soon enough. But you . . . you take care. Alp Arslan favors . . ."

Leo pressed Romanus' hand. "I will not go over to the Turks, do not fear that."

To his astonishment, Romanus squeezed back. "Rome needs her lions. . . ."

"I will stay."

He crouched there until the sky paled and Romanus fell into a murmuring, uneasy doze.

It was an effort to mount the next morning, as if Leo bore not only his own weight but Romanus'.

When he bent over to see that Romanus was as comfortably— now, *thère* was an irony—settled on his mule as he could be, the orange morning light picked out movement within the folds of bandage that shrouded the Emperor's eyes.

Silently, Leo gestured to the surgeon. He approached, bent closer. What he saw made him gag and hold his breath until he could straighten again and the wind blew.

"Maggots."

"They could at least have waited for my death," said the Emperor. *"Christe eleison."* He had a thread of voice left. Now it wavered up and down in the chants of the funeral office.

"Damn you, you didn't have to say it where he could hear!"

The surgeon shrugged. What was one more dead man?

The day was hideous, made more so by the fact that the Emperor was still conscious. His fever had lifted somewhat. Either that, or a cruel fortune had blown the clouds from his wits. Later that day, his head turned toward Leo.

"Sir? Do you want anything?"

"Do I want?" Romanus' voice cracked. "I would lament . . . if I had tears. Did you read, ever, of Hadrian, he in the West? In a rage, he threw something . . . and it put out a man's eye"

"Please . . ."

"No, listen. . . . Emperor offered him anything . . . anything at all . . . and all the man wanted was his eye, his eye. . . ."

His voice trailed off again. He had no tears, except the steady seep of blood and foul matter from beneath the bandages into his beard.

The night before they took ship for the monastery at Prote, the surgeon had soaked away the bandages over Romanus' eyes. After the first glance—and smell—Leo had not been able to look, and had stumbled outside to vomit.

He rose from his knees and spat, then went in search of water to cleanse his mouth.

"Sir?"

Leo whirled. His hand reached first for the sword he had laid aside, then for the obsidian blade he still carried, unlucky talisman though it had turned out to be. The man who approached him, wary though Leo went unarmed, was a *spatharios* in Leo's uncle's service.

He saluted Leo—*so even a renegade Ducas is worth that much!* Eyeing him curiously, the officer produced a letter.

The letter was unsealed. Well, that could hardly surprise him. What was surprising was that any letter came at all.

"From the City," he said. "For *him.*" He pointed at the Emperor's quarters. "I was told to give it into his hand."

"He's just got done with the surgeon," Leo said. He gestured at his stained clothing. "Let me take it to him."

"I was ordered: give it to him, or return it."

Maybe Romanus would be unconscious and the letter could be left beside him, unless, of course, this newest gadfly insisted upon tormenting the Emperor by his speech as well as his presence.

Leo turned abruptly. "Follow me."

The *spatharios* grimaced at the charnel reek beneath the fresh bandages. *Have you seen what you came to see?*

Romanus had nodded off into a fever dream. "Eudocia . . ." he murmured.

"What's that he says?"

"His own business," Leo told him. "You've seen him. Now give him the letter."

"It should be returned once he reads . . . once it is read to him."

"It will be." The steel in Leo's voice surprised them both. Men who chose the wrong side should speak more softly. "Now, go!"

The *spatharios* went, glad to be gone. Perhaps a miracle of pity had occurred, and Caesar John and Psellus allowed his wife to write to him.

"Sir . . . sir?"

Romanus jolted awake, stifling a moan as he jerked almost upright.

"A letter from Constantinople. Shall I read it?"

The horrible masked head turned toward him with more interest than Leo would have thought possible.

"Yes . . ."

He opened it, ran his eyes down the page. The hand was elegant, that of an imperial scribe or a trained scholar. The latter, he saw at a glance. The letter came from Psellus himself. Leo wondered that it did not scorch his palm.

"Michael Psellus writes you, sir," he said. "Do you still want to hear it?"

To his astonishment, Romanus managed a faint bark of laughter.

"What else . . . can he do . . . he hasn't done . . ."

Hurt you. Scorn you. The letters wavered in the dazzling sunlight, or perhaps it was Leo's own anger that made them dance. He began to read mechanically, then brought himself up short.

"What is this . . . ? Sir, he calls you a fortunate martyr! In the name of Christ and all the apostles, he says you are to be blessed because . . . 'deeming you worthy of a higher light, God deprived you of his eyes'!"

"Leo . . . please God he's right. . . ."

Against his will, Leo felt the tears come.

"What else . . . have I to hope for, son?" Did Romanus speak to him or the boy whom they could but hope was safe in Constantinople?

"That God will have mercy . . . what remains . . . I must get home. Home, my son." His voice trailed off in a mutter in which owls, Psellus, Eudocia, and cool water were jumbled. Perhaps he would enter a delirium from which, please God, he would never wake. If God were as merciful as Romanus hoped, his sleep would be pleasant and Judgment would rest easy on a man who had already borne too many burdens.

Leo bent his head. "Bless me, father."

Romanus put out his hand and rested it firmly upon Leo's head.

Psellus' letter dropped from Leo's hand.

Leo lay prostrate before his Emperor's tomb. The cold stone soothed his brow and lips. The deep-voiced sorrowful exultation of the chanting monks had subsided: even their echoes had died away. Now, only fragrant clouds of incense twined from the great braziers into the noble vaulting of the dome. Light pierced through the windows, dancing with the smoke and the beams of light that pierced through the lancets of the noble vaults.

Already, the incense had cast a faint dark pall upon the gold of the paintings and the mosaics, as if even the icons mourned in this church for the man whose gold had built it. Eudocia Dalassena had buried her last husband as befit an Emperor.

The peace of the monastery at Prote called out to Leo like water bubbling from a rock in a weary land. There was no haste here, no time but Heaven's own, but soon he would seek out a priest and shear his hair. Once he was a monk, he could settle himself faithfully at the tomb until his own life ended and he could be buried at its foot.

Summer had faded. Since no one had orders concerning him, he continued his self-appointed task of praying for the Emperor's soul.

"Leo Ducas. You were with him when he died."

A woman's voice. It was not loud, not in this sacred space, but imperially confident, as well it might be. For it belonged to the former Empress Eudocia Dalassena. Romanus' wife—widow—and now a nun.

Leo remained prostrate.

"Look at me, Leo."

He rose to his knees and looked. The rough black swathings of her order could not conceal that Eudocia was sadly changed. Her body had sagged during her exile, and her face was lined and pale. A short lock of grey hair escaped her veils. She no longer had the splendor she had once used as a weapon. But the hand she laid on her husband's tomb, workworn now from her convent's Rule, did not tremble.

"Leo, you were with him at the end. I would have given . . . much to be. Will you tell me?"

Leo had thought himself wept out. Now his eyes filled with tears.

"Lady, we shall have forever. I will not leave this place."

"No! You shall tell me now, this day, and then you shall return home. I know the temptation to renounce the world before you have played your part in it."

Leo gestured silently: *and have you not forsaken it yourself?*

Eudocia inclined her head. Her smile was bitter. "I see my husband did not love and trust a fool. No: you return tonight. Apart from my command to you, I shall tell you why I stay here and you may not. I was wife to two Emperors and mother to a third. This death finishes me. I am *tired*. Do you know what that feels like?"

The long night after Manzikert when the stars reeled like a drunken trooper; the retreat after retreat; and the terrible defeat of Romanus' death—oh, he knew. And now, with rest within his grasp, she denied it him? He raised his hands in supplication.

"You are *young*. Rest must be earned. I send you back so you may earn it. If you return, come back as a pilgrim, but come seldom! At the end of your days, you may desire to assume the habit of religion. If that is so, you will be welcome here. But I do not think you will. In fact, I hope you do not. Now, before you leave, come with me. I would hear of my lord's last days."

Leo rose and walked over to Eudocia. Greatly daring for a nun or an Empress, she embraced him. For a moment, they wept together. Her robes smelled of incense, and there was no comfort in her. Then she turned away.

Leo followed her away from his Emperor's tomb. The echoes of their footsteps died. The incense and the shafts of light continued their dance of sun and shadow by the Emperor's tomb.

Eudocia would have accompanied Leo to the boat back to Constantinople, had she dared. As it cast off, he felt himself alone for the first time in years. An illusion, he knew. Doubtless, at least three sailors and two passengers watched him and would bear reports back to various masters. Still, it was an illusion to be treasured.

The dark water lapped at the boat's sides. Lights reflected up at him. The walls of Constantinople reared up before him; beyond them loomed the sullen bulk of Justinian's great Church of the Holy Wisdom.

Leo swayed with the motion of the small ship, the wind stirring his hair, cooling his eyes. Too soon, its hull bumped against its moorings. Sailors shouted, ropes flew through the air, and the trip from Prote back to his world was over.

The gangplank slammed against the dock. Nodding courtesy to the captain, Leo disembarked. He had his sword again. No one, robber nor other watcher in the shadows, stood in his way. The cats that prowled the harbor went silent. They pressed against the crumbling walls, their eyes lambent in the scanty torchlight.

Leo's clothes were poor enough to let him pass up from the harbor unmolested. If he wished, though, to disappear into the shadows, perhaps he might find a taverna where his meager funds would let him drink until a wine-red haze befuddled facts and where he might find some comforting, convenient female body to sink into and clutch against his dreams.

He remembered the fine eyes and finer courage of that girl— Asherah, her name was, an odd name—in Cotyaeum. He had taken courage from her presence and her hand, light upon his arm. She was a Jew. He would never see her again.

No, there was no point of thinking of a taverna. He walked up from the harbor. The shadows twined and danced behind him. The reek of fish lessened. It was better than rotting flesh, but only barely.

Up from the harbor, toward the quarter near the palace where the patricians, even poor ones, lived. The lights of the shops that lined the Mese had all gone dark. Leo kept his hand upon his swordhilt. He had heard the robbers of Constantinople had grown bold. No one spoke to him or stalked him for the little he carried. When had he become so formidable?

Even his feet recognized the way individual paving stones had been worn down in the narrow street he finally turned down. The walls of home, a shabby fortress, loomed up.

A torch lit the heavy door. He knocked. It groaned open, as if entrance were begrudged. From within, a light shone. A servant cried out in astonished welcome, and the door yawned wider. Footsteps pounded down the passageways before him.

His father reached him first, still holding a letter. Leo knelt to be blessed—*Romanus' fevered hand pressing against his skull, "Bless me, father"*—but Leo's father was alive, was blessing him, pulling him up and into his thin arms, strengthened now by joy.

"This is my son who was lost and now is found," his father cried. Rapid footsteps clattered behind him. Leo's father laughed and passed Leo to his mother.

Fiercely, she clasped him to her heart, then held him off. He felt the sob that racked her—just one; and she put on her self-control like a veil. But, under her cosmetics, her face had thinned. The light of well-polished polycandela revealed that she had begun to wash her hair with henna.

"There is grey in your hair," she observed, and touched his cheek and newly trimmed beard. "Do you want something to eat? Will you wash first? Your room is ready."

He had feared how she might greet him, but she seemed almost shy, concerned only with his comfort. Weighed against what he had endured, there was nothing to fear here. Was there anything for him at all?

Leo went silently to his boyhood room. It was smaller than he remembered, and it smelled empty. A few moments more, and he would have to go downstairs, force down food, and meet his parents' eyes. He was not hungry, and his old bed looked inviting.

He took off his sword, placed it within reach, and lay down. Exhaustion drained from him into the familiar mattress; the old shadows from his childhood reached out to comfort him. He was aware of his parents standing at his door. He sensed their eyes upon him, their love and fear; and then he slept.

 13

The Emperor screamed in mortal anguish. Nearby, another *victim sank to his knees, the iron still in his hand, and wept for the crime he had been forced to commit. A young woman with eyes that hid old secrets knelt beside him and cleansed his beard.*

Get her away! Leo hurled himself between weeping man and patient woman as the ground shuddered more and more violently. They vanished.

He ran through a wasteland of twisted stone. The wind howled through it, striking up a wailing from the rocks itself. Something . . . someone pursued him, a horned crown upon its . . . no, upon her . . . brow. And where the creature walked, the earth cracked. A plume of white smoke rose from the wounded land. Fire lay below. His breath was full of ashes.

Leo hit the stone floor of his room so hard that his jaws snapped shut, cutting off his scream. Too late: footsteps scurried through the house. A servant peered in but did not dare to enter. His mother, for the first time that Leo could remember, looked at his father for advice. His father, kneeling by Leo's side, did not see as he lifted Leo against his shoulder.

"They are all dead," Leo whispered.

"Hush, my son."

"I should be dead, too."

He tried to ease Leo against his shoulder. "You are home. Let it be as when you were a boy. You will tell me what is wrong. We will reason it out and pray over it. And then, you will sleep."

"No!" Leo forced himself away from the temptation of comfort. His father was old and innocent; and he should remain so. He had not lain out all night at Manzikert and watched the robbers strip his comrades' bodies. He had not heard an Emperor scream as hot irons bungled away his sight. And God grant his father no idea, ever, of the dreams that haunted his sleep.

It was less trouble, in the end, to allow his father to sit with him for awhile than to persuade him to return to his own bed. Just so, Leo had watched over the Emperor: the illusion of protection, not the real thing. But there was love and trust. Through slitted lids he watched his father bend his head over his clasped hands. The older man's disappointed face turned serene. After a time, he could even feel the virtue of his father's prayer seeping into him as water seeps into thirsty earth.

He slept again, almost a waking dream. Again, he saw the girl Asherah's face beneath her veil. It dropped from her hair and rippled on the grass until it turned into cool water that flowed from a cleft in gray stone, warded on both sides by poplars, their green and gold leaves swaying.

In the greyness of first light, Leo stood by his window and looked down into one of the gardens. The roses were but a darker grey in this light, and their petals fell like drops of blood upon the ground before the garden shrines. Haze lay upon the Sea, hiding all but the masts of the ships in Byzantium's great harbor.

If he hurled himself from the window, would they think he fell? Or would they know? Christ would know; and Leo would be damned. It would be more familiar, perhaps, than the landscapes of his nightmares, but it would be hell, all the same.

As soon as he decently might rise, as if he simply were a young man home on leave, Leo dressed. The clothes of his former life were too loose, and their fineness offended him. What right had the likes of him to silk and fine wool? He chose the most somber and went down.

He sat himself at the old, scrubbed table with his family. Honey was on it, white cheese, and fresh bread, brought in by servants who had known him since his boyhood and whose eyes brightened—the more fools they!—at the sight of him.

Following his mother's example, Leo blessed himself and broke bread. He ate very little. She said nothing: merely watched out of those dark eyes of hers that missed nothing.

As his mother had always pointed out, they were not of the rich branch of the Ducas family. Father and mother had their appointed tasks. Leo busied himself in the garden as his mother supervised the cleaning of the shrines. The sun emerged as the last of the fallen rose petals were cleared away. The stone looked less as if it had been bled upon. He knelt before the shrine to pray and staggered when he rose.

"I beg your pardon," he told his mother. "I am still very weary."

He retreated indoors. He heard voices, quickly hushed. Even the servants, scrubbing down the stone, seemed subdued.

The door opened, then closed with a reassuring strength like the gates of a fortress. He heard a shout, followed by the rhythmic tread of litter bearers. His mother, he knew, had dressed as finely as she could and gone to the baths of Zeuxippos, there to speak to other women of her rank. In her own way, he supposed, she went to do battle.

He chose out a book from his father's collection and felt the older man's eyes upon him. Psellus had said Leo was no scholar. Psellus had said a great deal. He retreated into his room with it and waved away the servant who came to summon him to a meal. The small, clean chamber had the feel of sanctuary now, and he read until the light faded. He laid the book aside, rose, and stretched, preparing his mind as, in what seemed like another life, he had prepared his body to do battle.

The polycandela, freshly polished, gleamed. His mother, fresh from the baths, had a radiance of her own. Steam rose from a great silver platter of baked fish, pungent with liquamen; and Leo smelled the fragrances of his favorite lamb dish, fresh bread, and honeycakes rising from the kitchen.

How long had it been since he had sat down to a meal without the reeks of myrrh or rot or blood or dust in his nostrils? Not even when he had been a prisoner of Alp Arslan: the lamb at the sultan's table had been strangely, richly spiced. This . . . tears rose suddenly to his eyes. This was home.

"Good," said Lady Maria. "You are eating with more appetite. You were wise not to stay on Prote any longer. I . . . oh, I have so many people to speak to."

So Leo had been right, and his mother had gone to the baths as if into battle. His mother's original marriage plans for him, as he was not surprised to learn, had had to be scrapped. Already old to be betrothed—for it was hard for relatively poor aristocrats to marry off a son who had lately been set to the profession of arms and might be dead in the next battle—Leo could not expect a great match. But if a Comnena or Dalessena were out of the question . . .

He met his father's eye. His father shook his head. His mother would give no quarter. She had a son to protect, whether he wished to be protected or not. He was glad when his father retired to his study and invited Leo to retreat with him.

"Your mother," said the older man. "She took this hard."

"I am sorry to disappoint you," Leo said. He missed several volumes and a fine ivory that he recalled that his father had especially loved. Sold? And for what—bribes to officials?

"You are my son, not a disappointment!" His father was uncharacteristically fierce.

"And my mother's?" It was a swift, shrewd blow, and Leo was sorry.

His father shook his head and turned away. "You have no idea how much she loves you."

That night, again Leo dreamed. This time the figure's breath burned on the back of his neck before he screamed and woke.

The next day, wearing his darkest clothing, Leo ventured for the first time outside the walls of his family's home. The street twisted, carrying him like a spring stream into the Mese. Here, trade and people flowed, and the scents grew sweeter the closer you ventured to the palace. Here the finest of the silks were exhibited, here the jewelry, and here, the stalls brightly lit at all times, were the sellers of fragrances.

Men and women thrust past him, the busy, quarrelsome people of Byzantium, as quick to bless themselves as to curse when they got the worst of a bargain; moving fast, always, with their eyes darting about even faster. You had to keep your hand on your purse and your mind on the soundness of your doctrine, or the markets of Byzantium would strip you of money and soul alike.

Shouts rang out on the street: soldiers marching on endless rounds of duties on the city's great sheltering walls; boys calling out at the latest prodigy—this time, a troop of amber sellers, their hair as ruddy as the ropes of amber they bore. Someone tripped a wine merchant. Idlers laughed as beggars pulled out cups from their rags and tried to scoop up what they might before it grew too foul. Up by the palace, the streets would be swept.

Shouts rang out. Leo dropped into a fighting crouch and saw men back away from him. A woman shut down her stall, at least for the moment. One or two people signed themselves, and parents pushed their children behind them. Silence, more oppressive than the noise of the market, fell; and in Byzantium, silence could be a prelude to riot.

Do try not to act like a madman, Leo. He could hear his mother's cultured voice, edged with the deadly irony of the ladies of Byzantium. All this madness because of some outcry in the Hippodrome. Leo fought his breathing back under control. He consoled himself that it was not, after all, a total overreaction to be wary of the Hippodrome and anything that went on in it. Tens of thousands had died in an afternoon in that place because of the flash of a charioteer's color; and now people stared at him as if he were about to add them to its toll. Another shout rang out, the massed voices of 60,000 men of the city, from the lowest laborer to the Emperor himself. It was a game, only a game, he reminded himself. And he did not even have a bet on any of the events.

Leo moved his hands carefully away from his weapons: see? No danger. He dashed one shaking hand across his brow. Then he moved on, more careful now to slouch so he would look less like a soldier.

Spices prickled at his nostrils. Ah. The Spice Bazaar. Here the most wizened and wisest of Egyptian merchants hunched over their counters in tiny, airless quarters, lest a draft waft a few grains of precious spice away from their scales. Here the physicians of the city came for herbs and drugs and who knew what else? They appraised him from the wizened corners of their eyes. A man as young as he might be fool enough to seek out love potions: in that case, he was certain they would charge him handsomely or jeer him away.

It was not a potion that would win him a wife, he was certain. Unless, of course, there was a potion to bring power, which was in itself a potent drug.

One man met his eyes candidly. The colors and scents of a sun-baked land surrounded him, but, at his glance, the air turned chill.

You do not belong here. Go away.

Leo was easily a head taller than most of the people he passed, and his good dark wool garments were conspicuous in this covered arena of deliberately shabby robes. Nevertheless, he obeyed. As he left, only a man he recognized as the Emperor's physician dared to meet his eyes. A Jew, as the imperial physicians often were; and as shrewd as court politics made them. He eyed Leo, assessing him to his last coin and family connection. He bowed slightly, appropriate courtesy for even a disgraced member of the Ducas family intruding himself in matters that should not be the least concern of the likes of him; and then he, too, turned away.

Leo sighed. Even if he dared ask for drugs to ensure deep, dreamless sleep, he would find no potion ready mixed here for him to take away. The likes of him must see their doctors or their priests—or find an old woman, kin to those he had seen throughout the Empire, squatting by the roadside, gathering herbs.

Voices greeted him from the women's rooms as he returned home, high-pitched, excited, speaking the elaborately courteous Greek that aristocrats taught their daughters as well as their sons. The great ladies of Byzantium were visiting his mother. He thought of retreat, but their eyes were too keen to permit it.

"Oh! Is that your son, Maria? He is so pale now, so thin!"

His mother straightened her formidably straight spine at that covert assault. Even the air seemed to crackle with tension, like the moment before a charge is ordered.

"Nonsense, he looks like a soldier-ascetic. A young Saint Michael." This woman smiled kindly at Leo, and he found himself smiling back, bowing to her. Some sort of cousin to the Empress—the former Empress—Eudocia, he recollected. Had she been kin to the bride his mother had schemed to win for him; and did she regret the breaking of the contract?

"It is a pity, Maria," that lady went on with more kindness than discretion. "Your son is so handsome. Now, his Most Sacred Majesty, if he were not Emperor . . ."

"He would look like a little old man!" whispered a very young woman, who suppressed a yelp of pain from where her mother pinched her. After all, Michael was a Ducas, and this was a Ducas home—even if it held the likes of Leo, a mad poor relation who had turned, actually turned, on Caesar John's son.

"A pity indeed," his mother replied. "But Leo may choose as he sees fit." She smiled as she spoke, showing a faint edged glint of teeth. The other ladies nodded, as little as they believed it. None of the people in this room had ever had the right to choose as they saw fit. "We do not know whether he will return to the army. Perhaps some post in the City . . ."

Now, there was an absurdity. Psellus was *proedrus* of the Senate. Caesar John pulled the Emperor's strings. Leo as a civil servant? Perhaps—let us make this truly ludicrous—serving beneath the Master of the Offices. What better way for them to spy upon him than to seem to employ him?

"It is possible," said his mother, "that something may be done. A pity that the most excellent *proedrus* Psellus has no living daughter."

Leo suppressed a shudder. Reward a client's daughter with the hand of a son of what was now the Imperial house once more? If the son were disgraced, the bargain was too mean; if he were not, it was too costly. And Psellus would calculate either event to the last grain of gold in the family settlements.

Another woman with her hair henna-washed beneath her veils whispered something. Well-bred shrieks of laughter replied. *I am too old to be cut*, Leo thought at her. Leo's mother raised an exquisite eyebrow; the room chilled; and the woman left shortly thereafter.

In a dream, Leo said what he must, held himself as befit a Ducas in this assembly of silken, formidable ladies. Their laughter and whispers pulled at him like a perfumed undertow.

Raptures rippled about the Basilissa . . . "So lovely, so modest; but she is so *silent!*"

"That comes, my dear, of turning a deaf ear to her husband's verses!"

"And, of course, we are urged to imitate it and call it holy."

More laughter. Comments, claws sheathed in silk, about other women who turned deaf ears to *their* husbands' words. Lady Maria ordered more cakes to be brought.

Leo had the distinct impression that, were he absent, the conversation might turn disastrously candid in an instant. It would be cour-

teous to withdraw, but he caught his mother's glance, barring his line
of retreat.

Complaints about the price of gold and silk; Leo observed that in
the market that day, he saw merchants biting gold and silver coins, gri-
macing with disgust that was less than half feigned.

Sidelong glances followed at Leo's mother—at Leo himself.

"Is it true," the woman who had glanced at Leo asked, "that the Domestikos of the Scholae will winter in Constantinople this year?"

Lady Maria raised an eyebrow, then shrugged elegantly. *Why ask me?*
the gesture clearly asked.

Nettled, the woman replied, "One would think that you, of all his
kin, would know. At least, one would have thought so last year."

The silence that fell was even more horrible than that in the market when Leo had dropped hand to weapons. A tactful request for another cake from the lady who had compared him to a warrior saint broke
it. *Lady, if you have a daughter of suitable age, I would gladly meet her,* Leo
thought at the woman. *If you are certain you cannot do better for her.*

In this silken ambush, Leo dared not answer at random; he had the
sense that if he placed a foot wrong, he would find himself swept up in
that undertow and carried out into deeper waters than any he dared try.
His mother knew the order of this battle, and he looked to her. He observed its tactics: the elegance of the language, the sweetness of the
voices, the overpowering scents, and the clear-eyed ferocity of the
ladies to whom he offered wine and sweet cakes in such a way that his
mother smiled victoriously—*would your grown sons show you such respect by serving your guests so well?*—made his head reel.

Then the door opened, and the greatest of the City's great ladies
entered: Anna Dalassena, returned from exile. An icon gleamed on her
breast, but could not rival her eyes, or the warmth of her smile when
she saw Leo.

His mother let out a tiny gasp of relief. Leo rose in instant deference. Both he and the Lady had been exiles on account of Romanus;
and now they were both restored to their homes.

She smiled a private smile, just for him. "My son will be glad to see
you," she told him. "I shall bring him, the next time I call."

"I beg you, bring him soon," Maria Ducaina said, smiling with her
lips closed. Her color looked natural now, and she raised her head in a
triumph Leo did not understand. "The sooner we all go back to living
our lives . . ."

Anna Dalassena observed her with her wise, veteran's eyes. She
held out a hand to Leo, as she had done ever since he was a boy. He

went to her as if seeking anchorage. For a time, he actually found it in her presence.

That night, he did not dream.

Sooner or later—and sooner rather than later, if he were wise—Leo knew he would have to show himself in public places as befitted a son of his house. He was not sure that he wanted to. The people of New Rome might stare at everything, but he felt as pierced by their eyes as a dead soldier by arrows. Sudden noises still had the power to startle him in a way that could have proved positively disastrous in a better soldier.

Still, every day, after finishing her duties, the Lady Maria made herself sleek, veiled herself, and was carried out of the house to battle for her family's future among other great ladies. Leo had always thought her beautiful; now he saw how fragile the illusion was above the bone—how bravely she preserved it, and how it wore upon her.

Ducas they might be; but they were poor for patricians and, without money or standing, could easily be exiles or—worse yet—forgotten here in the City.

A sudden irony made him chuckle. Ladies in Byzantium were daughters of the Church and its teachings about women's place. They sat apart from men in church, left their homes veiled, when they left at all, and were legally subject to their husbands in all things. But when the ladies spoke among themselves—or in a certain way to the men whose word, presumably, controlled their lives, those men hastened to do their bidding. And, in many cases, walked very small, wanting more peace in their homes than ruled outside them.

Thus it was, at a word from his mother, Anna Dalassena's eldest surviving son presented himself at Leo's father's house. It mattered not at all that, clearly, he considered himself old enough to take up arms. He bore an aristocratic name. He had won through a monastic exile of his own. And he had come to nearly a man's growth.

Alexius would never be tall, Leo thought, as he embraced his friend, but he was very sturdy. Leo could only hope that Alexius would ask no questions that he did not wish to answer. *Probably, his mother has warned him about that.*

What impressed Leo most about his young friend was that, in the time since he had last seen him—well over a year, Alexius Comnenus had developed a poise that outdid an aristocrat's courtesy as much as a Varangian's courage outmatched that of a street fighter. He had always been clever. Now, beneath dark, arched brows, his eyes were full of life and thought; and he seemed *ready* . . . was the only way Leo could describe it, as if on a moment's notice Alexius could assess a situation and react correctly to it without turning a hair. Perhaps he would indeed have survived Manzikert.

I am glad he did not have to, Leo thought.

He met his friend's eyes and was again shocked at the intensity of the spirit that gazed out at him.

Then, out from the scholarly distractions of his books came Leo's father. The intensity Leo had sensed subsided into the deferential courtesy of a very young man greeting a friend's father. Lady Maria nodded as the three left the house, as satisfied as a *strategos* at the deployment of her forces.

The common sort had thronged before the Hippodrome since dawn. The instant that the gates were open, they had surged inside, scrambling for places in the tiers of stone seats of the arena. Not so Leo, his father, and his friend: for them, there was a box with a door that could be shut, off a passageway that could be—and doubtless was—guarded, not just from the mob, but from the aristocratic occupants of other boxes. For himself, Leo would have preferred a place less conspicuous: he felt displayed within the box like an ivory within a frame—as much under observation as he had been when his mother's friends came to call. But his father and young Comnenus struck up an easy conversation on the Gospels (to no one's surprise, Alexius' mind was wise beyond its years, and possessed a supple vigor of argument). Gradually, Leo was able to unclench his hands and lean back into the cotton and silk of the cushions that covered his chair.

The reeks of sizzling oil, of cooking lamb and fish and onions, of sweat, and of animals combined with the bray of horns and the roar of 60,000 men cheering as the *quadrigae,* with their matched teams, careened about the central *spina* of the great racecourse.

Today was a day for racing, not for animal hunts or bear fights. Leo did not think he could have borne a hunt, and he would have seen his dead Emperor in the baiting and suffering of any bear lured out into the vast oblong of the arena.

Alexius leaned forward, pointing at a chariot drawn by bays, their coats darkened now with sweat and dust. As the *quadriga* rounded the *spina* for the sixth time, he shouted like a much younger, much less self-possessed boy, leapt to his feet, and then seated himself once again. Leo's eyes flicked to the men seated nearest him. They too had favorites to cheer on, but time too for a quick, appreciative grin at the fine, enthusiastic boy's delight at picking what—yes, now the bays thundered past the *spina* for the seventh and last time—turned out to be the winning chariot.

Alexius let out one last cheer. With an uncharacteristically boyish bounce, he brought his head close to Leo's.

"Did you hear," he whispered fast, "what the Turk said when he heard about Romanus' death?"

At least, Leo had enough self-command not to recoil. Alexius and his mother had spent months in exile when Anna Dalassena had been accused of passing letters from Romanus. Had that, in fact, been truth—or did Alexius begin to intrigue for himself? He was a boy, only a boy—but what noble son in Byzantium was ever *just* a child?

"Alp Arslan?" he whispered back.

How had Alexius heard?

He must have given that question away with his eyes.

"I have another friend named Leo, you know," Alexius Comnenus said.

All this time at home, and he had never thought to inquire how the dead Emperor's sons were faring.

Alexius shrugged. "He will make a soldier."

Around them, the cheering rose to an even higher pitch. The victor held up his brass wreath so that the slanting sunlight of late afternoon struck it and made it flare up as if they sat under bright summer light.

"Did he tell you what Alp Arslan said?" Leo regretted the question in the instant he blurted it out. He forced a smile, acknowledging that Alexius would not, could not answer him.

"You met him, didn't you? He has more loyalty than I would have thought. I must remember . . . in any case, he called us Romans atheists and declared . . ." He wrinkled his brow, looking for all the world like a boy being questioned about race winners in days gone by. . . . "from today on, the peace with Rome is broken and the oath which linked them with the Persians no longer exists. From now on, the worshippers of the Cross will be immolated by the sword and all Christian countries will be delivered into slavery."

Leo blessed himself. "He is a man of his word. And he liked my Emperor."

"Quiet!" Leo's father did not lower himself to elbow either Leo or Alexius, but both fell instantly still. The older man looked pale.

"Shall I have wine brought, sir?" Alexius asked.

Leo slashed downward with his hand. He had seen his Emperor at Andronicus Ducas' table, had nursed him through the stomach gripes—hemlock, he would believe until he died—that, even before he was blinded, might well have killed him. It was dangerous to drink wine when you had not seen the seal on it broken.

All about the Hippodrome, sun glinted on armor. Surely, there were far more soldiers in the arena than there had been only moments ago. Trumpets blared out, overpowering the cries of winesellers, the cheers of winners, the howls of men who had wagered more than they could afford to lose.

"The Emperor!"

Leo's hands chilled again. His father rose to his feet as the Emperor and his suite entered the *kathisma*, the royal box linked by a covered passage to the palace. Leo rose, standing at military attention, Alexius quivering with eagerness beside him—or continuing to playact at boyish high spirits.

There stood the Basileus: Michael, seventh of his name. A Ducas and, as he knew he should think, therefore worth all of the betrayals and sufferings that Leo had seen. But his last sight of Romanus, his seared eyes rotting out, made him want to weep. Even dying that terrible death, the Emperor had gained a majesty he had never possessed in life in his response to his torment. While, this Michael—Leo had never found the man, only a few years older than he, particularly prepossessing.

Now, although Michael Ducas wore the purple and enough jewels, seemingly, to have paid an Emperor's ransom, he seemed even less impressive—as if somebody had dressed a scrawny pedagogue in silks and gold and commanded him to ape majesty. Michael, Pantocrator, *isaposteles*, Emperor of the Romans—for *this*, he had lost a ruler, Alexius had lost his freedom however briefly, the man's sons had lost their father, and now, it seemed, Christian Rome stood to lose its life at the sword and arrows of an outraged Alp Arslan.

Michael shambled to the front of his box. Following them were men wearing the robes of peace and the arms of war.

"We didn't know that *he* would be here, or even that he was in the City," Alexius whispered. He grasped his companions' arms. To his shock, Leo identified compassion in the boy's voice.

Didn't they? Leo had heard the murmurs in his own home, seen his mother's discomfort about speculation on the Domestikos of the Scholae, who now stood, the mask of Caesar upon him, his searching eyes raking across the amphitheatre.

Andronicus Ducas. At the sight of him, Leo's father stiffened. Leo had not been aware that bad blood lay between the two. Leo held himself proudly aloof. Let Andronicus see him. He had done nothing wrong.

Leo scanned the *kathisma* for Caesar John, his father and, next to the Emperor, master of the Ducas family. He was nowhere to be seen. But there was no mistaking the man, with his fastidious grooming at war with his scholarly stoop, who entered the box last of all, with a show of humility.

Psellus. Leo would have to concede that he was a handsome man, and his years scheming at the heart of Empire had given him undeniable presence. But if he saw him now, preening before a mass of men cheering their Emperor, he could also see him hiding in the crypt, awaiting glory or an ignominious end. A pity that the Varangians' axes had not slipped that day.

Michael seated himself, gesturing for the crowd to subside, to sit down, to let everyone get on with the business of entertaining himself. The sooner begun; the sooner over; and he could go back to his poetry, Leo thought. But Psellus' clever eyes scanned the crowd, occasionally pausing as if to read the soul of someone in the audience or to calculate what share of the homage granted the Emperor might be for himself. His eyes met Leo's.

Leo shuddered, feeling a cold that had nothing to do with the wind, and more with a sickness of spirit. Against his will, he thought back over the year or two since he had ridden out of Byzantium at his uncle's heels: rough hands seemed to poke through his memories just as a hoodlum might pluck his purse free and, in his own sight, turn it upside down to count his booty.

It was a relief when the entertainers ran in. Michael might turn his face away from the dancers, their legs flashing beneath brief tunics; but the audience greeted them with ribald enthusiasm. He glanced back at Psellus, who shook his head. Let them dance.

Races and dances finally finished. Leo was glad to go leave the Hippodrome. Servants and guards waited outside his house, armed and bearing torches to see Alexius safely home.

That night, in Leo's dreams, Andronicus Ducas pursued him and his family over jagged rocks through which the wind whistled. Leo was sobbing; his throat was dry; and instead of rain, ash was falling from the sky. He bared his teeth in defiance at it, and the force of his rage blackened his sight.

After a time, red and yellow streaks of fire lit the blackness, then formed themselves into a face with gleaming eyes and a scarlet mouth, drawn into a rictus that exposed sharp teeth. He wanted to whimper, but he was a man now, not a child; and there were children to protect.

If he were not silent, the enemies would come with their arrows, and there would be nothing for any of them.

Tears ran down his face. It was a wonder: they eased his pain. And, after a time, they touched his lips. A second wonder: they tasted not of salt, but of fresh water. His eyes did not burn as his poor Emperor's had; and the surprise woke him.

Leo sat up in the darkness of his boyhood room. It was silent, except for the rain outside, spattering against the walls and upon the pavement of the inner courtyard. He sighed with relief, not so much at the soothing rhythm of the falling rain, but at his waking.

For once, when the dreams struck, he had not waked screaming. But his cheeks were still wet from half-remembered pain. He touched them, touched tongue to the wetness: salt. How had he dreamed tears without salt? He had no idea, but the lassitude and comfort that they had brought him still hovered within reach. He settled back down, hoping that warmth and the rain would comfort him so that this time, he might slip into rest unblemished by fear or faces out of ancient nightmares.

Instead, just as his eyes closed and his body slackened into total relaxation, he saw dark, long eyes, half-hidden by a veil shot with gold threads. The veil dropped. Coils of dark hair fell upon it, framing a face he had seen only once yet never forgotten. He even could put a name to it.

"Asherah," he said, and fell asleep upon the sigh that was her name.

You might have told me Andronicus was in the City!"

Hearing his father's voice raised, Leo paused outside the room where his father and mother sat. Lulled by his memories of a woman he had seen but once, Leo had slept through the morning meal.

A lesser woman would have asked how she might be expected to know the whereabouts of generals when her husband did not.

"You have been much apart from us, husband," Leo's mother replied instead. "Preferring, no doubt, the company of your books to the comfort of your family."

"The comfort of my family. Aye," said his father. His voice carried an indefinable irony. "They stared at my son—Psellus—"

"Hush! He has His August Majesty's favor!"

"They both have my son's fate in their caprice, regardless. . . ."

"Leo is safe," his mother blurted. "I was promised!"

The pause drew itself out, became more painful than any silence Leo had felt since the time he had leaned over the stinking thing that his emperor had become and realized that, finally and thank God, Romanus had mercifully died.

"You knew, did you not, Maria?"

A long pause, even more excruciating than the previous one. A tactical error on his mother's part, trying to wait out his father, who had a scholar's patience.

His mother's assent, when she gave it, came in a small voice.

"You could have told me," his father said.

"I would not trouble you with every rumor," she said.

Leo heard his father sigh. Again, the silence. This time his mother filled it with talk of books, an outing Leo might enjoy. Her voice grew brittle, almost desperate.

It was time to practice mercy. Leo entered the room. Both greeted him with ill-concealed relief.

In silence, he was served. His mother, her voice still too bright and quick, insisted that he barely ate enough to keep a babe alive, that now that he had returned to Constantinople, it was her duty and her joy to feed him back to strength. . . .

How else had she cared for him? Leo had seen the rage and helplessness on his father's face when Andronicus Ducas had entered the Emperor's box at the Hippodrome. Shame swept over him like a wave of fire. *How contemptible you are, Leo!*

Smiling, the lady Maria watched her son choke down food he did not want.

When he had struggled with breakfast for long enough to reassure her that he was still her obedient son, she smiled and, from her capacious memory, produced her great concern: the list of eligible daughters of noble houses with whom she might ally him—and her own fortunes.

His father listened in silence only slightly less threatening than a storm.

"There is a price for such a match," he said. "How much do we pay this time?"

"Not more than I can afford for my only son," said Maria.

"We have paid too much already."

Leo drew back from the table, even as his mother pressed her hands to her crimson cheeks. How had his father managed to insult both his wife and his son at once? As God was his witness, Leo came by his bad luck honestly.

"No . . . Leo, my son . . . that is not what I meant. *You* are worth any price. . . . Oh, curse it . . ." His father rose and left the table. The sunlight that had sparkled on the pale-scrubbed wood and made the broken bread and honey glow seemed to diminish. Lady Maria cast a look at Leo, bit her lip, and withdrew in the opposite direction.

Andronicus Ducas had been in the City, and neither Leo nor his father had known. His mother, however, had; and the ladies she knew had taxed her with it. Now, she carried herself with the angry dignity of one who hopes to use her manner to overawe questioners.

The problem, Leo thought, had to have a solution. Abruptly, he was afraid to ask. He remembered Alexius' eyes: the boy had *pitied* his Ducas kin.

Leo left the table. With the door to his father's study already closed, the rest of the house seemed too small, too sweetly scented with care that had become a burden. He left that too, hoping thereby to shut his fears behind him within its massive door.

He strode toward the Mese. The clamor of a hundred trades warred with the chants from the churches that he passed, but he heard none of them in his haste to get away.

Leo had become adroit in avoiding precisely the sorts of meetings that the ladies of Byzantium thought would repair his credit—and his mother's—within the circles that revolved about the court. After all, he had just made a highly public appearance at the Hippodrome with his father and Anna Dalassena's son: that should content the tale-bearers, who might have been glad to say that he had withdrawn from the amusements of his class as well as its obligations; who might say he was ashamed to raise his head. There was truth in that—best not think of it.

For today, he resolved, he would not think. Today would be his. He longed for a clean time, a clean place—well, Leo, why not head for the Baths?

Because there would be eyes there, voices there, whispers and gestures there. In all the city, what could he seek that might be clean?

Inspiration escaped from the back of his thoughts and seized him. He had left the house on a whim and in fear. Now, however, now, he knew what he must do. He would recapture that sense of comfort with which he had waked.

Today, he would search for the woman whose face had eased him into the most restful sleep he had known for months. He doubted that the ladies of his acquaintance would approve of his plans at all. Certainly, they would not enhance his future, such future as he had. All the better. He straightened his shoulders and walked faster. A cook-stall drew his attention, and he devoured the coarse bread with more appetite than he had shown, even for his favorite dishes, painstakingly cooked, since his return to Constantinople.

The chilly air swept across the Bosphorus from Asia like an outraged Turkish horde, or the way that the City might view such a force. The City saw the Turks, by and large, as barbarians and pagans. He knew better, remembering the formidably disciplined forces that Alp Arslan had wielded with such deadly skill.

He was angry now, that courteous host and ruler who had saved Leo's life and given his Emperor at least a chance of regaining his throne. No, Alp Arslan was anything but a barbarian. But he was angered at the death of the man with whom he had signed a treaty and for whom he had truly felt some friendship. And he was right, pagan that he was, killer that he most certainly was—and all the sages and priests of Byzantium were wrong.

There was no accounting for these things. Look at Leo himself. He should be in Hagia Sophia right now, praising God that his family had taken him back and sought to establish him within the city. Instead . . . there was no point, he thought, in returning to the Spice Bazaar. He did not think that Asherah's father had been a spice merchant.

Up the Mese he strode, toward the finer stalls. It was a risk coming here: this close to the palace, he would most certainly be observed. But he could always say that he wanted a gift for his mother, or the Lady Anna, or even for a future bride.

Hours later, dizzy from the array of silks, patterns, and scents, Leo turned his back on the arcades filled with luxuries. The chime of coins, tested and stacked by the moneychangers, rang in his ears. Something—half monk, half madman—raved on a corner. From time to time, he edged against a wall: a litter pushed through, heralded by some August Lady's servants; or a noble rode by, eyeing him as if wondering whether or not to accord him recognition. Troops of soldiers marched by, deliberately not looking to right or left as they crowded merchants and servants from as far away as Egypt or Persia out of the street. They were bound for duty on the towers and walls that girdled the City. They had a cold day for it and would have colder days yet. Already, well away from the palace, officials had ordered the boards put up in the arcades, to give those beggars and paupers who overflowed the monasteries and workhouses some poor shelter.

More soldiers shouldered by, one party leading a donkey on which, face toward the creature's rump, a condemned criminal jolted. His hands were tied behind him, and he had no defense against the lash that had already laid open his back.

What crime had the man committed to be treated thus? Perhaps this man on his way to torment or execution had been a murderer or a traitor. Leo looked at the man's face, trying to read in it some evidence of evil, or of shame. He saw only the man he had tended so long. *You will not have much longer to suffer*, he thought and looked away.

He was hardly what could be called a good Samaritan: if he were not careful, he might find himself facing a mule's ass and execution. Leo muttered a prayer—as much for possible onlookers as for himself—and turned away.

He knew he wandered among pickpockets and prostitutes, both of which might regard him as rightful prey.

Perhaps he was. He was a son of Eve as well as of his mother (best not think of his father now): they were sinners all. He quickened his pace.

The information he sought might be found in the Mese among the merchants. But it would take him far longer than he wished to find it. And by that time—he did not want to think of why he had set a time limit on his search.

But his wanderings had given him a better idea. He turned and headed down through increasingly narrow streets, balconies overhanging them and shutting out the light, to the wharves. The great walls that protected the imperial City loomed, shadowing him, and making him shiver with the cold despite his warm cloak.

At Phosphorion harbor, near where the great iron chain shut the Golden Horn, a ferry took Leo across the water to Pera. Leo glanced about and saw no one who might be observing him.

Here, hemmed in by laws as well as walls, lived many of the Jews of Constantinople, a separate and accursed nation within the Empire. If Leo thought he had been out of place in the Spice Bazaar, here, he knew, he would be as alien as if he walked about unarmed in the midst of a Turkish camp.

They were a dark-haired, dark-eyed people, as sturdy as those he had seen in his campaigns East, and with a look about them of having outlived kingdom after kingdom. They went unarmed, and he knew the severity of the laws that guarded the Empire against the likes of them. But they did not look as if such laws were necessary. He knew the stories. He knew the reasons. But in a moment of desperate fear, he had glimpsed a woman's face, and the faith and courage in its eyes armored him.

Compared with that, what were those stories and reasons? The Jews were deicides. But Christ had been a Jew. Why would they have turned upon their own? *Politics*, he decided. He wanted to spit out the idea, but caught eyes upon him and thought better of it. The politics of Empire. Perhaps it had been pagan Rome that executed Christ, and not the Jews' fault at all.

His quarry watched him as he approached. He grew conscious of his clothes. They were of good wool, if hardly ostentatious; but they were the garb of a Christian, a Roman of noble birth. They made him as conspicuous as if he bore a mark of Cain.

Why had he come here? the silent faces asked, more than a hint of fear in them. They were wary, these folk. They had learned that a visit from one of the people under whose laws they tried to survive could mean them only harm.

The answer was simple enough. Once, he had seen a face, heard a voice that had held more comfort in a comfortless time than, even now, he could believe possible. He remembered the upright figure of the woman called Asherah, her anger at being exempted from the dreadful lottery that turned one of her brothers in faith into a torturer, the way she had dropped her veil to give a man about to lose his eyes one last fair sight, the way she had used that veil only minutes later to wipe the face of a man revolted by what he had been forced to do. Cool water in a desert, yes; and courage.

She was a Jew. Other women glided, modestly wrapped, past him. Without evident haste, they retreated. After Asherah's steadfastness, their departure struck Leo as worse than any court snub. Here were Jews. It might be that they would know of her and . . . what was her father's name? God, he was forgetting things again—and not those things he longed the most to forget.

He shut his eyes, trying to remember. The man's *name*, idiot! Joachim, yes, that was right. He must have heard someone say it. And the man who had—God have mercy upon him—been forced to put out his Emperor's eyes was Menachem. Surely, one person in this place might know one of those names. How many women like Asherah could there be in an Empire?

It was hard to remember anything but the face of the woman who had haunted his dreams and had driven out the nightmares that made him wonder, truly, if he were mad.

A tanner yelled abuse and hurled some sort of stinking offal at him.

It missed, but he whirled, hand on his dagger in any case; and the wretch recoiled, as well he might. God send that he think twice the next time he taunt his neighbors.

Into Pera itself he walked. It was poorer than the quarter in which he lived. And it was not just shabby, but constrained, restricted by walls and laws. Hard to believe; he had always thought—when he bothered to think of it at all—that the Jews were great physicians, great princes of trade. The Emperor's physician, alone of his people, had the privilege of riding a horse within the City. It was hard, too, to think that any people would have had less freedom than he, circumscribed as he himself was, by family, custom, and constant scrutiny.

They might be watching him now. In that case, God help any man whom he addressed. The women might know more, if they were anything like the ladies among whom he had grown to cautious manhood. But speaking to them might start a riot for which all would pay.

It had been a mistake to come here, but he could not turn and go home without at least some attempt at finding the answers he sought. He headed away from the water, up into the narrow streets. On all sides, young men, their heads bent together in the immemorial sign of concern, even of conspiracy, whispered.

Yet these men for all their stooped shoulders and long robes, looked strong. Their eyes, when they looked at him, blazed with outrage at what clearly was an intrusion. They were a turbulent people, these Jews. Doubtless, those earlier Romans in Judaea had found them so. Doubtless, they had gone armed and not alone into the Jewish quarters of the land they ruled. Patrician of this City Leo might be. But he was not welcome here. He saw the veiled figures of women urged away, into the nearest building. Most obeyed in haste: one lingered, and he half-heard the faint music of her voice; but even she ultimately yielded.

Two of the young men slipped away from the crowd. Did they go to bring others—or to fetch weapons to wield against him? Why even bring weapons? Pick up a loose stone, a sturdy stick, thrust him in between two of the narrow buildings; and his brains would spatter the walls. Thieves, they could say. Terrible thing, thieves in Byzantium.

Or perhaps they would blame it upon the tanners. In either case, Leo would be dead. It could happen. Keeping his hand away from his belt took all the courage he had.

Swiftly the young men of the quarter returned. Unarmed, thank God; but other, older men followed them more slowly, but with equal determination. They gestured the young, angry men—sons? nephews?—to remain behind, then approached Leo. Like him, they took care to move slowly, to keep their hands away from belts that might hold daggers.

The man who spoke first wore clothes finer than any Leo possessed. He held up a hand: well-tended, but very sure. Not a courtier, God knew. A scholar? A wealthy merchant?

"I saw you in the Spice Bazaar," he asked without elaboration of courtesy. "You should not have been there either. What have you come here for?"

A merchant, then? No. Leo placed him. A physician. The man from the Spice Market. The Emperor's physician. In that case, the man knew him and knew better than to use names. Perhaps he thought Leo had come to implore him to treat his family? It was their souls that were diseased, afflicted with betrayal and despair, not their bodies at least, not yet.

Leo paused. Other men stalked up behind the physician. They too were older, and they wore dark, full garments. They had a look about them, a look of priests. He had not thought before that Jews might have priests, men they held in honor. Though, he thought how, how could they not? Aaron had been a priest, and before him Melchizedek had been priest and king. But these men's faces were closed as the city's walls when a war was feared. Oh, these people understood walls and protection. They were their own fortresses.

Was this how Asherah had learned her strength?

"I seek a merchant and his daughter whom I met in Cotyaeum in the army's camp. They had been brought there with others. I heard the name Menachem. The merchant had a daughter . . ."

"Joachim . . ."

"You know . . . he traffics in dyes, in silks, in fine carpets. . . ."

"From the caravan routes, with the Radanites?"

"Hush!"

The physician held up his hand, restraining Leo's voice.

"What need do you have of these men? And by what right do you even mention . . ."

Leo met the older man's eyes. He was a physician; Leo was a soul in pain. Let him see that.

"I was one who was in that camp. I saw . . ."

"Let even the memory of those people and their names fade, August Sir." The words were a command, but the physician spoke them in a tone more like a plea.

"Their lives answer for this, as do the lives of every one of us in the

Empire." It was one of the dark-garbed men who spoke. His eyes flickered toward the house into which Leo had seen the women flee.

"I beg you, young sir, if these people deserved well of you . . ."

Leo began to speak of their courage, his remembrance of Asherah's
eyes and her steadfastness, but the other man held up his hand.

"If you think well of them, leave them, noble sir, leave them and
their people in peace. I can swear to you by the Ark of the Covenant
that the ones you seek are not here. Seek not to know more lest you
endanger all. I beg you."

The tone Leo had heard in his father's words this morning acquired
a name. Fear. Fear of him, what he might say, his very presence.

Leo was not his father, though, to retreat into his study. He held
out his hands, allowing the older man, the priest, to see the pain in his
eyes.

He shook his head in pity, but also in repudiation. "God pity you,
my son."

How odd that "my son" did not repulse Leo as he would have
thought it might. How very odd. People hurried down the narrow street.
No women could be seen now. Up and down the street, narrow windows, all but covered with shutters, lit. He heard chants rise from one
old, low building, too humble and too battered to be a fortress, but
hunched down on the street as if it were an old man protecting his head.
Leo had not known that Jews had separate buildings for worship . . . that
is, he had not known that the Empire allowed them such buildings.

"Reb Gamaliel . . ."

"I know, I know . . . it is almost sundown. But this young man is a
soul in torment, and I cannot leave him thus—any more than I could
leave one of our own people—until I know he . . ."

Leo realized that he was still staring at the man. The "Reb"—why,
that was like the word in the Gospels that they used for Christ! How
right he had been; this man was a sort of priest.

What if I knelt, what if I begged him to hear me?

Something snickered at the back of his mind. Excellent, Leo: abase
yourself in the middle of the street, as these men hasten toward whatever unimaginable rite . . .

They spoke of a Sabbath. . . .

He glanced at Reb Gamaliel. Almost, he was moved to act on his
desire to throw himself at the older man's feet.

But Reb Gamaliel, with infinite sadness, was shaking his head.

"God forgive me for being another such—what is that story of
yours? The man who passed upon the other side? I would stop to suc-

cor you, I give you my word I would, had I not my people to protect. In doing so, I protect you as well. I beg you, for all of our sakes—yours as well as ours, go away."

The sky began to darken. Beyond the water, the churches lit. He would not be able to hear the monks chant from where he stood. Leo looked at the Emperor's physician. The man seemed genuinely agitated.

Would he know if Leo had been followed?

Very likely, he might even recognize the Emperor's spies. Psellus' spies, that was.

"Hurry!" commanded the older man. "It is almost the Sabbath. You would not care to eat with us, and it would be more than our lives are worth to constrain you to spend this holy evening with us. You must go . . . now."

Against his will, Leo's gaze shifted to the physician. He shook his head with absolute authority and no fear at all. After all, he served a Ducas, had seen the head of that house, of the entire Empire laid low before him. He was valuable to the Empire as Leo was not, regardless of what bargain his mother had struck.

"It is better so, young Ducas." The physician's voice might as well have been a whisper over a deathbed. It was the death of hope.

The elders gestured, and the young men disappeared into the various houses. Leo found himself heading back to the wharf. The sun as it burned upon the water, one last explosion of glory before it set, dazzled him, and he stumbled as he walked.

As he boarded the ferry, he realized that he had bowed to Reb Gamaliel and to the Emperor's physician as if to his father's friends.

But he had not found Asherah.

And what had he wished to do? Asherah's tears had long dried, and the gold her father Joachim offered for water had been spent months ago. As for Menachem: Leo could say he forgave him for blinding Romanus, but could he ever forgive him for the pain his bungling had put the poor man through?

Back over the water he was carried. Lights reflected in it, cast from lamps and polycandela in houses. Surely those houses contained people, simple people, please God, whose enemies lay outside their families. The shimmer of that light, distorted as it was, made his eyes ache as if he recovered from a long bout of weeping. To that extent, at least, he had not fallen. But his eyes burned, all the same.

He flinched at that thought: he had seen what it was for eyes to burn. He had seen what it was when a man was forced to burn them, with his kin watching. It seemed hard that he would never again see the man and woman who had comforted victim and tormenter. He sighed. Only as the water carried him away from the people whom might have brought him news did he realize how much he had hoped to find the woman of whom he had dreamed.

And then what? Will you bring her home to your mother?

The water looked dark and deep as the sun set and its reflected fire died. Drowning, they said, was an easy death. He had but to hurl himself over the ferry's side. Aye, but how many of the crew, how many passengers who milled about the boat, might stop him? Leo drew his dark cloak more closely about his shoulders and shuddered, not from the cold.

A ll that winter morning, Justinian's great church of Hagia Sophia had filled. The heavy furs and brocades Leo's mother had chivvied Leo into wearing had sustained him as he had had to wait outside in the courtyard with what felt like half the City.

First, the Emperor had arrived. How cold the stone felt against Leo's lips as he reluctantly prostrated himself, colder than the earth on which he had lain that long night of Leo's lost Emperor's defeat, more than a year ago. Although the dome and lower roofs were still coated with snow and the trees still sparkled with it, at least, the ice on the paving stones had melted.

Michael looked spindly and almost lost in the gold-embroidered richness of his robes. His shoulders hunched beneath their weight. The strength of his guardsmen, grinning and ruddy in the snow, robust in crimson silk, made him look even more pallid.

Yes, His Exalted Majesty had never looked more splendid, Leo agreed—and hated himself for it. Here he was, outside the greatest church in the Empire. All his thoughts should be gathered into the contemplation of God, and instead, he must serve Caesar, even if Caesar were hailed as vicegerent of heaven.

Chants and prayers rose on the other side of the church as well. Led by a deacon with Gospel and censer, the clergy arrived, their gowns brushing the stone. Patriarch and Emperor met in the vestibule and proceeded through the Aurea Porta beneath a mosaic of Christ, before whom an Emperor Leo prostrated himself, and into the high nave of the church.

Leo had always thought Hagia Sophia a testament as much to the wisdom of mathematics as to the wisdom of God. Just entering it satisfied something within him. It had a rightness of proportion—galleries and nave were precisely the right dimensions to enable him to partake of the immensity and grandeur of heaven, while not reducing him past the (admittedly tiny) stature of a man. A man, not an insect: no matter how humble mankind was in the sight of God and His angels, Christ had become Man; and men had designed and built this place.

The pale light of winter crowned the nave, glowing above it like a diadem of aquamarines and casting a luster upon the thin panels of porphyry that clad the walls. And floating a hundred and fifty feet across the floor, like a celestial version of the Emperor's crown, was the great vault of Hagia Sophia's dome. Beneath it, worshippers were subtly contained, yet liberated as if they stood under a sky that was not of this earth, a sky that glittered and shimmered with the flecks of light from thousands upon thousands of golden tesserae that adorned the mighty church.

Across the nave swept the patriarch, past the circular pulpit where a guard of honor attended him, toward the sanctuary at the east end of the nave, down the carpet to his throne. A rustle sounded, oddly loud in the noble space, as the clergy took their places in banks of raised seats. The fumes of incense rose into the air, dancing with the dust motes that slanting rays of light caught and seemed to hold aloft forever. Incense— a millennium ago, it had been frankincense brought the length of the caravan routes, along with myrrh and gold, offered to the infant Christ: splendor, worship, and a preparation for the sorrowful mystery that must inevitably follow.

He knew that in this season of the year, sorrow should yield to adoration and joy. The congregation seemed especially rapt this morning: God knows, the City felt it had reason to rejoice.

For the same reason, Leo felt a traitorous desire to mourn. News had come, delivered by an exhausted man on a horse steaming with sweat and trembling with the effort not to collapse in the cold. Not "rejoice, we have conquered," and death to the messenger; but "rejoice; he has died."

Alp Arslan, the Enemy of the Empire, the man who had sworn to unleash his hordes upon it after Romanus was done to death, had himself died at the hands of a rebellious subject.

Was it wrong to mourn the death of an enemy? Alp Arslan, the mountain lion, as he had been called, had dealt with Leo more fairly than many a Roman. And—Leo had to admit it—he had respected the man, liked his fairness, the largeness of soul that could enable him to toy with an Emperor, then set him at his right hand and even advise him on the conduct of his armies. Alp Arslan had called Leo "lion's cub" and spoken him fair. And now he was dead, at far too little of the threescore and ten that, surely, God meant even Turks to have.

They would think Leo a worse traitor than ever they had if he admitted he mourned the man. It would be terrible timing: his mother had been proud of him this morning. When they greeted friends, neighbors, and relatives (far too often, not the same people), no one had looked at him askance or even hinted that he might well walk small. He was a Ducas son; he was home; it was right and proper that he appear in Hagia Sophia where his cousin sat enthroned. Doubtless, his mother was watching from the galleries right now—and being dissected by the other ladies.

At least, Andronicus had left the City, Leo thought. It was an unworthy thought. *He* was unworthy.

Best not think of that, not here in this church. Here, even he might release his spirit, let it soar like the fumes of incense, the deep-throated, multi-voiced chant, the light as it lanced from the windows below the dome onto men's faces so that the lines of care and fear that scarred them smoothed out for a time in worship.

And if, in that moment, he bent his head and breathed a prayer for the soul of his City's enemy, who would know? Only God and His Son. Alp Arslan had shown himself more forgiving than an Emperor. Surely, God would show himself more merciful than a Turk.

It was *right* to love one's enemies. God would not begrudge Alp Arslan a prayer in the center of an Empire that should have been his ally. Another thought insinuated itself, as subtle and seductive as the fumes of the incense that twined about the rays of light in the great church. After Leo had prayed for an enemy's soul, when his mind was most composed and pure, surely the Bearer of God would not object if he breathed a prayer for the well-being of the woman he had tried to find.

Like Blessed Maria, Asherah was a Jew. They were *sisters*, Leo thought audaciously. How should he not pray for her? He might even pray for the men who had stood with her, forgive Menachem for the torment he had never wanted to perform and think with admiration of the wealthy merchant who stood amidst soldiers and demanded water.

Yes. He would indeed offer up those prayers along with the other, more dutiful sentiments about the health of the Emperor that he was expected to express. No doubt the men who surrounded him would be

praying correctly—or would they? In the years since he had ridden from
Constantinople in his uncle Andronicus' train, the world—his world—
had become so full of doubt.

Light, incense, and music wreathed him about. He could sense the
worship in this place as yet another presence: in this moment, the City
seemed purged of its intrigue and devoted totally to adoration. In this
moment, then, he could love his enemy and forgive him. The light dazzled in his eyes. In a passion of worship, Leo bent his head to pray for
the enemies of his people who had treated him as a friend. As for the
kin who had treated him like an enemy—

Pain spiked through his temples. He pressed his hands to them, then
slid them quickly down his face to wipe off unexpected tears. Yet it was
no shame for a man to weep at prayer. Perhaps it was the light: he had
stared at it too long. Only eagles, or angels, may look thus directly into
the light. He would try again.

This time, the pain forced a groan from him. He sank to his knees,
rocking back and forth. Arms came around him, supported him. After
a time, his trembling subsided. The sweat stopped trickling down his
ribs under his heavy ceremonial robes.

He drew a shuddering breath and raised his head to nod thanks at
his father, who had sustained him. But it was not his father who smiled
as their eyes met. No: his father had withdrawn as if he had been commanded. *He will not abandon me!* A surge of pride in the scholarly, subdued man brought Leo's head up and steadied him. He could even smile
apologetically and shake his head—cautiously—as kindly men nearby
urged him to lean his head against the column in the northwest of the
nave where, it was said, Justinian had miraculously been healed of a
headache. He would be fine, his smile said. It would even allow him to
remove himself courteously from Michael Psellus' concerned grasp
without looking as if he flinched away from a poisonous snake.

Why wasn't Psellus in his own place? For that matter, why was he
not with the Imperials themselves? Because, judging from the smile on
Psellus' face, Leo sensed that it was Psellus who had cast him down—
and showed every indication that he would do so again.

Leo was younger than Psellus, and stronger, with a soldier's training. He had never thought of that before. How odd to remember it now.

Clearly, a breath later, it occurred to Psellus, too. He slipped away.

Once again, Leo composed himself to pray. His hands were cold,
and a rainbow haze danced before his eyes. First, he would pray never
to be struck by that sort of pain again. The incense prickled in his nostrils like some wraith out of an almost-forgotten time.

Leo buried his head in his joined hands. *Kyrie eleison. Christe eleison.* The mighty chant washed over him, a deep-voiced wave that swelled into the highest reaches of the dome before receding into silence.

Why, the holy music had drawn the pain from him!

In a passion of gratitude, Leo raised his face toward the apse, shimmering with gold. Suddenly, as if heaven twisted itself into earthly ken, the air seemed to twist and sparkle. It *filled*.

There, looming before Leo, enthroned on sunlight, the dust of the earth, and the fumes of incense, sat Christ Pantocrator, He Who ruled all that was on earth and in heaven: dark hair; pale face, melancholy at the world's guilt and the joint burden of his Incarnation and role as Judge; and his eyes—dark, all-seeing, all-knowing, compassionate, but capable of the ruthless choice between sheep and goats.

He held out his hand to Leo. *Leave father and mother and follow Me.*

Yes, he breathed. Oh yes! Leo started forward. He blinked back tears lest they blur for even an instant the miracle floating before him. He did not want to lose sight of that majestic face, of the wise, compassionate eyes.

Oh God, his eyes were burning out!

The stink of burning overpowered the fragrance of the incense. Once again, he saw his Emperor, weighted by shields and strong men's arms, saw the glowing iron, and heard the scream that marked the beginning of his death.

How have I failed this time?

Like Asherah, this time at least, Leo did not look away. Flame consumed those vast eyes, hollowed them until visions erupted in the waste space of their ruined sockets. Horses thundered across a plain, some as well-known and substantial as the cavalry officer Leo might have seen on the Mese the day before, others faint, with arms and garb such as he had never seen except in waking dreams. When the dust of their passing had subsided, mingling with the ash of the burning, rock towers loomed. Wind lashed them, wailing like damned souls, and the rocks split under its pressure, showing a path that must surely lead down into oblivion at the center of the world.

Throbbing battered his temples, like the beating of a gigantic heart. A heart in peril. In a moment, Leo knew it, the pain would start, and this time it would devour him. Psellus would not even leave him the sanctity of prayer.

With a strangled cry, he rushed from the sanctuary of Hagia Sophia, plunging out as if he were one of the rebel angels cast from heaven.

A wind blew in across the sea. A pall of grey clouds hid the sun.

Soon the sun would go down, and the ghosts of all the men and women who died outside Hagia Sophia and the Palace would throng the streets, whispering and drawing him with them. And one of them, a tall man with scarred eyesockets, would beckon him; and he would have to go. His mother would be furious. What was that, weighed against the damnation he felt waiting for him?

He knew now that there was no escape, no safety for him under heaven. But, like a wounded animal, Leo also knew what he must do: go to ground; hide in enveloping darkness until he could once again bear the light of day.

The streets narrowed as he fled Hagia Sophia. Not toward the Senate, no. That was Psellus' domain. If Leo had failed in the church, he would certainly fail there. Not in the Great Palace. But toward the Arch and to the refuge Leo knew was there.

The Cistern. Centuries ago, Justinian had built not only Hagia Sophia to bring nourishment to men's souls, but his cistern, to tap the sweet water that helped protect Byzantium from those who thought to sit outside its gates and wait until it died of thirst.

His eyes widened, accustoming themselves to the ancient blackness of the cistern's low vaults, hollowed out here below the streets of New Rome. Torches blazed at intervals, their flames reflected in the water. As he approached, ripples shivered across its surface. He seized a torch from the iron fastened to the wall. How very strange. The bracket was iron, not bronze, set into meticulous Roman stonework rather than the living rock of a cave.

The cistern's keepers maintained small boats for testing the water's depths or checking the integrity of the piers that supported its vaults. Leo cast off and rowed himself deeper inside. His boat left a wake of ripples; his torch left a wake of light and smoke, a tiny comet reflected in the water.

Gradually, the pain in his chest subsided, and he breathed more easily. He ceased to row, resting now, borne upon the water until it ceased to rock. The dampness soothed the ache in his eyes. He felt like a child who had cried himself out and might now rest in the safety of nightfall.

Here, no time passed, save as his torch flickered and burnt down to a ruddy flame and deeper embers. If only he could drift here forever, watching the patterns of light and water.

He would allow himself to be lulled by the silence, broken only by the occasional plink of a drop falling from the vaults or the whisper of water against the sides of his boat.

Now he drifted toward one of the piers that upheld the vault. It was sturdy, even squat. Leo put out an oar to prevent his boat from scraping up against it. He leaned over the side of the boat. He had not known how much older he had begun to look—his whole life wasted, before he was even thirty. His own face, pale, sorrowful, with hollowed eyes, reflected in the water, captured his attention again. His weathering was gone, his cheeks hollowed, and his eyes as remote as the figures depicted in shimmering tiles on a church's walls. To his surprise, his hair and close-clipped beard were faintly silvered.

Perhaps that was the flickering of his torch. Soon it would burn down to embers, then to darkness. The torch flared up into brilliant light, as if the fire had burned into a pocket of sap within the wood.

And a trick of that light exposed what lay beneath the water.

The cistern was old, but stonework even older still had been melded into its foundations. One such stone had been mortared into the base of the nearest pier—but surely not by chance.

The huge face carved into it had been mortared in upside down, so its pitiless blank eyes met Leo's as he stared into the water. The serpents that were its hair shimmered as if newly freed from the stone that confined them. Darkness formed in the pit of the Gorgon's eyes, as marble lids rose.

Too late! Now he would stay here forever, a stone man, his face twisted into a mask of terror. He wailed like a frightened child and flinched away. His boat rocked from side to side. His torch, falling from its holder, hissing into extinction. Leo clutched at the oars. Too far, too awkwardly—he could not recover, the boat was overbalanced, overturning. . . .

The water closed over Leo's head. For an instant he saw the its surface smooth and go taut above him. Then he collided with the pier, an ungainly kiss of the Gorgon's face.

16

A violent light exploded in Leo's face. His ears roared—was that the cooling tide of his own blood, or someone shouting at him?

Something tugged at his shoulders, his arms, even his hair—he was being captured again. He tried to fight the indignity, but his limbs moved so feebly! He could neither fight nor escape; but must submit to being drawn back into the world of whirling lights and loud voices from which the Gorgon had drawn him.

His captor dragged him through the surface of the water into icy air. The roaring subsided: the shouting rose in pitch.

"He's half ice!" the voice that had dinned in his ears now shouted.

"Get him out of that robe or he'll catch his death!"

"If he hasn't already. . . ."

"He can't!" The voice almost cracked. "He just can't!"

So the voice belonged to a younger man than he had thought. How very interesting that would be, if he were only not so tired. The blackness beckoned, only slightly out of reach. So warm . . .

Hands pounded his back and shoulders.

"Leo, Leo! In the name of God, wake up!"

That was Alexius shouting at him. And hitting him. Why was he hitting him? Leo had thought they were friends.

He opened his mouth to protest. No words came. Instead, he gagged, then hacked up what felt like half the contents of the Cistern. He lay gasping on the bottom of the boat as oars propelled it vigorously across the water. It crashed against the walls so hard that Leo's ribs protested.

The boy dragged Leo out of the boat. He lay face down upon the wet stone, dripping, gasping, and shuddering.

"The way he's shaking, if he hits his face, he'll break his teeth. Wrap him up in this."

The coarse blanket that dropped upon him almost smothered him from nose to sodden shoes, but it felt warmer than any furs from the Rus trade routes.

"It's those clothes. We've got to get them off him."

"And carry him naked through the Mese. In the winter. People will be certain he's disgraced or run mad. . . ."

"I don't call screaming in the middle of Hagia Sophia, then bolting out with the Emperor present particularly sane, do you? Maybe he's got a devil in him." Leo knew without seeing that the pause meant that the speaker had blessed himself.

"Leo's got to be all right!" Alexius protested to the other, older man. There was some family resemblance; but Comnenus was a large family. No shame to Leo if he didn't recognize the man, though there would be if he forgot to thank him—if he lived. And he had garnered shame enough as it was. Again, he coughed and choked and spat as he was hoisted from the icy stones onto the older man's shoulder.

"He doesn't live far from here."

"We can thank God for that." Head down, he was carried along.

Wind lashed him even through the blanket. Curious: this upside-down view of the streets he knew so well. How the people bobbed! No, he realized: *he* was doing the bobbing, jolting with each step the man took as well as shuddering from the cold.

The walk expanded into an eternity, made worse as his limbs, half frozen by the water, regained sensation in a barrage of tinglings and burnings. He bit his lip to distract himself with a more bearable pain. Romanus had not moaned.

Carried as he was, he recognized the scars left on the old wood of the door to his house before he could make out the house himself. The door slammed open, and the warmth radiating out from the house to envelop him brought hot tears to his eyes.

His mother stood amidst the house servants, so pale that Leo wondered if she had gazed upon a Gorgon of her own and turned to marble. She would have had to have a heart of stone to make the devil's bargain he now suspected. But would a woman with a heart of stone weep and wring her hands?

Controlling herself, she led the way to Leo's room, helped strip him, rub him dry, and wrap him in every warm covering she could find in the house.

Tenderly, she wiped away the tears as they dripped down his face. He was not ashamed of weeping before her and his rescuers: he was beyond shame now, beyond sorrow. Children wept when they were born; and he felt, in truth, reborn into a kind of puzzlement.

And then he felt himself washed beyond consciousness as well. Relief eased the tremor from his limbs, leaving only the wonderful unfamiliar warmth and the stillness of a long-lost safety.

Leo woke to the drone of a priest's voice. The holy words droned in his ears, and Leo listened idly. Miracles. Demons were being cast into the Gadarene swine, which was a good place for them—if they couldn't be cast into Psellus. No . . . Psellus *was* a demon, or maybe he had one of his own.

How pleasant it was to lie here, no longer shivering. He was delightfully warm, and his head did not ache as if demons were squeezing it in a heated vise. His throat hurt, but he remembered hacking up water when Alexius hauled him out of the cistern.

Warmth radiated from the floor as well as from the coverings in which he was wrapped. If only the priest would not drone on that way, or if he would at least read some more cheerful text.

His mother edged into the room with a steaming bowl. She would have fed him, but he turned his head away. It was too much trouble to talk. Better by far to drift away on tides of his own thoughts. Through lidded eyes, he saw her stricken look. That troubled him. Dimly, he remembered he had some reason—what was it—for this sense of estrangement he felt. He had seen her weep. What did she have to weep about?

Sorrow and anger flickered at the edges of his consciousness, but a yawn blotted them out. The priest's voice, his mother's footsteps, the creaks of the old house in the wind blown from Asia all faded. Leo felt himself sinking back into sleep, wrapping it about him the way blankets and robes had been heaped around him after he was pulled from the cold water beneath the streets of Constantinople.

Shadows stirred beyond the shelter of his eyelids. They melded, then split. Two shadows: slight ones. Not soldiers then, nor officials. Perhaps not even priests.

"This is the man you pulled from the cistern?" The voice was a child's.

"This is the man who stayed by your father until God took him to Himself." That was Alexius' voice, correcting the boy with him so subtly that he might not know himself to have been corrected.

Leo opened his eyes. His smile, much to his surprise, was unforced.

"How did you get in here?" he asked. *Idiot*, he reproved himself. *At least, thank him.*

Alexius smiled, an oddly adult expression for someone his age. It made them all conspirators.

"I am a dutiful son. I accompanied my mother, who is here consoling yours. We slipped away. I have two brothers named Leo. I wanted them to meet each other."

So, this was the elder of Romanus' two sons, the one who shared his name! Leo inclined his head, though the boy was no Caesar and might not even be allowed to survive to adulthood. Fevers, after all, were so common in the young.

Again, Leo raised an eyebrow, glancing at the dead man's elder son. Child he might be: he was perilous company in these times.

Alexius broke into a grin far more spontaneous than most of the expressions noblemen of Byzantium dared to wear, even in the privacy of a sick friend's bedchamber.

"You know my mother," he said.

And so Leo did. Anna Dalassena would despise the very thought of scorning a child—especially one who had lost both parents—in the hope of currying favor at court. She would hold her head high and insist on doing precisely as she wished, even if she risked exile again. Leo could well believe she considered herself justified—as she so often was. He wished . . . oh how he wished . . .

The boy, young Leo, drew himself up, catching his attention. "Sir, I want to thank . . ."

Leo shook his head. "No need. I am only sorry for your loss. Our loss."

He met the boy's eyes. They were filling, but they reminded him so much of his father's before they weighted him down with shields and forced the hot iron into the hands of a stranger.

"Leo?"

He and the boy turned to look at Alexius, who quirked an eyebrow at him. Quickly, Leo adjusted the expression on his face: best not to let the boy see the shadow he knew was there.

"Speaking of thanks," he began, "I owe you mine for pulling me out of the cistern."

Alexius gestured briefly and with surprising elegance, turning Leo's words aside. His eyes lit with curiosity. *I could tell him about my vision,* Leo thought. *But it is a heavy burden for one so young.*

Granted, it could be said that a boy with Alexius' talents and upbringing could not be considered particularly young, ever. Leo had always thought some fate surrounded him, like the halo on a mosaic saint. It was no real surprise that Alexius had rescued him. Leo's story would be safe with him. He longed to tell it.

But Romanus' son stood before him, and it would take torture with hot irons before Leo told the boy how he had seen the Pantocrator reflect his father's torture.

Leo's eyes slid to his namesake. Alexius nodded. The moment for confidences passed.

"Sit down, both of you," Leo asked. "When you are discovered, I shall say I heard you and invited you in."

"For which *I* thank you," Alexius said. "We are all grateful today, aren't we?"

That earned a smile from young Leo. "Will you tell me about my father?" he asked. "No . . ." He held up a hand himself in a studied, elegant gesture. "But about him and the Turk, Alp Arslan?"

Leo took a deep breath, as an ache he hadn't known he had eased somewhat. "How long I can speak, with this throat on me, young sir, I don't know," he said. "But I will try."

He more than tried. Ultimately, his success proved the undoing of all three of them, as their laughter and raised voices brought his mother and the August Lady Anna Dalassena to the door of Leo's room.

The battle was brief, its outcome never much in doubt. At its end, two chastened youths made their apologies to Lady Maria and somewhat hasty farewells to Leo. His mother escorted them to the door, though Leo knew she would rather have stayed. Their accounting could not be long put off: he knew that, too.

Vision, panic, and the shocks he had suffered in the cistern of Justinian, followed by the long, warm rest, had left Leo weak, but with a curiously clear mind. He rose from his bed and threw on the first clothes that came to hand. The floor was warm against his bare feet.

For once, miraculously, his father was not cloistered with his books. Leo seated himself in his father's customary chair and reached for pen, ink cake, and parchment. He drove his pen over the parchment with more assurance than he had done anything for years. He had been lost for so long, and now, finally, he had found himself a path that might lead, if he were luckier than he had been, to peace of mind.

He remembered that much from his vision in Hagia Sophia: the blessed silence beneath the earth.

Swiftly he wrote. The more rapidly he performed this duty, the more rapidly he could search for the peace and silence he knew how and where to seek. The scratching of his pen lulled him into . . . it was beyond resignation: acceptance. He should have thought of this earlier.

He had, in fact; but the Empress Eudocia had thrust him back into the world. Rest must be earned, she said. He had taken that as a command. Well, he had earned it now. It was not as if he had a great number of possessions to dispose of, but those few of value must be distributed in a worthy, responsible fashion. Arms and horse were luxuries, vanities, but he would need them if he were to reach his destination. Otherwise, Alexius should have them—not that the boy did not already possess far finer. A few books—for his father. A keepsake here and there . . .

"What do you write?"

Ever since his childhood, Leo remembered, his mother had the gift of soundless motion. He started, then sank back into his father's chair. She had arched her dark eyebrows, always a sign that she faced battle; and her eyes held the look he remembered from the day he had been carried home, half-drowned.

He laid down the pen. Soon he would have God's time—all the time in the world: he could well afford the virtue of patience.

"I am making my will."

Up came her hands, clasping as if in prayer, then dropping, twisting in the heavy fabric of her garments. Her face flushed. As if the sudden heat of her skin freed them, tears slid down her cheeks.

"So I lose you, after all," she said. "All I did to bring you safely home, and now . . ."

Her hands released the silk of her gown. Her face went suddenly gaunt. Leo had seen soldiers look like that after a defeat. He had felt it on his own. After Manzikert. When Romanus finally stopped breathing while Leo knelt beside him in his cell, but had no eyes left for him to close.

"I was not worth the sacrifice," Leo whispered, averting his eyes. It was the only kindness he could muster.

"So now you cannot even look at me?" Her voice was still low, but it had the intensity of a cry. "I wanted my son back, do you hear? I would have done anything to save you, far worse, even, than I did. And I would have thanked God for the chance!"

"In the name of God, Mother, *why?*" Leo demanded. So far removed from the world, are you, Leo my lad? he thought. So remote that she can catch you, snare you, and draw you back even more swiftly than the Basilissa? "Why not just leave it to God's will that I would have returned?"

His mother shook her head. Even in her tears, she could still be exasperated by what she considered stupidity; and, clearly, she considered Leo's question to be profoundly, hurtfully stupid.

"You were at risk, son," she told him. "A man of the same blood, the same generation as His Exalted Majesty. You might not have known what it meant when the *Proedrus* Psellus refused to teach you further, but I did. And I was afraid."

Leo let his pen drop to the table. Psellus had rejected him. That had meant, Leo feared, that he was a fool, that his understanding was childlike, that he had no future in a City that valued a keen, wily intellect almost as much as it valued faith.

"*Kyrios* forgive me," Maria said. "You thought it . . . you, foolish, Leo? To think thus is the only stupidity you have ever committed. There was a test. *He* . . ." A gesture of his mother's chin in the direction of the palace left no doubt of her meaning. ". . . had what was required. Which is to say, very little at all. *You*, however, *you* never yielded. Ever."

She sighed. "Thus, they feared you. And your father and I feared . . . this City is full of dangers. We prayed for you and we thought, since you were not to be a scholar or a logothete, that your strength might well make you a soldier. And it was in my power . . ." She shrugged.

Did my father know the bargain you struck?

Now that his mind was no longer crippled by the belief he was less able than other men of his age and station, Leo could follow her reasoning: The boy was bright and willful—far too strong. Best not advance him. Best, perhaps, eliminate him altogether. But if there were a reason why he must suffer no convenient accident, well, let him make war his career. He could go East, a veritable haunt of dangers; and he would go supervised by one of the men least likely to advance him. And why? His mother wished him to live and she had a claim—best not think of that.

"Why not one of the others?" he asked. "Caesar John himself, his sons . . ."

"They were too strong," his mother said. "And too well known. They would appear as usurpers. Though, when Eudocia married, I would imagine it was thought of . . ."

"None of the men," Leo mused. "And all of the women . . ."

"*Hush!*" His mother's elegant hands (*do not think of those hands, Leo, caressing, cajoling, or you will surely run mad*) reached out to shut his lips. "That was the problem. Not just a wayward mind, one immune to his tricks." She sighed. "It was hard . . ."

She loved him, had sacrificed for him, had suffered, and he had condemned her. Even his father had not judged her that harshly. *Let him who is without sin cast the first stone.*

His mother met his eyes with the courage he remembered from when he was a child. "*We* wanted to preserve our son's life. Sometimes," she added, "you win only by appearing to surrender. Now, it seems, we surrendered; yet even more is asked."

Her hands went up, covered her face; and her shoulders shook with her grief.

Almost against his will, Leo rose from his father's chair and put his arms about his mother.

"I do not go to die," he promised her, "but, for my life's sake, for my soul's sake, I go to seek a place where I may live in peace, without assaults upon my mind and heart. Alp Arslan called me Lion's Cub: you are the lioness who gave birth to me and sheltered me—bolder than any lion. Can you not understand that and forgive it?"

"Shall you go . . ." Her face lit. "You were at Prote, where . . . Romanus is buried. And Her Exalted Majesty the Basilissa Eudocia is there. It would be shrewd . . ."

She sank into a trance of connivance, both political and social.

Against his will, Leo found himself laughing. Whatever else might befall, his mother was herself again.

"Mother, I do not seek out the good monks for political advantage."

"You, a monk, withdrawn from the world?" His mother marveled. "A stylite, perched upon a pillar in the waste?"

Leo shook his head. "I have lost all my taste for heights."

"Then, where *do* you go? And why?"

"Because I have seen a sign, truly, I saw one in Hagia Sophia, Mother. The Pantocrator appeared to me. His eyes were full of fire, and I saw countless spires of rock in the waste. . . . Perhaps it is just a fever dream or the vapors of a diseased mind and soul. But I believe, truly I believe, that there is a purpose for me to leave the City.

"I shall go to Cappadocia and make myself useful there. I have no vocation, it is true; but my back is strong. I can hew wood and draw water for the monks while they praise God."

His mother's eyelids flickered. A true sign was a true sign: it could not be gainsaid by even the most skeptical, which no one in Byzantium dared be.

But Cappadocia was also Romanus' birthplace.

Leo nodded. "Yes," he said. "My emperor's home. There, I shall make my soul."

"But you will die in a cave! And I will never see you again!"

"It is as I told the Basilissa. It may be that I shall spend my life praying. But be assured, if I can come back to you, I shall; and I shall send word of my well-being, such as it is. Will that content you?"

He knew her so well, he thought, then realized that he had scarcely known one aspect of her at all. She wanted to say "no." "Yes" was too costly, but "no" was a lie; and there had been too many lies, spoken and unvoiced, between them. So, his mother said nothing for a long moment, followed by "I shall pray for it."

"And I. Give me your blessing," said Leo. "I have far to go." He held out his will to show her. "I must thank you, you know, for taking me back."

"You are our *son!* And you will always be our son. I beg you to remember that, even if you turn to lifelong holiness."

Leo promised what he must for his mother's peace. That he loved her and his father. That he forgave her. And that he would return to Byzantium and his position as a scion of the Imperial Family—however undesirable—if he might.

But he had not lied. Within the Pantocrator's eyes, he had seen the magnificent desolation of the cave monasteries of Cappadocia: the silence and the stillness; water running beneath the sun over rocks and into unimaginable crevices; the sanctuaries of faith and the darkness beneath the earth.

Heart and soul, he found himself homesick for a land he had never seen. For now, however, he let his mother rest her head against his shoulder and forgave her for helping save his life.

 17

C *louds hid the peaks of the Taurus range still far to the south.* The moon cast a silver track across the salt lake and traced the contours of the land. With the spring greens of the ground cover hidden by the night, Leo could imagine this entire land as the bed of some long-dried-up ocean, of which only the salt lake remained a prisoner, shackled by earth.

All the elements were mixed here: the water glittered, stirred by the restful night air. He had found slick black stone like his tiny knife scattered about by some subterranean crucible that had exploded, hurling fragments high into the air. Gazing out across the salt water, Leo found it hard not to think of a sunken sea waiting for flame to gout from the mountains.

A burst of noise from merchants and guards clustering around the fire disturbed the ancient peace of the night. Some fool had drunk too much—which could be fatally stupid out here, should bandits or Turks be riding on the lookout for easy prey. He had ridden with these men from Constantinople to Ancyra to Caesarea Mazaca. He would be glad when he could ride away on his own.

It would be good to walk now by the salt lake, perhaps to test whether the water were as buoyant as he had heard pilgrims claimed about the Dead Sea in the Holy Land: they said you could not sink. He would write of the lake, if he were permitted letters, to Alexius. After his labor in pulling Leo from the cistern, the boy would no doubt be relieved. Would Leo ever see Alexius again, or his home?

Constantinople is no longer my home. By the time spring came and Leo could leave the city, it was hard to say who was most relieved: the Emperor and his servants—for their power; his mother and father—for his continued survival; or he himself.

Out of fear, the unlikeliest assortment of travelers huddled together on the road. Leo was certain he saw Armenians. Traveling at the back of the troop rode Jewish merchants, who had paid handsomely for the privilege, including a veritable army of guards.

Emperors weren't the only ones who hired mercenaries. He himself could well have sold his sword. As a young man with army experience, he too would take his place among the fighters.

He would have preferred to walk in the caravan's dust, a nameless penitent. But "excessive humility is a form of pride," his mother had reminded him, her brows winging up ironically.

Meanwhile, the captain of the merchants' guard asked no embarrassing questions about why a man with no visible flaws of age or person was no part of an army. Most of his other men were older, glad for the pay and the reduced risk of caravan duty. One or two, watched askance even by their fellow soldiers, were Pechenegs. And one, who kept much to himself, had the long, fair braids, the pallor, and the blue eyes of a Northerner.

That man did not so much walk as march, his shoulders braced as proudly at the end of a day as at dawn, when the wagons first rolled. He had the discipline of an Imperial, right enough, but he did not bear the axe that unfailingly marked Varangian guardsmen; and Leo asked him no more questions than he wished asked of him.

The Northerner was of an age to have served in the East—to have served at Manzikert, even; he had sufficient scars and the withdrawn, over-the-shoulder look about him that Leo had seen in his own reflection. Once or twice, his and Leo's eyes had met. The man had run his eyes over the worn, finely crafted cataphract's armor that Leo wore when he must. They had no need to speak.

Uproar from the camp shattered the night's peace. Hard for Leo to believe that any of the guards could get that drunk on the swill that had been served out to them. Or perhaps it was the merchants, quarrelling. Was he their keeper? Soon, it would be Leo's watch. It would be better thought of, he knew, if he reported early. But his mind had strayed, and he had not yet completed his prayers.

He bent his head but a footstep brought him instantly alert. He crouched, his sword out, startling the merchant who approached him, backed by a guard.

"Sir . . ."

Leo straightened. "I know. I am due on watch," he said.

"Can you . . . young sir, it is one of the guards. We need you to talk to him. To control him."

The merchant glanced about, clearly perturbed at straying, even at need, so far from the camp where from all they could hear, all hell was breaking loose. No hoofbeats: no Turks. What had caused the uproar? Some blood feud suddenly erupting after generations among the merchants?

Leo raised a brow, inquiring of the guardsman. The man shrugged. "It is the big man. The Northerner."

"It is my duty to do what I can," he said, in his guise as pilgrim. "But surely, the captain . . ."

But the merchant was scurrying back toward the dubious safety of the campfires, not even waiting to see if he were followed.

"The Northman got drunk." The guardsman shrugged. "Can't imagine drinking enough of the swill they give us to get *that* drunk."

Leo raised an eyebrow, trusting to the moonlight that the guard would see it.

"He wasn't on guard. Ordinarily, the captain would fine him, or have him beaten, depending. Assuming he could. But . . . then he got strange."

More shouts, followed by the glint of moonlight on a sharp blade, caught their attention.

"So he *did* have his axe," Leo muttered.

"You think he was in the Guard? Why would he leave?"

"I think he has a right not to answer questions if he doesn't want to. If your captain had doubts, why did he hire the man?"

Too arrogant by half, Leo. Try to be a pilgrim for once, not an aristocrat, even a disgraced one.

"It's not hard to recognize a Varangian, even without his crimson tunic. They're good fighters; Captain jumped at the chance to hire him—until he started shouting and swinging that axe."

"Why ask me?" Leo asked. That was the real question. "I'm hardly a match for him even without that axe."

The men gestured at Leo's armor. "You didn't get armor like that just to go hunting. It's seen hard use. Rumor is, you can reach that Northerner. Maybe the two of you haven't spoken, but maybe you don't have to."

Ducas. His name went unsaid once again.

"Rumor talks too damned much," Leo said. "I'll speak to the captain before I go on guard if he thinks I can do anything he can't." Slowly, he started toward the camp. His overly aristocratic armor rustled and chimed about him, distracting him from the peace he had sought.

Behind him, the salt lake glittered beneath the full moon.

* * *

The moonlight glinted off the big Northman's conspicuous plaits of hair and his harness, half as broad again across the shoulders as Leo's. And, most to the point . . . and flat . . . and blade . . . the moonlight struck sparks from the axe that the man now bore. He spun, threw, and caught the deadly thing with the deceptive ease of an expert. He brought it down on an imaginary skull with such speed that it whistled as it cleaved the night air.

Better the air than Leo's skull.

Talk to the man. Stop him. A Varangian who had left his service. A Varangian who was drunk and toying with his axe.

They didn't ask for much, did they?

And why? Because camp rumor, an effortless source of truth as well as entertainment, pegged Leo as what he was . . . almost: a son, however disgraced, of the Imperial Ducas line and therefore the likeliest person here to control a former Varangian guardsman who looked as if he were running mad.

Had the moon maddened him? Easy enough to see tricks and figures in the light, on the flat ground, in this old, haunted land.

At a distance, Leo stopped. Holding his hands out at his sides, he waited for the man to pause in his whirling, stalking assault on moonlight and shadows. The axe whistled and cut a few more glistening spirals and circles in the air. Then, the former guardsman stopped and raised it to inspect the edge. Finishing his task, he looked up and saw Leo.

He grinned. The moonlight flashed off his teeth.

"So they found someone they could talk into sending out after me, did they? Do you really think you can take me, or are you drunk too?"

Keeping his hands at his sides, Leo accomplished a shrug and several steps forward. The Northerner's eyes widened, but he shrugged and tossed the axe from hand to hand again.

"Captain says you're scaring the merchants."

The Northerner snorted. "I'm scaring him too. He hired me. If the merchants get scared enough, they'll cut his pay."

He cocked his head slightly. "Why don't I scare you?"

"I don't scare easily these days."

The big man nodded and lowered his axe. "You went East last year, too."

"I was with His Majesty when he died."

The former Varangian muttered something guttural in one of those barbarous northern tongues. "It should have been me, Greek. Me and the rest of the hearth companions.

"But this time, I was lucky." He snorted. "At least, I didn't have to see my ring-giver die. Not this time. Bad enough to see him betrayed."

Leo let out a deep breath. *Keep him talking.* "You think he was betrayed?"

"Man, we all saw it. Saw the reserves turn around and just ride off, with about an ocean of Turks riding at us; and us circling around the Emperor. It's my *wyrd,* my fate. Let me give my pledge to a lord, and the man dies."

He sighed. "The priest calls that kind of thinking *wanhope.* Says it's a sin. It's not a sin to say what's true."

"I had a choice," said Leo. "I could stay with my . . ." What was that word the Northerner had used? Best not mangle it. ". . . Emperor, or betray my kin."

"You had kin with the reserves?"

"My uncle led the retreat."

"Mother's brother?"

Leo managed not to flinch.

"I called him uncle. Actually, the relationship was a little more tricky."

This was the tricky point, if the guardsman decided that Leo's kinship with the traitor meant some kind of blood feud.

The ex-Varangian breathed out explosively. "Then I saw you, riding up to the Emperor like the *berserkrgang* was on you." He grinned again, that unholy flash of teeth in his beard. "No wonder you came out to talk to me."

"I'm on watch." Leo shrugged. Where was he getting this composure? The answer came, unwelcome. From Andronicus.

"You're not part of the regular guard the captain hired." A flat statement.

Leo gestured at his gear. "I may not be part of the Emperor's army any more, but what kind of fighting man would I be if I let this fat flock wander around without trying to herd them?"

"One of those eunuchs they have in the palace. Or a merchant yourself!" His companion laughed fit to make the salt water shimmering to their left ripple, as if it, too, paid attention. "Can you see any difference?"

Leo shrugged again. "Eunuchs have more gold, maybe. More courage, too. After all, emperors come and emperors go; but the eunuchs abide."

The Northman laughed, and Leo joined him, surprised at himself. He set aside his axe and looked about—for more to drink, perhaps. Which was precisely what he did not need.

"Still, if you can't sleep, why not stand watch with me?" Leo sought for a distraction. "I'd be glad of the company."

God credit it to him for a kindly lie.

By the time they circled the camp once, the moon was rising to its height. The fires were dying. The air grew cold. Somewhere a cat yowled. Leo blessed himself. The Northman reached for something at his throat and shivered.

"If you're not a merchant, and not a monk, and not an officer any more—and you can't very well return home, not if you walked out on your uncle's side . . ." The words burst out of him, but he managed to break off before he actually asked the question.

"My dreams are bad," Leo said. "I'm headed to Hagios Prokopios and the brothers. Maybe Peristrema. I hear it's quiet there."

"So you'll become a monk? Waste of a fighting man."

"Don't know yet." Leo clipped off the words, just as he had heard fighting men like Attaleiates and Scylitzes do. The less said the better, especially if—and it was true—his dreams were bad.

"What about you?" A question for a question; and the Northman had asked first.

"Me, young Greek? You should keep your distance, you with your purple, bloody name—oh yes, I know who you are. I was in England with Hardrada—he was a guardsman here, an officer, once, did you know that? Well, he died; and I had cousins in the North on the other side. Good family, much as you all believe we're all bastard pirates. They'd spit on me now, if any of them stayed alive. *Stay with us,* they said; and so I did, and I took service again with my cousins. Then Harold died too, killed by the Bastard's archers. . . . God, I hate archers! They say he and his people were some kin of ours, way back. So, after losing two kings in one year, like as not, I came east."

"You said your first king, Hardrada, was that his name? was a guardsman?"

"Senior officer, no less. That's what gave me the idea. You see how well it turned out, too."

They walked further, again in silence. As they turned, Leo and the Northerner spoke at once. "Have you got a name you use now?"

They laughed, somewhat uneasily.

"Leo," he said. "Just Leo."

A nod. The moon cast a silver track on the water and made the

Northerner look as though he wore a mask. "You can call me Nord-briht. Hardrada fought under that name in Miklagard. I don't think he'd grudge it me."

"Nordbriht." It wasn't that hard a sound in the mouth. "So now what, Nordbriht?"

"Now?" Nordbriht paused, considering it. "I may turn *wraecca*. You would say wanderer. Or maybe outcast. I have outlived three ring-givers.

"And you, Leo?"

"I seek to mend my soul. Hew wood, draw water for the brothers. Turn priest, if God speaks to me."

"Ah. So you will be a penitent. We have kings who turned to God. The Saxons have more. Which is why they lost their kingdom."

"So have we."

Nordbriht shrugged. "There is no place under heaven for a man ac-cursed as I. My skies are dark." He cast an eye up at the stars and the rising moon.

Something yowled. The big man's eyes shifted, and he drew a shud-dering breath.

"There is always mercy," Leo said.

"A lonely man often longs for mercy, his Maker's mildness, while his mood is dark and he must journey, striving with oars . . ."

". . . the wine-dark sea?" Leo was as astonished as Nordbriht to hear himself interrupt.

Nordbriht shook his head. "Not wine-dark. Silver . . . grey in the North, where the gannets stoop. Is your 'wine-dark' from a Greek song about the sea, then?"

"I will never see the sea again," Leo murmured.

"Our songs speak of it as cold with frost, the path of exiles. My path. It is great sin to say so, the priest in Miklagard says. He calls it despair—ugh!"

A cat yowled, joined now by others and by the deep-voiced bay of a hound.

The big man whirled, his axe coming up, his free hand rising to the amulet at his throat.

Leo unsheathed his sword. "You think it's Turks?" he asked.

The Northerner was sweating. "No. Not Turks. Worse than Turks. *Seithr*, ill magic, you would say. Greek, go away. Get away while you can."

"Damn it, man," Leo said. He dared lay a hand on Nordbriht's shoulder. The man's flesh, even through his harness, damp now with his sweat, burned. Nordbriht stopped in his tracks and slumped to the ground.

So he had finally passed out. There was a sheltered place a little further on, nearer the water. It could not be drunk, but it might suffice to bathe a fevered man's face.

Leo draped Nordbriht's arm over his shoulders, levered him up, and started toward what little safety he could see. The bigger man tried to push away. "Easy. We'll get you settled and then I'll think of what's best to be done," Leo tried to soothe him.

"Too late . . ." Moaning, as if so small a motion was against his will, Nordbriht turned his face to the moon. His moan turned into a howl of pain. He sank to his knees, taking Leo down with him. The Varangian's hand twisted the chain of the amulet he wore. Abruptly, it—massy silver, at that—snapped, and he flung it from him in a long glistening arc. It splashed into the water, disrupting the track cast by the full moon, high in the sky.

Leo's eyes followed the path of Nordbriht's amulet, where it splashed into the salt lake. The ripples were spreading out, subsiding. As he tried to steady the man against his shoulder, Nordbriht's hand closed on his arm.

As if lacking what scanty protection it afforded, Nordbriht drew in upon himself like a babe in the womb. He shuddered violently, then twitched and mewled.

And Leo saw the night as if through Nordbriht's eyes. Darkness grew as familiar as day, though more terrible. The stars pulsed and beckoned like torches on a battlefield. Among them, shining horses soared. He could see the long hair of their riders and hear their silvery, lost laughter.

"Women . . ." he breathed. Goddesses in the sky. . . . He thought of Artemis of the Silver Bow, shooting swift death from the sky. He had no hand free with which to bless himself. God have mercy.

"Not women," Nordbriht whispered. "Battle-maidens. I told you . . . run *now*. . . ."

"If I did not run at Manzikert, I won't run now."

"Fool!" Nordbriht cried. His voice caught. "You damned fool!"

His voice rose in a howl, first of pain, then of pure longing. And down the track cast by the full moon upon the water, their hooves as insubstantial as their road, came dark horses with flaming eyes.

"Nordbriht," Leo shook the sick man, "who are those riders?"

The horses tossed their heads, their manes turbulent as stormclouds, lashing across the sky. And then their riders came into focus. Some wore the armor of cataphracts, riding the company of Turks. Some looked much like the man he tried to restrain.

But others . . . more men ventured out onto the moonlit track, some riding, some walking; all warriors, but all different. Some wore tunics, some trousers and furs. Some carried the iron and bronze and flint of the earliest people who tilled the soil here. Some scarcely walked like men at all.

Leo had reached that last moment where sense and reality look at each other one last time before the mind snaps and the madman begins to rave. He would not go alone; he had a companion, pale as death, with a grinning mouth.

The water beckoned as the water in the Cistern had beckoned that winter. He was mad, he could hurl himself into the water and drown; and none would call it suicide.

"The hunt . . . my old home's Wild Hunt . . . it followed me. See it and ride with it forever. . . ." Again, that unearthly howl.

"*What* hunt?" Leo demanded.

"The Master . . . the Master comes!"

Nordbriht pulled away from Leo and ran toward the shore. As he ran, he tugged off his clothes and crouched lower and lower, as if avoiding a blow. His run became a shamble almost as bestial as those last almost-men in the hunt's trail, those who bore arms of flint and sharp-edged black stone.

"Wait for *me-e-e-e!*"

At his wail, a rider paused and turned in his saddle. Upon his head was a crown. It was not of thorns, which might have meant that the pale rider on his dark horse had some mercy about him, but it gleamed darkly, and it shifted. At one point, it seemed to be three crowns, one resting atop the next. Thunder pealed overhead. The man shifted form. Now, his crown seemed to be the antlers of an ancient stag, so vast Leo wondered how the man could bear them.

He ran after Nordbriht at the shore, straight into the path of the dark crowned rider . . .

. . . and met his eyes. They flamed, then burnt out with a hiss such as Leo remembered from when Romanus was blinded. Clean bone shone in their sockets; the demon on the horse was sightless, yet he still faced Leo down, laughed, and spurred his ghostly horse. . . .

"Away!"

Nordbriht's shoulder took Leo in the belly, and he went sprawling at the Northerner's feet. He looked up at the man, dazed, his throat exposed, his arms and legs sprawled out, helpless on the earth. Nordbriht's face had coarsened, distorted. Now it seemed covered with hair. His brow was flat, his jaw drawn out into the muzzle of a beast: not a man at all, but a wolf who howled and ran forward on two legs.

Into thy hands, Leo thought. How could he fight that?

Then the man-wolf who had been a guardsman howled again and swerved—between Leo and the wild hunt, luring the others away—

Hooves thundered overhead. Leo heard howling, then lamentation; and then nothing at all.

Someone was slapping his face gently, while another man held a flask of thin, sour wine to his lips. Merchants' babble in the background assaulted his ears.

A vision, a swoon, and a rescue: this happened entirely too often to him.

Nevertheless, Leo sucked gratefully at the flask, grunted thanks, then pushed away.

"What happened?" he demanded, thrusting aside hands and the usual, useless counsel to rest or lie back or not to worry. "And where is . . ."

"We found you lying here on the shore. And . . ."

The shore was empty. Even the moon-track was gone. Only the axe lay upon the ground.

"I'm all right," Leo insisted.

"The big barbarian . . ."

"Nordbriht? I spoke to him. Then, he went to walk by himself and think. Leaving his axe." For the other man's soul's sake and whatever might be salvaged to him of a future, best not tell what Leo had seen. Best not tell for his own good, lest Leo find himself shut up in those monasteries he feared, where the brothers were skilled in the care of the hopelessly mad.

"We will get you back to camp—"

"No!" Leo almost shouted it. He pushed himself upright. "I have a watch to keep," he snarled as fiercely as any man-wolf. "Leave me."

And, in the end, he watched out the night. Leo spent that watch praying for the man, or beast, who had him in his power, but who chose to thrust him from the path of that dark king, and then ran away himself, rather than endanger a fellow man.

At dawn, Leo saw the hoofprints of a great riding, and the remnants of the host—coins of awkward shapes and sizes, cast-off spearheads, broken beer jars. Sprawled amid them lay Nordbriht, his scarred body half-covered only by a cloak whose very patterns seemed to shout immense age. Around him lay Nordbriht's own clothes. And, of course, his axe.

Cautiously, Leo approached Nordbriht. Carefully, he gathered up his clothes and weapons. Carefully, he brought them to the man as he lay face down by the lake. And, most carefully of all, he dared tentatively to shake his shoulder.

Nordbriht's eyes flickered open. They were blue like lapis or the sky overhead. And filled with loathing.

"I didn't . . . no, you live. Once again . . . I tell you I will not live to suffer this again!"

He struggled to his feet and headed at an unsteady run toward the lake, clearly determined to hurl himself in.

Leo's shoulder hit him in his midsection and brought him down.

"It's *salt!*" he shouted, blurting out the first words that came to mind. "You won't sink, fool! You can't even drown yourself."

Nordbriht stopped and turned to look at him, pivoting so rapidly that he overbalanced and fell. To Leo's astonishment, the Northerner burst out laughing, a deep-throated bay that sounded somewhat like his howls of the night before, but that, strangely enough, did not frighten Leo.

Thank you, God, Leo thought.

"Now what?" Nordbriht demanded.

"Now?" said Leo. "Now, I have saved your life, and you are bound to me. I am Leo . . . Leo Ducas, and I go to Cappadocia to be healed. You, who have left an Emperor, will you join me and seek healing and your soul's salvation?"

Nordbriht rose.

"I kill the men I swear to. I told you that."

"I don't want a guard. A friend at my back, maybe."

The guardsman paused, considering it. As the sun struck him, he seemed to realize, finally, that he was naked. Slowly, he stalked over to the pile of clothes and arms, dressed himself as best he could, and rummaged through the wrack left upon the shore. Then, he took up his axe and knelt before Leo, lowering his head until he lay hunched over on his belly, in the prostration that he would accord a reigning Emperor.

"I will swear to you," Nordbriht said. "Pray I do not betray you too."

About noon, the wind went breathless. Ahead, the cone of Mount Argaeus, touched with snow, emerged from the clouds like a mother's breast. Odd thought, wasn't it, Leo, for a man who was about to vow celibacy?

But it was better to think of it as a breast than how it had appeared to him last night, rumbling and gouting fire and exploding rock. Had there been a face amidst that fire, a woman's face, all bright eyes and feral teeth and ancient rage? He had seen it before. He feared he would see it again and again until the holy monks took it and all other evil visions from him.

Leo squinted at the mountain. Sometimes, his eyes ached so badly from the glare that he wondered how he could open them at all. At least he still had his eyes—*if you think that way, you will go mad.*

His thoughts rushed ahead into the land toward which he and his companion rode where he might seek the shelter of the holy caves. The men who dwelt there were blessed, safe beneath the ground, not ice-encased like the stylites atop their pillars or, like the monks of Athos, lashed by storm and wave . . . though, very likely, storms rushed like tides over the great plain across which they rode.

These were not, he thought, Psellus' magics: those had to do with the lamp, the book, the city Leo had fled. *You have your will, mage. Leave me in peace,* he had implored silently once, and more than once. He thought that in that much, if nothing else, he had succeeded. But other torments succeeded to their place.

The air as the sun soared toward zenith was warm, moist on Leo's tired eyes. He let his horse slow to a walk. Behind him, Nordbriht reined in his heavier mount. They stopped, and Leo's horse swung his head down to crop at the sparse greenery.

"Do you want to stop?" Nordbriht's voice at his shoulder, deferential, giving away nothing.

"You woke me last night. Again. I am an unlucky companion, always to dream in the night and rise screeching. I owe . . ."

"As I recall, between us there is also the matter of a lake, a huntsman, and a man who hurled himself across my path. So let us have no talk of who owes what."

Nordbriht's beard and braid were streaked now with silver, and his eyes, even in daylight, preserved a reddish glint as if embers still lay buried far within. Had it aged him to see the Hunt, to set his will against that of its fell master?

He remembered Leo commanding him not to throw himself into the salt water: Leo remembered a wolf that had walked like a man, hurling himself between Leo and the alien damnation that had made itself a habitation now in this land.

Had the Northerners, when they came to New Rome, brought their people's oldest curses with them? For that matter, what had his own people, who had ridden back and forth across Asia since Alexander's time, brought—and before them, what monsters stalked these plains?

"You screamed once about some woman. I was certain that the crones were at their weaving, and it was your entrails they used to thread their loom."

Leo shuddered. "I've had that dream. Perhaps I should have gone to Mount Athos," he mused. "They allow no women there, not even female goats."

Nordbriht grinned, exposing strong, yellowed teeth. "Then is it like tales of Jomsborg, but they are all pagan there. Two things they forbid on the island—women and fear. Yet how should that be, turning away the shieldmaids who come to bear heroes away across their saddles after they die in . . . at least, that was the old error," he finished up.

Did they ban women for greater holiness or lest they distract men from the more important business of war—or because they feared them? If asked, Leo would have weighed in on the side of fear.

The plain stretched between Mount Argaeus and themselves un-rolled before them like a vast tapestry of greens and tans. Woven, as Nordbriht said . . .

Leo kneed his horse. "Let us ride," he said.

If Nordbriht pressed him, he would attribute his heaviness of spirit to the sun-dazzle in an overcast sky and the growing heaviness of the air. Clouds were gathering; the sky was growing dark. Lightning darted about the peaks far to the south. Leo counted three separate storms, separated by clear air. Within each storm, lightning glittered fitfully inside the piles of clouds that made each storm look like a warrior, marching across the plain.

"That could reach us," Nordbriht said. He glanced around: no shel-ter of rock or bush offered within a quick ride, and the horses were tiring.

"We should find a town soon," Leo decided.

Nordbriht's nostrils flared. He pointed at a coil of smoke rising in the sky, and unslung his axe. They rode toward the smoke, and Leo's shoulders under the mail felt as if someone used them as a target.

Not long later, he rose in his saddle to survey a cluster of houses. While smoke could mean a baking day when all a village's ovens would be in use, he had long ago learned to choose caution over hope. Even his horse seemed to pick its steps on the road. Nordbriht muttered to himself. It sounded like a growl. Leo's horse shied at a shadow and what even Leo, with his weaker, human nostrils, could smell now. An old man lay across the road, feathered with arrows.

Leo blessed himself, and Nordbriht fumbled after the amulet he no longer wore. They took the long way around the village. They would report its death at the next—if that one still lived.

Not daring to light a fire that night, they ate but meagerly and lay out beneath their cloaks. Rain beat down upon them. Flames lashed through Leo's dreams, then were quenched by rain and sweetened, after the rain, by the gentle face that appeared in Leo's thoughts, its eyes meeting his with joy.

Rainstorms marched across the horizon like patrols guarding the land they sought to reach. Between them swept thin veils of cloud: the day had been dark and cool, easy to ride in. And then, late in the day, the storms faded. Only high fresh winds remained. They left the land smelling clean, green, with a faint hint of salt and the sky scoured clear of the clouds that had veiled it all day.

Heavy, slanting sunbeams accompanied them into a realm that was not so much desert as a wilderness of stone: ruddy in part, with striations of tan, copper, even pale green glinting in the rock. The rain had laid the dust in the road and was drying in gleaming pools. It wound along, a well-beaten track, then edged beside a cliff.

Leo reined in.

"God the Savior, will you look at that?"

Over countless years, since this land had risen from the seabed, wind and rain had carved the soft stone until a field of tiny volcanoes and chimneys reared up below them. The sun painted them copper and bronze, with a hint of green where stunted pines fought up through the grit, all that was left by cones scoured into the ground. Trees and cones and spires cast dusky shadows on the shining ground. Glints flashed upward as the sun picked out the glassy black of stone hurled from Mount Argaeus untold years ago.

"Miniature mountains," Leo marveled.

"You can see where people have carved into some of them." He pointed. "Can you imagine the work?"

Nordbriht dismounted and scooped up two chunks of stone, a black fragment like a dagger and a lump of tufa. He discarded the black rock and showed Leo the softer, lighter stone. "Both of these rocks come from fire. When you pass them through the fire, it hardens. And if not . . ." His strong hands clenched, crushing it into a trickle of powder and grit.

Leo laid a hand to the pouch in which he had hidden the ancient rock he had been given long ago. Hard enough to hold an edge or work stone, it was. Or to serve as a weapon.

He pointed with his chin at Mount Argaeus. "But one day, the earth shakes again, and all this . . ."

Did the Northerners always look into darkness and ruin? It might account for why Leo found this man so congenial. What would he do among the monks?

No wonder monks had come then to such a place, to serve God in a wilderness fully as desolate and stranger than the deserts of Egypt or the mountain fastness of Athos. All of them looked as if they bore God's curse, not a blessing; yet, out of them had come sanctity. He removed his helmet, and the growing wind flicked at his damp hair. The wind wound about the cones and spires that stretched out as far as the eye could see into the haze before the true mountains began. A crooning seemed to rise from the pipes, as if the wind and rock conspired to become a huge instrument.

"Do you suppose," he asked Nordbriht, "that when we reach Hagios Prokopios they will house us in a cave?"

"As long as they have food for us, I do not care. You are not a monk yet to fast; and God is not so foolish that He will call me to become one."

By the time they rode into Hagios Prokopios, purple shadows slanted from the spires and chimneys that overhung the well-worn track. The music of wind playing on spire and chimney murmured at the farthest frontiers of Leo's awareness like the words to a song that tease an old man's awareness just as he falls asleep.

With an explosion of pale wings, a flock of pigeons erupted from windows carved into a cliff. Nordbriht followed them with appreciative, covetous eyes.

"Usually, they're asleep by now," he observed. "Someone must be cursing." He paused. "I wouldn't mind bringing down a few of them. They make good eating." He paused, then added regretfully, "But they belong to someone. I guess I'm not that hungry yet."

Leo sniffed. *And their dung goes to the fields, to enrich them.* He could well believe it: whatever fields men tilled here would need all the help they could get. Where there was so much more stone than trees, it made sense to carve pigeon-houses into the hills—but people's homes, too?

Lights glowed up ahead, removed at some space from the side of the road from just such homes. He could smell bread baking and roast lamb. Despite his resolve to eat as sparely as the monks he had come to live among, the temptation to dismount, to go into one of those dwellings, and claim hospitality by the fire made him feel empty inside.

"We should disarm," he told Nordbriht.

Eyes on the pigeons, the Northerner snorted. "Two men are not a pack of bandits. Or invading Turks. If the people here have sense, they know that men who ride alone must protect themselves. Besides, the sooner we are lodged, the sooner we are fed."

Nevertheless, at Leo's raised eyebrow, he slung his helm and axe. The braids on his shoulders hardly looked familiar and reassuring, but at least he did not appear ready to charge.

Hagios Prokopios was a mingling of homes and churches, built of battered, re-used wood or carved into overhangs of rock. Beneath each cliff, piles of stone and grit lay tumbled, the result of decades of wind and storm, eating at the friable stone.

Lights glowed within the cliffs. There might be comfort in living thus, within the rock, perhaps within hearing of water running perpetually beneath the surface. It would be like a child, really too grown to be nursed like an infant, retreating to his mother's lap.

If he had had a home like this rather than a shabby mansion in Constantinople, perhaps he would not be a stranger, not in a strange land, but in his own home. Well, he would be going to God's home now. Once settled, perhaps some kindly superior would permit him to write to Her Imperial Majesty to tell her that, after all, Leo Ducas had chosen to join her in holiness. He hoped that his Emperor's widow would not judge him harshly.

Though the sun was going down and all about, stalls were shutting, talk still filled the streets. Leo and Nordbriht let their tired horses pause, dusty hoofs crunching on a road that was stone, grit, and something that looked like ground-up potsherds.

From one enclosed, unusually wide stall dug into the stone hillside, he heard merchants chaffer in several tongues. Cups and coins clinked seductively. In the mellow light of new-kindled lamps, gleamed the deep, colored geometries of fringed rugs strewn over the dusty floor. A merchant laughed and clapped his hands. Two younger men unrolled an even more vivid carpet, a veritable mosaic wrought of wool and dye. From near that stall came the groan of tall beasts, swaying down to rest.

Camels! Leo had seen them during the campaign East, sturdy, vile-tempered, stinking of dung and the grasses they munched and spat whenever strangers came in range. By lamplight or torches, men unloaded their packs. The men's voices were impatient: it was growing dark; they were tired; and they wanted the reassurances of a roof, a fire, hot food, and the laughter of companions.

Where there was trade, there was need for guards, even if Leo doubted Nordbriht would want ever to journey east again. But something must be done for him after Leo entered his long-fought-for sanctuary. Could Nordbriht earn a future here?

Leo stared down the dusty road. Women walked alone or in groups, their dark, narrow garments sweeping after them. They moved swiftly, but without the guilty, hunched scuttle of wives or servants out far too long and answerable to authority the instant they returned. The wind blew, and he turned his head at some poignant memory of a sweet scent, some glimpse, out of the corner of his eye, of a veil the colors of sunset floating in the air behind a figure whose movements were almost a dance.

Incense wafted out from a church, overpowering whatever he thought he had smelled. From the weathered, low building came the clamor of a wooden semantron and bells, summoning the pious to worship. Many of these, he noticed, were the tall, severe women he had noticed earlier.

Kyrie eleison.

Here, in the dead emperor's native earth, Leo could finally pray for Romanus' soul. Here, God would surely hear him, and the blessed Bearer of God would intervene. And no time like the present to begin in the work of piety that would last him, if all went well, the rest of his life.

"We stop here," he murmured.

Nordbriht shrugged, resigned. They dismounted before the church. Like many of the buildings here, it was half wood and masonry, and half cave. Incense clung to the air inside, darkening the stone and all but obscuring the paintings and lines from Scripture daubed on the rough walls. They blinked until their eyes adjusted to the darkness and stopped prickling from the onslaught of the incense in the cool air.

Leo turned his attention to the apse. There, above the altar was not the figure of the Pantocrator he might have expected, but a depiction of a woman, standing, her hands upraised in supplication. She had not the sweetness that Leo had always associated with the Bearer of God, but a kind of ferocious concentration more like his mother than any icon had a right to be.

Fearing the last time he had looked into the eyes of such a holy image, he dared to meet Hers. No flames lashed over the fixed intensity of her gaze, reminding him of the old crime and the gates of hell; but he had the sense, when finally he lowered his eyes, that he had done so by her permission rather than his own will. About the image's feet, sibyl-fashion, coiled a serpent. Like the women Leo had seen in the road, she was robed in black, unrelieved by the mosaic gold and gems that she would have worn in Byzantium.

Those women who were her image were here too, prostrating themselves before the altar until they looked like black boulders scattered within the church. Leo remembered Empress Eudocia, praying before her husband's monument. Had Cappadocia lost so many of its sons that this many pious widows were left to mourn them?

He sank to his knees in a rustle of mail, a creak of leather. Behind him, he heard Nordbriht sigh at yet another postponement of his dinner, then struggle downward, a fierce guardian even in prayer. Listening to the chant, Leo stretched out in the darkness humbly on his belly, letting the waves of holiness wash over him.

Except for the voice of the priest, the chanting was borne on women's voices, powerful, even edged as the prayers rose as high as the crudely carved ceiling of the cave church would permit. What were these women doing out in the world? Surely, they would sing in their own communities, not here. . . .

He deafened himself to the questions that threatened to storm his mind. It felt good, so good to be here in the grasp of a kindly mother, here beneath the stone where lights and shadows flickered the way nightlights had when he was a child. He yawned as he prayed, and tears came to his eyes.

The clamor of bells and semantrons broke his reverie, and he levered himself up in time to see a file of tall, black-robed women stride out. Behind him, he heard Nordbriht's stomach growl, reminding him of his own hunger. He regained his feet and went to seek the priest to beg a night's hospitality.

Above his black robe, the priest had a gray beard, bright eyes, a hooked nose and dark brows: a strong face that reassured Leo with its familiarity. He named himself as Father Demetrios, raised eyebrows at Leo's names, but blessed him in any case. He even achieved a nod and smile of greeting for Nordbriht.

"A night's lodging?" He made hasty, dismissive gestures with his hands as Leo reached for his purse (though Leo rather thought a donation to the church would not come amiss). "It is I who should thank you. It is more blessed to give than to receive; and too often it is I who have not had the opportunity to give. Come this way, sirs, come this way. You have horses, servants, perhaps? My house is not large, but . . ."

No, the priest's house, once they entered an arbor, then a reception chamber painted white, and then a dining room hollowed from the rock and imperfectly sanded smooth, was not large. But it was clean and, like his church, it gave the sense of shelter.

One of the black-clad women brought out bread and olives, a sharp, strong wine, and a salver of fish, which Father Demetrios served his guests with his own hands. Gladly, the priest would have loaded their plates and stinted himself, but Leo's frown forestalled him.

"A miracle!" said Father Demetrios. "The loaves and fishes have been multiplied and produced a feast. We are far inland for fish, unlike you of New Rome. We do keep a few trout in pools; but for the most part, it is mostly lamb here and goat."

"I no longer eat meat," Leo told him and knew that Nordbriht had again sighed.

"And have you yet taken vows and been commanded to that penance?" asked Demetrios. "No? You are my guest and shall, of course, do as pleases you. But speaking as a priest, my son, I shall tell you that it is better by far that you eat what is set before you rather than make yourself singular."

His eyes twinkled, and when the meat indeed came round—freshly roasted and served with warm bread, Leo helped himself. The food tasted better than any meal since his first dinner in his father's house when he was first home. Nordbriht attacked the lamb like a wolf, if a mannerly one.

"Tomorrow," said the priest, "you shall rest if you choose or—" he held up his hand "—ride out to Peristrema. It is too far to reach in a single day."

Leo felt the man's eyes upon him.

"We do not dwell apart from the monks here, my son. The Holy Basil set our Rule: morning and evening services, in accordance with general church usage, plus other prayers five times a day."

Nordbriht could be heard to sigh.

"It is no more than the *Didache* recommended for the early Church," the priest reproved him. Leo hastened to nod.

Distraction came with a swish of skirts as a black-clad woman removed dishes, tended lamps, and brought more wine. Nordbriht muttered thanks and wiped his chin, shining with grease. The woman smiled, pleased by the amount he had eaten, and offered more.

"I wish to retire from the world," Leo said. "There is much trade here. While I rejoice in your town's fortune in having it, I should wish to withdraw. . . ."

"Still so austere?" The priest eyed him with gentle irony. "Your sins

are so great as that? You have not yet told me your story, but I judge
that you have been a son, a good one, and a soldier. Surely, you . . ."
He was a mannerly man, if ironic, and he broke off as Leo flinched.

"Peristrema, then," said Father Demetrios. "It is some distance from
here, and your horse should rest before you go there. Tomorrow, you
shall bide here"—*and tell me what you have left unsaid*, came his thoughts,
so strongly that Leo could sense them—"and I shall give you a letter
to Father Meletios, a saintly man. His servant will be here that day. He
is both eyes and hands to the blessed man, and he can guide you."

The footsteps behind them ceased as if the priest's housekeeper remained to listen.

"I know, Xenia," said the priest. "You could guide our guest just as
well as the young lad. My son, Father Meletios came to us from Egypt,
where the rule separating monks from the world are even more strict
than here. Who would have thought it? Years ago, monks and nuns both
lived out in the caves in the gorge. But the holy father expelled the nuns
that the monks might live the purer of thought for their absence."

"Hard on the nuns, wasn't it?" came Nordbriht's rumble. "If it was
the women's land to start with . . ."

Now even Leo could sense the tension in the tall woman standing
behind them. Had she been one of the banished nuns? Would that order
of exile account for the dark-clad women he had seen, with their blend
of humility and impatience? Surely there had been holy women in the
deserts of Egypt: there *had*, Leo remembered, but some had been a
temptation and a snare to the men who lived withdrawn from them.

It is not as if it were their *fault*. He looked up at the tall woman removing the dishes from the table. Serving him, expressionless, in silence. Serving Nordbriht a second time. He had, after all, expressed
regret for the women and their plight.

Father Demetrios blessed the room, then looked over his shoulder.

"Thank you, Si . . . Xenia," said the priest. Dismissed, she had little choice but to withdraw. Leo heard reluctance in her firm footsteps.
He was not surprised. There was a mystery here, old stories, old guilts—
and as a penitent, a hewer of wood and drawer of water, he would not
be asked to bear a part in them.

Leo thanked his host, bowed his head for a blessing, and found himself led to a small, windowless room, whitewashed and chill. It held a
chest and a narrow bed, heavy with blankets woven from the local wool.
Tomorrow, he would rest, if he could rest; and the day after, he would
ride out to this place and give himself away. Give himself—he corrected
his thought—back to God. There would be prayer. There would be hard

work. And at the end of the day, and of all his days, there would be rest.

And that would very much be that. Resolved, he blew out the ancient lamp that had been left for him. The darkness was absolute. He had a moment's fear—of Psellus in Hagia Sophia, his eyes of Christ in Majesty burnt out in his presence, the evil dreams sent to torment in Byzantium that had all but cost him his life. He yawned. Perhaps—please God, no writ ran here, not Psellus' nor any other sorcerer's.

The blankets were as comforting as his earliest memories, and sleep came quickly. There were no dreams.

19

*S*hould *he take his sword or not? Leo asked himself as he pre-* pared to leave the room Father Demetrios had made over to him. He heard Nordbriht's rapid stride and quickly picked up his weapons: he did not want to hear what the Northerner would say if he left weapons behind, nor did he wish to be guarded.

He had tried to quarrel over that the day before.

"If you do not ride armed, I must guard you," Nordbriht had said. "Even if you ride armed, I shall watch your back."

He had no response for that. How had he and his ever considered the Northerners to be *barbaroi* or lacking in wit? This one easily got the better of him. So, Nordbriht had companioned him when they had ridden out to view the monastic community that Leo had always assumed he would join before Father Demetrios suggested this site in the valley upon him as being more remote.

"I release you from your oath. You do not owe me any service," he had told Nordbriht when the man's presence looming before him or guarding his back had caused the monks to view them both with suspicion. "I am no prince to require a man with a great axe to guard me."

Nordbriht had merely raised his brows, a gesture he had, worse luck, learned from his years in Constantinople. Leo was Ducas; a Ducas was Emperor; therefore, Leo was of an Imperial family and, by Nordbriht's reckoning, a prince.

"Remember: when I take vows, I will surrender even my name."

The road twisted through a desert frozen in stone, but as much a refuge as the pitiless sun and sand in Egypt. Rain spat down briefly, and the wind blew, piping eerily through the chimneys carved by centuries of wind and water. The road dropped off.

Abruptly, they found themselves in a weird geometry of cones, chimneys, and spires. Nearby loomed a cliff, striated like the rest of the rock: perhaps, ages ago, this had been level ground, perhaps even a seabed. Leo thought of waters rushing back in to fill it, shuddered, and shut his eyes in brief prayer. Surely, people contemplating such a cataclysm must have thought it the end of the world. But it had not been: and perhaps what he had lived through was not the Last Days either.

When he opened his eyes, the winds had dispelled some of the clouds, and the sun, even though it had reached its zenith, was not as oppressive as he had remembered, sheltered as he was by the sand-colored cliff. Studding it, much worn away, were doors and windows such as one might see in some back-country basilica, all wrought of the living rock of the hills. The face of one cliff had fallen away and lay in rubble at the foot of a huge hill.

Peering within, Leo saw the remains of chapels and corridors. He could see figures within the ruined chapel, striding down toward the altar, wrought of one block of stone, behind which generations of humble workers had hollowed out an apse and painted it. More figures, their paint rapidly faded now with exposure to the air and rain, stood arrayed upon those walls. Among them were images of robed women, whose faces were scored and scratched out. As Leo watched, a monk walked by the ruined church. Something on the ground caught the man's attention. He picked it up, then hurled it at the wall with an exclamation of loathing.

Leo tensed, and Nordbriht was instantly at his side.

"Potsherds," the big man said. "I saw them in the town. They have old marks on them, like butterflies. The holy men say, though, that they are women's bodies—which shows you how little such men know of real women—and so they break them."

"Soon I shall be one of them."

Nordbriht shrugged. Leo, his gesture suggested, would not be such a fool as to be shocked by pottery.

"Do you not understand me?" Leo demanded. "You may wish for—what did you call it—a ring-giver. I am not he."

"You drew me back from the Hunt," Nordbriht said simply.

A file of monks in dusty robes wound along the path among the rocks.

"They've seen us," Leo pointed out to Nordbriht.

Three monks left the line and approached them, offering hospitality. Slightly behind them was a shorter figure, not quite out of boyhood. He moved hastily, trying to catch up despite a bad limp. As he reached Leo and Nordbriht, his knee twisted beneath him. With the uncanny silent speed Leo had first seen under a full moon, Nordbriht leapt out to steady him.

"I would not have fallen," the boy said. "It is my duty to greet pilgrims. I am quite fit."

"No doubt, young sir," Nordbriht said and stepped back. He released the boy, who bowed to Leo with far more formality.

"The stranger did not know that, Theodoulos," said the elder of the monks. "After all, you have had such a long ride that anyone might falter when he dismounted. You owe him your thanks."

Leo restrained a faintly malicious smile. The boy's face, ruddy and somewhat round, despite the thinness of all of the monastics, flushed. He looked even younger: black-haired, black-eyed. Then, he regained his composure, and his features settled into a mask that should have been absurdly dignified on a lad so young. He greeted them with the manners of a prince and an accent that somehow escaped all rusticity.

In vain, Nordbriht shook his head and would have edged behind Leo. The monks insisted on greeting them both and inviting them both to join them at their meal. Leo ignored the Varangian's silent plea to be dismissed.

He had chosen to follow: this could just be his reward. And if his head scraped on the stone doorframes as they visited the churches, or his knees jutted up as he sat with the monks in their refectory, tables and benches carved in site from what had been solid stone, he attempted to keep watch and what decorum he thought might be appropriate among these strange ascetics; he even tried, when he saw them holding back from taking food, not to eat more than the others. Theodoulos, however, was sharp-eyed and brought him more bread.

The boy's name was Theodoulos. He was no resident of that community but there on a pilgrimage to one church where the wall-paintings were all of serpents: when Leo rode out to Peristrema, the river valley where Father Meletios ruled, the boy would ride with him, home to the hermitage where he served its master.

"Are you coming? They wait for you outside."

It was victory of a sort that Nordbriht called to Leo without insisting upon a formal title. But the former Varangian had let all of the others assemble while Leo lingered in the priest's house as if they had nothing better to do than dance attendance on a spoiled princeling. That war remained to be fought.

It would be fought by others once Leo put himself under obedience. Leo wondered how this saintly Meletios would dismiss the Varangian.

Theodoulos, no doubt concerned that his twisted leg would cramp on the long ride to the valley, had dismounted and limped over to supervise the loading of supplies on pack animals. Leo saw him in the company of several of the dark flock of tall women who served the church and were such a presence in the town.

"You must eat!" One handed him a packet that looked like honeycakes. A second smoothed his hair and tried to make his coarse robes lie more tidily on his shoulders, while a third worried that there were nowhere near enough supplies, that the roads became hot and dusty, and who knew whether they would be safe to travel later on in the year.

"Supplies are stored underground in the cities. . . ."

"Hush!" The tallest of the women blessed herself and looked around. She and her sisters had been exiled from the valley, but seemed to feel bound to keep whatever secrets it might have.

Whose son was Theodoulos? He was his master's servant, Leo had heard the boy explain to Nordbriht who, unembarrassed, made his share of the honeycakes disappear. Perhaps the youth was the posthumous child of some soldier and one of these black-robed women, consigned to holiness as soon as people realized his leg would prevent him ever from becoming a fighting man.

Seeing Leo, Theodoulos hugged the black-robed women like a much younger boy, knelt for the priest's blessing, then mounted quickly. Leo and Nordbriht mounted with a clash of armor that drew people's attention. But Theodoulos bore not so much as a dagger.

"You're determined to come?" Leo asked Nordbriht once again.

"I can't let you and a bunch of monks ride out there by yourselves. God only knows what sort of barbarians you might meet on the way." The big man grinned at him.

After so long in the saddle, Leo was certain that the sun's rays hitting the earth sent up clouds of dust. He shut his eyes against the glare, then flinched: even worse than the reek of beasts, of sweat, had been the stink as his emperor's eyes rotted out beneath their fouled bandages as they rode, always pushing the pace, from town to town, exhibiting the man who was no longer an emperor and scarcely even alive. The sun had beaten down upon Leo's head until he thought it would boil in its helm; but not to wear the helm meant brain fever.

Soon, he would find quiet, disturbed only by the singing of holy men, and the darkness of caves, lamplit so that the saints painted on the wall seemed to come to life. Soon.

He forced himself back to awareness. Like it or not, the others still saw him, armed, as a fighting man: he could not let Nordbriht guard this troop alone.

Gradually, the glare faded. The road swept them past what looked like a desert, frozen in time. Shepherds on the road gave way to them (the sheep showed less deference). A tree clung, twisted from the years that storms had buffeted it, to one small hill. It was hollow: Leo saw a watcher retreat within it. Later on, a boy who waved as the troop ride by appeared, as from the ground itself.

"They say this whole land is hollowed out," Nordbriht muttered. "Cave cities all around here. Malagobia, with its deep wells, and Ene-gobi, which is smaller. They use them for storage and to hide in from the Turks."

"Are these cities linked?" Leo's head came up.

When he looked about for someone to answer his question, he found the monks' attention curiously elsewhere. He pointed that out to Nordbriht.

"I heard mutters of a road underground. Thing is, no one knows if the story is true. For my part, I prefer Turks and the sun on my face. Riding underground, I would worry if every step would be the one that would set the earth shaking and bury us all. But that doesn't seem to trouble *them*."

This rock-strewn plain guarded as many secrets as the court. Others were welcome to seek them out.

Gradually, clouds veiled the sky, hiding Mount Argaeus as if it were shrouded in its own smoke. The clouds thickened, shielding and revealing the road they travelled. Now they had the wind at their backs, and driving rain. The clouds scudded toward the vast horizon. Once again, Leo imagined that he could see figures marching in the land, helmed men and women, gods and goddesses from before the time that civilized people had come here.

Don't see such things, don't think of such things, he warned himself. Don't fall into illusion now that you are so close to holiness. Not even Psellus' spells or spite can reach you here.

Perhaps, in the secret safety of the valley toward which he rode, he would even consent to be exorcised.

Theodoulos' shout—that of a boy in sight of home—recalled Leo to himself. Ahead, the earth was cleft, following the track of a river, that ran too fast to be choked with leaves from the trees that lined it—or branches from the treetrunks that it had engulfed, swollen as it was by the spring rains. Sunlight glistened on the troubled water, hundreds of feet below.

The packtrain halted. At Theodoulos' direction, Leo followed him toward the rim of the cliff. The ground seemed to shake, or perhaps that was just the effects of a long, long ride. He stretched out on his belly in the grass and stared into the valley. Grass crowned the cliff on the other side of the river that had gnawed, century after century, into the soft rock through which it ran. On either side of the river were tumbled piles of rock. Many of them were marked by the rough-cut openings that Leo knew meant doorways. Peristrema. Perhaps his home from now on and his salvation?

Did any of those doorways lead to the underground towns of which Nordbriht had spoken?

He promised himself not to care.

In the valley, men in brown and men in black, but no women, went about their tasks beneath the long shadows of the poplars. They moved without haste or idleness, though, from time to time, a monk might pause to look about the valley or study the river, slowing now after the storm, sparkling in the sun. Carvings gave jutting rocks above and beside the entrances to the caves the semblance of ancient temples.

How fortunate the monks were to live in such splendor. No wonder those formidable old women in town still mourned their loss.

Not far from where they paused, the road halted. A rough stair, carved into the rock and kept in good repair, snaked down into the valley.

Gesturing them to follow him, Theodoulos started down the stair. Very soon, his limp became more pronounced and he was sweating heavily, but he refused to rest or give place to the others. Nordbriht edged down beside him.

"Let me give you some help with that." He gestured at the pack that Theodoulos had insisted on bearing.

"You are my guests!" he said, the first young man's pride Leo had seen in him. "The path can be tricky. I know it; you don't."

Nordbriht lifted the young man's burden from his back. "You may be strong enough. But you are not our pack-horse."

"Father Meletios would expect me to guide you."

Nordbriht clapped him on the shoulder, careful not to strike too hard and push Theodoulos off balance on a turn in the stair.

"By God, we'll make a fighter of you yet."

Theodoulos looked uncomprehending. Nordbriht laughed.

If the Turks struck this far into the land, they might all have to turn fighters here before the day was done.

It would be a pity if battle ever came this way.

Ever came this way again.

What had put that thought into Leo's head? He pulled off his helmet and let the breeze cool his face and dry his matted hair. Here in this hermitage, the breeze and the swift-rushing river seemed like luxuries all the greater for their simplicity. He found himself smiling at the surface of the river, like some fine, ever-changing brocade—sunlight striking it from above; rocks and branches pressing from beneath the surface.

Perhaps it was rockfalls from the protecting cliffs and the way that some of the temples—a strange word to use for cave churches only slightly simpler than those outside Hagios Prokopios—had fallen into disrepair that made him think that there had been battle here before.

Light flared, and he spun about.

"Father Meletios knows we are here!" Theodoulos cried. "You must all come now!"

Despite his limp, he started up the twisted narrow path to his master's retreat. Three slabs of rock that looked as if some giant had untidily piled them framed a dark entrance.

"Looks like a barrow," Nordbriht muttered.

Leo chuckled. "And do you think that monsters from the ice will leap out at you? Here, in a Christian land?"

Nevertheless, he peered ahead, as if trying to see the holy man before he actually was admitted to his presence. Like an Emperor, this man had power of life and death—not only over his future in this world, but in the next. Qualms, such as he had felt before battles, made him glad he had eaten very little that day.

"I don't think that *anything* is beyond belief among you Romans. I am a stranger here in a strange land." As he probably intended, the scriptural allusion brought Theodoulos around in shock. The boy had the wit, though, to laugh at himself as he beckoned to them from outside the cave.

Shaking his head, Nordbriht followed. The sunlight glinted on his pale braids.

A deep voice rang out from the cave, echoing from the valley walls. "There are no evil spirits here, man of the north."

20

Nordbriht's hand went to his axe, and Leo's to Nordbriht's wrist. Although the voice from the cave carried out to them, it nevertheless preserved the peace of the valley that its owner ruled. Assurance rang in it, but no false pride, as if, like the rocks of the ancient cliffs here, sun and wind had honed the voice—and its owner—into some essential form.

Theodoulos' face lit, and he rushed inside the hermitage. More slowly, drawing himself up as if before entering the palace in New Rome for an audience with the Basileus, Leo followed. Nordbriht waited until Leo had passed, then fell in at his shoulder. His guard of honor: for once, Leo did not object.

They bent their heads to enter the cave, then more deeply yet in reverence to the old man seated on a slab cut from the side of the rock wall. Sunlight beamed out at them from a highly polished shield he had no doubt set to draw them in.

"Kindle a lamp, my son," the holy man told his servant. He pushed a small oil lamp toward Theodoulos, who took over the small task, then knelt for his master's blessing. A long hand cupped the boy's head, then slid down over his eyes.

"And did you find your honeycakes, my son?" asked the monk.

"They made me bring some back for you, Father," said the boy.

"Will those women never stop trying to tempt me? If I had not packed them all off back to their homes, I would be as wide as this valley by now. Well, the birds will be thankful."

Leo glanced away from the light of day outside the cave and the column of light that flared from the shield that had been the old monk's beacon, letting his eyes grow accustomed to the softer light of the small oil lamp. It was very old, almost as old as the pots and bowls neatly stacked upon the rock tables and shelves hollowed into the cave walls. Some of the bowls bore faded paint. And at the table by Father Meletios' side lay not holy words, but . . . no, it was not a statue of some blessed saint, but an image, blank-faced, rich of breast and belly, such as he had seen other monks smash as abomination.

The mellow oil light was kind to the austere dwelling. Its flickering shadows hid the scars of chisels and torches where they had carved out and hardened the rock into rough corners. But they could not conceal the man himself. Wind and years had left him sere, brown, flensed of all but essential flesh to house a spirit that glowed of its own strength. But not in his eyes: they were dull, had been dull for years, Leo would guess—burnt quite dead by the pitiless ancient sun of Egypt's deserts.

"Welcome, my sons," said the monk. "I am Meletios, the younger of that name and quite unworthy to share it with the blessed saint. And your names? You, man of the North?"

Nordbriht came to what salute he might in the tiny compass of the entryway, then knelt. His head was still level with Father Meletios'. "I am called Nordbriht."

"But you have other names. If you seek admission here," Meletios raised a slender eyebrow, "I shall have to know them."

The big man's face, even in the dim light of the cave hermitage, paled, then reddened, and the expression of horror on his face drew a laugh from Theodoulos.

"I but accompany my . . ."

"I am Leo Ducas." Best cut Nordbriht off before he ran through Leo's full panoply of names. No parade of family, loyalty, or titles for him. Leo knelt at Father Meletios' feet. He would have bent his head to the rock floor in the full prostration he had wanted to refuse his kinsman the new Emperor, but the monk's hand went unerringly to his brow and restrained him. From the dry fingers, their pads callused from decades of sweeping them across stone to guide himself, Leo felt a surge of vitality akin to standing out in the open, thunder rumbling from afar, before a storm strikes.

"And this is Theodoulos, whose father's name we do not know. Except that he is *my* son, as are you: both worthy in the eyes of God. Theodoulos has proved his value and loyalty to me over the years, young Ducas. What will *you* do, young Ducas, to be equally valuable to me—and, of course, to God?"

"I seek entrance to this community."

"As monk or priest?"

Leo shook his head. "Until I know how I am called, I am content to be a hewer of wood, a drawer of water. Father Demetrios said you were a holy man. I have need of holiness. And healing."

Meletios's hand slid over his brow, down his face, "seeing" him. It awoke a memory of his emperor's hand, blessing him or reaching out in an appalling need for comfort, before fever snatched his wits and life away.

"You, who bear the name of an Emperor's ruling house?"

"In my own Emperor's memory."

Leo was weeping, he knew it. The long, bony fingers wiped his tears away, then withdrew. Leo bowed his head now, resting his brow on the rough floor. It smelled of cleanliness and age. Immense age.

"You seek a refuge, do you? But there is danger in Peristrema, young prince. And danger in too great humility. We are not simply penitents here, but guards. If you live among us, or even if you do not, you will learn that."

"Nordbriht says there is danger all around us."

"Your friend who hides his name? Let me see you too, warrior."

Nordbriht edged closer, side by side with Leo, to the blind man. He had feared neither Turks nor the Wild Hunt, but he tensed visibly— "Be easy, son," said the old man who could *not* see the sudden tautness in shoulders and neck—although Meletios' hands "saw" him as clearly as they had seen Leo and Theodoulos.

"Yes, you have need of the mercy, haven't you, my son? And of forgiveness, too. At least once, you have sought to lay violent hands upon yourself . . ."

"Paws," Leo heard Nordbriht whisper under his breath, but Meletios gave it no attention.

". . . but you did not. You must not. There is mercy; there is always the mercy for sin if it is truly repented of. Go and sin no more."

Nordbriht almost snorted.

"King David was a warrior, and he sinned mightily. Yet, the Lord loved him because he was always so wholehearted in his repentance. It may be that we will need your sword. And I see you have no desire at all to be a monk."

Nordbriht's laughter at Meletios' complete acceptance was surprised, and, even more surprisingly, found an answer in Meletios' own.

Then, the monk turned grave. "I didn't think so. But what do you seek? One last battle against the curse that stalks you so you do not have to take your own life? Oh yes, I do see that a curse lies over you—or what you perceive as a curse. Try a little harder, and rest in the mercy. Yes, I know it is a paradox, just the sort of thing that sacred madmen spout and that a man like you cannot wait to escape. But one last fight? Seek, and ye shall find. Once, I thought otherwise, but now I fear me that this is a time for warriors. It may be that your mercy may bring us all whatever hope we have."

Was it the darkness of the cave, or did Leo actually see the old man ruffle Nordbriht's hair as a man might dismiss an unruly lad? The oil lamp made the long braids seem to glow.

"Now, walk outside in the sunlight, away from shadows. And let me speak with your companion, who will not permit you to call him master."

Shaking his head, an animal freed from the pain that has been gnawing at him, Nordbriht rose. Light from the entrance to the cave cast the shadows of his head and shoulders, immense on the painted wall behind the old priest, almost the shadow of some monster from the harsh, cold North. Outside, birds sang, and the air that blew into the cave was fresh and sweet. Nordbriht's shadow dwindled, and Father Meletios nodded as if he could actually see it shrink to the size of a man.

"Now, for you, Leo Ducas. Please be seated. Theodoulos will serve you wine. And, if he has not gobbled them all, some of the honeycakes from the women in town. Excellent women; but let them bide there, not here." Meletios blessed himself. "Never here again."

Leo accepted rough wine with the thanks due a far finer vintage and sat, his thumb caressing the cup. When he looked down at it, he saw that it was ancient pottery, incised and painted, red, and black, and white, with what looked like a butterfly. He had seen monks outside Hagios Prokopios smash such things; Meletios put them to use instead.

"This cup is very old," politely, he gave voice to his thoughts.

"Trash, they call such things, and worse names in the village, but I see no need to waste what has been given. Like us, it is wrought from the dust."

The statue lying on a rock shelf glinted in the lamplight like the eyes of a willing woman: gleaming obsidian, a black Aphrodite perhaps as old as the world itself. As Leo stared at it, the statue seemed to take on added luster.

"She knows you admire her, my son," said Meletios, uncannily perceiving where Leo looked. He laughed. "I was a young man once, with wine and fire in my blood, hard as it may be to believe it. And the sun of Thebes can strike sparks even from the coldest chastity: look at Thais—or do not look, as I learned. *Never* look."

Leo turned his eyes to the roughly cut and painted walls. Here too were figures of men and women. Again, odd: twice now, Meletios had spoken of how he had driven the women from their own worship in this valley. And yet, the women's faces on the walls were as cleanly painted as any of the men's, not scratched out.

"You are curious, my son," Meletios observed. "You do not simply accept, submit. And you are still so very young. Are you certain that the life here is what you seek?"

Leo swallowed and muttered what sounded like assent.

"Truly? Let me hear you. A temporary anger with the world is no reason to renounce it, you know. Here is no place for men to hide in preparations for eternity. Oh, they may stay long enough to find some peace and to know where it is; but in the end, it is back to the world such men must go."

"Was I wrong to come, sir?"

Meletios was silent for long enough for Leo to hear the poplars' leaves brush against each other in the wind, to hear the river ripple over the stones, to hear Nordbriht's heavy boots scuff over the stone as he climbed toward the higher shrines. A bird sang overhead, and Leo's eyes filled with tears. Soon, the sun would begin its long decline toward the horizon. Night would come, and stars would sparkle, reflected in the swift river, until dawn. Or rain might muffle all other sounds and send rest to the community when their prayers were over for the moment. And then dawn would fill this place like a chalice. Day and night and day for the rest of all his life if he could but remain here.

Meletios' burnt-out eyes were blanks; the droop in the thin lips, the hollowed temples gave him his answer.

"It is never wrong to give grief and faith and humility their proper play, but wrong to make of them little icons to blind men to their proper work. You are welcome to make such retreat as you will."

"Sir . . . father . . ." Leo's eyes filled with tears.

"My dear, dear son," Meletios said. "I do not forbid you a retreat, a time spent dwelling apart. But to stay here forever? As well to cage a hawk. It is not in you."

"From touching me . . . and listening, you know that?"

"I *saw* that," said the old man. "When the sun burned out my eyes, I found in the darkness another kind of vision . . . yes?"

"Psellus . . ." Even in this hallowed place, the name came out like an angry hiss.

"Not a holy man for all his learning and his vows?" Meletios' voice was fearless.

Leo flung out a hand, as if beseeching the harmless old man not to speak words that might condemn him.

"His writ does not run here: I do not fear your Psellus. Be easy, son. What did the man say?"

"He told my emperor that he had been deprived of the light of his eyes in favor of the light of heaven!" It was the cruellest thing, the un-bearable savagery of Psellus' cultivated Greek; and it had torn Leo as if each letter had been a poisoned fang.

"I found it thus. But I was priest, not Emperor and warrior."

Leo looked up sharply. Father Meletios's voice had changed, hollowed out as if spoken from the bottom of a deep well; and his burntout eyes seemed to stare like the eye-sockets of a skull upon a fearsome eternity. The bones beneath the spare flesh seemed to light: Meletios was not so much man, but a lantern for the spirit that possessed him.

"You breathe a word you dare not say, young sir," Meletios said. "Haunted? This very place, the land itself is haunted, and you have seen it. Once this land was part of the seabed; now, above it, it is like a shoal upon which ancient castaways wash up. Some die where they lie; others would rise and walk, were we . . . were I . . . to let them. The desert sun blinded me, but when the anguish faded, I looked into the darkness, and I saw a deeper, truer light. If thy right eye offend thee, pluck it out. . . ."

Leo stiffened. Oh God, Meletios was going to prophesy, to share that lightning that had replaced his ordinary sight. *I do not want to know* warred with *How can I write this down?* in Leo's thoughts.

"For the sins that I have sinned against Thee . . . oh, Lord, what is Thy will now? I drove out the nuns, imperfect as they were, servants of darkness. God forgive me that *I* was not strong enough to restrain the men who might not resist them. Yet I, who am blind, may stand before the leopard altar and see not, fear not—how is that a woman's task, a woman's place? And yet, I thrust those worthy ladies from their ancient homes, oh woe . . ." Meletios raised his voice in a soft wail that reminded Leo of the wind blowing about the stone chimneys of this ancient land.

The saintly old man seemed to age before Leo's eyes. Then he shook himself, as if dispelling some long-held grief. Light filled his sunken eye-sockets, and his voice tolled like the music in the Church of the Holy Wisdom.

"The time may come, the time will come when the Wolf and the Lion's Cub sink beneath the earth to the lair of the leopard altar. The earth itself shall shake and split asunder. Then shall light emerge from blood and darkness."

The light faded in the blind eyes the way Leo might snuff out a lamp. Father Meletios jerked forward, his mouth opening in a huge gasp for air, almost a death rattle. Leo leapt forward to catch him.

"Bring wine!" he ordered Theodoulos. His own breath came as if he had been running. Meletios' sere frame shuddered, the tremors passing into Leo's body as he tried to keep the old man from falling.

"He doesn't drink wine, except for the sacrament!" Theodoulos protested, even as he poured the thin stuff into Leo's cup. Together, they got the wine into him. With the last drops, Meletios flailed out, and his bony hand dashed the painted cup against the wall. Along with the crash came uneven footprints.

"If he's not used to it, maybe it will put him to sleep. Ah . . . will he remember what he said when he wakes?"

"This way, sir; his pallet is here."

"That's never warm enough, not for a man who spent so many years in Egypt. Give him my cloak, too. No, Nordbriht, there is no trouble. Father Meletios had a vision, that is all."

Even in the shadows, Nordbriht's face showed what he thought of "all."

"Shall I carry him?" he rumbled.

"There is not room enough for all of us in this cave," Leo replied. "We would suck the breath from him."

They settled Meletios on his pallet and covered him warmly. Underfoot, the ground shuddered slightly. When Leo looked out the entrance to the cave, from Mount Argaeus rose a faint plume of smoke. Light flickered on the last of the wine, still beading the shards of pottery where it had fallen. Leo picked up one shard and tucked it into his pouch. He would toss it into the niche at Hagios Prokopios, trying his luck like the other pilgrims.

But what would he wish for?

The sun beat on Leo's back in rhythm with the blows of his hammer on the crumbling stone of the rock face. A chunk dropped free at his feet, sending up a plume of dust. He stepped back, coughing and wiping his eyes.

When his sight cleared, he paused to check on his progress in turning cliff into cave. So what if he were covered with dust, except where sweat runnels washed him clean? The rock face he was attacking looked somewhat more as if, one day, he might even be able to hollow out a cell within it. A very small cell.

Behind him came the crunch of heavy footsteps and the welcome gurgle of water in a leathern bottle. Water or perhaps, and better yet, wine: at this point, Leo did not care.

He wiped his hot face on his sleeve. The coarse fabric stung it where rock shards and dust had nicked him more shrewdly than a razor.

Stone dust and sweat marked the cloth. He could not remember having labored so hard.

He straightened to spare his back and barely escaped banging his head on the ceiling-to-be. Still too low. After his hours spent hacking at the rock, then bending over, grubbing out the rubble, carrying it out of the burrow that was taking form with agonizing slowness, then repeating the process, he ached as if he were eighty. Offer it up? Leo choked off a grumble that showed appalling signs of turning into a moan. Or a curse.

"If you had hit your head," Nordbriht remarked, coming up behind Leo with water, "perhaps you would have knocked some sense into it. And asked for help, or given up the whole idea."

"This must be my own work," Leo insisted. He turned to take the bottle from his—what was Nordbriht? His friend? His sworn man? A comrade in arms? After so long squinting at the rock, Leo's eyes dazzled in the bright sun. Nordbriht appeared as a shadow crowned with that incongruously shining hair. A Varangian icon. He hid his grin with the water bottle.

"A rat digs its own burrow. Does that make us admire rat or burrow the more?" asked the Northerner. "We might have had lodgings in the town. Or the priest would have given you, at least, houseroom. But no, you will be holy if it kills you. You mortify your flesh, but must you also mortify mine?"

Such a fine, stubborn length of limb to mortify!

Leo shrugged, pleased that he had managed not to flinch at the gesture. *You do not need to remain.* Nordbriht ignored it, as he ignored the subject every time it came up.

Leo drank again. Faintly astringent, the faint sourness of wine mixed with water washed the dust from the back of his throat.

He turned back to the rock and began again to hack away at it. Nordbriht's immense height shaded him for a pleasant moment. And then, muttering barbarian imprecations that Thor's hammer could make quick work of this stupidity, the big man joined him in hewing at the rock. So much for "this must be my own work" or any other orders Leo might try giving him.

With the strength in Nordbriht's shoulders from years of axe drill, they would soon excavate a sizable room. And then would come the task of firing it, finishing the hardening that exposure to the air began. An interesting way to build, Leo thought. For himself, he was more used to the stone and masonry of Byzantium, of churches built on the pattern of Justinian's, bright with mosaics and all the colors of the rainbow shimmering to delight the eye and stir the soul. Here, they carved churches from caves and painted them in all the colors of the earth—reds and browns, golds, and dusty greens.

It was not only churches, though, and holy cells that the people here built in the living stone.

"Like digging a grave," Nordbriht muttered. "A barrow . . . which God the Father avert. Hew wood and draw water, indeed; but in the station to which God has called you," he remarked. "Build your own habitation, if you must, but use the skills you already possess to serve these people."

Toward the end of the day, Leo laid aside his hammer and traded his worker's tunic, if any worker would wear a thing that ragged, for one that was merely shabby. Nordbriht had found a tavern where, he claimed, the lamb was so tender that going meatless was like a sin—a dubious piece of theology to which Leo's belly growled fanatical belief. He allowed himself to be persuaded. Besides, he told himself, in Hagios Prokopios, he could buy the supplies that would mean he could spend less time away from his work.

People eyed him and Nordbriht as they rode in. Not that he himself was anything that unusual among the dark-haired Romans with their eyes, melancholy, as if contemplating their sins, until something—business or faith—caught their attention. Farmers, laborers, and potters from the next town pushed through the dusty streets, shoulder to shoulder with the tall, proud women Leo had noticed the first time he had come this way.

How many of the older ones were former nuns? he wondered. If he told them of his talk with Father Meletios, would they spit on his shadow—or the old monk's? He had done his best to obey the monk's instructions. When he was not carving out his cave, he rode back and forth between the town and his hermitage-to-be, his hermitage and the cave churches, even, once or twice, making the long trip to Father Meletios in Peristrema. He visited the sick, brought food to the poor (a blessedly small number), and even tried to help the halt bring in their flocks. He was *not* very good at herding sheep, he realized, but at least he made the lads who were smile at his clumsiness.

But I know enough what I saw. Quick those boys were, but not so quick that they could conceal from Leo what he expected to see—entrances to caves and to more than caves, a network of them lying beneath the earth. Malagobia, it had been called, the place where life was difficult, despite deep, deep wells.

Meanwhile, Leo sensed Nordbriht's impatience, honed by the

smoky, fatty lamb they both could smell. They headed toward the center of the town, pausing frequently to greet people.

The younger women met his eyes, then looked away. Presumably not in shyness, but because a man in a drab tunic was hardly worth their attention, he thought. Not with a man like Nordbriht at his shoulder, his grin at war with his watchfulness. He treated them with the courtesy he would accord ladies in Byzantium—and a watchful eye out for nearby fathers or brothers.

Many of the younger men went armed, though Leo had seen not even so small a trace of a Turkish raiding party as a discarded bowstring. They swaggered in their weapons, thrust into new scabbards. But for all their unfamiliarity to arms, these men were fit, with an ill-concealed anger about them that reminded him . . . where had he seen that? Where? Memory flashed behind his eyes: the young Jewish men in Constantinople had had that same sullen readiness for trouble.

Horsehooves pounded behind him, drew up fast. A man dismounted, bowing with precisely the degree of deference that Leo's former rank required. What a time for a courier to come and find him. His heart pounded. Nordbriht closed in. Surely, if they followed Leo's doings in the capital—he had declared himself dead to the world, but he would not be the first imperial to have been resurrected—they knew he did not go unguarded.

The courier's eyes were blurred, but fearless, even when he saw the former Varangian. No, if this were an arrest, the man would have been flanked by soldiers.

"The Esteemed Lady Maria Ducaina sent me with letters from her and your noble kin. She will be glad to know I see her son well."

That was court courtesy; Leo knew he looked like a laborer, if a laborer to whom a courier from the capital must bow. Hagios Prokopios had one thing in common with Byzantium: the curiosity of a feral cat. Soon, a crowd would gather. Best send this courier on his way. Leo took the packet of letters, weighing it in his hand. *You have been weighed in the balance and found . . .*

Who had written? His mother with prudent admonitions; his father, with his detachment and his trust; perhaps even Alexius, who must be training for a soldier about now. God forgive him, they seemed more real than the people he met here every day. He had not yet forsaken all attachments to his old life, had he? Another sin with which to barrage the priests, if he were ever to be one with them.

"Greet the Lady for me. And for yourself. . . ."

He reached for his slender purse. Some gold was left; he could reward his mother's courier as the man had a right to expect.

"Sir, the Lady your Mother says you have given yourself to God. How shall I accept reward from a servant of God?"

Now *that* was a shock, Leo thought: a man of Constantinople refusing gold.

"Then give it to God in my name as in your own, with prayers for my salvation," Leo intoned blandly.

The courier bent his head for a blessing. The idea was incongruous enough that Leo gave it and hoped the presumption would not be held against him at Judgment.

He moved on. Gradually, the knots of men, whispering intently, loosened and dispersed. One group, which did not, stood almost in his path.

Leo had no choice but to acknowledge them. And so he nodded respect at a knot of youths better dressed than the press of farmer's sons and junior merchants: minor nobles, he suspected. At home—no, now his home was here—they would be nothing to him; here, he must show them respect.

One, the youngest, the back of his neck shaved in imitation of the City's mercenaries, jeered after him. A lump of dried mud—or maybe dung—flew and shattered against a wall.

The pad-pad-pad of Nordbriht's tread paused. Deliberately, the Northerner turned to survey the men, little more than boys, their blood high, as he might regard unfit recruits.

"Little boys," he snorted. "One good battle, and their nurses would have laundry to do once they finished wiping those fools' . . ."

Leo glared at him.

"I was going to say, 'wiping their *eyes.*' "

"Of course," Leo agreed, nodding courtesy at a very wide and very eminent merchant. The man returned the nod, calibrated to reflect Leo's no-doubt-lean purse, then turned to bow more deeply to a finely robed merchant of a distinctly foreign cast.

Leo remembered his inquiries in the Jewish quarter of Constantinople. This merchant might well have been at home there, or in company with the Emperor's own surgeon, searching for spices, medicines, and knowledge. From the man's robes, he might be a dealer in spices, perhaps or silks. With a beauty for a daughter. Leo wondered that he would expose her to the town's gaze. He had seen no women there; and when he had asked . . .

Forget they exist, Leo had been told in essence. He had not been able to forget; and now, here, he saw a man much like the one he remembered.

Behind him walked younger men, dressed like him, only less richly. Leo had seen such young men in Pera, suspicious, even eager to fight. There always were people angry with him when he sought answers to questions. Fearing stones hurled by young men whose anger could set a city ablaze, Leo had turned away.

In the midst of these young men, temporarily intent on their work, not their pride or self-preservation, walked two women. One, heavier and older, he dismissed: a nurse, perhaps, of the type of whom Nordbriht had made his joke. But with her walked a woman smaller than the wives and nuns of Hagios Prokopios, and far more finely made. Those women were foursquare or thin almost to gauntness. Beneath her robes, this woman—this lady—blossomed into gentle curves, a more refined version, perhaps, of the figures Leo had seen sculpted of dark stone.

He flushed, ashamed that at the very time he prayed for a vocation, he could eye a woman and think of how she might look without those cumbersome garments sweeping the dust behind her. *If thy right eye offend thee . . .* Oh God, don't think of blindness; think of anything but that, even carnal thoughts of women . . . *Oh God no, his mother and Andronicus, not even to save his life . . .* He managed to look down before the lady felt his eyes, his hungry eyes, upon her.

At least, he could hope that she had not met his eyes and seen the hunger in them! Her face was veiled, but not hidden, so fine was the silk that covered it. Metal threads glinted in the weave; and from its pretense of modest retreat, bright, dark eyes surveyed her world.

The woman whose pride had shamed Andronicus Ducas had disappeared into air, she and her father, or into the obscurity of caravan routes and the secrecy wrought by their age-old and notoriously secretive people. Whatever else might be said of the Empire's Jews—and much was—they looked after their own.

His hope that she might not see him, or that she would simply pass by went, like most of his hopes these past few years, in vain. The lady quickened her pace and pulled at her father's sleeve. The man paused, turning to look toward Leo. Yes, he had indeed seen that face before. Judging from how the man furrowed his brow, Leo suspected the merchant tried to place *him*.

Only a moment ago, Leo's belly had been growling. Now, it chilled. He had asked among the Jews about a merchant and a woman—a lady— and had been sent away. The man, or priest, who had dismissed him had been afraid. The pounding of Leo's heart made him suspect that these were the people he had met and sought.

If I call his name, will he turn to me, or will he send his servants to drive me off? Leo brushed at his dusty, tattered clothes.

Joachim, or his twin, made his way toward Leo, his hand already reaching toward his purse. His daughter took a step forward as if she too would give alms.

He bowed with the grace his mother had insisted he learn for a career at court, if all went well. Even in rags, he was a Ducas, not a beggar: insufferable to be an object of charity!

So much for humility!

Something about that delicate, costly veil—*she had knelt and wiped sickness away from a sobbing man's face.*

"Do you have water?" her father had demanded. "We have gold to pay for it."

They understood pride, these people. Again, the woman plucked at her father's sleeve. The man nodded and returned Leo's bow.

"Do you require employment?" he asked. "Anyone in the market can point out the merchant Joachim's house."

So it was Joachim after all. Leo had fled the world only to find other remnants of his old life washed up upon this shore. A hand on his arm, trembling slightly; rapid breathing, catching in revulsion at the moment that her countryman's irons struck the Emperor and went awry; a scent of sandalwood and roses—

The lady had unveiled so that Romanus' last sight might be of a fair woman: he might as well think of her as bubbles in a fountain—brilliant and quickly vanished. Her father's strength: it was only an illusion. Neither could have a thing to do with him. They were Jews, and he would be a monk, serving God. It was sin even to think of this woman, even though her face had haunted his dreams.

Let them pass.

Leo shivered and let Nordbriht steer him into the tavern he had scouted out. The lamb was tender, savory, but it might as well have been Dead Sea fruit, turning to ashes in the mouth.

"You have merchants here," he said to the innkeeper. "I would imagine they bring you much trade."

"Not they. Jews, you know. They keep to themselves and eat apart. God only knows what filth they eat or do." He blessed himself with one greasy hand, licked his fingers, then shouted for empty plates to be carried out. If God was kind, the tavern's kitchen was cleaner than its master.

"What do they trade in?"

"Rugs from the East, if the godless haven't burnt it out. Silks from the City—you'd know that better than I, young sir. Spices. Gems from Persia, maybe—how should I know? And perhaps that is not *all* they trade, seeing as they travel to the East."

Spies, he meant. That was another reason why the Jews were watched, one reason why they had feared so when a nobleman came asking for a man of their blood. It was not at all uncommon to wipe out a nest of spies. Fool that he was, he might have signed the death warrant for an entire people.

Best make amends as best he could. "A Jew named Joachim offered me employment."

The innkeeper's eyebrows wagged, and he slammed fresh cups down upon the table.

"One of the richest," said the man. "Richer even than a City man like you, young master."

Leo sat, waiting, not daring to ask for more information.

"He is a decent man, even for one of *those*. Likely, he's spent enough time—and made enough gold—trading among Christians that he knows a good man when he sees one."

"What about his daughter?" a voice asked from across the table.

The innkeeper straightened up. "No one has starved since her father opened his house here. Jephthah, not Joachim, his name should be, though, please God to a far better end for him and his daughter Asherah. She is a good woman, for all she is a Jew. I have said more than I should even in naming her."

Asherah. A hand, delicately poised upon his arm. Hair tumbling down a back as straight and supple as a swordblade. A voice as cultivated as . . . as his own mother's, though husky from speaking languages Leo would never know, demanding to share her kinsmen's risks as a way of making them the lighter. A pride that might beg to save a life, but that would never, never break.

To dispel the heat that flooded through him, he reached for his mother's letter, opened it, and read: Turks in Anatolia; civil strife among the Ducas; the last witticism Psellus had made and in whose heart it had struck home. A warning that Cappadocia yet blamed Michael Ducas for the death of Romanus, a native son. *You may be the son of God the Father, hallowed be His name,* his mother wrote in elegant Greek, *but He has a greater Son by far; and you, for whom I have sacrificed more than ever Hannah gave for Samuel, are the only son I have. Since*

I can do no more, I shall implore the Blessed Virgin, the bearer of God, to keep you in a mother's care.

Leo reached through a blur of tears and hearthsmoke for his cup, drank deep, and set it down. Overset it: it spilled on the rough-planked table, and a man across from him jumped back with an oath. His garments were good and had been better once.

"I was clumsy," Leo said. "Forgive me, sir."

"Moonstruck," Nordbriht struck in cheerfully. "Or perhaps touched by too much work. My . . . friend has been cutting himself a monk's cell in the side of a hill."

The man nodded. Nothing ever went unnoticed in a small town: merchants, strangers, a young man turned to holiness.

"Is this some discipline that has been set for you?" he asked, the Byzantine's fascination with God gleaming in the dusky room. "Surely, there are caves enough, even hollowed-out rocks in the wilderness. Or room and to spare in the cities . . ."

"There are cities underground?" Leo caught him up. "I saw entrances to caves, but thought they were for storage. Or housing for birds."

The stranger's mouth thinned. Quickly, Leo poured him a cup of the sour wine.

"Storage, certainly. But some of them are large enough to hold a village. There are churches down there. A trusted man might ask leave to tend a shrine."

"Barrows," Nordbriht said, and won a blank look from their new companion. "Like the grave. Why would a man live down there before his death? No one is *that* holy that he shuns the light; Our Lord established light from darkness."

"Yellow-hair, when the Turks come riding with their bows and their devilish swift horses, you may be glad to shelter in such a cave."

"And what stops the Turks from sitting down and starving people out like rats in a trap?"

The man shook his head, stung. "You haven't been here long. That much is clear. Those caves go down level upon level, room upon room. Roll a rock before the entrance, and no one can get in unless he tunnels; and the corridors double back and forth. The air is fresh, and there is water. . . ."

He looked about, then lowered his voice impressively. "I have heard that if you descend far enough into the caves, you find a great smooth road that links them one to another: a great highway beneath the earth. And men say, even, that if you go on that highway, you will find a city richer than . . ."

"You say too much, don't you, Paulos?" Casually, the young noble who had sneered at them earlier that day sauntered over to the shabby man, plucked his cup from his hand, and spilled it on the floor. "You talk *far* too much to a traitor and an enemy of our land."

Leo levered himself to his feet. The bench screeched on the tiled floor, tottered, badly balanced as it was, then toppled.

"You have a name, no doubt?" he asked, turning the elegance of his City accent like a Syrian blade upon the newcomer. "And . . ." He let his voice rise in doubt. ". . . a father?"

"We know you, *Ducas*. Go home to your palace. Unless you're afraid they'll burn your eyes out too?"

Leo's eyes filled with flame, his mouth with bile. The stink of burning flesh in his nostrils and of the fever and maggots thereafter. At the end, it had been hard to see his Emperor in the husk he had tried, and failed, to keep clean. If he had tried harder . . . If he did not try to restrain himself, he was going to kill someone.

Why try? He might be blind with rage, but his hand could still feel its way to his knife.

Nordbriht leaned forward across Leo, Varangian in all but the red tunic and the axe. One of his large, scarred hands slammed down right in front of Leo, waking him from his own fever-trance. He wasn't just defending an imperial scion from attack—but from himself.

"In the North," his voice was a low, almost feral rumble, if perfectly polite for the moment, "we have many stories of how easy it is for men to boast when they drink—especially when they drink too much. Our stories are sad because they tell how dire it is when a man speaks too rashly of what he does not understand or cannot do. That is wise, do you not think?"

The noble rose.

"I asked, and nicely, too, 'Do you not think this is wise?' "

Paulos grabbed the young noble's hand before it could drop to his belt and the too-new dagger exhibited there. *Think, man!*

"And yet," Nordbriht said, always in that pleasant, purring voice, "fools call us barbarians. You do know what fools are."

Disgusted, Leo threw down silver for the meal that burned like coals in his belly. He left the tavern, Nordbriht padding after him.

Laughter rose at his back. Leo did not think that it was aimed at him.

"You have made an enemy," Nordbriht warned him.

Leo made himself shrug.

"Yes, a boy and a rash one, but shamed enough to become even more rash." The big man laughed at the night sky.

Leo glanced upward. The moon was almost full.

 **22**

A sherah's torch guttered and drew black streaks on the rock of the tunnel. She was small, but she had to hunch almost double as she climbed back toward the light. Her back protested, but she ignored it: she had not made the long ride from town to yield to discomfort. Resolutely, she entered the underground city that people here called Malagobia. A hard place to live, indeed: but she sought not comfort but knowledge.

Now, Asherah ran her fingers along the rock, counting: like countless generations of passersby, she felt for marks in the rock other than the scars of the tools that had hollowed it out.

The opening on her left led past an air shaft, one of many. Yes, she had counted the steps and turns correctly. Here, wind from the upper air whistled and whispered. Behind her came a choke, quickly suppressed. In the first days of Asherah's exploration of the underground, her poor maid had listened to the same stories that she had. But where Asherah had been enthralled just with the idea of the subterranean cities, let alone the possibility that a great road might connect them all and lead to one queen city, her maid feared being trapped alone in the dark while random breezes seemed to whisper her name like evil spirits approaching from behind.

Here, in the very shaft that brought them life-giving air, there was also danger. She must guard her torch. Light might be seen from the surface. Or if a stray gust put it out, Asherah thought she knew the passage well enough that she and her maid would not wander in the dark until her father's servants came, or they went mad before they died of hunger, or the underground city filled as villagers fled down into the dark that they feared as much as the Turks.

No one knew better than her father's heir and confidante just how likely that was. Caravans had been attacked. For now, her own family's camels and horses, and the treasure that they could carry from city to city, here into the West had halted behind walls; and it lay in the hands of the Almighty whether they would be safe or not.

Never mind the camels and the silks, the spices and the treasure: if the Turks struck here in force and these later Romans struck back, she and Joachim, her father, together with the other Jews in the Empire and throughout Persia, would be lucky not to be ground between them. The villagers and those who dwelled on outlying farms might view the merchant lords askance, but they shared the same fears, the same problems—and *they* might not have willing access to the underground cities if war came. At least, not yet. All Asherah's charities in the town and fields might not suffice to correct how the villagers thought of the Jews—though that was not why she had performed them.

No one minded now when she visited Malagobia or Enegobi, provided that she was discreet; provided, too, that they did not know how assiduously she hunted. So far, however, what had she found? Dry stone, scarred by tools and fire. A few broken tools. A chip or three of pottery, such as she might find in any abandoned house. Once, she had found a tiny idol; but better were to be found in many places roundabouts—including (as she had heard) the valleys where the monks lived and prayed within the rocky spires. Such trove as she had found dangled from a bag at her girdle. Such symbols as she had seen etched or scrawled upon the carved-out walls were recorded in her memory.

"Not much longer now." Asherah hoped her maid found the sound of her voice encouraging. She would never say it, but she found the sound of actual, sunlit cheerfulness an intrusion here.

What if they hear you?

Be quiet, she told herself. *There is no* they.

None that she had found. Yet.

Tzipporah, as she often pointed out, was older than she. The damp made her knees ache. It was cruel to bring her here, let alone to descend level upon level armed with no more than a torch and the knife Asherah had been taught to use; but her maid and her father were united on this: Asherah must not explore the deep ways of the city-caves alone. Perhaps, no certainly, a manservant would have been better for the task of companion, but Asherah had bent custom and braved comment as much as even the sole heiress of a wealthy merchant might dare. Even if the merchant heiress was a Jew.

It was not the Christians who would comment that Asherah, daughter of Joachim, wandered about companioned by a man. They knew so little of her people, and condemned all of it, that they would not know how great a violation of custom it would be for her to spend time alone with a man, especially in the dark caves outside the town. If she could gratify custom and her curiosity both, how much the better for her. Her conscience smote her at her maid's attempt at a brave reply. The shadows danced as Tzipporah's torch wobbled. God send that the damp had soaked into their clothes so they would not go up like tinder if a torch brushed them. Her heavy garments were a sad nuisance; but man's clothing was forbidden.

Asherah stopped so quickly that Tzipporah almost walked into her. She shut her eyes. No, it was the wind, not a voice at all. She sighed, echoing the sound. At times this trip, she almost thought she had found it. Whatever "it" was: some prickle of power, some trace of it, even a rock curiously carved or a shard of pottery, or scrap of metal—something that could *not* be traced to the villagers who now maintained these cave warrens as storages and refuge in times of raid.

Almost.

She heard Tzipporah's sympathetic response to her sigh. At her age, her maid had a child at her hip, another at the breast, and one in the belly. Easy enough for Tzipporah to ascribe these trips below the earth to a longing to get away from from the duties of her father's heir as well as the keeper of his home. But Asherah was as strange as her name, and had always been so.

That was how she survived, she and the people she loved, some of the time. The darkness brought back memories, memories of fear, of power prickling behind her eyes, of voices in her brain calling her name, demanding that she *pay attention!* Or, like a tardy schoolboy, she would face the whip. The lashes of that power in her mind were not a punishment she would choose.

Around this curve. Bend down. Put out your hand—just so! yes, and support yourself against the pillar that some kindly artisan had carved here, no doubt for just this purpose. What was that she felt incised into the rock? A butterfly? A figure of a woman, such as the monks vied in smashing? Or was it only a slip of the chisel? She ran her fingers along the grooves. No . . . letters, a maker's mark. One *D* . . . *U* . . . *K* . . .

Behind her Tzipporah murmured in dismayed impatience.

Asherah moved on, her garments sweeping against the narrow passageway. Had the mark been important, she would have sensed it as fire behind her eyes, or a pressure so demanding it would force her to her knees until she gave voice to it.

The time they had fled Baghdad, for example: as a child, she had waked screaming in the night, just enough time for servants to snatch up arms and defend them, winning the precious hours they had used to retreat. Or the time a cousin bought a house she did not like. It had burned, and it was only through the mercy of God that no lives were lost. But who listened to a child, unless she screamed?

More people, Asherah realized, than listened to an unwed maid; and it would be many years until she grew old enough—God grant she lived through them in health—that she would be listened to for her wisdom. And yet, wisdom of a sort there already was, honed by study. And her senses grew keener as her body ripened. At first, her women blamed her moods on her new womanhood.

She had wept when her mother had left their house with her brother to show her kin her baby son, and wept harder, for no reason, they all said, all one night. For months, Asherah had dreams of bones covered by drifting sand, or raiders sweeping down. For months, they waited for a letter from her mother's people, then for some word from the outposts along the caravan routes, then for any scrap of news or rumor at all from the net of spies her father cast into the sand. Like water poured onto the desert, her father's gold, like her mother's and brother's blood, had been spilled out into the sand; and no one would see any of them again.

In comforting a child who seemed likely to run mad with grief, Joachim had become aware that his turbulent daughter's dreams were more than a child's mourning. He had not become rich, not survived by ignoring what was put before him—in this case, the history of his daughter's outbursts and what followed them. Another man might see her as a witch, a danger to him and to the safety of the people. Joachim saw the promise in his daughter's painful gifts!

How much Asherah loved her father, not least because he called her curse a gift! But he too had sought out truth as eagerly as trade all his life. Finding his daughter of even more interest as a mind than an agent of family bargaining, he had kept her by his side: a good daughter, a loyal girl, and his dearest ally.

If he had given her life, she had repaid him several times. On the road from Samarkand once, the sight of a pool of water had sent her retching to her knees. That sight had cost her father a prospective son-in-law, as frightened by the way her fears had been accepted as he was revolted by her loss of control. Joachim accounted the continued health of their pack animals and, of course, of themselves as rather more important. Aided by substantial gifts to his family, her father found it easy to convince the youth (who wanted to be convinced far more than his family had ever wanted her for a daughter-in-law) that fear and fever had made him see what he had not. Now, her father's drovers looked to her as much as to her father. Well enough, since she was now his sole heir. Better still, now that she was known among the great trading families to be sufficiently odd that she might better, for all her youth, her virtues, her wealth, and the Law itself, she might do better to remain thus.

Only once since her mother's death had her foresight, refined now by study and prayer and practice, failed even in part. Menachem, she thought, had been pressed into service to torture an Emperor who had already lost his diadem and must lose his sight. She had failed to warn them when the soldiers came. One young soldier had taken pity on them—she remembered his cleanliness and strength beside her as he fought for courage in her presence. No harm had come to her or any of the Jews herded into the camp—except that Menachem had left them and gone to Alexandria where, please God, he too would learn to heal.

She had feared her powers were failing but, "Who else was there to comfort the Emperor?" her father had comforted her—when he too had stopped shaking. It was a good deed, a great deed; but it was a deed she could have done without. Its immensity, and its power to have destroyed her and hers, terrified her. So, she had been well pleased to attend her father here, to this Imperial backwater that had been the birthplace of the Emperor she had watched be destroyed.

True help, she raged to Joachim, would have been to free him. Since she had had her women's growth, he had introduced her to some ancient scrolls, some from Alexandria and some, older yet, from Babylon. They had awakened her to ideas that desperation might have made her try. She had feared for her father, the other men, and for herself. She had even feared for the young officer, who had offered her protection although, white and anguished himself at his Emperor's fate, she thought he needed it even more than she. His determination and loyalty—like his Emperor's courage—deserved better recompense. And so she had drawn upon her power . . .

. . . and felt her father's *voice* inside her thoughts, forbidding her as surely as if an Archangel barred her path with a flaming sword.

And then the iron had struck, bungling the hateful task, once, twice, a third time; and the time for intervention was far past. Menachem had collapsed, and what she could do by compassion and courage must be done.

But she had taken the subject up with Joachim later on, as they hastened into the South. With luck the Ducas Emperor now in power would not know them from any one of a number of clans of wealthy Jews. Even his own surgeon would help conceal them. If true danger came, they could be gone in an instant, bound for the caravan routes that were marked more surely by the names of merchant families that were kin to them than by the shifting roads across the sand.

"And what then, daughter?" he had asked. "Let them see what you know and they do not? No quicker way to the torturers ourselves!"

"He might have been grateful!" She had railed.

For the first time in her adult life, her father had laughed at her. "Grateful to *us*? What is the measure of a king's gratitude to the Children of Israel? A quick death, perhaps, if we are fortunate. No, we truly exist to serve God and to save a remnant of us alive that we may continue to serve Him until, finally, at the end of time, we establish *our* Kingdom. That is why we are alive, and not washed away like sand upon the shore. Like the others."

The others . . . up the rocky stairs Asherah trudged, one stair to every vanished empire. The Egyptians. The Babylonians. The Philistines. The Greeks. The Romans. This latest empire of Christians who called themselves Roman. Was it too about to be swept onto the shoals of time where empires that had been cast down went to be forgotten—by everyone but her?

It was hard to watch and wait. But, for Asherah, it would have been harder not to know at all.

One last stair there. She ducked to avoid the bulge in the rock that the carvers had not smoothed when this tunnel was burrowed out of the naked stone. Almost free. Now the passage evened out, went from tunnel to sloping chimney within instants. She began to see light up ahead. The shadows plucked at her clothing as if seeking to draw her back into their midst: *come; we will give you all you ask*. She pressed on, calling on strength that prayer and constant walking had allowed her to sustain. Hard enough it was to negotiate the twists and turns, to learn the stairs and ramps of the underground ways without the constant need to *listen* with all her senses, not just for water, but for whatever man or beast might lie in wait. Or even for the whispers that the knowledge that she sought was here. Use these places the villagers did, and must; but they feared them.

Past the millstones and the heavy doors that could be drawn to bar the way within. Up uneven stairs, rough-hewn once, smoothed now by the passage of centuries of feet. Asherah urged her maidservant up the last steps toward the light.

She raised her head, smoothing her veil over hair that she knew was sadly tumbled. The sky was darkening from gray to indigo, a few last banners lingering at the horizon in a futile contest with the rising moon.

And then she smiled. Along with the servingmen, her father was waiting for her. And smiling. Guilt twinged deep within her. He was too old to ride out this far. But he smiled as one sure that he had given a joyous surprise. She would not have to travel home by night accompanied by a tired maid, sullen guards, and questions such as "did she run mad this time?" mouthed behind her back. Sometimes, those unspoken accusations weighed on her more than any other burden she might bear.

"Are you content, daughter?" Joachim asked her with an answering smile.

"I shall be content," she said, "when I find the entrance to this roadway to the center of all caves the Christians talk about when they think we don't hear them."

Joachim laughed.

"And what did you glean today?" he asked. "We should call you Ruth. Surely, no corn is as alien as what you seek."

He gestured at one manservant to take the bag tied to her belt, at another who must help Tzipporah mount—which she did with precisely enough moaned complaints to let Asherah know she had exceeded her bounds. How long the road would be to their home. But Tzipporah, like Asherah, had traveled the caravan routes to the east: she could ride in her sleep, if she must.

"You think there is treasure in there?" She met her father's eyes. Merchant that he was, she had grown up familiar with the feel of the finest silk in her hands. She could count the knots on the rugs loaded upon the swift, sullen Bactrians that plied the caravan routes. She was as able to judge the flaws in rubies as in pomegranates. But it was not such treasure that she sought below the earth—little as any of her father's friends or the villagers of Hagios Prokopios might believe her.

Asherah sought knowledge and the uses to which that knowledge could be put. Knowledge that, thus far, she had not gained, but that she planned to continue to seek.

"I came out to tell you," said her father. "The packs from Babylon arrived. There is a shipment of clay . . . no, not the pottery, but clay bricks, unglazed, and marked with symbols such as I have seen before. We shall see if they are words that we can try to read."

He pulled a tablet from his belt. Asherah closed her hand eagerly upon the clay. In the light of the full moon, she saw marks she had last seen at the feet of an idol. Or thought she had: half the inscription and almost three quarters of the image had been smashed by previous travelers, whether Christian, Jew, or Muslim, indignant at such abomination.

The hope of knowledge, of secrets plumbed and known, prickled along Asherah's spine. There had been great mages among the Chaldees. Perhaps these tablets held their secrets.

One of the drovers gestured urgently.

Joachim came alert. "Quick! I hear something," he whispered.

Asherah scrambled onto her waiting horse. She might have had an Arab, but the rocks here would have been unkind to such a pretty creature. Better to ride one of the ungainly horses she had seen in her travels in Persia and Ferghana, valuing them for their strength and endurance. Not for the first time, she was glad she could mount by herself and ride. It was quicker, if far less proper, than any closed chair or carriage, quicker even than the veiled enclosures perched atop camels that had borne her in the deserts east of Persia and in the highlands where a noble woman must be secluded.

They set out quickly. Beside her, Joachim set up a humming on several notes, a song of passage that she knew carried other meanings as well. She joined her voice to his, setting protections that had nothing to do with the armed men who surrounded them, invoking the archangels to surround them, a second and far more powerful circle of protection.

Pass unnoticed, like sand falling in the night. Pass unnoticed, like moonlight bathing ripples of water. Pass unnoticed. We are safe within the circle of archangels. You do not see us. You sense only the rhythm of the night. You see nothing: a trick of the light—no more.

Sometimes, it even worked.

The full moon made their path clear over the rubble-strewn ground: just as well, lest their horses step awry on the track, perhaps on one of the sharp pieces of obsidian that glinted darkly before them. Asherah's humming took on words, becoming a soft-voiced chant. She drew the light and strength of the full moon to help her. So much depended on the moon, which, for the Muslims as well as for her own people, established the times and seasons of the year and its holidays. Moonbright: Asherah was certain she had seen mentions of a female power, if not the false beings worshipped by the ancient Greeks, in Muslim texts. But in her own holy words? God was God; and that was all there was. Yet Wisdom was a woman, and the moon governed women as surely as the tides.

As above, so below: as within, without; the ebb and flow of tides of the seas and the blood tides within a woman's deepest privacy. It was woman's magic, this looking to the moon. She had learned it for herself. No need to tell her father: if it protected him, she would take the blame for any idolatry upon herself and atone for it when the moon proclaimed it to be time.

Her mare settled down from her initial trot to a smooth walk she could keep up for the hours the trip home would take. She too would not be dazzled by the moon nor spooked by the shadows cast by the rocks through which they rode, but would gain strength, Asherah hoped.

Ahead of her, were two men riding, one far taller than the other. She reached *out* with her senses in the way she had been taught—a fragile tendril of awareness she thought of as a shining thread spun from her mind and soul and body. Yes, others waited for them. She could hear their horses shift from hoof to hoof. The men moved to stand on either side of the road. An ambush, then?

She could hear them cough, or mutter to each other; she could even hear their breathing, smell the wine upon their breath. The heated courage inspired by the wine was cooling now, but a cold anger underlay it.

They waited for their enemy. The murderer of their lord. Kinsman to the hated man who had stolen his place, and who had—less important, if more immediate—faced them down. He was but one, and his friend, though fearfully strong, was only one more: they could take both men and make certain. . . .

Asherah shuddered. Death ruled the watchers' minds. They would kill the men they stalked and then, no doubt, hide them in the underground ways. In times of trouble, Asherah knew, people died in those caves. The dead were carefully preserved in special crypts until they could receive proper burial. She had never found such places, but she had no wish to come upon some moldering *thing* during her explorations.

The two men rode closer. A moment more and they would ride right into the ambush she foresaw.

She tugged at her father's sleeve.

"They mean murder!" she whispered.

Joachim signaled for the guards he trusted most.

"Get her away!" he ordered in a hiss.

With a shout, the ambushers surged up and over the men for whom they had lain in wait. The moonlight let Asherah see them clearly, even to the details of their clothes and weapons. Young nobles, eager to prove themselves, if not to put themselves in much danger. Fine warriors, those. Contempt, more chill than anger, made her dizzy. Such men, such noble men to lord it over an Empire and oppress her people and kill strangers.

In an instant, they'd have their victims off their horses.

"We must stop them!" she whispered. A man reached to take her reins and lead her safely away. She jerked her horse's head away.

"*You* must be safe!" her father said. She was what he had, and all he had left. But if she allowed herself to be put in safekeeping like some useless treasure, what, indeed, did he have? A scroll of wisdom kept wrapped up because it was too precious to be read? That was stupid!

They were down now, or at least one man was. She saw his face as he fell. . . .

Salomon had her bridle now, was drawing her away. By now, Gershom would probably have had to gag Tzipporah unless she convinced herself that this would mean another attack upon the People unless she kept silent.

The other man cried out as the nobles clubbed him.

"We'll dump them in the city for now. They'll keep until we decide how best to bury them. You sought our treasure, *Imperial Highness?* The rock and shadows that are all you robbers left us? You'll sleep with it till doomsday!"

She could feel his eyes and hearing go wild as he searched for help. That man's face, strained and pale, its dark eyes flashing up to the moon, around, as if seeking help. . . . *I lift up mine eyes unto the hills whence cometh my help . . .*

She heard the name "Ducas." She knew that face. And she knew whence his help must come.

She had felt this kind of rage before, when her powers failed and she had been swept up by officers into the soldiers' camp. She had demanded to draw her own shard in the hideous lottery that would determine which of her people would have an Emperor's death upon his untried hands: one less chance that the lot would fall to her father. Failing in that, she had been escorted to where the Emperor's last sight would be of her.

He had spoken fairly to her, summoning his courage lest she be more afraid than she was. He had even sent his servant to stand by her, a man he treated as his son. His hand had shaken as he guided her, but she had gained courage from his will, not to fail before one given him to protect. And he had seen her and the others safely from the camp.

He had a life's claim upon her.

"Father," she cried despairingly as Salomon pulled her reins from her hands, "this is the man who saved me!"

Joachim would know which man she meant and where.

"The man we saw in the town? The one I told to come see me if he needed work? I shall see to this, child. Go home."

She would have stamped her feet and shrieked if she had time or safety for such display.

She brought her nails down upon Salomon's hand and when his grip faltered, wrenched her reins free. The way her horse jerked her head, its tender mouth aching from this treatment, only fueled her anger.

What was the point of training a daughter like a son—and the Wise Son at that—if, at the slightest danger, she was to be led away like a solitary, precious lamb? Lambs too could be sacrificed: she would far rather go down fighting.

The man about to die understood, had understood when she refused to hide under the guise of tender lady and be led from his Emperor's sight when there was a kindness she could do. He had treated her like a comrade and an equal. He should not die if she could save him.

"We must not be involved!" her father whispered. "You most of all."

She wavered, seeing the fear in his eyes, not just for her, his only surviving child, but for her, because of her visions, her powers in a world that would treat her as a witch.

"He would not have forced Menachem to blind the Emperor. He helped me tend him!" She had never begged in her life and would not begin now.

But she had begun to shake. It made her furious as well as terrified. This was the worst of it, had always been the worst of it. As a child, to *know* what would happen and never, never to be believed. As a woman, to *know* and to understand, but never, never to allowed to take a hand in events.

"If Moses had not listened to his sister, we never would have crossed the Red Sea!" she cried. Like Miriam, Asherah was a prophet. Her father had tested her, trusted her: why could he not make *use* of her gifts?

She flinched as she heard the young aristocrat groan. If they fancied themselves alone, they might take their time in slaying him, might kick him to death, judging from the sounds she heard.

"They're killing him!"

Salomon had wrested control of her horse from her again. Asherah slipped from its back.

"Mistress, this is a bad time. . . ." He dared argue with her as if she were some creature fit only to bake bread and tend babies? He knew better than that.

"Asherah, my child, my child, wait!"

Joachim's footsteps grated on the rocky soil.

Wait. Again, wait. Time, time, it was never time to *do*. Always, they must speak softly, wait, hide, flee, bide their time—and for what? Until the Messiah came? And she had seen her mother killed, her friends and family dispersed. She had been spied upon for madness, had lost homes without count, and would never, never, never be trusted to *be* the mere bread-baker and baby-tender that Salomon tried to make her.

"Why couldn't God save her?" she had asked during the days of mourning for her mother, too young then to see her father flinch at the grief her question had renewed.

Why, indeed? Why had God not saved her mother? Why not their friends, their cities, their holy kingdom? Why have powers at all if they were only a study, not a weapon?

Indeed, they *must* wait until the Messiah came to bring them courage, if nothing else.

All during her childhood, Asherah had railed at that and had been told, "If we showed what we know, all the nations of the world would band together just long enough to wipe us out. Truly, we exist—we *must* exist—only to praise God. And to keep alive that a remnant may be saved and, at the end of days, rebuild God's Temple. That is why we are alive, not tossed onto the shoals of time like the powers we have outlived—as we will outlive this one too."

But, Lord of Hosts, it was hard to take the long view when a man was being blinded or kicked to death before your eyes.

This time, she would not wait. She ran toward her former rescuer, her hand going to a little dagger she always wore.

If she waited much longer, another man would die. And his help had saved her, and perhaps all the Jews in Cotyaeum.

Her father ran up behind her, old as he was. He caught her by the arm. She had not the heart to pull free, assuming that she could.

She looked up at him and let the tears of anger come. "He was kind to me. And . . ."

"Because of that, daughter . . ." Joachim might wish to hide her away like an unread scroll, but he seldom refused her anything else she asked.

"But you will let *me* lead."

She obeyed, glad to seem meek now that she had gained her will.

Joachim extended his hands. No humming now, but the full-throated invocation, here beneath the moon and stars.

Power prickled along Asherah's spine and grew to be a roaring in her ears. Her father had not yet begun, but she could feel the strangeness start within her, the roaring in her ears and heart and brain that meant, as it always had, some use of magic. She was floating, floating above the battlefield. In an instant, she would see. . . .

An actual roaring drew her back to the world, as if a beast leapt from a cliff into the midst of a den of thieves. Joachim and Asherah whirled around, Asherah's hand, with its puny dagger, going up before her, her father pushing her behind him and drawing the sword he had learned to use, after a fashion, unlawful though it doubtless was.

A creature had indeed leapt between the murderers and their prey. Half man, half beast, it seemed and wholly huge, like some demon ravening out of the Persian hills. Its long muzzle opened, it bayed at the moon, showing darkened teeth, as a man broke and ran shrieking from the carnage on the ground. The creature leapt after the man and onto his back, bringing him down with what appalling grace.

The ambushers' horses screamed and broke free. They were too well trained to do that, except in the case of fire, or blood—or something completely unnatural.

"Demon," she whispered.

To her astonishment, Joachim chuckled. "I heard such tales of men from the North and never thought to believe them. And yet . . . yes." He drew a deep breath, a warrior finding the weapon of his choice.

"Now," he demanded, "will you believe there are some things in which I am still your teacher? I shall restrain the Northerner. You, since you wish to be a second Deborah, guard your old guardian."

The moon was high now, occluded only by a few fast-moving clouds. Asherah could feel Leo's desperate grasp on awareness fade, like a man struggling back over the lip of a cliff, whose fingers scrabble and falter. He was fighting to live, and yet—she screamed with the pain she felt, roused to panic at the sight of a dagger held before his eyes, silver-bright, not red-hot, but just as deadly. . . .

Again, the creature, the man-beast snarled, its voice rising into a howl of fury and, much to Asherah's surprise, anguish.

Joachim's hand gripped her shoulder. *Yes.* That was the way. Closing her eyes, Asherah added her strength to his, invoking the archangels, especially Michael the Warrior, whose dark hair and eyes had reminded her of this man's ever since he had led her from an Emperor's execution.

When she could open her eyes again, she saw that the young man was up and fighting as best he could. His sword was long lost; they had disarmed him before anything else. Yet, he was trying now to defend himself with the shreds of his cloak wrapped about one arm and what looked like a dark light glinting in his hand. Asherah turned her attention to his weapon: it was a dagger chipped from black stone, the sort of crude, final weapon someone might use only if he had nothing else, not even hope.

How long had it been since this man had dared to hope? Since before his Emperor lost his eyes?

She knew him again now, remembered his name. Ducas. Leo Ducas, his name was. God protect him. Light formed about her and her father, a sphere of protection, moon-shining, that expanded until it touched the fighting men. As the light brushed one of them, he screamed and ran. Leo dropped to his knees and slashed at the calf of another: hamstringing was highly effective, if not at all the type of blow Asherah expected an aristocrat of Byzantium to resort to. His chest was heaving, and his head moved from side to side as if his vision faded and blurred. He was losing strength.

What they had done was not enough.

And with the sphere of light came sigils. A star of five points. A star of six points—the seal of Solomon, greatest of mages, to bind and to control the wild creature that had once walked like a man in the marketplace.

The light grew brighter and brighter, sun-bright, and then exploded in a conflagration like a burning ship when its supplies of sea-fire are breached.

The last attacker took to his heels. If their working had been spectacular enough, perhaps that, combined with the apparition of whatever creature he had seen, would suffice to silence him. It might even be enough to prevent him from trying to kill again by stealth and in the dark.

Asherah had escaped peril of her life before, and on less assurance. But it still was not good enough! Her mind screamed in rage. She was a stranger in a strange land: this man was one of this land's own.

As if the beast that leapt onto four legs from two could hear her, it loped after the last attacker and brought him down with a casual swipe of a huge paw across his neck.

The people here would never, never think Turks capable of such a killing, would they? she asked herself, afraid that even the help of that creature would not avail them much.

They feared. They hated. They would think the Turks capable of anything.

Better the Turks than her own people, she thought, and hated herself for it. Hatred, within the wards themselves: another sin for which she would have to atone.

Asherah wanted to run to the man whose life she had helped save, but the wards of protection must be taken down, the powers thanked, and her father seen to, lest this working have proved too great a strain upon his heart. Though the time seemed long, it was only perhaps a moment or so until she could drop to her knees by the young Ducas. He lay prone, his head in the dust.

The other thing, the man-wolf, padded over and sank down at her feet. It whined, put its nose down between its paws, then raised it and howled once more. The desolation in that cry brought tears to Asherah's eyes. Poor monster, poor thing, to know itself a monster . . .

"Don't let it touch you, child!" To her horror, the voice belonged to Tzipporah, who had come panting up with one of the manservants. He was at her side in an instant, holding another sword—where *had* her father secured these weapons, forbidden, as she had always thought, to Jews? Along the trade routes, she was certain, but where? She must learn before much longer.

"Why aren't you safe?" she demanded of her maidservant.

"Leaving your mother's child in danger? May my right hand wither first!" Tzipporah's right hand shook, but it held a knife, and she contemplated the creature lying nearby as if she planned to use it.

The wards still shimmered about her. "We will not harm you," she spoke to the creature as if to an enormous dog. It whined again.

"Did they hurt you?" she asked.

Behind her, she heard Joachim's low-voiced laughter. She knew she would hear later, "Daughter, one does not treat a man-wolf as a dog." She would tell him that she saw no reason why *this* creature might not serve as just such a guardian. After all, he clearly had set himself as protector to the Ducas.

But she would have to see that he lived, and that her own servants did not hack him to death as they clearly had a mind to.

Time to change that. Asherah raised her hands and eyes, invoking Gabriel and swift healing. Moonlight washed over the creature. Its shape shifted again, into the body of a scarred man. A much-scarred, naked man, she noticed and quickly looked away.

"Throw a cloak over him," Joachim ordered the servants who had ridden up. His hands, far more expert yet in knowledge than hers, though hers would be the deeper gift when it matured, prodded at the two men for breaks and wounds.

He nodded, satisfied. "Lay them across the horses and take them home. I ask you as your friend, not as your master: let none of you speak of this to anyone. If you cannot remain in my service because of it, I will see you safely away. But I will implore your silence. And may the Shield of Abraham ward us all."

Low-voiced mutters of assent rumbled from the men. Asherah found herself able to breathe freely again. She had not realized until that moment just what her impulse to save these two men might have cost. And yet, to pass by on the other side—the Christians had one story, just *one* of a Jew who had done just that, and they never let her people forget it. Perhaps she had lived too long among the Christians, but passing by upon the other side shocked her to the core.

Carefully, Asherah helped her father roll Leo over and examine him for wounds. His eyes opened as they moved him. At first, they searched about wildly.

"Nordbriht," he muttered. "Don't hurt him. Don't tell. He hates this."

Under his cloak, Nordbriht flattened himself into the dust of the road, rather like a dog caught stealing food, as if he were still the beast who had hunted down would-be murderers.

"Be easy, stranger." Joachim laid a hand on the man's massive shoulder. He wrapped himself more fully in the cloak and turned, pale eyes watching as Asherah's father turned back to the other man. His hand opened, and something dark and bloodstained dropped from it. Joachim wrapped his hand in a fold of his ample robe and picked up the object: a tiny knife, wrought of the shining black stone one found here even in the roadbeds.

"Your friend is safe," Asherah said. "He has"—how could she put this?—"returned to himself."

Her voice brought Leo's head around, and she flushed: recognition shone in them, recognition and, despite his ordeal, delight.

"And are you still so sure, lady," he whispered, "that they would not harm you?"

He caught at her hand and pressed it against his face in a way she was certain her father would not approve and that made the air chill where Tzipporah was standing.

Never mind that. His eyes demanded an answer.

"I was afraid then, too," she whispered.

She found herself smiling. And then she shook with fear—shook again at her confession.

23

F rom her bath, Asherah contemplated tasks yet undone. *Here* she was, guests in her house, the house in an uproar from the very nature of those guests, and Tzipporah had imprisoned her in hot, scented water and was turning out the finest contents of her clothes chests and jewelry coffer. In addition to the daily obligations of her father's accounts, the house, and her own studies (examination of the clay tablets her father had brought her would have to be postponed), she faced sacred obligations of hospitality and healing. Meanwhile, her maids enjoyed a flurry of excitement right out of the stories of the Gentiles that, frankly, she was surprised they had even heard of.

A son of the Ducas line always turned out to be the hero of such stories, she remembered. At least, the women would attribute her blush to the hot water.

She rose from it and reached for her robes before she could be surrounded and enveloped in the richest of them with what she privately considered to be far more flutter than necessary.

She shook her head. No, not the purple. The Empire's laws forbade that she own anything finer than purple of the second class; and this was a City man of the highest family, used to the finest of dyes. Purple was for Empire. It was not, however, as if Asherah had objections to splendor, though she rarely resorted to it before Christians: judicious display was a weapon in any merchant's trading arsenal. And fine fabrics and rich colors gladdened the eyes and could lift the mood. She nodded approval at the Persian brocade, indigo with a peacock sheen, held out next for her approval. (She remembered how much she had bargained—in gold—from its initial price and smiled private satisfaction.)

The silk was cool even against the sheer cotton her maids drew quickly over her scented skin; and she shivered with pleasure. But enough finery! She was mistress of this house and she need not jangle with all her bracelets, necklaces, and rings when she had tasks to perform. For modesty, she draped a veil over her dark hair, but she took pains to untangle hair and veil from the long earrings, studded with sapphires, that she did consent to wear.

"You look like a princess," Tzipporah murmured.

"No, a bride!" her youngest and newest servingwoman said, as the others laughed and clapped their hands. Then they hushed, no doubt at a glare from Tzipporah.

Caring for them, Asherah could not tell them that their dreams of what a real life should be were not hers, and could never be. Not when her childhood fears of madness had yielded to knowledge that made the moonlight itself hers to weave; not when the visions that had cooled suitors' pleas could be channeled to coax the archangels to aid her.

I would give anything to be as you are, she thought at the women as she studied her reflection in her mirror. *Except what I already am.*

They loved her. They wished her every happiness, except the ones that *she* knew.

Were they still thinking of those imbecile songs? Send the young lord back to his people; go with him as hostage and as prize herself, just in time for the next story? They were different, the Ducas and her family. Centuries of Imperial law and the threat of death made that all too clear. Rescue the prince, yes. Send him back, yes. Above all, send him on his way and forget, except to pray that punishment would not come again—and that, if it came, it would not be more than she and those she loved could bear.

She fretted through an application of kohl to her eyelids, then reclaimed her freedom to race to the kitchens, then into the room in which her father received his most honored guests. Despite her preparations, she was gratified: she was the first to arrive, Tzipporah following in her indigo brocade wake. A servant laid down the last dish of heavy silver, then vanished.

Asherah inspected the dishes, the cushions, the goblets. It was not often that her father ate in company with outsiders, especially Christians, or whatever the tall fair man was. Perhaps, as an unwed girl, she should efface herself, seeing to her father's and her father's guests' comfort from a discreet position between this room and the kitchens.

But she was Asherah, her father's heir and keeper of his house and secrets. And she would serve her guests herself.

They knew him, Leo thought, and gave him more honor than his own family. Why else would they have dressed him, after treatment by a skilled surgeon and a bath that made him think he had returned to Constantinople, in heavy silks, rich with purple and embroidery in the Persian fashion?

"All you need is your axe," he told Nordbriht, who marched along behind him, splendid in crimson silk that, for a wonder, did not strain over chest and shoulders.

The Varangian shook his head. Lights from highly polished poly-candela struck highlights from his braids and beard. "I should go back and tend to those bodies," he muttered. "Small enough price to pay: these people spared my life. They saw me as I am and they spared my life." It had become his litany.

A servant beckoned them toward a door. He nodded respect at the doorway, then knocked. The carved door opened from within . . . into a room Leo might have envisioned in Samarkand or Susa, but never in Hagios Prokopios, so far from the center of Empire.

He had lain a prisoner in the Turks' hands, yet had entered Alp Arslan's tents to be stunned with the richness of rugs and cushions strewn about instead of the squalor he had expected after a night spent dazed on the field of Manzikert.

What had he expected of the merchant Joachim's home? Some garish combination of tavern and blasphemy?

No mosaic tiles winked up at him from the floor, as he would have expected in a great house in Byzantium. Instead, the rugs piled one on top of another on the floor were even finer than those deemed fit for the sultan Alp Arslan to walk upon. Cushions lay atop them. Some were also made of squares of carpet, wool or silk. And some were brocaded silk that seemed to shift color in the light from the lamps fastened to the walls. Overhead, casting a glitter of light and shadow, hung a great bronze lamp, cunningly pierced in a thousand places.

Against the walls stood ancient, broken columns, each smoothed off into a flat surface on which rested some treasure: beasts of lapis, malachite, and jade; a fluted bowl of rainbow glass; a chipped dish incised with butterflies like those Leo had seen in Meletios' cave; the head of a young hero, his nose smashed, his eyes looking into forever; the statue of what looked like a woman with tiny head and feet, but with the belly and breasts of a mother of many children.

Aside from the lack of icons, they might have been in the home of any aristocrat Leo might have visited, if the aristocrat had been a man—or woman—of sufficient wealth and vision to amass treasures from the caravan routes and all the ages. How much of this was the father's choosing, and how much that of the woman, scarcely more than a girl, sitting so demurely near her father's feet?

Nordbriht drew in his breath. Leo agreed: the smells of cooking in the room were distinctly tempting, far more so than silks or cushions or the most prized wares of what, clearly, was a highly unusual merchant. Low tables stood by each pile of cushions. On a longer table rested covered dishes, heavy plates bright with patterned glazes, and massive breads, wrapped in immaculate cloth. Beads of moisture trembled on a silver pitcher with a neck curved as gracefully as a dancer's arm.

Joachim the merchant allowed them to get their bearings, then rose to greet them. "You are welcome to my home," he said. "Our clothes become you. My daughter chose well."

"You would honor us," she said softly, "if you kept them as our gift."

Leo found himself smiling at her voice. In this island of wealth and peace, it had finally lost the strained courage he had always heard in it. Asherah. The woman he had been told not to endanger by seeking. *I know you, Lady*, he thought.

As if she could hear him, she glanced away. When he and Nordbriht had come in, she had not risen, choosing to remained curled on a cushion somewhat to the side and behind her father's chair. Trying to fade into the background? This room's splendor made it impossible for any of it to fade into the shadows. Asherah had dressed to match it in a flow of iridescent blue and green, matched by the gems she wore, and outshone by her eyes.

Now she rose and gestured at a door half draped in silk. Servants emerged with soft towels and basins. The water for washing was scented with lemon: father and daughter washed too.

Joachim beckoned them further into the room, to the waiting cushions. Leo sank down well enough, despite his soreness from the fight that had almost killed him . . . *that these people had saved him from*. Nordbriht proved more of a problem. Asherah laughed and gestured a servant to bring him more cushions.

Going over to the table, Joachim broke apart a loaf, murmured words over it, and handed pieces to his guests and to his daughter. Dishes were brought and passed, far richer and more plentiful than in his father's house, rivalling the feasts at which Alp Arslan had treated his emperor like a guest, not a captive. Joachim refused thanks, refused talk of the night's . . . excitement, as his daughter watched lest dishes or cups become empty. From time to time, Leo heard laughter from the cushions on which Nordbriht sprawled attentively. Apparently, his ability and his willingness to devour as much food as they wanted to press upon him delighted everyone involved. Even Asherah laughed before gesturing for more food to be brought and insisting that he *must* take the last of the roast kid or Tzipporah and she would both be desolate.

Leo caught Joachim's eye and found himself laughing ruefully. He too had seen how easily Varangians, one step removed, perhaps, from *barbaroi*, could charm the cultured ladies of Constantinople when they had a mind to. This time, however, his heart rejoiced. At least, Nordbriht showed no signs of trying to hurl himself into the nearest lake.

At length, Nordbriht polished his plate with the last of the bread, wiped his hands and handed the towel to a waiting servant, then sagged against his cushions. Replete, for a wonder; and, for a greater wonder, sober. He looked about, briefly abashed that he was the last to finish.

"Sir," he turned to Joachim. "You saw . . ."

"I saw men attacked by wild beasts," Joachim said firmly. "Including you and your friend."

Oh, they were all very civilized, very careful in this room, pretending not to know one another's pasts and shadows; but they were there: they overhung each person seated in this splendid, discreet place like the shadows cast by the glittering bronze lamp overhead.

"Accept my thanks," Nordbriht said in a rush of words, as if he had gathered up his courage and must now charge ahead, "for your hospitality and for saving my friend's life. Mine, too. And give me leave to tend to the men lying in the road."

At that, even Asherah quirked up an eyebrow.

"What?" Leo murmured. "And are you now become as tenderhearted as that kid you wolfed down?"

Nordbriht brought his massive fist down on his silk-clad knee. "What if we were seen?"

Father and daughter shook their heads. Remembering the thrum of magic shrewdly used, Leo was inclined to agree: no, they had not been seen. His would-be assassins had planned carefully for everything, but a young woman's being met by her father and servant and escorted home from—where *had* Asherah been?

"Even so," said Nordbriht. "The bodies will be found. Those fools were of some name, I gather, in the town. Their families will be looking to cut somebody's throat."

One of the servants uttered a faint moan of protest.

"Tzipporah," Asherah's voice was level, "this is not a song we have strayed into. If you are going to dine with warriors, you must accept that their after-dinner conversation may not be what you would hope."

"Your pardon, noble ladies." Nordbriht flushed the color of his tunic. He looked down and shifted uncomfortably on cushions that suddenly appeared too small and tumbled to hold him. "But, after all, they call me *barbaros*."

Joachim nodded, assuring Nordbriht he understood the term.

"You, however, you . . ."

"I am hardly *barbaros*," Joachim cut in. "What you mean, I think, is that I am not of the fellowship of Christ. Are you?"

Nordbriht barked out a laugh. "I have, in any case, had the water sprinkled over me and the priest's mutterings. I would not have your throat cut for my . . . my trouble. And I don't know if the countryfolk or the nobles roundabouts here are stupid enough to believe the Turks could do—apart from knifework—what, what I did to those men."

"What would you suggest?" asked Joachim calmly. "My workmen have bows. Shall we shoot arrows into the dead? Let us be at peace, here, while yet we may." His tone became a command. "People will believe an enemy to be capable of any violence, any vileness at all."

"Just look at the stories they believe of *us*," Asherah cut in.

Leo met her eyes and found himself laughing without mirth.

"I tell you, the villagers expect the Turks to invade. I have seen load after load of food, of bedding, cheese, and skins, carried down into the caves. The people prepare for attack. This will only make them work the faster." She turned to her father. "About that last shipment . . ."

"In the morning, daughter. Not now."

"Lady," Leo said, "I have been a guest in your house and it desolates me to speak against anything you say. But I have guested as well in the tents of Alp Arslan, who treated me and my Emperor . . ." The words came hard, even to one who had witnessed it. ". . . Better than my own kin."

Asherah inclined her head. "We are not talking about reason here, but terror. And hate." She rose and poured wine for all of them.

"Lady, against those, there is no argument." Leo drank, then reconsidered. "Except knowledge. And I gather that you are as expert in that as you are at welcoming a guest."

Joachim smiled proudly. " 'But wisdom, where shall it be found?', is it? It is the custom of ladies of Baghdad and Alexandria to study, if they have the aptitude and desire. My child has both. But, sir, I am forgetting honesty. Let me return your property to you."

From the folds of his heavy robe, he produced a tiny, gleaming blade. "This fell from your hand on the road. It is very old, I judge, and very curious. Were I you, I would take great care of it. It might be of some value beyond its age." Carefully, he tested his finger on the shining thing, then handed it to Leo.

"It was a gift from a prophetess. I shall keep it forever now."

"There is a great deal of that stone here," Asherah ventured. "Wherever the mountains smoke. Father, do you recall if Plinius mentions it?"

Joachim shook his head. "My memory is not what it was for Latin. But the black stone holds an edge and carves well. Show our guests the black figure."

Asherah rose and went to one of the columns that served as display stands. Carefully, using both hands, she picked up the figure Leo had noticed before, of a goddess with child, hugely swollen, but with tiny head and feet, and brought it to him. With equal care he took it to examine, trying hard not to flush at the idea of holding a figure of a naked woman in the presence of his host's daughter. He watched his fingers glide sensually over the curves of the figure's breasts and belly and the incised triangle beneath them. This time he did flush.

The light struck the statue, and it seemed as if it glowed from within. Or at his touch.

And he didn't know whether he was more relieved or more embarrassed when Asherah laughed softly. "It affects everyone so. I tell my father that he retains this ancient idol because it has charmed him."

"It was a gift," said Joachim. "From your holy man Meletios. You ride to see him, I have heard. He is wise and good. Oh—what do we talk about? Egypt, of course. I spent some years in Thebes before my daughter was born.

"To answer more of your question, daughter, they used this stone in Egypt during surgeries, opening even the skull. I think there is some story about Moses and the black glass, too—that as an infant, he was tested to see if he had special powers. Pharaoh had him shown glowing coals and the black glass. A babe would choose the coals, but a wise soul in a baby's form would know to pick the stone. Naturally, being Moses, he would know which was the more precious—but an angel whispered to him, and he reached for the coals and carried them to his lips. Which was why, ever after, he was halt and thick of speech, and Aaron the Priest spoke for him."

Asherah laughed and shook her head. "Father, surely, Moses saw onyx, not obsidian."

Joachim imitated her head-shake. "Does it matter? We are dealing in symbol here, not in fact. Never have daughters, sir. They feel free to argue with you, far more than sons. Did you not feel as if your sisters took unfair advantage?"

Leo found himself laughing, more at ease than he had been for months. "I had no sisters, sir. But I knew no lady among my kin who was not a better general, in terms of the ordering of her life and the lives of those around her, than many in the field."

Leo handed the statue back to Asherah.

"It is very beautiful. Sir, do you discuss such stories with Father Meletios, or such statues?"

Joachim smiled at him. "Mostly, we argue. He is a civilized man, despite the wilderness he chooses to inhabit. Do you not find him so?"

"He is a hard taskmaster," Leo admitted. He found Joachim easy to talk to, much like his own father, only as adult man to adult man, not father and son. "He tells me I am not cut out for life as a hermit or as a priest, but that I may build my own refuge and try to pray for a vocation. If all goes well, I shall have no daughters."

"And you will have missed out on one of life's greatest blessings," said Joachim.

Asherah set the statue back on its pedestal with a tiny clash of stone against stone.

"No doubt, you have found him to be a sane and practical man as mystics often are. Ah, Asherah, come back to us. My daughter does not approve of the valley. She is angry for the sake of the women who were cast out. Child, at times, I think I should have named you Deborah, not Asherah."

"She was a wise woman." The laughter was back in Asherah's voice.

"And led her men in battle—no, she told Barak to fight, and so he did. But you, you would be a Deborah who led her own soldiers, perhaps both men and women?"

"Father, I am certain that the time may come when we will all have to fight. That is why the people fill the caves, why . . ."

"My daughter studies history. And since coming here, she has become convinced that the history of this land can be read in its very rocks. The very presence of the black stone indicates that once, Mount Argeaus did not just loom on the horizon; it, or others like it, belched fire and molten rock."

"Is that why you go to the caves, lady?" Leo was glad of the excuse to speak directly to her again. "Or do you, too, search for the road they say connects all the cities below the earth and the great treasure in their midst?"

"Ah, the caves have you in their spell, too!" Asherah said. "I should explore them in your presence; you would grow tired less rapidly than Tzipporah."

Her waiting woman straightened, flushed, and proclaimed her willingness to clamber in the dark for as long as her mistress desired. Asherah, Leo knew, was being outrageous; women of good family in Constantinople would not have gone on such expeditions unaccompanied except by a man who was no kin to them. In fact, such women would probably have seen no secular advantage in such expeditions at all. Clearly, however, Asherah did.

"You seek treasure, lady?" Leo asked again. "What would you find? The jewels of Helen or of some unknown queen?"

"Wisdom," Asherah declared, "is the treasure I seek. But it would be good to see, to know whether those roads exist and where they meet. And treasure . . ." She shrugged. "A little treasure would not come amiss. Too much, and there is enmity. But a little . . ." She looked at her father and laughed. "I am a merchant's daughter, sir. Would you expect me to protest I have no eye for value?"

"Not if you created the beauty in this room," Leo told her.

"You see," said Joachim. "You must have daughters. My child is my great consolation."

"I did not create the beauty here. I found it. This is an old land, a haunted land, with many shards from old cultures tossed up on its fields. Perhaps that is why I find it beautiful. But still, I thank you."

"You do not fear the old things, lady? In the town, they break them."

Asherah shook her head. "How shall I fear them? They are old, but so are my people. I feel at home among them. Your people, however . . . only a thousand years, an eruption of Turks; and you fear world's end. We have seen many such, survived many such deathbeds, perhaps, of Empires. . . ."

"Asherah," Joachim cautioned, and the woman fell silent.

" 'Strength and dignity are her clothing, and she laugheth at the time to come,' " Leo quoted softly.

Asherah's silks fell about her like water as she rose from her cushions. Color more angry than modest stained her face, and her eyes were bright and enormous. "I must go speak with the servants. Forgive me." She swept from the room.

Leo looked about it, as if for clues to her sudden anger. "Forgive me, if I offended."

Joachim held out his hands, a baffled, conciliatory gesture.

"It is not from *you* that my mistress should hear such words," Tzipporah rustled to her feet more slowly than the younger woman had. "Those are words with which a husband praises his wife." She left the room, her back too straight.

"I may have erred," said Joachim. "My daughter is not just my daughter, but my only son as well. We value such women, but their lives are not as easy as their more sheltered sisters. Do the ladies of your City find it so?"

Leo thought of the Empress, mock-demure despite how Psellus praised her. Of the redoubtable Anna Dalassena, who, he was fairly certain, had never pretended to anything in her life. Of his mother, ambitious in the world, but fiercely contrite. The Empress Eudocia, resolved to spend her life in prayer. They would have things to say to one another, he thought. And to this woman, this stranger in a strange land, who might be the strangest and most accomplished of all of them.

I have dreamed horrors, Leo thought, and always, then, it was your face that brought me rest from them. What are you, lady? Aside from forbidden to me, by the salvation I seek, by your people, and by mine?

Perhaps it would not be that great a tragedy if Father Meletios were right about Leo and his vocation.

"I should beg her forgiveness," Leo said. "I meant no harm."

"I hope you will come again to do so, and to speak with me. You are a civilized man, Leo Ducas, and civilized men are rare at times like these."

Leo bowed amidst his cushions, a grace he had learned from his time among the Turks. Would they indeed overrun this land he hoped to make his home? He hoped not.

"With your permission, I shall indeed come again to apologize, at least."

Joachim inclined his own upper body with even more ceremony than Leo. He rose. Perforce, Leo and Nordbriht rose too.

"It grows light outside. I shall have you shown to rooms where you can rest until dawn or however long you require. I have morning prayers, but I shall be here to say farewell to you."

24

The hot wind plucked at Asherah's clothing as she watched the file of women and children carrying provisions into Malagobia, the more remote of the two major cave cities. Other refugees, she knew, prepared to move into Enegobi.

If she ruled here, she would have ordered those children loaded onto her father's camels, would have slung them up into the carpeted saddles herself rather than see them serve as beasts of burden. All their willing labor now: and for what? To retreat into a fastness their parents only hoped would withstand attack, and attack by a race known to be swift, thorough, and merciless.

The villagers had found more than just the bodies of the . . . she dared not call them assassins; words like that, slipping unwarily from the tongue, betrayed as subtly as human traitors. No: the nobles whose bodies they had found lying in the road had been young men, cruelly ambushed by raiding Turks, cut off in their prime, and all of the other truisms that she, outside the Christian community, need not repeat with the women of their families, who had little enough to say to her outside details of trade.

Matters had not stopped there. The villages had suffered other raids as well. Alp Arslan was dead. Fierce as he was, he had been at least honorable, as Leo had told her and her father. Now his successors made him seem a paragon of peace and restraint. The earth itself had trembled, and the cap of Mount Argaeus seemed whitened with a smoke plume rather than its perpetual snow. The churches, needless to say, were crammed.

More than one storm loomed over Cappadocia these days.

She shut her eyes against the sunlight and the ugly visions that tormented her: men and women dying in a misty land, the unity of God the last words on their lips before the screaming started; men drawing lots and slaying their families, then slaying each other, before the last man slew himself. Why hide when you could flee, saving what brands you might from the burning, to live and thrive another day? Honor lay in survival of the people. Survival of the children. And extolling the unity of the name of God.

Open your eyes again, Asherah. What do you see?

A brazen sky, with flat, sullen clouds moving in too fast.

The hot wind lashed at her as if she stood in the deep desert far to the East. To her left, like a fist of clouds, a storm center hammered the horizon. It would strike here before long. When you faced such storms in the desert, you wrapped yourself and your camels in felts and huddled down to wait before moving on, always moving on.

Here, it would be safer to flee indoors than to try to outrun the storm. Safer yet, to seek the refuge of the underground in this land. Here, the earth was its own protection. Having herself fled so often, she felt this rootedness, this faith in the old, rich land, as a seduction.

How tempting to say "here I am and here I remain." It was an attraction that should not be for the likes of her. Long ago, her people had lost their land. But they remembered it always, dreaming of the day—even if it came at the end of time—when they might be restored to it and, this time, please God, hold it forever.

"For we were strangers in the land of Egypt." They were strangers everywhere their feet touched, Asherah thought with the sorrow and anger the words always brought: useful for their talents and their wealth;

valued, sometimes, for their knowledge; but never trusted, never permitted to remain.

Perhaps these people, these stolid, sturdy people, who dug themselves into the land itself, had the right of it: scurry into sanctuary, abide, let the waves of Empire wash over them; and, when the waters subsided, emerge again to till the soil, lead the flocks to what greenery remained in the summer, raise the children, and show them how to survive the next assault. Ararat lay far to the east, Asherah recalled. It made sense that from this land, the world would be rebuilt.

Safety argued that it was time and past time to leave here. They had received packets of letters sent from up and down the caravan routes urging them to move on; yet she and her father had not done so. Not this time; and she had not forced herself to speculate why.

"My father judges it safe," she told a woman with two children clinging to her shabby skirts. "*I* remain here."

"But when there is danger, you will be gone?" A flash of resentment: dangerous as sparks to dry leaves if that rumor spread.

"I am my father's daughter and must obey him." A woman's obedience was almost always a safe thing to invoke: everyone paid it lip service before going about her business. "But I do not always give in without a word—do you?"

The woman smiled, and they were friends again. Or friendly. Once again, Asherah set about her self-appointed work: getting those people out who wished to go. Saving brands from the burning. No, she assured one woman, if she wished to send her son to her kin, he would be brought there "out of the land of Egypt, out of the house of bondage." But the story of the Exodus did not reassure the woman. No, Asherah assured her, they would not seek to make a Jew of him. He would not be cut, though they did that in the capital. "We have sons of our own," she reassured her.

Only, Asherah had no sons and was not likely to. She remembered from her lessons in Greek how long ago, there had been a princess whose name meant, quite literally, "spirit." Beautiful, Psyche was—accomplished and wise, she was admired, but not beloved. Never beloved.

But Asherah was no princess to wait for fate or fortune. Never mind her Greek lessons, set aside now in the face of commerce and danger. Never mind the face of the man she and her father had rescued, and who had rescued her in Cotyaeum, or the way her heart had lifted when he had smiled at her—*he remembers me!* It was not only her maids who had heard too many stories; as a scholar, she had heard far more.

And it was past time for her to set to work. Allowing herself to be distracted by greetings, by details of stowage or a child's illness, she proceeded toward the caves.

Why is today different from all other days? she asked herself. Her heart raced; her breathing came fast. Because today, she would return to a deep, deep passage that led to a way she had glimpsed as her next-to-last torch flickered. Something about the rock had drawn her attention, and she would gladly have tested it, had she not been forced up from below by voices echoing around a corner and her maid's terror.

As if reluctant to allow her to descend, the wind tugged at her as she headed toward the rounded entrance to the city, twice a man's height, branching off into rough chambers with columns scraped clear of the living stone like immense bones.

At the entrance, two men tested the balance on the millstone, almost the color of the grain it should have ground, that would block access below. Women wiped down the tables, also carved from the rock when the chambers were hollowed out, while their daughters fitted bedding into alcoves carved into the walls. One family; one room. It was said that thousands could live for months in these warrens. Asherah hoped she would not have to learn how.

The storage bins were filling. The water tanks were full. In a room with carved arches like blind windows, a young priest spread out cloths and bowed before the altar, carved from a block of stone, a cross incised in its front. A boy wrestled a wineskin into a room that reminded her of a refectory. The main church was far below: she would not go there, being unsure of her welcome.

Moving on, she saw her household's marks on bags and boxes. The priests and monks would eat well at the Jews' expense, and the Jews, for safety's sake, dared not begrudge it. Perhaps, if the Turks swept through the town, her household too would be permitted to find refuge here. But refuge was not a thing that could be paid for. It had to be earned in honest liking and trust.

So far, no one had thought to blame them for the deaths of the men left by the road. Wild beasts, the rumor went. Some blamed the Turks, as Joachim had thought they would. Other fools, with more humor than taste, had looked at how they had died and suggested that the stone lions that, occasionally, one found buried in rubble had come alive and mauled them. Asherah suspected that such vile humor helped guard them from their fear of Turkish raids.

For the most part, as merchants sought to send their wares out of danger, the men in the town formed into troops of guards. Leo had broken off work on carving out his hermitage, to move into a room in the priest's house and drill the younger men. He had, of course, to attend the funeral for the dead assassins—a ceremony Asherah was devoutly grateful her faith (and theirs) forbade her to attend. She could imagine Nordbriht trying to dim that sunbright physical splendor of his that had dazzled the women of her household.

All except her.

His name is Leo Ducas! *she told herself again. He is practically a prince, or would be if he hadn't chosen the wrong side of the Christians' last ridiculous civil war. Even so, he says he will take vows; and he is true to his word. And then, where will you be? Men befool themselves for ideas far more than for women. Or, say he gives up, and goes back home. Never mind his talk of learned ladies, they will match him up with some small-dowried second daughter who will make big eyes at him, do all his will, and give him a baby every year. And bore him senseless.*

She must forget his kindness in Cotyaeum, the slender, distinguished height of him, even in the rough clothes he wore these days, or how gently he spoke to her in her father's house. She must regard him as just another of her father's friends, another exile washed up on the same shore. She always promised herself that, when he called, she would withdraw to her own rooms and the company of her maids. She had never kept her word yet.

At least her maids had not commented. She could bear anything but that—except her fear that they were too kind to tease her.

She caught up torches from storage and started downward. At the first bend, from a niche carved into a ruddy column, she lifted the hammer and some iron tools she thought she could use as scrapers that she had left there against the need she hoped to have. It would be better to have help, but any of her father's men would tell him, even if they obeyed her; and her women were out of the question.

Again, the faces of Leo and his guard came to mind. She had seen them in the caves—Leo more frequently than Nordbriht. They marked places for ambushes by the doors that separated parts of the city from each other. They measured storage bins to see if spears could be propped upright within them, and set the strongest men to dig traps in the cave floors, trying to disguise the airshafts lest their enemies roll stones over their mouths and snuff out the refugees' lives with their air supply. He spoke of sea fire, stored in ceramic jars, if it could be begged from a garrison in time and set alight as a weapon of last resort before the sur-

vivors withdrew below. He had even written to Byzantium, jeopardiz-
ing the fragile quiet he had won here.

He had more important things to do than quest with her, for treasure or for wisdom.

How cleverly she had distracted her women with errands—and
necessary ones at that—in the town. Today, she had vowed, she would
descend as far as she might. She had achieved the ninth level the last
time, and only Tzipporah's fear had restrained her from squeezing herself into a passageway narrower than she had ever dared before.

Facilis descensus . . . no, this was not time for Vergil, and, in any
case, it had been years since she could decipher the language of the
Western Empire with much facility. Easy is the descent to hell: she remembered that much. Strait as this stair was, she would have to pray
it led to somewhere else.

Now her robes swept the sides of the narrow passageway that led
down into the lower levels. Dampness rose from the walls, and through
the air shaft that she passed, she heard the rush of wind, the rumble of
thunder that found response in the tremors of the earth. Rain was lashing down, she discovered by putting a hand out into the shaft. But it
vanished quickly. The land would reap no benefit from this storm or
the ones to come.

Behind her, the tumult of children fleeing from lightning and rain
subsided.

Around this bend. Down this flight of stairs. Careful of the hollows
in their centers.

A gust of wind from the airshaft jeopardized her torch. From here,
she must take the greatest pains not to let it be extinguished, or to walk
longer than it would take her to return using her second torch. Otherwise, Tzipporah's worst fears would come true, and she could easily wander in the dark until she lost the power to tell up from down, left from
right, and collapsed, perhaps only a wall or a bend in a wall from help,
or so mad she could not discern friend from phantom.

That made life harder in this haunted land. Even friends labored
under the burden of old spirits.

Downward. And still down. She must be below the level of the
church; in fact, she had not thought the ways ran this deep. Here, the
rock was damp and chill. She fancied that she could hear the water in
the deep wells. When she thrust her torch in at openings, she saw
rooms that bore no evidence of having been used even for the rough-
est storage. And yet, they seemed smaller, rougher, older than the levels up above.

Don't think of that, she warned herself. Don't think of the weight of rock and earth above you, the distance between you and the open air. The thought of all that mass could bring one gasping to her knees in panic, which could kill more cruelly than any dagger.

But she *must* think of it. Something, she told herself, did not make sense. She stopped to work it out. These chambers were disused. Well enough. These chambers seemed older than the ones above. No. Try again. How could these chambers be older than the upper rooms, seeing as men would have to cut their way down this far into the rock before they could excavate them?

Asherah shuddered. Her hands chilled, and she drew a deep, quivering breath. There was only one way the rooms down here could be older than the levels now being prepared against attack: if this cave warren had been cut starting from *below*.

That meant that the diggers had had to break through from somewhere else.

Setting down her tools, she shut her eyes and pressed her forehead against the stone, willing vision to come. It had come so much more easily when she was a child and did not want it. Now that the fate of all she cared for might hang upon the powers she had feared were madness for so long . . . the stone gritted against her brow, chill and rough.

Ahhh, there it was. Even as men worked the stone high above, passing the shards and grit and pebbles back into the light, hand over hand, others scraped far below them in the darkness, taking away the detritus through a longer tunnel, hollowing out rooms, building a foundation for a new city, then pulling back. Perhaps last of all, a clever mason patched the wall, blocking this new city from the roadway under the earth until the right time came.

Say it never did. Say the secret was lost. And when workers broke through to these lowest levels, they found only unused rooms. What they could not explain, they feared and thus drew back from.

What if Asherah could find the entry to that road?

She could try.

She lifted her brow from the rock wall and dashed her hand across it. Odd: she had not thought that the rock was wet enough or soft enough—her stomach twisted with fear at the thought of the upper levels caving in upon her, crushing her into a bloody smudge.

She smeared her fingers across her forehead once again and examined them in the torchlight. Not mud, not grit; but paint smeared her hand. Backing away from the wall, she played the torch over it, careful not to stain the pictures with soot. There were figures, crudely daubed, of men bearing spears and picks, of women wearing intricate headdresses towering high above them, and, at their ankles, cats and a long, long painted serpent leading . . . leading to a space bare of goddesses or workers or even snakes. The stone here looked rougher, too. So far below the earth, it would not be exposed to weather, would not wear down into smoothness as it did on the surface.

Again, terror and excitement rushed through her, like a river overflowing its banks and sweeping toward the fields. Was it unbroken rock there on that wall, or had it been cobbled together from behind it?

She wedged her torch into a crevice in the rock. Awkwardly, she lifted her pick and scraped it across the wall. The noise set her teeth on edge; its echo made her glance around. Had she been heard? She paused, listening for footsteps, and heard nothing except her heartbeat and her rapid breathing.

What was on the pick? No, no paint at all. She pressed in toward the rock face, holding up the torch to examine the whole blank area. Yes, at some point, the paint *stopped.*

Experimentally, Asherah tapped the pick against the wall, then elsewhere further down the corridor. The sounds echoed, then died. She heard no difference, and her heart sank with disappointment.

Strike harder, fool. The thought possessed her with the power of the strongest dreams from her childhood.

She traded pick for hammer and swung it against the wall: here, the solid crash of hammer against stone (and the serpent's head); here, against a soldier's shield, too; but here, in the empty space, the crash was hollow, as if here, she struck not solid stone, but a thin wall.

Joy made her tremble; fear made her ice cold. She had found the way within. What might lie behind the wall? The long road? Treasure? Nothing at all?

Whatever lay behind it was unknown; and knowledge was the treasure that she sought.

Her trembling ceased. She braced her hands upon the hammer and swung with all her strength. The impact knocked her halfway around. Try again, Asherah. Brace your feet and try again. Again, she swung. A small piece of rock flaked from the vacant wall. She attacked the stone before her in a frenzy.

When Asherah finally had to pause, coughing from the damp and the rock dust that her flurry of blows had stirred, she saw how little progress she had made, and her heart sank. This was not how workers did it. Workers picked one spot and struck at it repeatedly. A trickle of dust. A scattering of pebbles. A chunk of rock segmented from the wall and burst into powder. She bent to examine it: this *had* been assembled from broken stone.

She spared a glance at the torch. It had scarcely burned halfway down, and the spare was yet untouched. She had time, assuming her strength held out.

If only Nordbriht were here, with his immense strength . . . not Nordbriht, who might change into a beast; and this time, he might not crouch with his head at her feet.

Again, she struck, a measured set of blows, and paused, head down until her breathing steadied.

Then she heard the pad, pad, pad of footsteps coming up behind her. She whirled, grasping the hammer as she had seen fighters grasp an axe and held it between her and whatever might approach.

 25

L ady," Leo Ducas said, holding aloft a torch. "Lady Asherah. What are you doing here?"

Startled past bearing, Asherah screamed and tried to swing the hammer. He darted forward and pulled it from her grip. The torchlight flickered. She tried to dash past him, but he caught and held her. She twisted, trying to bring up her hands, or reach the knife she carried, or fight free.

"I am sorry," he said, "Asherah, Asherah, do you not know me? Forgive me for frightening you. Steady there. Steady. I know you can control yourself."

He let the hammer fall. It rolled near where his torch had fallen. Leo looked down, pushing her away from the dying flame. She shuddered again: if her clothing had caught fire, she might truly have reason to be afraid.

"You have nothing to fear. Not while I'm here."

He spoke to her so gently, as if to a madwoman or to a child. But then, he always spoke thus, not like the nobles she had seen, or her own clever people, who expressed love in other ways.

She sighed deeply and let her head drop onto his shoulder. Just for a moment, let her feel shielded. She would not indulge herself for any longer; but she would allow herself just that much.

"Leo," she murmured. "How foolish I have been."

"How foolish *have* you been?" he demanded. "I saw your women in the market, without you. When I spoke to Tzipporah, she told me you had come here. Alone. Don't you know . . ."

Let a man, any man, catch a woman in an adventure of her own, and he took it upon himself to lecture her as if he were her father. Just as well: otherwise she might imagine this one to be a paragon when he was only a man.

"I know the story Nordbriht told, about the woman whom a comrade in the Guard tried to . . . to attack. She killed him, and his former brothers ceded her his property and threw his body out. *He* does not think I am helpless."

Leo laughed. "Where Nordbriht grew up, the women were six feet tall and had shoulders almost as wide as his. Which, you will forgive me if I point out, you have not. So it is foolish for you to wield hammer and pick when you have a friend who will do it for you. Remember, I am much in practice from carving out my own hermitage."

Asherah looked away, appalled to find herself sulking.

"Come now, is it that you do not want to share what you have found? You told me you were looking for the underground ways, remember? I could say, 'Tell me and I will not tell your father that you slipped your tether and came down here alone to hack at the stone like a child playing stonemason,' but I will not. Asherah, we are friends. What do you think you're doing?"

"You will think I am possessed," she burst out with her secret fear, which was far worse than simple terror.

"No more than some people I left behind thought I was. And I gave them considerably more reason to believe I should be locked up. You know, lady, you and I share an uncomfortable passion for the depths. In Constantinople, there was this cistern. . . ." Leo gave a bark of laughter that hurt Asherah to hear. "I saw a Gorgon in its depths and fell in, terrified of what was simply an old piece of stone, mortared in upside-down. A boy pulled me out.

"I'm babbling. That's a sign of insanity too, they say. Some day, we must compare the evidence against us and determine which of us has the greater claim to madness. But for now, tell me what you've found."

"The rock." She pointed. "It sounds hollow when I strike there. The rest of the wall is painted. But that place isn't. I think they sealed it behind them when they left."

" 'They'?"

"Whoever built the road between the cities, the road everyone whispers about but no one has ever found. Look about you, Leo. The rooms down here are older than the ones above. You can see it from the stone. *They built from both ends.*"

"From both ends?"

Asherah hissed with frustration. He was a Byzantine. Next to the Jews and the Syrians and Persians and the Phoenicians, they were as clever as any people in the world. Why was he so slow-witted?

"Yes. The caves down here are older. So logic demands they had to tunnel through from somewhere."

If her madness didn't drive this man away, a parade of logic surely would!

He nodded. So she had convinced him. She attempted to conceal her surprise. Then, he stooped and picked up her tools. Asherah tried to soothe her cheeks with her freezing hands, then raked them through her tumbled hair. Her veil hung wildly askew.

He tapped the wall, just as she had done. "Hollow, indeed. I have broken enough stone to know. When was the last time *you* dug out your own hermitage, lady?"

This time, his laughter made her warm again, almost relaxed. It was painful when he picked away at himself and his memories, as if hacking at rock that could bleed. She had learned very young that people flinched at such remembrances, and had always taken pains never to inflict her own upon the unwary. Leo, though: she could hardly call him unwary, or unpracticed in strangeness. They were alike in that, and it marked what friendship they had built, even from the moment he had struggled to her side.

More strangeness still: here they stood on the edge of amazement, in a land awaiting attack, and he could smile at her as if they sat at dinner. *He is gracious, your father's friend and yours. Do not expect more than he will give. Or you will weep when he goes away.*

Leo rekindled his torch from the one she had wedged into the rock. "You seem to have made some progress. I suppose Nordbriht could make a faster job of this, but Nordbriht hates the depths. He calls these caves pure barrow, probably complete with monsters from the frozen North."

Their eyes met, confirming what they knew as truth: Nordbriht had a right to know and fear such creatures, tainted as he was.

"So, I have even more practice than he at breaking rocks. Now, if you will step back, while I put my back into this . . ."

He swung with practiced skill. The wall did not so much flake away as disintegrate. The stone might have had centuries to set, or longer, but it was soft, fractured; and Leo was determined.

Asherah backed up, hands over her ears as he battered at the wall. Finally, he paused to draw a deep breath. Despite the chill, sweat showed dark on his clothing, pressing it against his body. Setting down the hammer, he rubbed his hands over his arms.

"Another blow or two and we'll break through," he told her. "Do you still want to?"

In the torchlight, she could see his eyes, kindling with the curiosity of the Byzantine and something more, something akin to her own passion for knowledge. Knowledge meant survival. Knowledge meant power. And the passion for knowledge was more powerful than the lust for gold or for . . . protected by the shadows, she flushed deeply.

Asherah drew a deep breath to steady herself. "We can always block the passage afterward." She offered tribute to a practicality she did not feel.

Leo's grin showed he did not feel it either. He raised the hammer, then set it down.

"The air could be bad in there," he said. "So I want you to get behind me. Well behind me."

He pointed with his chin up the twisted passageway. She measured the distance as if she planned to bargain for it in a bazaar. She would not be able to escape upward and fetch help in time if he were overcome.

Asherah shook her head. "If you fall, I shall cover my face with my veil and drag you out," she told him.

Why did I say that? she wailed to herself. *Watch him choose retreat before embarrassment. And watch him call it prudence. Like all the others.*

"I am certain I should not allow . . ."

She stamped her foot, stung by his tone into a display of temper that would surely dash all of Tzipporah's simple-minded hopes—not that the presumptuous thing had any right to them. "*I* found this cave. And if you had not come, *I* would have broken down the wall. It would have taken me a long time, but I would have done it. Now, are you going to finish what we started or . . ."

Leo drew a deep breath and swung.

Crack! The rock crumbled before them. For an instant, Asherah disgusted herself by throwing up her arms, as if they could protect her foolish skull from any chunks of rock that might shake loose from the ceiling. Both of them coughed, hunching over in the puffs of rock dust that rose despite the dampness this far below the earth, from the wall. And from the hole that Leo had battered.

He stood back, pushing her with him. *Let it settle.* They both

breathed shallowly as the dust eddied into the cave, obscuring the figures that had led Asherah to this spot. When it subsided, and they had
not fallen choking to the ground, Leo reached into his tunic and pulled
out something dark and shining.

"I have my sword," he told her. "But you . . ."

"I have a dagger," she said.

"Use this instead," he asked. His eyes lit. Asherah had seen that look
on men about to take a mad risk for the joy of it, and in that moment,
she felt it in herself.

She took the weapon. It was the small, obsidian blade that he had
used as a final weapon the night he had been attacked. Had he given
it her for luck? They all grew superstitious in this haunted land. She
smiled and lifted it to him in salute.

Lifting one of the torches from its improvised holder, he kindled
the other and handed it to her. Raising the other torch, Leo bent down
and thrust it into the darkness beyond the broken rock.

It flared brightly. Undoubtedly, the unknown, ancient engineers
had equipped their creation with air shafts, like those the cave cities
boasted.

"I must see!" Asherah's hands tightened on torch and dagger. They
pulled her forward like iron to lodestone.

She was so much smaller than Leo she could duck beneath his arm
and find herself within. Too quick for him to stop, she suited action to
her thought.

Panting a little, she stood within a passageway, wider than any in
the underground cities, except for their vast, main caverns. And it was
more finely carved, the walls more truly vertical and smooth, the corners carved more finely. In the torchlight, paintings flickered on the
walls: women again, but in no manner of garb she had ever seen; women
with cats and serpents; men in triple-crowned headdresses, marching
down the long corridor until it turned sharply, hiding what might lie
ahead from sight.

With a quick oath, Leo scrambled through to stand beside her. He
was taller by far than she, but, nevertheless, his head did not touch the
ceiling; and five men his size could have marched abreast.

"Get back outside!" he whispered harshly. The command echoed
down the passageway, idle, useless. He might as well, in the golden days
before the library at Alexandria burned, permit her to stand before it,
but forbid her to enter. Her breathing came rapidly. She could hear her
heart pounding, a drumbeat that, in another instant, would set her to
dancing forward.

Her hand shook, but she raised her torch and played it on the walls. Reddish light danced off the figures in their endless procession down the painted walls. Asherah thought she could see their eyes light with awareness: after all these centuries, to hear a voice again.

But who knew what they spoke among themselves once this corridor was sealed off and the builders withdrew, abandoning them to their unthinkable privacy?

"I have seen men and women like these carved into the side of a cliff," Leo said. "Storm gods."

"And I have seen idols thrice the height of a man carved into rock," Asherah murmured.

"In tombs?"

She shook her head, already, in her thoughts, starting down the corridor, around the bend that might lead to . . . to what?

Leo stood at her side, his breathing rasping even more deeply than hers. She would have been afraid without him here. *He will leave you. He is not for you.* But in this moment, he was here; and this adventure and this knowledge were adventure and knowledge shared. *This much, at least, I have.*

"Best not to go too far," he said, prudent far too late. He realized it and flashed a conspirator's grin at her.

She handed him back the obsidian dagger.

"Keep it."

She shook her head. "There's no danger here. Not now."

Exasperation flared in Leo's eyes, to be replaced by a wary respect. "If I asked how you knew . . ."

"You would truly believe I had gone mad. Unless, of course, you chose to believe me. You really might try that some time." She had strained every sense, including that strangeness within her that had told her so often whether danger lay ahead. Danger always did, these days; but for now, they were safe. No enemies would stalk them down this long, strange corridor; no enmity hovered in the still air.

Leo sheathed his sword. Asherah blinked away unexpected, unwelcome tears and decided she had seen a wonder. He wanted to know. For once, knowledge—or curiosity—had cast out fear. In that regard, Byzantine and Jew were very much akin; but that knowledge was unwelcome.

Half-abstracted by the lure of the opened passageway, Leo propped his torch in an ancient bronze torch holder that had not been removed when the builders withdrew. He kindled a fresh one from it. The third fire bloomed in the corridor, catching glints off the rock surfaces left unpainted.

Down the passageway, boring straight through the living stone. Down to where the passage curved and seemed to start downward; but forward, always forward.

"Look at how much finer the work is here than even toward the end of the tunnel." He gestured with his chin. "And down there a ways, do you see those openings? I wonder if they lead to rooms or other passageways."

How long had they been down in the lowest depths of the underground, and how long had they delved? Here in the firelight, time aboveground seemed like an illusion: there was only firetime and shadowtime now that the unimaginable silence had been breached. The figures watched them from painted eyes. Many were no taller than Asherah herself: dark-haired, dark-eyed beneath their pointed crowns; sturdy in their archaic armor or draped gowns.

"I have seen women like this painted in the valley," Leo said. "Did your father tell you about them?"

"On icons?" Asherah felt her voice rise skeptically. "They hardly look Christian."

Well, if it came to that, they hardly looked like Jews either, not that there should be graven images in any Jewish shrine. She thought of the underground ways in Rome in which Christians had hidden, in which they had worshipped, and which they had made bright with symbols of their faith: men praying, shepherds, vines, cups. Catacombs, those Roman hallows had been called.

From whom had the builders of Malagobia and Enegobi and all of the other caves felt they had to hide? Or was all of this a maze in service of some nameless god? *Next time*, Asherah thought, *I shall bring a clew of thread.* She would not think of the Labyrinth of Crete or what Minotaur might lie at its heart—or the betrayal of Ariadne, the traitor who had revealed its secrets to save the life of the prince she loved, who abandoned her not long afterward.

These figures marching down the walls in solemn procession looked far more fierce—dark of hair, dark of eye, intent of purpose. None wore any garb that Asherah saw men and women wear today, and her wanderings had taken her very far. But some: she imagined that the men with staring eyes and fiercely curled beards could have borne names like Nebuchadnezzar or Nimrod; some looked Armenian; some tall and fair; and some, for whom she had no standard to refer to, looked far, far older.

One woman's figure stood facing forward, as if it would confront her. Asherah went up to it and looked into its ancient face. Save for its immobility, its darkened skin, it could have been her own.

"Don't go far," Leo warned her. Asherah shook her head, preoccupied.

She stared into the painted face. The torches burned brightly: the air was good. The builders had built for comfort, she decided, as well as convenience. She wondered at the roughness of the caves beyond the broken wall. What catastrophe had made them begin work, then leave it in so crude a state?

She found herself smiling as she stared at the image. *Greetings, Sister.*

It seemed to smile at her as if seeing her, knowing her better than she knew herself. Her heartbeat and breathing were settling, deepening. *One day*, she promised herself. *Soon.* Soon, she would take the passage to wherever it might lead.

She glanced up at her torch: time still remained before she must return, but not as much as she could long for. Air stirred within, and she fancied she could hear music, a faint piping that drew her onward.

Her heartbeat grew louder. Abruptly, her clothes clung to her, too heavy, though it had been chilly in the caves earlier that day. She put up a hand to touch not her face, but the goddess' as if she wiped a bead of sweat from it. Her fingers came away dusty. She brushed them down the painted figure. More dust, which she had taken for pigment, fell away: the figure beneath was fair, totally bare, and ripely female, like the graven image her father insisted on keeping in their house. Her own body, if she forced herself to strict honesty, curved thus, not like the tall, more spiritual forms that the Christians painted in caves and icons, or picked out with shimmering tiles.

One must favor the spirit over the flesh, said the theologues of Byzantium. Oh yes. They said, they always said so very many things: especially if they could speak in a tone of utter command to women. But in the depths of the night, when the blood heated, and the pipes played, it was not the spirit alone that drew men's hearts. Not the promise of spring, but full, rich summer such as this. Even after all these years. They had known it in Canaan. And they had feared it. Why else would the priests thunder so loudly? They must have felt it themselves.

A thread of something heavy, dark, and sweet, such as might be carried at great expense and peril from the lands of incense, wafted through the air. *I am dreaming*, she told herself. The painted goddess smiled without parting her lips.

Asherah put her hand to her own brow and started forward, her torch flickering bravely. There would be time to see what was in at least one of the side-passages, if she hurried. She suspected from the footsteps behind her that Leo was already exploring too. She wanted to call out, tell him to wait for her or at the least tell her what he saw. Something choked her speech, and she could not move for the heat that spread throughout her body. All she could manage was his name; and even that came out half stifled.

"Asherah." Leo had come up close behind her. He set the torch in the nearest holder, illuminating the shameless figure on the wall.

Again, the painted goddess smiled that knowing smile. Again, his heartbeat and the warmth of his body, the smell of his sweat, the dryness of the dust that dulled his hair mingled with the incense.

The music and the incense joined with her pulse, intensified into a thrum within her.

"Asherah." No "lady" now; unease trembled in his voice, but not more than his hands shook as he clasped her shoulders as if to shake her free from some strange dream. Instead, the dream wrapped itself about them both more firmly, drawing them down into it.

Yes. The figures marched down the corridor, to some ritual in which she must participate—but not alone. Here was her match, if their courage and desire held.

Greatly daring, Asherah smoothed the dust off his hair and looked up into Leo's eyes, black and wide in this hidden place. Within them, she saw herself. That strangeness in her that she knew had driven away the sons of merchant princes and made even scholars and physicians recoil waked now and shone in her, full force.

He saw her as she was. He saw all that she was. But his eyes held her reflection, but no fear. His hands slid over her shoulders, drawing her close against him. Again, he breathed her name, making it sound like a sigh of longing and need from a man waking in the depth of night and turning to his beloved.

The beat of her heart and the illusion of music and incense in her mind heightened. As his arms closed about her, she let herself yield. It was that or dance down the passageway to what unimaginable ending she might reach before her light guttered out and sanity and life followed it into the dark. She would take, she determined, this much to remember even on the edge of the storms that her father said thundered on the horizons.

Don't think of your father, she ordered herself. Not now. He *likes* Leo, something in her mind protested.

Don't think, the command came again, this time backed by the scents and in the air, or in her mind, her own mental voice reinforced, as it seemed, by a darker, richer music that seemed so familiar now that it had been awakened in her thoughts. And in her body.

Don't think. Not now.

The air was hot. Her clothes were heavy. Leo's touch and the throbbing in her temples and her body made her head spin and weakened her knees. Before she shut her eyes, she saw the face upon the wall. Its gaze seemed to intensify, the eyes to enlarge. And to approve.

For a moment, Asherah rested against him. Leo's hands stroked her body, caressing it the way she had watched him touching that statue the other night. His hands on her sides, sliding to her hips, were increasingly insistent as he bent to kiss her. His lips were thirsty as they sought to part hers. As her mouth opened under his, she flung her arms about his neck, making herself vulnerable to the seeking hands that moved up to cup her breasts, his thumbs rubbing over and around her nipples until she gasped with pleasure.

Laughter bubbled from Leo's throat into her mouth. He slid his hands away from her breasts, laughing again when she murmured with growing delight, flicking her tongue with his own. Were these refinements that Christian nobles learned in Byzantium as they learned the trade of arms? Or was it simply that he knew more than an unmarried woman—or even that the compulsions here that had driven them into each other's arms were teaching him, minute by minute, how to excite her?

He slid his hands down until he could push her hips against him. She tried to recoil, a last instinct toward modesty, from the urgency she felt in him; but his hands forestalled her long enough for her own body to take fire from his. A slow, aching pulse burned deep within her where she had always known she must not touch nor permit anyone else but perhaps a midwife someday, to do so. Her thighs opened before she willed it. Leo worked one hand around to press her mound. The sweet, unfamiliar ache heightened. *Comfort me with apples, for I am sick of love.*

As Asherah felt her knees give way, Leo swung her up and carried her into the darkness of the room from which she had called him. The light from the torch above the goddess-image was enough for her to see it: a carved table, much like she had seen in the upper reaches of the cities; an alcove.

Leo set her down carefully as if upon a bed, bare of the sheepskins that, in the city they had left behind, she might have expected. He edged himself in beside her, kissed her again, then pressed her back against the stone until his body covered hers. Again, he kissed her, and she closed her eyes.

He would flee her, as they always had. At least, this one desired her for now, and she wanted him. For once, she thought, she would risk taking what she wanted. She was a woman grown with a woman's craft. If that failed her, as, clearly, her good sense had, there were herbs and discreet midwives. There was even exile, which would be better than knowing that this man too had not just feared her, but repented of her.

But for once, she would know what it was to be desired, rather than respected like one of the icons these Christians knelt to. Leo plucked free her veil and kissed her again, twisting fingers in her hair. Wanting him made her ache as if an ember smoldered inside her, just where her thighs met. Slowly, she let her legs part. Her body moved beneath Leo's, seeking a way to yield herself without seeming too eager. Perhaps she could even imagine just for a little while that she was beloved.

When the kiss ended, she found herself clasping him, arms and legs. The pulse that had first aroused her drummed now in the hot air. The incense she fancied she had smelled earlier seemed mixed now with musk. Leo's mouth pressed against her neck. His face was wet as he murmured her name, first against the hollow in her throat, then upon her breasts, already half-bared from his caresses. For a moment, he relaxed as if, for the first time in years, he could permit himself that much ease. He trusted her as much as he wanted her! The shock held her motionless long enough to feel how utterly his body trusted, resting on hers.

Whispering to him, Asherah ran her hands down his spine, then up his back again. He lifted his face from between her breasts to look into her eyes.

Asking her consent? She would give him anything. He had only to take it—and her. Again, his hands moved over her, holding her heartbeat in his hand. She had raised her knees, but she was still guarded by the heavy fabrics of her garments. As he began to coax them away from her, she remembered how intimately his fingers had traced the shadowed delta so lovingly carved between the thighs of the statue he had held. She had flushed at the sensuality of that touch: he had reddened to find her watching his fingers. This time, he would be touching her, rather than lifeless stone; and she would open for him and be joyful. He wasn't a priest. He wouldn't ever be a priest. And for now, he was hers.

Asherah closed her eyes and let desire wash away fear of the unknown. With desire came vision. The goddess she had seen: she saw her, bathed and oiled by priestesses, led to recline in such a place, softened by pillows, waiting for her consort.

Now Leo rested his hand upon her inner thigh and traced it delicately. Upward. Yes; further upward. This was no dream. It was no dream that she should dare be dreaming. Leo's breath hissed between his teeth. A moment more, and he would touch the fire within her. She should cry out. No one would hear her if she cried. She should call this abomination, flee it, repent of it. It had been abomination so long ago in Canaan when the priestesses called out to the men of the Twelve Tribes, and the men from the stranger-tribes with their dark eyes reached out their hands to the daughters of Israel.

She would do nothing of the kind. It was no stranger whose touch made her tremble and gasp now: it was Leo, not an enemy, an outsider. So righteous the old fathers were: so stern. They too had known this. But they had been afraid, where there was no need for fear.

In her vision, the woman lying on the altar wore her face and nothing else. And the man who came to her, dropping his robes, was Leo. She watched him, in her dreams, her eyes flicking to the mysteries at the center of his body. He was ready to take her and bring them both to the fulfillment that was counted here as worship. He lay beside her, then over her; and her knees came up to clasp his legs. She felt the heat throb in her core, the opening of her body, the tracing of the folds within it, and then a triumphant cry and union.

Wind blew into the tiny room far beneath the earth. Outside, in the hidden corridor, one of their torches flared up, then into darkness, heavy with the smell of smoke.

They clung to each other in the thickening shadows. Leo's eyes were as dark and wild as Asherah's own. Instinctively, and as one, they both pulled back. Leo slid his hand over her hip, up to her breast again, but they had lost whatever urgency had compelled them into each other's arms. Her eyes filled, and he kissed the tears away. They had lost the moment. What had they gained?

"I should have stopped before," he whispered. "This isn't how . . ."

Had he wanted her, dreamed of her? Her heart leapt beneath his hand, and he fondled her again.

"I didn't want you to stop."

His arms tightened around her, but she knew that he had turned his head and was staring out into the corridor. The pulsing in the air had stilled; smoke from the burnt-out torch annihilated the scent of incense; and the music in the air was drowned out by fear of the growing dark. It was one thing for them to take each other in the heat of the moment, another now that the wind—wherever it had come from—had snuffed out one of their torches.

What had possessed them might be worship, but it was not her way.

Still, she put up her hand to his cheek and turned his face back to hers. She offered her lips to be kissed again and again lost the power to speak.

When his mouth reluctantly left hers, she smiled. "Leo?"

He still caressed her, affectionate now, rather than intent upon possessing her. "Do you know, Asherah, how tempting you are when you welcome me like this?"

Again, he kissed her. "When shall we finish what we've begun? Now?"

The ache in her core was beginning again, but she pushed at his shoulders. "Leo, listen to me."

He raised his head, watching her with a smile that pleased her even more than his touch. "Tell me."

"Leo," she said. "I do not think you are cut out to be a priest."

She had a sudden, intense memory of the way his body had pressed against hers. *Not cut at all, thank God.* She could still feel him, hard against her, even though her clothing—and that unexpected draft—had preserved her virginity. The memory brought with it a spasm of regret.

He laughed merrily.

Do you hear that? she asked the shadows. *Not just passion. Not just worship of whatever kind you demand. Two people together who like each other. And who laugh together.*

"They all tell me that. But you are the best argument of all. Asherah, unless you tell me 'no,' I want to talk to your father. Ask him for you."

"The laws against Christians wedding Jews are strict," she ventured. If she did not control herself now, as the surprise and exultation leapt within her, she would disgrace herself; and then he *would* reject her and go away.

"Meaning that there have been many such. How could anyone not prize you? Say I may speak to Joachim." He kissed her breathless, eager as a boy. "Say it."

"You may change your mind. As you did about being a priest." *Don't tempt fate,* came the wise, somewhat cynical female voice within her brain she had heard once or twice, but tended to disregard. *I want him honorably and wholly,* she argued with it, *or not at all. There will be no tricks.*

Not even whatever ancient tricks lingered in these passageways.

"Not this time," Leo told her.

Asherah shut her eyes. Let the rocks bury them now or the storm sweep over them. She had this moment, and in it, she had everything. And, in her next words, she gave herself away.

"He will make a merchant prince of you."

Leo laughed. "You are my princess."

Reluctantly, he moved away from her and sat up, awkwardly, before putting up a hand to raise her. For a moment, they clung, unwilling to separate.

"We must go back now." She did not know who said it.

"Separately?" It was almost a test: would he involve her in intrigue, seek to meet her here again, enjoy her entirely—or would he go honorably to Joachim as soon as possible?

"I have been your father's guest," Leo said, kissing her hair lightly. "And yours. I found you underground alone, and brought you back in safety. What could be proper, more natural?"

The way their bodies had almost fused, Asherah thought, though that was hardly proper. Best not to think of that for now.

One torch burning, they retraced their footsteps past the goddess, who seemed to watch them from the corners of her long eyes, through the breach in the wall, and back into the rough-hewn ways of the city that they knew. Both knelt and heaped up the shattered rock: a temporary barrier they hoped would escape notice.

They threaded their way through the maze of corridors and chambers. Their torch flared and sputtered as the gusts from air shafts blew this way and that through what teemed now with agitated men, women, children, and even, God help them if they planned to spend some weeks down here, goats. Armed men pushed through files of children carrying small parcels or parcels not so small. Women sorted and stored supplies, talking even more rapidly than their hands moved. Some of the children pushed and shoved while others had already taken on that preternaturally still look that meant too early and too great acquaintance with fear.

Asherah felt her own stomach clench. In returning to the world, she returned to consciousness of danger, danger in the upper air. Still, she spared a secret smile at Leo as she saw a woman fitting sheepskins into an alcove like the one they had warmed.

Up into the waning light of day. The rain had fallen and dried. For now, the air was clear. The wind blew, though, forcing wailing notes from the rock chimneys that studded the blasted land, a dirge Asherah could hear even over the crowd outside the caves.

Herdsmen and shepherds led flocks off the road into hiding. Lines of villagers awaited their turns to carry their few valuables into the caves.

And there, calm, instead of fretting as was her way in times when nothing was wrong, stood her own servant, accompanied by one, two, no, four of her father's guards. That very number alarmed her. What was more, it meant Leo would have no excuse to guide her to her father's house. Another test: see if he would keep his word. God knows, she wanted to believe he would; God knew equally well, however, that a harsh school had taught her wariness.

"That's Theodoulos!" Leo pointed at the youth, who pushed forward despite his withered leg and the tall, black-clad women who tried to steady him. Had the boy ridden all the way out from the gorge? In another life, Leo would have said it was a miracle that some raiding party hadn't picked him off; in this one, he thought it very probably had been.

Nordbriht shoved past some of the local notables, past men who bore the unmistakable impress—and scars—of veterans. Some were nobles, even more heavily armed than usual; and were farmers or herders who had grabbed up spears or knives or slings, or even their scythes, and followed their headmen here. Leo even saw one or two of the Armenians who had resettled here less than a century back and who were therefore still outsiders. They pressed forward, but Nordbriht blocked their way just with sheer size (and the horses) but by his immense presence. Exiled, he might be, and bearing a curse. But he bore a letter that carried heavy seals; and in that moment, he was still a Varangian of Byzantium.

He handed Leo a letter. "You wrote the City, asking for reinforcements. Here's your reply."

Leo eyed him. The seals were unbroken. He split them and read, Asherah staring shamelessly at the cultivated Greek hand.

"Cut off, by God the Father. Cut off!" he hissed. "Alyattes blinded, no troops sent. . . . That damnable Psellus—he throws away a whole region to . . ."

Asherah dared lay a hand upon his arm. "Not to rid himself of you. This is Romanus' land. It suits Psellus and his puppet well to throw it to the Turks. They have no desire to see us defend ourselves."

"Well," said Leo, "I cannot say I am surprised. Enraged, yes. Surprised . . . ?"

Asherah pressed his arm, pursing her lips in a signal for him to be silent. "Don't let them know," she whispered. "They may hate the City, but your tie with it—perhaps you can use it with these people."

Leo blinked at her, then grinned. "Lady, your wisdom shames us all." Perhaps it might. But now, she knew, she had to withdraw before she was pulled away by her father's people. Where men fought was no place for her. She let herself be drawn from Leo's side. He would not miss her. Please God, he would come in search of her, as soon as he could. If he could.

Nordbriht held his ground, his face unwontedly severe. Clearly, he expected an Imperial to show more sense than Leo had, at this moment.

"This isn't all that makes you hover like a storm crow, is it, man?" he finally managed to ask.

Nordbriht shook his head. The wind swirled about him, and his eyes glowed so fiercely that Asherah glanced quickly up to see whether the moon was full. Hoofbeats pounded upon the dried land like the thunder she had heard that afternoon: all that was left of the force of Cappadocia—in its prime, nineteen fortresses and four thousand men—now discarded. Instead of an army, they had shards; and they would have to make do with them.

"There's been another raid," Nordbriht told his master. His eyes gleamed almost as redly as under the full moon, when the Change came upon him.

"They sent me from town to guard the priestling here." He jerked his chin at Theodoulos, who flashed a white grin out of a dusty face while a black-robed woman glared at such disrespect.

"He rode in just a few hours ago, long enough to snatch a meal and close his eyes. Father Meletios sent him. Armed only in his own faith—" Nordbriht snorted. "—which is not how I'd treat a lad under my care. I'm afraid the holy father is looking for you too. Theodoulos, lad, come here!"

The boy limped up. Leo fought not to put out a hand to catch him as he wavered. Mostly, he had washed—or had washed for him—the grime from his face. Watered wine and a good meal had put some color back into his face. His eyes were still ringed with exhaustion, but they shone.

"Father Meletios told me to bring you to him. He has had a vision. The wind is rising fast, he says, and this storm could wreck us all."

26

Nordbriht led up Leo's horse, loaded with the arms he had hoped never to have to wear in battle again. The men clustering tightly around him muttered to each other and exchanged significant glances. It was going to be a damnably long ride, most of it in the dark.

How many times had Leo warned Nordbriht that he wasn't Leo's swordbearer! More to the point, Leo realized with an even bigger chill at the belly than he had felt before, he wasn't the Acolyte, the Varangian whose privilege it was to follow the Emperor most closely.

He feared how the men of Cappadocia might interpret what they saw. A Ducas in Cappadocia, home of Romanus, served by a Varangian; local nobles killed; a battle to come—he would pray, he thought as he wrestled with his armor, that Meletios was right and that the City's writ no longer ran here.

It could endanger Asherah, he thought, in sudden terror. An Imperial, allied to a Jew. Perhaps you might fear to strike at the Imperial, but the Jew—Leo might be fair game; but Asherah was easy prey. He looked frantically about for her, but two of the local nobles blocked her from his sight.

Leo raised an ironic brow at the northerner. "You think I ought to go out there and see what he means?"

"*We* go," said Nordbriht. "Take the boy back to his master. Find out what the old man meant."

"Bring him back!" cried one of the farmers, glaring at a noble who thought to frown him into silence. "Bring all the monks into the city where we can protect them!"

"A prophecy! We have to hear this," shouted the oldest of the Armenians, whose harness and arms looked older by far than he.

"Ioannes, you've ridden on pilgrimage to Peristrema, remember?" a burly man asked his son. Leo had seen them in town: minor nobility. Neither precisely well-off nor inclined to tell tales of woe, they lived contentedly on their land with old horses and their grandfathers' arms, as much the backbone of this country as the footsoldier was the backbone of the Emperor's army.

"But, sir, isn't leaving the monks there just the same as staking out a lamb for wild beasts?" his son ventured. So much for the armor of faith!

The boy found other men's eyes upon him and flushed.

Leo gestured, "Go on," at him. The boy flushed more deeply: *Christ save us, he thinks I'm a prince.*

"Bring them among us and . . . and . . ." He drew a deep breath and, seeing his father more beaming than displeased (although embarrassed), then continued more boldly. "We could protect them, *and* we would have the blessing of their presence and the wisdom of their counsel!"

That drew shouts of approval. Ioannes's father blushed with pride and flung an arm about him.

"My boy got his sense from his mother, God reward her," he announced. He blessed himself, and the others followed. Even Nordbriht touched his chest. The wind piped about the rocks. It was not a good day to go unblessed.

"Who'll go with us to fetch the monks?" Ioannes the elder asked.

Swords beat on battered shields. Nordbriht grimaced. "They're even more drunk on glory than recruits. Heaven spare us all.

"At this point," he muttered to Leo, "Father Meletios, blind as he is, will see us coming with a whole damned army, and he'll probably have us struck down with plague for crowding in upon his prayers. That is, if the Turks don't get us first."

Do something, his blue eyes told Leo. They were cold now, the way they got when it looked like Nordbriht might have a fight on his hands.

Leo signed. Once again, he must be a Ducas. A leader. "I'll go," he said. "Holy Meletios asked for me. I don't want a whole troop with me— we can move faster and safer with a few good men, riders with some experience, maybe even some practice fighting Turks."

He turned to the noble and his son, the Armenian leader, and the other headmen. "Sirs, you know these men far better than I. May I hear your suggestions?"

By the time Leo mounted and exchanged shouts that, in a saner world, might have passed for advice and plans about the remounts that ran with them, the guards, being met outside the valley, reinforcements, and regular patrols with half the headmen in the area and at least ten of their wives, Asherah had long since disappeared. No doubt, her father's servants had swept her into such safety as might be from the on-coming storm: they had aspects of being a defending army as well as a caravan. He would have liked to see her once more, even if he could not hold her fully against him as he longed to do, and to have her eyes assure him that what had passed between them, far beneath the surface of the world, was not a mistake she already regretted.

No use regretting what would not be. If a battle came, Joachim would pack her out of Cappadocia to wherever might be safe for the moment. In that case, he would never see her again, unless a kinder fate than ever had been his decreed that he would be allowed to seek her out. It was not likely. Even if he survived the coming years, her own people would protect her from even being named. Still, he would know, at the very least, that she was well.

And that would be enough, Leo told himself, knowing that he lied. He wanted peace. He wanted to be back in the hidden passageways with Asherah, feeling her tremble under his hands and mouth as she surrendered fully to him. He wanted his son in her arms and long years with her at his side.

But at this moment, he must be grateful simply to live past the next minute. And if, to do that, he had had to play on these men's belief that he had yet some influence with his kin *plus* their old Emperor's voice and should therefore command them, so be it.

His horse broke into a trot, then surged into a gallop. Outriders, heavily armed with weapons plundered from armies of at least three generations, flanked them. Ioannes and his son, yielding to the argument that they knew the land and the men on it better than any townsman, rode off to speak to the veterans who had turned farmer when they left the army, but who were still of fighting age and strength.

Leo felt Ioannes's eyes on his back, coveting his horse, his Guardsman, and, no doubt, his mail, as they rode off.

Be careful what you want, boy.

For banners, they had the sunset, beginning to flare at the horizon. He glanced over his shoulder: to Leo's relief, Theodoulos rode better than he walked. He would not need to be nursed all the way to the valley.

What a liar you are, he told himself. It was not enough to know Asherah was safe, even from him and his perilous family quarrels. It was not even enough to see her, or to hold her and exult in the discovery that he could love a woman, and that she would not flee him as she would a madman, capering and leering on the street.

What would be enough? He shifted painfully in the saddle. Not merely to possess her, though he still ached with wanting her so that riding was a torment. That would subside. "Enough" was a life with her at his side, her wildness and her wisdom balancing her need.

His heart pounding with joy and fear, he rode toward Ihlara. If this were a normal day, Leo would be happy enough to allow Father Meletios the victory of laughter at Leo's dream of a vocation. He loved, which was a blessing. But he loved a Jewish lady, and he dreaded what the monk would say to that. He wondered what, after the initial horror, his mother would make of Asherah and her wit. Or the redoubtable Anna Dalassena. It was probably just as well he would never find out: he had enough to do with a coming war and with worrying what Asherah's father might think of *him*.

He knew what they would say at home. But it was not, however, as if he were going home.

My home is here! he told himself. That is, if the Turks, sweeping over the Empire in a wave, left anything of "here." And if Asherah remained.

If he survived today, he would speak to Joachim and plead to wed his daughter quickly, quietly.

As the night engulfed the day, Leo slipped into the trance that made long rides or marches survivable. The miles fleeted by under the stars. Turks did not attack by night, he remembered: all night at Manzikert, he had lain beneath the stars as they wheeled and formed patterns that would have held meaning for him, had he only skill enough to read them. Once again, he saw faces in the darkness; and one of them was Asherah's.

His horse was lathered, but it ran until, out of pity and fear for the fine creature, he coaxed it to slow. Armed men fanned out around him, Nordbriht, the priestling Theodoulos, and the black-robed priest, girded with a sword, who insisted on riding out to the valley at this of all times.

His back itched as if, at any moment, Turkish arrows might whine through the air. He had learned to fear Alp Arslan's archers on their ponies, tireless, quick to change directions, skilled in ambushes. Why, at this moment, Cappadocia could be filled with small, deadly raiding parties.

All the more reason to see that Ihlara was secure. Like the cave churches clustered in the shadow of Hagios Prokopios, the vale of hermits was the pride and the responsibility of the entire region. It might be, Leo thought, he would suggest that the monks evacuate to ground that was safer because it was more closely patrolled by such troops as the town had available to it. But again, the question of safety was a knotty one: with noble and worker, Jew, Christian, Armenian Christian, Imperial and Cappadocian supporters, men and women glaring at one another, like as not Hagios Prokopios would rise against itself before the first Turkish archer dared enter.

So it was as well that he rode to see Meletios now, lest his existence prove tinder to the fire that could be made of a town he had come to cherish.

They paused to rest and eat somewhat. Nordbriht eased Theodoulos down from his saddle and gripped and rubbed his lame leg with those big hands of his until the boy bit his lip. But he did not flinch away, and when the time came to mount again, he walked to his horse more easily than Leo would have believed possible.

The air hummed and whispered. Stray breaths of air teased murmurs from the rock hillocks and chimneys that they passed. The trees, thirsty, sighed. At this time of the year, even the swift river that fed the valley would be much shrunken.

The earth shivered underfoot; and Leo's horse, too tired to dance with unease, fretted. He laid a hand against its neck, still held high, which was a miracle. *You ought to have a blanket on your back, not a man in armor,* he apologized in his thoughts. *A groom should walk you till you cool, then feed you mash. Forgive me for driving you.*

That he drove himself even harder mattered not at all.

The horse snorted, dropped out of its trot, walked for a space, then picked up speed. Famous as Cappadocian horses were, ponies bred and trained by the Turks could run for far longer. But they never had to bear a tall man in cataphract's armor over the miles.

By full night, when they finally reached Peristrema, Theodoulos' horse limped as badly as its master. Faint moonlight glimmered in the much-shrunken river, as it gurgled, cutting through the soft rock as it had for thousands upon thousands of years. The poplars whispered, like workers tired past sleeping. A stray torch gleamed far below, in one of the hermitages; and guards met them at the path leading to the valley floor. Even at this distance, they could hear deep-voiced chanted hymns.

"Careful," the guard told them. "We've had rockslides. Perhaps you should wait till dawn." He meant Theodoulos, who ignored him. More used to the valley's ways than all the others, the boy led the descent. He had to be exhausted, but he paused only when Nordbriht restrained him forcibly.

A rock rattled down the cliff face. One of the guards gasped.

"Nothing up there," Nordbriht rumbled out. He muttered to Theodoulos, who guided them to the left where the rock, overhanging their narrow path, might provide some protection.

Leo tried not to think what would happen if the cliff wall itself collapsed: in its own way, this was as bad as descending into the cave cities. If only he could tell Meletios what Asherah had found—well, not *all* of it, he corrected himself with an inward grin! But Meletios was her father's friend, not hers: knowing Asherah and loving her, Leo wanted her consent before he told the old holy man of their discovery.

"Steady . . . steady . . ." Nordbriht chanted it as if he manned an oar on one of the high-prowed ships of his homeland. His quick eyes spotted every hand- and foothold, and he seemed always there, to steady someone whose footstep went awry. Leo ached in shoulders, back, and thighs from hacking at a cave wall, the long, long ride, and now the climb down treacherous rocks.

How long had it been since he rested? Only that day, he had lain with his cheek against the softness of Asherah's breast, her arms encircling him in such rest as he had not known for years. His face heated at the memory, and his blood sang in his temples. Careful, Leo: if you fall here, you will *never* rise.

The wind picked up, chillier now than it had been for weeks.

How long since he had slept? He must have slept the night before. He remembered waking in the dawn. The nights had been too hot for slumber, but now . . . now, he thought he could sleep, if Meletios and his monks had no urgent demands to tend to first.

The rock seemed to come up to meet his feet, and he stumbled.

"Steady now. We're down." Nordbriht's hand clasped his arm.

Only then, Leo realized that he had tried to step *down* while the ground remained level. His knees sagged.

Theodoulos lurched toward the pile of rocks that concealed Meletios' home. His limp was worse than Leo had ever seen it, but he moved fast, nevertheless, his hands thrust out to touch the familiar rocks of home, push off from them, and move even more quickly along the upward path. Staggering almost as much, Leo followed him.

Flint and steel were struck up ahead: Meletios, blind for so long, never failed to provide light for others.

Flinching somewhat from the light, Leo entered. He peered up at the holy man's words of greeting, lurched to his knees for a blessing, then sagged to the clean-swept rock of the cave floor. He heard a rumble of explanation, Meletios' serene assent, and other people settling nearby.

"I have a message . . . we've come to fetch you to Hagios Prokopios . . . it's safer there. . . ."

"Are we under immediate threat of attack?" Meletios asked, his voice delicately ironic.

An immense yawn choked off Leo's denial. This was ludicrous. Heroic rescuers did *not* yawn in mid-speech: young Ioannes would be appalled. But fortunately, young Ioannes was not here. As it was, bad enough that Theodoulos had to stifle a laugh.

"Then we can wait to hear your news until you are rested enough to give it."

Leo's head sagged forward. Someone dropped a blanket over him. Its weight felt like a cope of lead on his aching body until his eyes closed.

Shouts and a crash dashed away the remnants of a dream of a woman who held him close, comforting him.

Those thrice-damned Turks *had* struck by night! Well, he, Leo Ducas, would show them. . . .

With a shout, Leo thrust himself up from the rock where he had lain, grabbing for his sword.

But if the Turks were close enough to attack while you were sleeping, they were already much, much too close. Blessed Mother of God, let him not be a prisoner again!

"Be easy, my son, easy." The speech of an educated man, the city Greek overlaid with an accent that made Leo think of sun and sand: Father Meletios.

"You—they took you too?"

"They are taking us nowhere, my son. We are in the valley. You are *safe*. Now, put away your sword."

Outside, the shouting formed into words: Theodoulos' orders that the paintings were not to be defaced, the carvings left untouched, the stone and pottery shards brought to the Holy Father.

"I regret that we have iconoclasts of our own." Now, Leo could hear the gentle irony in Father Meletios's voice.

Leo sighed and set down his sword, then dashed his hand across his brow. Be easy. From his first visit here, he had felt this to be a place of peace. But that peace was shattered now, along with the ancient shards and statues that Theodoulos and his master had been unable to protect.

"Give me your arm," Meletios said. "This valley is a sacred trust and must not be violated."

He could not *see* the statues, could not see the wall-paintings. Daylight lanced in from the entrance of the cave. Even here, the figures painted so long ago upon the walls, though faded by exposure, looked like the ones in the underground passage he and Asherah had uncovered.

Uncovered. He wished Asherah were with him right now, even here in this place from which women were barred: perhaps not as she had been, abandoned to whatever impulse had possessed them both: his Asherah, with her kindness and her wisdom and the sense he had always had about her that she was a well of warmth and repose, set in a garden. What a joy it had been to discover her, even more than the underground passageway, and to know from her touch how totally she would give herself.

"So, you have learned something, have you?" Meletios chuckled. "Truly, you're not a monk, are you?" His hand patted Leo's arm as he might a favored grandson upon the announcement of his wedding. Meletios might live withdrawn from the rest of the world, even from the rest of Cappadocia, but he was not deaf, as well as blind. It was ever so: monks were the worst busybodies.

Or perhaps what they said of Meletios in Hagios Prokopios was true, and he had powers beyond the human. Leo was inclined to agree.

Leo flushed. "You will think we are very different," he began stiffly. "We are of different faiths. . . ."

Meletios put up a thin hand.

"First, my son, you must tell me who this lady is. She must be a pow-erful logician indeed, to persuade you where I failed." Meletios smiled.

"She has no need to persuade where she can smile," Leo said. Mother of God, he sounded like a proper idiot, didn't he? "But she is accounted very wise." *Get to it, coward!* "She is Asherah, daughter of Joachim, the merchant."

If Meletios sighed, he recovered himself quickly. "Joachim has spo-ken—not much, but as much as is fitting—of his daughter's charm and wisdom. She has never accompanied her father. Who knows? Perhaps you will bring her to the true light."

Leo chuckled wryly.

"No? In any event, I would see this woman."

See? Meletios would never *see* Asherah, but perhaps he could meet her, talk to her, put his hand in blessing on her soft, dark hair. If she would permit it.

Voices erupted outside the cell. Meletios rose and signaled to Leo to accompany him—he needed no guidance—to the entrance of his cave. The old man put up his face toward the sun. He no more needed that guidance than Leo did. Perhaps even he, practically a living saint, craved the reassurance of human contact.

"There is no need for this panic!" Meletios shouted. "Where is your faith? God will protect us!"

His voice echoed from the valley walls. The wind twisted it and car-ried it into the gnarled rocks, and the shrunken ripples of the river bore it downstream to the rustling poplars. Leo thought of them as flames in the night, giant torches kindled by the Turks in the battle to come, and flinched. Once again, Meletios pressed his arm.

"This is not the end of the world!"

"But it's the *Turks*, the Turks!" cried one of the younger monks. So much panic in a name. Leo saw Alp Arslan's dark, profoundly civilized face, heard the sultan's cultivated voice, a purr in it, greeting his Em-peror and calling Leo himself lion's cub. The Turks were fierce. They were not world's end.

"I have fought Turks," Leo shouted when Meletios did not reply. "They are mortal. They can die. They can be conquered. . . ."

"If there is no treachery!" came a howl from a nearby hermitage. For the first time, Leo did not flinch. He was no traitor, even if his uncle had been.

"I have also been the prisoner and the guest of Turks," Leo added. "They are fierce, but they are not monsters. And they respect shrines."

They respected their *own* shrines, in any case. And these Turks were not Alp Arslan but, from all he had heard, a force far less under control: raiders, not a royal army. Still, Leo must, at all costs, prevent panic here. God forbid he had to comfort panicked monks. He stood as if to inspection. Unworthy he might be, but let the monks see him, fully armed, a symbol of the Empire's power . . .

. . . on which, he knew, they dared not rely. Still, he was here, and he was theirs.

Meletios' voice washed over him: reproofs, exhortations, commands that all retreat to their caves to fast and pray for better heart.

"And there will be no destruction!" he commanded as he turned, as a Parthian archer might fire his last arrow before he withdrew.

When the old monk signaled that he wished to return to the cave, Leo guided him, helped him seat himself upon a chair carved from the rock, then crouched upon a boulder.

"I have been asked to bring you all hence," Leo told him. "You first, so you can form part of the council taking shape now in Hagios Prokopios. The town fears for you. They sent me to escort you into safety."

Meletios laughed. "Just you and these few others? And, of course, my servant? You count yourselves sufficient to fight Turks?"

"We will be reinforced along the way," Leo said.

But Meletios was smiling. "Truly, what safety is there? My son, we face such a storm that we are all shards tossing in the waves as they sweep over this land, which once they covered. Wave upon wave upon wave. This is an ancient land, you know. It has been possessed by many powers. Sooner or later," he dropped his voice and, had he not been blind, Leo swore that he looked about furtively as if seeking eavesdroppers, "it will react. Rise up against invaders and retaliate."

He drew a deep breath and put his hand out to touch one of the statues he had saved from this last wave of iconoclasm. Leo reached for a pitcher and a cup, poured for the old man, and held the cup to his lips.

Meletios drank, and sighed. "I have discussed this with only one man. Joachim. Your lady's father. But several nights ago, after my prayers, there was a storm. And though I cannot see face to face, in that darkness, a greater light opened within the storm, and I saw . . ."

"Come with me," Leo pleaded. Not prophecy on top of everything else: not now!

"The others will come if you do," he urged. "Please let us save you. Then I can bring Asherah to see you. She says this is no longer a place for women, especially such as she," Leo told the monk.

"Ah, you wish me to meet Joachim's daughter. Is that as much your reason as carrying us all to safety?" Meletios laughed softly. "Well, even storms bring with them rains that water the fields."

Leo flushed, like a boy caught in mischief. He even felt his shoulders slump into the way such a child stands in the instant before "stand up like a man!" and punishment fall upon him.

Meletios smiled although, surely, he could not see how quickly Leo diminished from protective warrior to embarrassed lad.

"I will not abandon this place, to the storms *or* to the Turks," he said. "I told you. It is a sacred trust. But I will ride back with you to talk with the others and to see how we can guard against this storm to come."

Leo had hoped to leave as soon as the horses were rested enough to travel. But, naturally, before they could ride away, taking Meletios with them, an argument had to race through the valley. Meletios' intent, Leo realized, shocked the monks as deeply as if they heard Saint Simon Stylites had slid down from his ice-girded pillar and demanded a bath, wine, and silk garments.

How long had it been since the old man left his valley? Since he had been guided here after the journey from Egypt where his sight had been burnt out? Perhaps if the monks saw that their leader was content to leave, they would be more willing. Perhaps, upon his return, Meletios would order them out of the valley, or at least give the youngest ones a chance at life.

No, at this point, Leo did not at all believe his hopeful words about the Turks. Or about anything else. The storm was coming, and, unfit shepherd though he was, he must guide his people into shelter.

When had they become *his* people? He would ask himself that again when . . . if he had leisure. And if he survived the storm to come.

Theodoulos knelt nearby, packing his master's few clothes and trying to keep the tears from running down his face.

27

W hat sleep they had snatched the night before was not enough, but it would have to serve. At least, this time, Leo was clear enough of mind to strap his armor to his back before starting the long climb upward to where the horses had, he hoped, been walked, and cooled, and fed against their return. The morning was cool. Nevertheless, he was sweating heavily by the time his head cleared the edge of the cliff. The weight of his harness and the sweat stung the galls the chain mail had scored upon his shoulders.

He turned to offer a hand to Father Meletios.

"Take His Excellency's hand, Father," Theodoulos urged the old, blind priest. The boy had bounded back more rapidly than Leo would have expected from exhaustion: perhaps feeling himself responsible for his master helped restore him. Nordbriht towered like a wall at Meletios' back, one hand on the rock, the other steadying him. The old man had made the climb bravely and in silence, flinching only when his aged joints troubled him, or when, heedlessly, his guards pushed the pace.

Obedient, Meletios stared upward with his sightless eyes and extended his hand.

"Here, holy sir." Leo reached down and caught his hand with its dry, dusty skin and its long bones, like so many twigs ready to be broken into kindling. As Nordbriht pushed more or less subtly from behind, they raised the old man out of the deep-carved valley that had been his hermitage so long.

For a moment, Meletios crouched on the hard earth, heedless of the unseen edge, regaining his breath. Then he rose as if scanning the horizon he would never see.

Leo laid a hand upon his shoulder, pointed out the direction of Mount Argaeus, then the direction they would ride. Why was he bothering? Had Meletios ever seen this land, or had he been blind when he came here from the Egyptian deserts? Somehow, though, it seemed discourteous, indecently so, simply to haul the old man onto horseback and lug him like a bale of fleece or fodder. And, from the way he turned his sightless eyes up to the heavens, who knew what he "saw" that normal eyes could not?

A warm wind scrubbed across Leo's face. He shut his eyes to the vast horizon, savoring the way the wind soothed his skin, the respite from climbing, the silence in which he could hear the song of insects across the vast plateau, the rumble of thunder in the Taurus range, and the reluctant clopping of horse-hooves led toward him from the stables above the gorge.

He opened his eyes. The horses looked better than he had any right to expect. And remounts were sound, too, which was a relief: no matter what Meletios might think about humility, let alone ease of riding, he must bestride a horse, not a donkey if they were to make the speed they needed. Leo gestured to Theodoulos, the lightest of the party, to take the horse Nordbriht had ridden and for Nordbriht to move to a fresh horse: he had seen the Turks shift from mount to mount to ease the burden on their horse-herds, and it made sense—especially if they had Turkish riders as their enemies.

Father Meletios turned toward the cliff, blessing the valley and all who lived therein. Then, he sank to his knees in prayer. Leo glanced briefly away. It would shame the old man if he were afraid and they even took note of it.

He eyed the kneeling figure narrowly. Before the years had bent him and his disciplines turned him gaunt, they might have been of a height. That decided him.

At a gesture from Nordbriht reminding him, Leo pulled the bundle of his mail from his back. The rustle and clangor of its rings drew the old man's attention. Carrying the mail shirt over to him, Leo laid it over his hands.

"I want you to wear this, holy sir," he told Meletios. They would find something else for Theodoulos to wear among the collection of spare leather and chain mail oddments among them.

Meletios pushed it back at him. "I am armored in faith," he said. Then, as if forestalling Leo's protest or making sure he would not issue a direct order, he added, "Let me be, my son. I am strong enough, perhaps, to ride to Hagios Prokopios if I do not bear that burden. If I falter, tie me to the saddle."

Will we reach it safely?

The blank eyes went dark and terrible for a moment. "We *shall* arrive safely. More or less, we shall . . ." his voice trailed away into the muttering aftermath of a prophecy.

"What about Theodoulos?" Leo asked.

Meletios' hand clasped his. "I would see him safe. Promise me you will care for him."

"As if he were a son of my own."

Meletios chuckled, a surprisingly worldly sound. "Perhaps he will care for your son to come," he added. Leo narrowed his eyes at the holy man again. Was this more prophecy?

"Let Theodoulos decide how he will ride. He knows the road and his own risks."

The boy, too, rejected the offer of Leo's mail, though he was glad enough to wear the leather shirt and helm produced for him. He had a sword now and even a bow; and heaven only send that no one had to rely upon his skill.

Leo struggled into his harness. Groaning inwardly, he distributed its weight evenly across his shoulders. How much more easily he would be able to ride if he didn't wear it—not to mention the possible risk to the men he rode with if Turks saw them with what looked like an Imperial officer. There was risk if Turks saw them in any case, he thought; and soon they would be reinforced, please God.

Gesturing for Nordbriht to guard priest and servant closely, Leo tested the girths of their horses, then his own.

After what seemed like too long a time to him—and was probably far too short a time of parting from his retreat for Meletios, he signaled his men to mount, then to ride.

The sun beat down upon his back. Apprehension prickled along his spine. Where were the men who were supposed to meet them on the road? Don't think of that; don't wait; just fare forward and hope that whatever guardians protected Meletios would have an eye to his fellow riders.

The dusty road scrolled out before him.

They paused at noon to eat, to rest, and to cool the horses. Nordbriht crouched by Leo as he rested in the shadow of a reddish rock, striated with purple, and softened with tiny mosses.

"How's he doing?" Leo asked in an undertone. Lacking eyes, Father Meletios no doubt had ears that were doubly keen, to compensate.

"He may make me *really* believe in the White Christ yet," Nordbriht replied around gulps of watered wine. "He'll make it. He isn't even stiff, he says. Praying all night has kept him in condition, or made him used to discomfort. I'd like to see the Acolyte try it on recruits."

The Northerner laughed, showing large, white teeth.

Involuntarily, Leo glanced up at the sky.

"Nowhere near full." Nordbriht looked away. "I could wish it were. I hadn't wanted to mention it, but near the full moon, just before I . . . change, I feel stronger. Sharper, somehow."

Leo laid a hand on the other man's arm. "I wouldn't ask it of you.

But you have always been the guard I send before me, little as I have liked doing so. Moon or no moon, do you sense anything out there?"

Nordbriht nodded. "So does he. You saw his eyes, such as they are, go strange this morning. Oh, we're *for* some sort of fight; but he'll come out of it. And," he said after a pause, "so will you. But you won't like it."

That much Nordbriht did not need to say. Leo had never been one to take joy in fighting. It was one of the ironies of which his life was full that now he must function sometimes as scout, sometimes as *strategos*, and even in his old role as messenger.

Beneath a rock of his own, Father Meletios chanted under his breath. Theodoulos knelt before him. So did several of the men who rode with them. If they died this day, their sins at least would be forgiven.

Nordbriht stretched out upon the ground, lying motionless for so long that Leo thought he must have dozed off. He was contemplating how best to wake him without provoking an attack when Nordbriht raised his head again.

"Hoofbeats," he said. "I hear them."

"Ours?"

"Cataphracts ride heavy on the ground. These are lighter. Might be our reinforcements . . ."

"Reinforcements probably won't all be mounted, you know that. They stripped us, last time the call went out."

Then the riders were probably Turks.

"In either case, they're coming toward us." Nordbriht leapt to his feet. Leo followed him as he emerged from the shelter of the rocks in which they had set up temporary camp to point down the road. No dust rose from it: whatever approached was riding or marching cross-country.

They had been so thirsty at Manzikert. Leo remembered choking on the dust as he galloped, head down, shield up, between the Emperor that had been and his uncle. How innocent he had been then. It took ranks and ranks of men, their shields up, to withstand a Turkish charge, then override it with their heavier arms and horses.

He marked in his mind's eye the next likely rock barrier: anything but be caught in the open when the archers charged, shooting as they rode. He could almost sense Nordbriht's regret. Were it a full moon, he would shift shape and prowl, trusting in Father Meletios and whatever other miracle that, so far, had kept him from rending friend as well as foe.

And what odds would anyone lay that the Cappadocians themselves would not come upon him and, taking heavy casualties to do it, shoot him full of arrows or hack him to pieces that, at dawn, changed back into the arms and legs of a man?

Romanus had had cataphracts, archers, slingers, and spearmen. Leo had a blind hermit, a lame servant, and four mounted men, one of whom was about as mad as he. It was past time to pray for a miracle.

And time to ride. Turks tended not to fight at night. But a raiding party this far from its base might dare anything; and these were Turkmen, not the more cultivated people who had followed Alp Arslan before he fell, and then his son.

As the hours wore on, their horses tired, from the heat, the burden of their riders, and their riders' fear, which the horses surely sensed. They tossed their heads; their eyes rolled—all except Father Meletios' mount, which picked its way along the smoothest part of the road while the old monk sagged comfortably forward, chin drooping on his chest as if he slept. Theodoulos, scarcely less at rest, rode beside his master, guarded right and left by men who knew to cover them with their shields.

Leo and Nordbriht led. The sun beat down upon his helm, which gripped him like a vise. He coughed in the dust until he was dizzy, and his vision blurred. He drew a deep breath, bracing himself against gagging at remembered stinks of sweat and ordure and rot as a man decayed before he died. Almost, he swayed in the saddle, but Nordbriht was at his side, his immense bulk shielding him from the sun long enough for him to recollect himself.

He shook his head. "Old memories." It was all the apology Nordbriht would get.

"The old man's doing better than we are," Nordbriht said. A rush of tears cleared Leo's eyes. This time, thank God, he had an old man, not a dying Emperor, to shepherd. Christ have mercy, he thought: all his life he had thought of shepherds without thinking how terrifying, how hard their job must be when the wolves and thieves prowled about them.

He allowed himself a glance back at Meletios and found in it his reward. The old monk rode serenely, swaying, but not quite asleep.

Leo looked up at the sky. This late in the afternoon, he could see the pallid crescent of the moon.

The crescent, though—that meant Islam. God forbid that it be an omen of defeat. He would not survive another defeat, he thought.

No sooner than Leo thought that, Meletios' head came up.

Leo reached for his shield, Nordbriht for his axe. The other riders closed in before Meletios and his servant.

If only Leo knew what lay ahead upon the road.

As if sensing his thought, Theodoulos dodged out of the rough formation in which he had been guarded. He trotted up to Leo.

"Get back where you're safe!" Leo ordered.

"No one notices a boy," Theodoulos told him. "You need someone to ride ahead. Let me go."

"If anyone rides out to scout," Leo snapped, "I shall send someone who can fight."

"Sir, if you go, or if you send someone armed like *him*"—Theodoulos gestured with a sharp chin at Nordbriht—"everyone will know that something's up. But who looks at a lame boy? Some of the farmers here know me; the rest won't bother to care. And if Turks are on the road, the most they'd do is steal my horse."

There's nothing wrong with your mind, never mind your leg, boy. But you are my charge, Leo thought. *Christ, don't let me fail again.*

He tried to wheel his horse around the eager boy and ride on, but Theodoulos, greatly daring, put out a hand and grasped his reins.

"Let me, sir. Let me. I made it to Hagios Prokopios to fetch you, didn't I?"

You're a boy, just a crippled boy, Leo would have said if he had not bitten his lip—and knew Theodoulos heard the words anyhow.

"What would your master say?"

Leo glanced over at Father Meletios. As if conscious of that gaze, the old man raised his head and hand, muttering something.

"See? I have his blessing. I beg you, let me go." He pulled off the harness he had put on earlier with so much eagerness.

Leo met his pleading eyes. Hard as Leo found it to be a shepherd, no one denied him the right to run his risks, aye, or choose what risks to run. They might treat him as a madman or an enemy: the truth was, they treated him like someone who had made the passage, strait as a second birth, into manhood. Just a boy? he wanted to call Theodoulos? No boy was just a boy, but someone who must seek his manhood where it could be found. Theodoulos, lame and the servant of a monk, had fewer opportunities than most.

Could Leo deny him this one, even if it killed him?

"Ride with God," he muttered. "But take *care.*"

Theodoulos urged his horse forward: difficult to say which one preened worse.

"You're not on parade!" Leo called after him. "You're not even a scout. You're just a tired lad lucky enough to sit a horse's back, not a donkey's. Don't be an ass!"

Theodoulos waved jauntily, grinning at the pun Leo would rather have been hit than make. He gritted his teeth and compelled himself to wave back.

Theodoulos let his shoulders slump. As he loosened his reins, his horse dropped his head; and boy and horse ambled forward at a walk, as if heavy tasks awaited them when they finally, reluctantly were compelled to return to whatever farm owned them and their labor. Why send him after all? He would never cover any ground at that pace, Leo groaned inwardly.

What then? Would you have him gallop? This way, at least, he may escape attention.

A few hundred feet up the road, Theodoulos turned off onto a side-path and edged his horse into a smart trot.

He knew this land, Leo reminded himself. *Please God, let that be so.* He would know where men would be likeliest to meet. And, if all went well, he would find them and bring them. Or—the possibility had to be faced—he would die with them. It would have been easier to go himself than entrust the task to a lame boy.

Leo signaled for his small band to start forward once again. He glanced back at Meletios, who rode as calmly as he might have knelt in prayer. Probably, he could storm heaven from either position.

After an hour or so passed during which Leo heard no death shouts, no arrows whined to seek homes in his men's flesh, and the worst trouble he had was the weight of armor on protesting muscle and bone, he let himself relax somewhat. If they returned tonight, he would stop long enough to bathe, he promised, and then he would seek out Joachim. Asherah should not have to wait and wonder if Leo had thought better—or worse—of what he had said in the underground city.

And he would see her. Oh God, he would look into her eyes, although with her father there, he would not presume to embrace her; but her eyes . . . he remembered how, in the firelit darkness, her eyes had widened and he had seen himself transformed and glorified in them.

Meletios cried out like a bird over water.

Leo backed and wheeled his horse so swiftly that the poor beast, tired as he was, tried to toss him from his back. Swiftly he drew his sword. Nordbriht came alert, rising in his saddle to scan the land with his sharp senses, even in this guise, almost beast-keen.

"What is it, blessed sir?"

"My son, oh my son . . ." Not panic but pain echoed in the old man's voice.

You set a cripple to do a whole man's work.

The deed would be on his soul forever. Not even Asherah's love would wipe the memory away.

"There!" Nordbriht pointed. "Look how the little rat rides!"

At first, all Leo could see was the wide land, broken here and there by eerie rock formations. Then, he saw a cloud of dust . . . no, two clouds.

Theodoulos raced toward them, clinging to the saddle, his arms flung about the lathered neck of his horse. He had lost his weapons. It did not so much gallop as run, the flat-out panicked gait no rider liked to see— and certainly no officer. At any instant, he might fall, or the horse stumble; and they would be lost and all the news they had died to bring him.

He nodded at Nordbriht. "Bring him in."

His larger mount lumbered forward, then picked up speed, meeting the boy halfway and turning fast. He had his arm about the lad, was supporting him as he sagged in the saddle, then brought him back to the others. Even Meletios crowded up to hear.

"Turks!" gasped Theodoulos. "I told you. They saw me. Someone pointed, but the others just laughed."

"How many?"

"Ten, maybe fifteen . . . no, I'm not thirsty. . . ."

"Not a word till you drink," Nordbriht growled.

Theodoulos gulped obediently, then pushed free. "I saw Ioannes, both of them, some slingers . . . about five others. Oh, hurry, hurry. We have to help them."

"Can you take us back there?" Meletios asked. He held out an arm, as if he would reassure his servant, but Theodoulos held himself proudly straight.

His eyes met Leo's fully for the first time since he had known the boy . . . no, the young man. "I can guide you, sir."

"Good man!" Hadn't Romanus used just those tones on Leo when he had appeared at his side on that dreadful day at Manzikert? Leo suppressed a shudder.

Ioannes and his son were outnumbered. Even if Leo threw his tiny force after them, they would still be outnumbered; and they were fighting a scourge of God. And that was assuming he did not leave at least one man behind to protect Meletios and Theodoulos both. Perhaps it was his duty . . .

Time slowed while temptation writhed out from the darkest part of his soul, and he contemplated abandoning what should have been his reinforcements to their fate.

What manner of monster are you? he asked himself, *that you would go off and leave men—and that gallant boy—to certain death?*

You are Ducas, the reply came. *Like your uncle, no better.*

Bile rose in his throat, and he spat.

"In the name of God," he blessed himself, "let us ride."

He heard a voice so hoarse he could hardly recognize it as his own instructing his men in what they should shout as they closed with the enemy; he showed them how to hold their shields against horse archers; and then—and how grateful he was he had the strength to have made the choice!—he dropped his arm, signalling the charge.

Nordbriht tried to dash out before him, but he was heavier; and that slowed his horse just enough that they crashed through the back of the Turkish line simultaneously. Turkmen, all right. They bore no insignia that Leo remembered from his time as a prisoner.

The men they rescued shouted—premature triumph. The swordsmen pressed forward once more, shields out to aid the spearsmen. The slingers, stocky, dark-haired countrymen, their eyes on fire, took aim, swung, then launched their missiles. Turks fell, their skulls crushed, or their ribs smashed in.

Together, Nordbriht and Leo flashed out their steel, slicing and sluicing red from swordblade and axehead. Red dashed over their hands, a red almost matched by the distended flare of his horse's nostril, the open, screaming mouth of Nordbriht's mount before an arrow brought him down.

Shouting, Nordbriht toppled, rolled, and fought back to his feet. Leo kneed his horse in beside him, and Nordbriht grasped its reins. One of his men took an arrow in the chest. He had time to scream once before blood bubbled out of his mouth, and he fell.

Another held the reins of Meletios' horse, sheltering the monk behind his shield. Theodoulos, facing close-in battle for the first time in his short life, hung back. Then, at a gesture from young Ioannes, half hidden behind his father's shield, Theodoulos rode forward, his jaw set. Ioannes leapt forward, as if to bring him in.

In the moment he left himself uncovered, an archer fired—and his father hurled himself across his son to take the arrow in his eye. Ioannes cried out in shock, then stood still.

"Give me his sword!" screamed Theodoulos. "Give it to me!"

His scream woke the dead man's son from his trance of horror.

Scooping up his father's sword, he tossed it to the other boy. Together they advanced . . .

. . . and two at once attacked Leo. He had all he could handle, and then some. His arm ached from the clash of swords against his shield, dropping somewhat as an arrow glanced off his mail. He could feel the point go in: no harm, he told himself, and forced his shield back up. Meanwhile his swordarm wove a deadly, shining shield before him. Before him, guarding him, Nordbriht swung his axe. He was *singing*. Enough blood had splashed him that he seemed again to be clad in a Varangian's proper red.

A rasping voice tried to scream and tried again. With horror, Leo heard it for his own. His was the only voice to scream the battle-cry: the others had all fallen silent.

"They can be killed!" he shouted. *"Nike!"* The word had blood in it, as it always did. His voice broke into a racking cough.

Over by Ioannes, Theodoulos sank to his knees, to retch, rather than to pray. Ioannes the younger threw his shield aside and hurled himself upon the body of his father, who had died for him.

"Wait till they're all dead!" Nordbriht shouted. He swung his axe above the supine body of an archer. The man's eyes bulged in terror before it embedded itself in his chest. Nordbriht pulled it free and cleaned the blade.

The horses stopped, trembling. No one shouted. No one moved. After a moment or two of utter silence, insects began to chirp, scraping their wings, buzzing overhead. The stink of blood and ordure drew them.

Leo dismounted. To his shock, the ground did not give way beneath his feet: no, that was the weakness in his knees. He clung an instant longer to his saddle.

"The wounded . . ." He gestured. "And if any horses are too badly wounded . . ."

Drawing his knife, a slinger approached a horse that rolled in pain, his foreleg snapped and useless.

Meletios edged his horse forward despite Leo's order to his guard to keep the monk away.

"I hear boys' voices," he said. "They are weeping. Bring me to them."

Meletios dismounted by the grieving boys. His voice, sere and sure and oddly beautiful, floated over the bloodied land. "Your father lives in you. Do you remember the words of the Psalmist? 'Oh Absalom, my son, my son. Would God I had died for thee!' It is the way of things that son outlives his father. You must not despise the gift of life he gave you—that he gave you twice. There, my son, there. Cry it out now, then never again. How do you hope to rule your family, fill your father's role, if you cannot rule yourself? You, Theodoulos, fetch him water."

Leo walked about the tiny battlefield. They would have to move quickly: these raiders they had killed were too small a party to be the only Turks for miles around. Others would seek them out; by that time, they must be long gone.

Manzikert, he thought, had inured him to carnage. This was Manzikert in miniature; and he was not inured. At least, the wounded horses were all still now. No one cried out. But a flutter of cloth, spied from the corner of his eye, drew Leo around, and he strode toward a Turk who lay half pinned beneath the body of one of the sturdy steppe ponies.

His mouth was shadowed with pain—small, his horse might be, but it still was far from light—and blood from a bloody lip smeared his face. But as Leo approached, the man looked up, blinked, then stared at him more closely.

"Allah be praised, it is my lion's cub."

28

Leo looked down into the face of the gulam, *the soldier slave,* who, upon the day the world seemed to blacken, brought the Emperor of all the Romans before Alp Arslan as his prisoner.

"Kemal," Leo said. "By all that's holy."

The Turk moved his head from side to side. "Nothing is holy about this horse lying on me. . . ."

Leo's bark of laughter brought the others' heads around to see their leader talking to a wounded Turk. Laughing at the sight of him as if he were a friend, not some demon-spawn from off the steppes. *They'll lock you away. You'll never see Asherah again.*

"If I ever deserved well of you, young Ducas," Kemal said in his atrocious, stilted Greek, "heave this carcass off my legs. It grows too heavy to be borne with ease."

"Kemal," Leo groaned. "Must everything slip through your fingers? Wealth, freedom . . ."

"My horse's reins . . ."

"Didn't you get enough gold for taking the Emperor to make you rich? One day you were a hero. But now, here you are, riding with the

Turkmen, not even your own people. Did your master lose favor with the winners? Or did you lose him, too?"

"My sultan died," Kemal said. "I had no wish for a lesser master, and none trusted me. You should understand that."

Better a tail to lions than a head to foxes; and Alp Arslan had been a mighty lion indeed.

At Leo's nod, Kemal flicked dust from his hand into the wind. What had happened was what was written; it was past, and now one waited for what else was written to reveal itself. Leo knew that was all the answer he would ever get from the man. He sighed.

Having unburdened himself, in spirit, if not from the horse lying upon him, Kemal made himself grin, showing white teeth between split lips. Leo found himself grinning back.

An enemy, a captor had proved to be a likable man, and far more to be trusted than his own kin. They *both* could think that, Leo realized.

"We have to get out of here," Leo said. "I assume you came with more of a force than these. . . ."

"My cub grows wise with power," said Kemal, committing himself to nothing. "I may no longer be a hero, but I do not betray those who fed me."

They might not be his kin, but the Turkmen were Muslim, therefore his brothers. Leo found himself laughing helplessly on the edge of ruin. They would have to bury or burn the bodies of Greeks and Turks alike, or at least, lay them out decently, then flee this place with a blind monk, a lame servant, exhausted horses, and now, of all things, a wounded Turk; and here he was, matching wits with a man who had saved his life when he had sought only to toss it away.

The laughter brought young Ioannes's head up from where he grieved beside the body of his father. "There's a Turk left—kill him for my father!" he screamed and launched himself from the bloody ground toward Leo and Kemal.

"His father died saving his life," Leo muttered. To his shock, the words came out almost apologetically.

"We all lose our fathers," said Kemal. "I lost mine before I was born. Not that I ever knew for certain who he was. But my sultan . . . and yours, my cub. I was sorry to hear . . ."

Leo laid a hand on the *gulam's* shoulder. "And I, about Alp Arslan. But you must be my prisoner now. It is the only way to save your life."

"That is," said Kemal, "as Allah wills. Still, if He does not object, I do not complain if you serve as Allah's aide. It is, I think, a promotion from serving an Emperor. . . . ahhhh! easy, cubling, I am not made of wood!"

"Can you slide your leg aside?" Leo asked.

Nordbriht crouched beside them, lending a shoulder to Kemal to lean on as Leo probed his leg. Ioannes leapt at Kemal with his bloody knife, and Nordbriht thrust him off almost casually. He hunched a shoulder, fending off Ioannes and his bloody knife.

"Why do you try to save him?" Ioannes screamed. Tears cleaned his face in streaks.

"He saved my life," Leo replied. "He saved the Emperor's life—your fellow countryman, remember. And, besides, we may prevail upon him to tell us of the other raiders. . . ."

"A traitor and a filthy Turk!"

"Leo," murmured Kemal, "this child needs his clouts changed, or a good whipping."

Leo sighed. Try again. "They brought us before the Sultan in chains. This man, who found us, had the chains struck off and presented us to Alp Arslan. He treated Romanus like a guest and a brother, more kindly than his brother Christians—and my kin."

Ioannes' face twisted. He looked absurdly young and anguished to contain such rage.

Leo wound strips of cloth about Kemal's leg, splinting it with the remnants of a spear that was not too badly hacked.

He was shaking now with reaction from the battle and the pure shock of finding Kemal, too unstrung to be politic.

"You want him dead?" Leo asked Ioannes. "Fine. You kill him. Let's see you try."

Kemal's black eyes shot pure fury at him, then glittered with malicious humor, even at his own impending death.

He took hold of the ground, as if bracing himself and his courage for the deathblow and met the boy's eyes.

"Another cub," he muttered. "After all my kindness to you, was it too much trouble for you to procure me a warrior's death?"

Leo shook his head. *You're not going to die.* Careful footsteps, a blind man and a limping boy, were coming their way; and Nordbriht knelt at hand. But it were as well to see how Ioannes, his grief fresh, the power to kill handed to him, would behave.

Ioannes had stopped weeping. His knifehand had become unnaturally steady. He raised it, paused, raised it further, and launched himself forward, to stab repeatedly at the earth, sobbing as he stabbed.

"I'm a coward!" wept Ioannes. "Kill me too!"

Meletios knelt. "To kill in the heat of battle is bad enough. To kill in cold blood . . . if we lose our decency, we are not men, not Christians at all. May the Blessed Mother of God bless you, my child, for your mercy."

Kemal drew a deep breath. "You had best be getting moving," he told Leo. "They will miss us and send out more riders. And I do not think they will be pleased with you."

"*We* move," said Leo. "I told you, this time, you are my prisoner. We'll get you to a physician."

"Not one of your Christian butchers!" Fear, much more than he had shown in battle or facing Ioannes' desire for blood, rang in Kemal's voice.

Leo found himself laughing again. He choked it off, hearing the low-voiced rumble of Meletios's prayers, first blessing young Ioannes, then blessing the dead. He would bring Kemal to Joachim: hardly the most politic or the kindest infliction upon a man whom he wanted as his father-in-law. But Leo specialized, it seemed, in insulting family; and Joachim would know how to deal with it, if he were half the man Leo thought he was.

What had Asherah told him about their time spent in the caves?

And if her father could not cure Kemal, Asherah would, though her presence might make Kemal expire from fright.

Leo wanted to be around to see *that*. And to let Kemal know that the lady was to be treated with respect.

"Lad," Nordbriht's voice rumbled behind Leo. "By now, you're empty inside. If you think you're done heaving, I want your help."

Theodoulos muttered something.

"I tell you, you did fine. You brought us word in time, you didn't run, you waited till things were over—even comforted Ioannes before you were sick. You didn't even foul yourself. Now, I have to help load the prisoner. You lie there and listen for riders. You'll hear them through the earth, long before anyone could see."

It would help, Leo thought, if Kemal would tell him what kind of force they might expect. He gestured for his men to mount. There were enough horses now for all of them, even the reinforcements—assuming two men did not mind riding Turkish-style, and Ioannes would consent to ride with the priest's boy.

"Hear anything?" Nordbriht asked. He wiped his hands down his filthy tunic. His offer to tie Kemal to the saddle had been rejected with a hot display of offended pride.

"Thunder under the earth," murmured Theodoulos. "Over and over. Thunder."

"They're coming," said the Northman. "Damn! I hoped we'd have more time."

Kemal shrugged. "It is the will of Allah," he said. "The storm will come, not this battle perhaps, but one that will make the battle where we met look like a rainshower. As for these men, if they listen, I will say you saved my life."

"We'll run as far as we can," Leo decided.

"And them?" Ioannes gestured at the dead, including his father. Leo knew he was half a moment from refusing to leave his body.

"Load them on the remounts. They are ours; we do not leave them or our decency, as the holy father said. We'll bring your father home, lad."

He turned to Meletios, reaching out to take his reins, as Nordbriht took Kemal's. "I wish we had Joachim here. He and Asherah saved my life one night."

Her name tasted sweet on his cracked lips, salving the dryness, the sickness, and the fear. Such a lady should not be named by outsiders, the Jews in Pera had said. She was a secret, a garden, a hidden treasure. God grant Leo saw her again. He remembered her valor and the lights that wreathed her and her father the night they struck at his assassins.

The lights.

"Father," Leo leaned forward, "have you and Joachim ever discussed . . ."

Under the color that the desert sun had seared into his flesh, Meletios blanched.

"You have," Leo stated. "You know what sort of disciplines he's learned. You probably know them too, those that are permitted to Christians, and, I'd stake my life on it, even some forbidden ones."

He would have to stake his life on it. Heaven only send the priest did not curse him and refuse to ride further in his presence.

Meletios went silent. Despite his blindness, he had always managed to seem as if his eyes met Leo's, as if they kindled with agreement or compassion. Now, they went as dead as they were in truth.

"Can you tell me, Father, on your faith, on your immortal soul, 'No, I know nothing of such powers?' Remember, silence is also an answer of sorts, and I have spent most of my life among liars."

Meletios flinched. His face dropped. A sighted man would have looked away.

"You are our prophet. You will get us home."

"My son, we might be better off cleanly dead. *They* will hear. *They* will answer."

Leo rose in his saddle. Nothing lay ahead save rock and scrub— nothing he could see. Nordbriht waved at Theodoulos, who pointed. The "thunder in the earth," as he called it, came from behind them. It might be better to disperse and let each man or youth take his chances—*so the Turkmen could hunt them down, as if in sport?*

No. The time for flight was gone. He remembered Romanus' retreats overmountain, losing men and hope at every step.

"We could use some answers, Father."

"These are answers no one wants!" cried the priest. "God knows, I do not, I never sought them when I was given the valley as my charge."

Leo's hand tightened on the reins of Meletios' horse. He was an old man, a frightened man, holy and blind besides: and would Leo really shake the truth from him?

"I want those answers," he repeated.

Father Meletios shook his head. "This much I will say: this is an old land. Nation after nation has marched across it, bringing their arms and their false gods. The land itself cries out underfoot."

A tremor shook the earth for less than the blink of an eye. One of the horses shied and cried out shrilly. An armsman struck it. The Turks might hear such noise.

"I want us safely home. So long as I get that, I don't *care* what your answers are, at least not for now. Can you help us, Father?"

The old man was trembling. Leo lowered his voice. To think how sure he had been the old priest could assuage his nightmares. What a fragile reed he seemed now to rest their lives on!

"They're getting closer," Nordbriht warned. The sky was darkening, and Nordbriht's other senses kindled with the coming of the night.

Kemal's eyes flickered, then closed in on themselves, giving nothing away.

"In God's name," Leo pleaded with the priest.

"Joachim warded you. Set up defenses so that you could walk unnoticed through the valley of the shadow of death."

"Can you do that? Apart," Leo's mouth twisted, "from your role as priest?"

"I wish now you *had* been one of my monks. I would have put you under obedience. *Yes*, I can allow you to pass by, hidden from the sight of Turks. But from those others . . ."

Meletios shook his head.

"Upon my head be it," said Leo.

"You had best beg God the Father, God the Son, and God the Holy Ghost, if you have not abandoned them, that such judgment *not* fall upon your head. But . . ." Meletios sighed. He drew himself upright and breathed deeply, as if drawing sustenance from the earth up the column of his spine and into head and heart.

"In my father's house, there are many mansions," Leo quoted. "You dwell in one, Joachim in another. Now, for God's sake, get us to one of them or to the other!"

"You had best tie me to the saddle," Meletios commanded, his voice already remote.

Leo obeyed, perhaps a little too briskly at first. As his hand touched the priest, he suppressed an instinct to pull it back: heat seemed to shimmer off the man's sun-darkened skin, as if he were stone left out too long in the desert sun.

"In the name of God, priest, pray for us," came a voice, thickened by pain, out of the growing darkness: one of the men at arms, riding by a dead man, draped across a tired horse. "I can hear them now. They are coming closer, riding fast."

Leo reached for his sword. Probably, he should cut Kemal free, give him a chance at such life as he might have, lacking fortune, kin, or lordship. The last of the daylight reddened, then turned darker. Long violet shadows stretched across the hardened dunes.

Nordbriht keened, a beast longing to hunt.

Meletios' low voice cut across his, a chant, but from no liturgy that Leo had ever heard, no Greek he knew, not even the complex gutturals Joachim had used.

The Northerner fell silent. Even the wind sank. Their horses' hooves, striking the sunbaked ground, sounded muffled. Then even that sound died.

Leo thought he heard a piping sound, accompaniment to the priest's chant. The music from the pipes rose above Meletios' voice, a hollow threnody that wove about his words and seemed to wreathe about them all.

The light *bent*. It wrapped about them until each of them seemed surrounded by a halo, such as glorified the saints in the great churches of Byzantium. The light fragmented into rainbows that clung in glory to their shoulders, then slid off, casting no shadows. Shadows streamed from the rocks and the brush, even from the clouds high overhead; but, if light and shadow were any indication, Leo and his troop were not there.

Nordbriht whistled, then fell silent. Father Meletios' chant reached a triumphant climax, then subsided.

Now they rode as if through a tunnel of altered light. Leo kept an eye out, not only for Turks, but for shadows such as he thought he had seen far below the surface of the earth: ghosts of sensations—though there had been nothing ghostly about how he had felt when he took Asherah in his arms. Best not to think of her now.

Father Meletios' voice sank into a mutter, and the pipes—from wherever their music had emanated—grew more faint until they could be heard only at the very threshold of awareness.

"They're here." Leo did not so much hear the words as see their shapes printed on Theodoulos' trembling lips.

Turks galloped into sight, dashing from the protection of stone dune to dune, their bows already drawn.

"*Kyrie eleison, Christe eleison, kyrie eleison . . .*" They should have heard those gabbled prayers all the way to Baghdad, but they did not. Leo could not hear the Turks' horses' hooves or the faint deadly melodies as armor clashed upon its rider.

"Allah!"

Leo knew when Kemal prayed. His prayer might or might not be answered: after the first exclamation, it certainly was soundless.

And there was silence in heaven for the space of half an hour. . . .

They rode as if in a tunnel of light, armored against the sharp eyes of Turkish archers, muffled against their too-keen ears. Bearing their dead with them as Father Meletios chanted in a whisper, they rode across the plain. Hagios Prokopios appeared in their sight, made strange and dark by the errors in the light that guarded them.

Under their silenced horsehooves, the land trembled.

The land itself cries out, Meletios had warned.

Men rode out past them, their mouths squared in silent screams of battle rage toward the Turks. Folly, Leo thought. They could not afford to lose a single man. They did not dare reinforce them or do aught but ride forward, guarding the priest who spent his strength guarding them.

They rode past perimeter guards whom Leo was frankly glad to see. Some, graying under battered helmets, were clearly veterans. He saw one or two Armenians, and even men whom he knew to be in Joachim's pay: caravan guards and drovers would know more of Turks than most farmers.

Leo leaned close to the priest, resting his hand on the man's wrist. It was burning hot.

"We're home," he murmured. "You did it, my father. Thank you."

The light altered. The rainbows died, restoring the men that light had protected to the world. Meletios collapsed, sagging onto the saddle. Leo leaned in to support him, controlling his horse with knees alone as it sidled away from the priest's tired mount and yet another slight earth tremor.

At a villager's shout, Leo ordered, "Get the priest. Get Joachim from the markets."

"You just appeared here," a merchant pointed at them. "No one saw you ride in. What sort of . . ."

"They have a Turk with them . . . a Turk!"

Father Meletios' head lolled onto Leo's shoulder, a dependency he never would have permitted if he were conscious. "He is old, he is blind, but do you doubt he can work miracles? Now go!"

Torches appeared on all sides, and men shouted.

In an instant, they would have a panic on their hands, or what was worse, a riot. Already, the rougher townsfolk were looking for likely rocks to hurl—and in Cappadocia, rocks were always close to hand.

The guards who had ridden out heard the shouts, sent scouts back, then returned—a bad moment, that, when Leo's men found themselves surrounded by mounted soldiers. Even if they were not Turks, the assembly of nobles, Armenians, and God only knew in the dark what else was alarming enough; and the way they glared at Kemal did not augur well for his future.

Finally, too, the priest ran out, his robes flapping. Tenderly, he helped a black-robed woman cut Father Meletios free of the saddle and lift him down, all the while barraging everyone with questions.

Nordbriht dismounted and stood, holding his axe, staring at the outskirts of the town, the dying sunlight casting bloody shadows upon his face, braid, and gleaming weapons.

Women and children ran, and even guard dogs barked in shock, fear, and welcome, as Leo brought his charges to Hagios Prokopios and what sanctuary an unwalled traders' town might offer them.

29

Tumult *outside, an explosion of shouts and horses' hooves,* brought Asherah out of her meditations with a cry. Footsteps pounded down the corridors toward her quarters. The walls were thick; it would take some time to burn them or break them down.

She reached for the pouch of gems and the dagger she kept by her in case she had to flee.

Father! She knew what his orders to her had been should catastrophe strike them yet another time, in yet another place they had hoped to make their home. She hoped she was an obedient daughter—most of the time. She knew she was a loving one. And so, perhaps, she would be forgiven if love won out over obedience.

She pressed her hand to her heart to keep it from pounding through her ribs, and pushed by her maid into her father's rooms. To her astonishment, Tzipporah followed her.

Joachim would want her to flee. He had ordered her, in fact, to do so; she knew where the gold and gems were hidden and how to gain a place on any one of a number of caravans.

She had fled thus before: never again. She would stand firm, as she had when an Emperor was blinded. Or she would fight and die.

Let it not be Father who was hurt. *I would know it if they struck at him,* she told herself, falling back on the old, familiar madness. *My dreams would have brought me awake, screaming. . . .*

The horses outside were Greek, and a new terror seized her. Let it not be Leo, the dark eyes glazing, those clever, tender hands of his going lax in death. *Please God, spare Leo, even if I never see him again.*

Asherah burst into the room in which she had sat and listened to Leo and her father. Already, her father's men had turned it into a welter of warriors, snapped commands, and flustered, frightened servants. Some of the men tried to push between the soldiers and the maidservants, while they shoved furniture to one side or cried out in pity at the injured men. Nordbriht had shoved aside the heavy columns on which ancient statues rested and now bellowed for order. A streak of blood defaced one white wall.

Not again, Asherah could not help thinking. *Not the killing again. Oh, please.*

And this time she even knew the soldiers. That did not reassure her. Knowledge had not spared those she loved before.

But there was a difference. This time, it seemed, they had come not for plunder, but for care.

To *ask,* not demand.

Perhaps the world could change. Slowly. Perhaps.

Joachim clapped his hands, gaining the silence that Nordbriht sought. As always, when a storm was rising, he created order. In the quiet, his calm voice ordered medicines and cloth brought from Asherah's own stores. She must match his courage with her own.

Summoning all her courage, Asherah looked about. Her heart almost exploded, and she leaned against a wall for support. Leo stood there. He was watching for her, she realized; and his face lit when he saw her. No wonder the soldiers had come here. Leo knew she and her father would take them in.

Father is alive. Leo is alive. Now I can go on living, too.

Leo half-carried, half-supported another man whose leg was crudely splinted. Both of them were filthy, both stained with blood. Tzipporah tumbled cushions into a pile and gestured for Leo to set his burden down.

"He'll spoil your cushions," Leo protested. Even the man he upheld recoiled. So he was civilized, too.

"Better ruin cushions than lose a life!" Tzipporah cried. Two servants helped her settle Leo's companion. Waiting for medicines, she held his hand and did not flinch from the blood on it or its hard grip.

Asherah met Leo's eyes, which searched hers for shared memories. The impact of those memories halted her in her tracks: just like that, not caring when a maid's shoulder pitched her forward.

Leo strode forward and steadied her. Briefly, she was in his arms again, resting in that warmth, near that remembered heartbeat. For an instant, she closed her eyes to savor his touch.

He set her back on her feet, but his hands lingered on her shoulders. Despite the tumult in the room, her father saw and raised his eyebrows. Asherah felt hot and chilled all over. The moment had come before she realized: Leo's gesture had been a declaration as telling as a formal announcement—and to think she had worried that he might regret his promise to ask her father for her! Her eyes filled with tears of relief that Leo had proved true. And yet, his truth could put them all at risk. He was willing, he was willing—and yet, she must pretend for just a moment longer. She raised her chin proudly, then turned back to Leo and the prisoner . . . no, the guest he had brought.

"Esteemed lady, I have brought you . . ." Leo's voice was husky from the road and battle. ". . . a very dubious guest indeed."

She looked up at him, standing so close so that her hair brushed his shoulder. He reached out his hand toward it, then let his fingers fall before he could touch her.

"Another ambush?" she asked.

"Not assassins. This time, the storm we spoke of. It's struck."

She glanced down at the injured man in the torn silks, the battered leather, the torn mail of a *gulam*—oh, she knew the signs, knew, in fact, where that harness of his had been bargained for.

"Your prisoner?" The words tumbled out breathlessly. It was a foolish girl who spoke, not the sensible, calm woman she tried to be. He had fought Turks. At this moment, he might be lying outside, pierced with arrows. Here he was, alive and standing before her, bringing her his prisoner and all but embracing her before her father. She had nothing to fear, had she? Still she flung out a hand for support, lest her knees collapse beneath her.

"This time he is. Last time, at Manzikert, it was Kemal took me and the Emperor captive. He saved our lives, you might say. So, when he said he feared a Christian surgeon—he called them all butchers—I ask you, Asherah, what was I to do?"

"Precisely what you have done," Asherah said.

She might say much else to this stranger, starting with her thanks for saving Leo's life so long ago. But the best things she could give would be hospitality and healing. She greeted him in Persian, a tongue she knew better than the language of the steppes, and saw his dark eyes flare.

"Ah, lion's cub, do you make of this gazelle your lioness?"

Much was said of what brutes Turks were, how they slaughtered children, how they ate their meat raw. Many other such lies were told of Jews: if it did not make for common cause, it at least made for a kind of wry sympathy. Turks were Muslims, therefore people of the Book, therefore, as Asherah accounted it, civilized—at least as much so as Christians. And she had never known one to be less than shrewd—including this one. He even spoke in an undertone, as if protecting his captor's secrets.

"Quiet, you!"

Leo's hand came down to cuff his prisoner into silence, if not courtesy.

Asherah stepped between them. "You shall wait until he is healed to beat him," she said.

"Just let him try it," Kemal chuckled.

Astonishingly, Leo laughed too.

She could smell the sweat, the blood, and the fear on him. He had been much afraid, for friends as well as for himself. They wavered on the edge of war, she knew that. But, here in her own house, standing so close to him that his shoulder braced her as it had before the Jews in Cotyaeum drew lots to see who must blind an emperor, Asherah had never felt more secure.

Had the *gulam* saved Leo's life? Then he would never want for anything, she decided. She would tell her father. She felt her stomach chill with fear, now that the moment was upon them. She had never, in her life, failed to win what she would from her father: not until now, when her whole life hung in the balance.

"The lad, Ioannes, is it? Son of Ioannes?" Joachim gestured off in the direction of the dead man's land. "He lost his father, but lasted out the fight. I turned him over to the women to mother. As long as he's well, he can be ashamed of himself in the morning for wanting to be a boy again."

"The other boy, Theodoulos, is with his master. The priest came for them. The holy father collapsed—"

"After that long ride and a battle?" Joachim interrupted. "I should think so. Leo, why did you roust him out of the valley? The ride from Peristrema must have been hell on a man that old. I don't think he's stirred from that cave of his since he came here from Egypt."

"The word was that they needed him in the town. Needed his wisdom." Leo's voice lingered on the word and his eyes narrowed. "And you and he are friends. You *talk*. I thought you might know what ailed him. And how to help."

Asherah caught her breath. The night that assassins had stalked him, Leo had seen her and her father wreathed in lights, invoking the archangels to preserve him. They had been immune, even, from the fear of the wolf-thing that Nordbriht had become. Asherah watched her father. Part of what made him such a successful merchant was that he could communicate without speaking. *Why did you come here?* he asked Leo with a glance.

Leo looked down, gesturing at Kemal. *Where else could I have brought him?*

Joachim nodded. Part of what made her love him was that he not only listened, he understood.

"The Turk will not want to be tended by women or those he considers infidels," Joachim told Leo. "Bring him into the anteroom."

"A little further," Leo urged his captive and heaved the man's arm over his shoulders.

Asherah following, Joachim ushered them out of the crowded room into the anteroom he used to show valued guests or customers treasures from the East. Rash enough that his daughter and his guest betrayed themselves before a room full of soldiers, prisoners, and servants. That answered one question that he had. Now, in a place of his own choosing, as safe as he could find, he would ask those other questions that were his duty and his right. Please God, let him understand the answers she and Leo would give.

Joachim busied himself, washing his hands in the basin a servant held, untying the battlefield dressings. Asherah bent to assist, hiding her face, listening with all her heart.

"I take it, Leo, that the holy Meletios did not collapse from merely too much riding," Joachim remarked in Greek too rapid for the Turk to follow. "Did he?"

Leo shook his head. "We needed his help. Turks were coming, too many to fight, too fast to outrun. I had to insist that, if he knew anything to do, this was the time to do it. He was afraid, sir, said there were consequences I had no idea of. But I didn't think they would mean his death. After all, you . . ."

You did not falter when you saved my life.

Joachim had to hear that as clearly as his daughter.

"I had help, Leo, though you will never hear me admit that again. There are better physicians than I, but I know better even than to try to suggest summoning one of them. So it must be me.

"Now, do you suggest that I go through the streets where, I hear, they are practically rioting out of sheer panic, knock on the priest's door, and offer myself—dressed as I am, known as I am—as physician to a living saint? What if my old friend dies? And what right do I have to leave my daughter unprotected?"

"Nordbriht owes you more than his life," Leo said. "He will guard you as though you were an Emperor. And, sir, you must know I would lay down my life for Asherah."

Asherah set down the bowl and rose, folding her hands. The moment for her and Leo to tell all the truth had come. Kemal looked at her. His eyes were half shut, but she thought he winked at her. Leo would not need to beat him, Asherah decided. She would do it herself.

I do not want Leo to die, but live! Asherah's eyes filled. Blindly, she reached out and felt her hand taken in a firm grip—her father's.

"Child, this is hardly the match I planned for you," Joachim said. "I had hoped . . ."

"I know what you planned. That I would be son and daughter to you both. I succeeded, and you saw what awaited me—wealth, solitude, and whispers about Joachim's daughter, witch even to my name. You tried. I even tried until I was ashamed. They didn't want me!"

Joachim shook his head, his own eyes, the canny eyes of a merchant prince and scholar, filling. He had not wept the last time they had had to flee. So he had seen what she had tried to conceal from him. He had seen and sorrowed for her, preparing her as best he could, teaching her to try not to mind that the powers that made her strong had made her a stranger to her own people.

"Leo's family cast him out, too," Asherah went on. "So here we are, washed up on the same shore."

Her father flung up his free hand. "I had so hoped that . . ."

Asherah raised his hand to her cheek. "I am the woman you raised me to be. I will grieve if I have caused you pain. I will mourn if you cast me out—"

"Asherah, daughter, how can you even think of that?"

She laughed, though it tore at her heart. "You always raised me to consider every possibility."

"Check your reasoning! For me to disown you—that is not even an improbable possible!" Joachim interrupted. God bless her father. Even on the verge of war and of seeing his only surviving child join hands with an unbeliever, he stubbornly invoked Aristotle. The absurdity made them both smile, easing the moment.

"I am sorry now to hurt you," Asherah kept her tone soft. "But I tell you now, I will not give him up."

"They rejected me," Leo put in. "You—from the moment that I saw the two of you in Cotyaeum, you behaved with such strength and dignity. I tried to seek you out in the City. They told me to go away. And when I came here and found you, which was luck I never dreamed of having, you treated me with more honor than my own family."

Leo flushed, but drew himself upright. He let Asherah's hand fall. "Sir, one thing more. You treated me as a son in your house. I would not have you think I betrayed your trust."

Asherah's cheeks went crimson, and her mouth dry. To think he made that confession before a Turk!

What made it worse was the entire truth: if Leo had not betrayed Joachim's trust, it was not for lack of opportunity. Or desire.

Joachim nodded solemn acknowledgment to Leo. Then he sighed. "I had thought that you might stay with me in my old age, Asherah." *Let all of them live to see it, that was all she asked.*

"We both will," Leo said. "If you consent. And if not, I promise Asherah will always be safe and cherished."

Joachim pulled the hand he held forward and took Leo's with the other. Sighing, he joined them. It was not the ritual of go-betweens and contracts, of family rejoicings. There would have been a contract. There would have been gifts. For the daughter of a merchant prince, those gifts would have been lavish if, say, she had joined with the son of another wealthy family, rather than a Christian outcast from an imperial family. And, when and if the time came when such things were possible, Joachim would not even be able to give his child the wedding that, no doubt, he had promised her mother he would provide. God only knew who could be found willing to wed them.

After all, canon law forbade marriage between Christian and Jew. Forbade it very loudly and very strictly. Which told you just how often it was disobeyed.

I do not care, Asherah thought, and knew it for the truth. She let her father see her face so he would know it too.

The tightness around his mouth eased somewhat. Joachim almost smiled.

"Be as a son in this house," he told Leo. Asherah suppressed a sigh of sheer relief. *"Be* my son."

Leo knelt. How strange, to see him kneel that way to her father: it must be a Christian thing. They were so very different. It would be a hard road to travel. Well, she had traveled harder ones.

And this way led to life.

Joachim pulled his hand free of Asherah's and laid it on Leo's head, blessing him. "Get up, get up," Joachim told him. "We have work to do."

So, it had happened. In the midst of war, she gave herself away to a stranger who drew her as no one ever had. It was not what she had hoped for. It was more than she had ever hoped to have, and more than anyone had ever thought she would have.

Leo rose. For the first time since Asherah had seen him, he looked young and glad. The gladness faded on the instant as the welter of tasks and cares he faced came flooding back; but she had seen the joy in his face, akin to hers, and that too was more than she had ever dreamed anyone would feel for her.

"Are you content now?" her father asked her.

"Thank you, father," she whispered. "Thank you." She bent to kiss his hand (he tugged it away, mortified), and that too was a gesture new to her. It was over. Whatever curse had dogged her, it was gone, and she had won. She had won even if they died in the next minute. But let them live.

"Don't be abject, child. You should not have doubted me. That is not how I raised you. Your promised husband will have a surprise coming, if he expects a puppet, not a wife."

Leo's surprised laughter made the room ring.

"You take a first wife, lion's cub?" asked Kemal with a sly smile, finally daring to speak.

"Not just a wife," Leo said. "A queen."

"Ah," said Kemal, "I wish you many strong sons." His bloodshot eyes evaluated her as if she were one of the sturdy Turkish ponies, and he nodded approvingly.

Joachim nodded. He parted the curtains of the anteroom, then pushed past them, a little blindly. They had loosed their handclasp as the curtains parted, but the servants turned to stare at them. One or two of the injured men managed to smile at their commander and their benefactors.

Tzipporah, ripping cloth for bandages, looked up. She always could read her Asherah's face and eyes like a child's first letters. Her face glowed like sunrise. This was like a ballad to her; it was beyond any of her dreams. She sobbed once, and Asherah braced herself for the inevitable smothering embrace; but Tzipporah knew her duty. She finished her bandages, and now she bent to wind them about a bloody arm.

Kemal, half-forgotten, stumped after his captor. Tzipporah, finished with one patient, bore down on him with threats in her eyes of what would happen to him if he did not instantly rest. The strain in Joachim's face lifted somewhat.

"Your people do not drink wine," Joachim told the *gulam*, "do they? You are a guest in my house, you and these others, and I would not insult you or your ways."

Her father's eyes met hers, amused. Dietary laws, too, were forbidden: theirs, most assuredly; and those of Islam, assuming the Christians knew of their existence. With, of course and always, the exception of her Leo. *You are becoming maudlin, Asherah*, she told herself in imitation of her father's earlier reproof.

"Sometimes we forget. But I would drink to my friend—and, of course, to ease the pain."

"See our guests have wine and food, will you?" Joachim asked Leo. "My steward will take your orders while my daughter tends the people you have brought her. My child, I think our life from now will be . . . extremely interesting."

Joachim clapped his hands for the steward, then turned to leave.

"Where are you going?" Asherah managed to ask.

"It has occurred to me that the last time we were accused of passing by upon the other side, the Samaritans got all the glory, and we got all the blame. Rather than risk that again, I shall go tend my friend Meletios. You and your . . . Leo may stand as my guides, you know. Times like this force us all to become braver than we have been. Perhaps I can even partly redeem the ill that our kinsman Menachem wreaked upon my new son's"—yes, decidedly, he savored the word— "Emperor."

30

A t least, the townspeople had agreed to meet not in the church, but in one of the largest of the storehouses behind the market. Those farmers and herders who heard the summons in time crowded in. Some, like the well-off widows who kept their half-grown sons close at their sides, were accustomed to the town. Others, like the herders, seemed to fear the crowd, though doubtless, they feared the Turks more.

Asherah, seated to one side on a bale of carpets, tugged discreetly at her veils. The meeting was not a victory, of course, though her presence was.

"You may attend," her father told her. "*If* you can be quiet." He had shrugged at Leo, who would just have to get used to the independence of a daughter whom he had raised as his heir. From what Leo had said of his own kinswomen, he would have little trouble. Asherah sighed. There were secrets about Leo, stories from his childhood, that only his mother could tell her, but they would probably never meet.

Back to reality, she cautioned herself.

In a crowd this mixed, the mood could turn ugly in the twinkling of an eye. The Christian house of prayer was hardly a place where armed men, bloodied men, angry men could meet and shout. So their priest would forbid assembling there. At least, that prohibition removed one danger—if a slight one—from her and her father. They could be present, yet need not fear some hothead deciding to take offense at the presence of Jews in his holy place. Privately, Asherah did not think that God would be so inhospitable—anybody's God, including the one she worshipped—as to begrudge them room. But the market was a space common to all.

It was not an opinion she voiced, and it was not one asked of her. For that matter, her presence had not been requested and probably was not wanted. She was here, she realized, as nurse and prop to her father: as much a servant to the men who reeked of fear, anger, and excitement, as the black-robed women, exiled from their shrine, were servants of the sere old holy man—and as little.

Not even the priest had frowned when Joachim remained by his old friend's side, quick to sense his need for quiet or for a restorative Joachim kept to hand. "Brought from Egypt," he had explained. Everyone knew the fame of Egyptian surgeons and drugs. They even knew that the Emperor himself kept a Jew as a physician.

They knew her from her work in the underground villages as a generous lady and a willing worker, if a stranger and a Jew; but they knew nothing of her other skills. Somewhat against her father's will and Leo's, here she was, an attendant to Kemal, who was such a man as she might have been shielded from on the caravan routes from Baghdad. He had to be here, a trophy and, perhaps, a source of information; and he had winked at her again and hinted that his well-being relied upon her skill.

Shadows clustered at the back and by the walls—the black-robed women. They whispered among themselves, one or two smiling behind veils as Theodoulos limped past, his head up, side by side with young Ioannes.

In the center of the room, with the priests, the headmen, surviving local nobles who were not now out raising troops, and Father Meletios, lying on a pallet, stood Leo.

He was another reason that she sat here so securely in the presence of former and—who knew?—perhaps future enemies. She could not take her eyes off him. Just this once, thank God for veils. He caught sight of her and smiled, ever so slightly.

Leo had snatched a few minutes to bathe and dress himself in the clothing of a man of the great city. He looked like what he had been born to be: Ducas, knowledgeable in the Empire's ways, poised near its apex, and as confident as if he expected reinforcements to march in down the road.

Nordbriht, reclaimed from her father, stood behind him. He had rebraided his hair, and he too had changed, into a crimson tunic—so *that* was where the rest of the red brocade had gone! Asherah thought with an inward crow of glee. Although he lacked his axe, he and the message he conveyed were unmistakable: he was a Varangian who guarded a prince. He glared across the room at the only men who had been permitted to enter it armed. They watched Kemal, Leo's captive and, in a strange way, his friend. How strange that Kemal had insisted on being present. He had, he said, somewhat to tell the Greeks.

Ioannes, in clean, dark garments, stood nearby, forcing himself into the manhood that war had thrust upon him. His father would be proud. Asherah murmured a few words under her breath. The man was dead; he could not object to her prayers, and his son needed all the help prayer could afford him.

"What news from the City?" One of the Christian merchants from

Hagios Prokopios was first to shout. "Will they send us troops to protect us?"

"Who's he?" Asherah heard the whispers start. "Ducas. A young one. Served with our Emperor before . . . you know. He brought us the good father to speak to us. Let him speak!"

Leo stepped forward, drawing the attention of the room about him like a garment an actor might wear. "I think," he said, "we should ask Father Demetrios to conduct this meeting. And allow others to speak who have lived among you longer."

He gestured, ever so slightly, at Father Meletios where he lay. Joachim nodded at him: Good. So the old man was strong enough to speak.

The town's priest, his black robes brushed, glowed visibly. "Perhaps the holy man would bless us, then speak to us."

Beneath her veils, Asherah bit her lip. Moments like these meant risk for her. She knew what to do: Hunch down, bow your head, do not draw attention to yourself.

Leo knelt by the old man's side, helping to support him. Now that was a relief, and clever of Leo: at least, her father would not be seen propping up a Christian priest. Despite Asherah's apprehensions, she was struck by the cultivation of the hermit's Greek and the sere beauty of his voice. She had seen glass plucked from the desert—thin, graceful shapes glazed by sun and sand until they shimmered with rainbows. Out of the waste, a treasure.

Joachim respected him. Leo revered him. Even the black-robed former nuns, angry as they still were after all these years at their exile from the valley, bowed their heads. One wept at the sight of him, so wasted and laid low.

Sighs gusted across the room, then subsided. Asherah tested the quality of the silence: tension, not contemplation.

"Are the armies coming?" This time, it was a noble who threw that demand at Leo.

He rose. "This is why *my* Emperor fought in the East and why your sons went with him. I do not speak of my kin. I left them to come here."

"So we're cut off?"

"No!"

"Have you sent a messenger to ask?" One of the women asked that.

Speak quickly, Leo, Asherah thought, or these people will get out of hand. Already, some of the younger men had stiffened their backs, were drifting oh-so-casually toward the corner where Leo's most trusted soldiers guarded the *gulam*.

"They won't come," Leo said. "This emperor wields a pen better than a sword. His clerks control him. . . ."

This Emperor Michael was a coward and a fool, Asherah had long since decided. Leo had said very little of him, but she had pieced it together with accounts brought from Constantinople by other merchants. A coward and a fool, dominated by unscrupulous kinsmen and by the scholar who had all but driven Leo into madness and suicide. No wonder he sounded as if he were being strangled.

"They would not come in time, my daughter," Meletios' voice cut in as shrewdly as if he had not spent decades praying in the wilderness.

"We are blessed here. We have each other. And we have our friends. I have seen what I have seen—and what I see is a storm so great that the tree that attempts to stand tall against it will only break. And here is my counsel to you: we do not fight—yes, I know, but where is your humility? We lower our heads. We let the storm wash over us. And we wait for it to pass. Time is on our side."

"You saw fighting in Egypt!" Young Ioannes shouted. "How can you tell us not to fight? The whole Empire will fall!"

"My son, it has already cut you off. I am a shepherd, not a prince. And I say, if my flocks are safe, I have not failed, no matter . . ."

Meletios bent over, coughing. Joachim pressed forward, holding out his restoratives, but the old man waved him away.

We agree on one thing at least, her father had told Asherah after he returned from a visit to the valley. *We both see the day when this Empire will fall. Odd, for a Christian. Must be his time in the desert, that graveyard for empires.*

He seeks to save a remnant, Asherah realized. To save *us*. All of us. And Leo is his agent.

Still, the room was filled with young men, angry men; and the counsel of submission was never attractive to such as they.

"Esteemed and learned sir," came a voice huskier than the priest's, but equally cultivated, "it takes great courage to retreat, sometimes more than to engage in battle. Is there, perhaps, another reason why you enjoin this on your people?"

Had her father gone mad that he spoke up in this group? Asherah pressed her hand to her heart and calculated how many steps it would take her to fight through to his side.

Meletios smiled. "I would remind my friend Reb Joachim—oh yes, we have disputed many times, that this is a very ancient land, known to both our peoples. I do not think open war is the will of God. We saw our Emperor fall—or you did, and this young man at your side. If we persevere in this course, well, as I said, this land is old. It shudders underfoot. Who knows if it would not crack asunder and swallow up evildoers, as it did when the Israelites fled from Egypt. . . ."

"God has sent the Turks to scourge us for our sins!" A young monk—and Father Demetrios laid an arm about his shoulder, comforting him, calming him, and forcing him back onto a convenient bench.

"Perhaps the old man is right. Perhaps we should repent and not fight," said one woman wearing the black that the nuns exiled from the valley had clung to for all these years.

If it came to that, she would have made a formidable enemy. Asherah had seen her in the fields once, wielding a scythe. The memory made her shiver.

Now, the tall old nun rose and made her way toward Father Meletios, her bony figure casting a long shadow over him. He lay looking up at her, prepared to endure whatever she might say or do.

She knelt and bowed her head. "Give me your blessing, Father," she said. "Here at the end of all things."

Meletios laid a hand upon her head. "At last. My daughter, blessed are the peacemakers. It eases my heart to reconcile with you."

She looked at him. "But now what?"

"You can't fight us." Kemal's wretched Greek rose over the quarrelling voices of his guards. "Even after my sultan died, they keep coming. Alp Arslan was a prince and a warrior, but these men are *hungry!* What was that in your Book about a plague of locusts? That is what we are, thousands and ten thousands of us, tribe upon tribe. Locusts with bows and swords. For the sake of my friend here, I hope you will all flee or accept us. I would not see you resist and die."

Leo grimaced in pure frustration as the room rang with curses and howls of outrage. Kemal's tact, clearly, was as lacking as his luck. *He's not taunting you!* Asherah wanted to shout. Instead, she clenched her hands. It was terrible to see, terrible to know, and terrible to realize that if you spoke out you'd only make things worse—and she didn't know if she were thinking of Kemal, or of herself. Asherah watched Nordbriht push through to the back of the room and stand with the Turk's guards. He turned and gestured at Leo: *you had best say something fast.*

"People," Leo shouted. "People, listen to me! This man saved my life when he might have killed me, long ago. He rode with men not his kin or they would have killed him. He does not taunt you. You heard him yourself. He would not see you die."

The crowd exploded into shouts and quarrels. If they didn't die of

their own accord, blood might flow. Leo and the priests had agreed: disarm the men at the door. Asherah was not fool enough to believe that
they had gotten all the weapons. Even if, unfortunately, they *had* collected Nordbriht's axe.

"And who are you? Ducas! Princeling from the city that throws us
away. . . ."

"He came here, turned his back on them . . . he was to be a
monk. . . ."

"Some fine monk, visiting the Jews' house!"

"Look at him, city man with that great monster in the red tunic always stalking alone behind him. Needs only his axe—I tell you, he's
going to use us for an army to go back and become Emperor himself;
and then what? Throw us away again?"

"Say, he's a good one. He fought for us. Brought us the hermit. If
he says he turned his back on his fine folk, I believe him."

"You really think he's going to make a run for the Empire, if what
you say is true about the girl?"

"Shut that down. How'd you like someone speaking that way of *your*
daughter? And she's sitting right there, quiet as you please. . . ."

Asherah was too old, had seen too much to blush this way. She nodded, practically a bow of gratitude at how the merchant had intervened.

"What's it to *them?* Any time they want, they can get out of
here. . . ."

"Look, the old man, the chief Jew, you know which one, wants to
speak again. You'd think he would keep his mouth shut in this town
when it's not a matter of trade, wouldn't you?"

"They're crazy. Why else would they deny Christ? But they're not
cowards. Come on, brothers, let the man speak!"

"Good people, let me speak." To Asherah's utter horror, Joachim
rose again. She twisted fingers in the folds of her robes to conceal how
they trembled. The somber luxury of her father's clothing fell about
him, giving him a quiet dignity equal to that of the priests. Too often
and too long in this Empire, they had to conceal themselves. Let the
Christians see.

"I need not tell you I am a stranger in a strange land, a guest in your
country," he spoke quietly, without rhetorical tricks or a hint of foreign accent. "I know the risk that I take in setting my word against that
of a holy man, though he has allowed me to call him 'friend' for many
years. But listen to me!

"One thing we Jews know . . ."

"Is how to turn dung to gold!"

"Or anything else!"

At least the laughter that followed those interruptions was good-natured, for now.

Joachim shook his head. "It's true that God has blessed my hard work with success, which some of you have shared. Now, I have not survived to this . . . somewhat surprising age of mine without knowing *how* to survive and how to face facts. Here are the facts I would lay before you: we are far from the Empire's great capital, and the roads—I do not think we can rely on them for messages or help. Empires rise, and Empires fall. And right now, I fear we are on our own to thrive or perish as our wits and strength serve us."

"So, do you run, old Jew? Is that your way? Grow rich here, and, as soon as you see danger, run away?"

Asherah clenched her hands in her lap, thankful for veils that concealed what she knew to be a dagger-glance. These fools, these fools saw courage only in the sword. What did they know of the courage that made you run and live when lying down to die would hurt less? What did they know of the pride that forced you to rebuild, when you might have wallowed with *pigs,* of all unclean things, in their sties? They spoke of an ancient past: compared with hers, what was their Empire but the twinkling of an eye?

"Here I am, and here I stay!" Joachim shouted back, taunted beyond his facade of humility. "I tried to send my daughter away. She is the only hope of my house. Do you think I do not want her safe? But she will not go."

The people turned toward her. She relaxed her hands and raised her head, trying to look fearless, like a great lady in whose presence people should not jeer, rather than a disobedient child. Leo caught her eye and gestured reassurance at her. The yells died down to mutters, then subsided.

"She insisted on coming here tonight, too," Joachim forced a rueful smile, as if he had been overruled by a much-loved child. "But, if any of you have children of less spirit, I will gladly find places for them in my caravans—those that the Turks let through. You choose."

"You say we're cut off, then?" demanded one of the merchants.

"We don't leave our land. Ten generations on it and buried in it . . ." a farmer shouted. "Too bad if I'm the eleventh, but that's how it is."

"Then, what do you intend?" Joachim cut in as smoothly as Asherah had ever seen him press a point. "If you will learn from me and my people's history: we have seen enemies come and enemies go. Pharaoh, Antiochus, Herod: they came, they conquered, they faded into time; and we remained. That Turk can tell you. His kin respect people of the Book."

"They respect courage too!"

Underfoot, the ground rumbled. Joachim swayed somewhat.

"Yes, they respect courage. There are many kinds of courage. Which will you choose?"

"My children . . ." Meletios' voice was very faint. Leo made frantic gestures for quiet. "Thank you, son. I shall be better as soon as I can rest. My friend Joachim and I, though we differ on points, as we have ever done, agree upon one thing. We cannot muster an army. We have no army to muster. He gives you the example of his own survival. I offer you the shield of faith.

"Just like the valley I have been chosen to guard, this place has become a place of refuge, not just for men and women, but for what they believe. Thus it has been for untold years filled with prayer. Now—and this is a great mystery that I would not reveal to you if we did not stand beneath the shadow of death—in all those thousands of years, do you truly think that all the men and women who have lived here have vanished without a trace? Or that their beliefs have passed into silence? How can we say that when, every day, we live amid the relics of their errors—and when we have men and women who still cling to old ways among us?"

I hope he knows what he is doing, Asherah thought. *And that it's not "kill the Jews" again. The line of reasoning Meletios pursued could lead either to tolerance or death.*

"I am proud to call Reb Joachim friend. Some of these others, though, who died before we were born would never have been friend to me or anyone else here. I believe their spirits yet remain, inquiet among us, their spirits and those of their false gods. Like the plotters on Constantinople, they linger in the shadows, wishing to rise, yet unable to seize power for themselves—

"Until such a time as now! If we fight a war, I tell you, I fear that war is likely to make this land erupt in fire or sink in earthquakes or back into the sea from which it rose. It is for us to exorcise the land itself, to heal it. And we cannot do that if we fight!"

Asherah met Joachim's eyes, and he shook his head. The man was old and sick, dying perhaps. And all these years, she had stubbornly refused to meet him. It was time to change this as so much else had changed. She rose to her feet, her silks flowing about her with a splendor that other women noticed and sighed at, and made her way to her father.

"This crowd is too much for him," her father told Leo. "But if I say 'take him outside,' they will swear that the 'old Jew' means to smuggle him out of the way, then kill him."

"I can arrange that," said Father Demetrios.

He gestured, not daring, despite his priesthood, to clap his hands. No young men with strong backs—and hard heads—came promptly up; they were all shouting. Instead, the tallest of the former nuns approached.

"The holy father is ill and would rest."

Sister Xenia nodded. The former nun beckoned to her sisters. "If you permit, we will bear you hence," she offered. She paused, as if waiting for a protest, either from Meletios or from the other nuns. Here, at what seemed like the end of their world, it was forgiveness of a sort.

The old man sighed, submitting to a return of good for exile. "It is as it must be."

Their active lives had kept the nuns strong, despite their age. As one, they stooped and lifted the pallet on which the hermit lay, and left the room, marching as if in some procession.

Sister Xenia swept her eyes across the room. They fell upon Asherah and paused. The tall old woman strode toward her, seized her by the wrist, and pulled her along until she stood before the ancient priest.

"Do you think we don't know why you have not shown proper respect to your father's friend and a holy man?" asked Xenia. "We are going to forgive him now. So are you."

Asherah suppressed a laugh that might have caused a riot. If Father Meletios wanted the Jewish woman to accompany him, then she would—whether she chose or not.

She lifted her veil and sank down. She did not kneel, she told herself, before a holy man, but in order that she could meet the eyes of her father's friend.

No, that was wrong, too: Meletios was blind, wasn't he? She could not think of him as a blind man. His eyes lifted, then, and she saw that they were dark, quite burned out by the sun or some other affliction. The thing that made her trust her dreams resonated within her, and she knew he saw her with eyes other than those of the body.

"So you are my old friend's daughter? And have you forgiven me for taking your father from you at times, and for barring women from my valley?"

"If the sisters can put anger aside, it is surely foolish in me to hold such anger now."

"I would bless you," Meletios said, "but you are your father's daughter, stiff-necked as he—and all your ancient kind. But there is one gift I would give you. Will you will take it?" His voice trailed up, and he raised his hand. Asherah caught her breath at how the thin brown fingers trembled as they groped for Leo's hand.

"Come here, my son, just for a moment, while they shout at one another. Here," Meletios whispered. He held Leo's hand and reached out for hers, just as her father had done.

Father Demetrios' face, though he dared say nothing, went blacker than his robes. The nuns sank to their knees and whispered. "I knew from the moment she came here that she was the one chosen," Xenia whispered. "Praise . . ." her voice trailed off into prayer.

Asherah placed her hand in the old man's callused, dry one.

He joined the hands he held and lowered his head, murmuring prayers Asherah had never expected to hear, least of all for her.

Leo's eyes sought hers, shy, after what had passed between them. He flushed deeply: well enough, she too found herself hot with blushes. He bowed his head and murmured as the old man instructed him.

"Canon law forbids . . ." Joachim commented.

"Still clinging to the letter of the law, are you? For once, let a Christian get the better of you, old friend. In this case, I think we had best obey its spirit," said the old man. "I have done what I can. You will no doubt insist that your own holy men can do it better."

He turned to Asherah. "Now, daughter, you repeat . . ."

Tears sprang to her eyes. This was not what she had been led to expect; she had been led to expect nothing. But Leo's hand held hers, and she found breath and voice to whisper her unexpected vows.

Leo reached for the veils wreathing Asherah's hair as if they were a marriage crown. The assault of sweat and sheep and spices and fear upon her nostrils gave way to memories of incense and cinnamon and of thrumming in her blood. She swayed toward Leo, who reached out to embrace her.

"Later," said Father Demetrios. "Let them know outside, and you will have a riot instead of a wedding feast." There would be no time for such a feast, but he looked as sour as if the food lay spoiled upon his table. He was being sensible, Asherah knew: Meletios' impulse was likely to strike a lot of people here as a violation. Leo pressed her hand.

"Lift me up," Meletios pleaded with Leo. "Help me!" He looked at Joachim.

"He is exhausted; he should rest. I could tend him." Pity made her blurt it out.

"On your wedding night, my daughter? Ah, I shall be resting sooner than you. I beg you, just let me speak, and I am done."

"He's probably never begged in his life," Joachim told Leo. "Better do as he says."

Leo gestured to the nuns. *Will you carry him back outside?* He released Asherah's hand.

The buzzing in the outer room swelled into a roar as they entered. Leo entered the room and shouted for quiet.

Meletios raised himself on one elbow. Asherah sensed the prickling of energy, summoned and waiting for use, waiting for a sick old man to draw it from the earth, up along his spine, and let it manifest to the nuns and the town priest. A light gleamed about his face, and they gasped.

He was consuming himself, and he knew it as well as she.

"One thing more," the hermit said. "I am leaving you now. Tell the others. This too I leave with you to tell them, whatever you decide are the fit tasks of younger men, yes, and women too. I commend you all to God's mercy. My task now is simple: guard the way and pray for all your souls. I have never ceased to pray. As soon as I can, I shall take up the role of guardian again."

Meletios sagged back. This time he did not refuse restoratives. "Now, take me from this place," he said. "I want to go home."

Joachim nodded. This sounded too much like a conspiracy for Asherah's liking: get her out of there; it was no place for a woman; we want you safe. At the same time, Meletios had just joined her hand and Leo's. She could remember the pressure of his fingers and the warmth of Meletios's hand, protecting both of them. This might be all the marriage she was going to have, and she hardly felt like spoiling it with a quarrel. But she would have to be, she saw, very, very watchful lest her father and—would the Christians really consider them wed?—her husband Leo ally against her to keep her safe and ignorant.

Just let them try.

Once again, the nuns picked up Meletios' litter. Hardly a bridal procession, was it? Her eyes met Leo's. What she saw in them robbed her of breath and made her kindle again as if they stood in the deepest city-caves and the seductions of incense, music, and ancient memories ringed them about.

Leo's eyes darkened as they had in the underground ways when he had spoken her name in a voice that made her shake; and his breath came faster.

Asherah replaced her veil, but not before she let her father and her new husband see her ironic smile. For now, she would obey, because it suited her. Later on, it would suit her to extract from them every detail of every decision that was made. She stopped on a sudden revelation.

Leo would be returning home with her. "On your wedding night?" Father Meletios had teased her gently. Beneath her veil, she raised her fingers to her lips. They were trembling as if Leo had already kissed them to breathlessness.

31

A yowl, a scrabbling of claws on stone . . . instantly, Leo awoke, sweating in fear. He forced himself to lie motionless, eyes closed, even as he eased his hand toward the weapon he kept hidden beneath a tumble of pillows.

There. The touch of the deadly metal strengthened him. Leo tensed, waiting.

Another yowl. Something struck a wall, followed by an oath, as if someone had thrown a rock at one of the strays that prowled throughout town—and missed.

Leo loosed his grip on the hilt of his sword and lay back, sighing with relief. The silk under which he had hidden the sword comforted his sweaty hand. The room in which he lay was fragrant and hung with heavy fabrics that glowed in the faint light of the tiny alabaster lamp glowing on a low table. Thank God, no danger this time. He raised his hand to bless himself and hesitated. Not here. There were no icons in this room and never would be.

At least, the noise and his sudden alarm had not waked his wife of but a few weeks. The idea of Asherah in danger, Asherah needing protection, Asherah with only him and his pillow-sword to rely on made his heart pound in a very different way from other kinds of thoughts about her. At least, she had not seen him glance about instinctively for an icon.

In sleep, Asherah's face was as serene as the statue of the goddess he had caressed in another, lonelier existence. The light glowed on her shoulder where tangled skeins of dark hair and the bedcoverings parted to reveal it. She had been brought up to modesty, but, since their marriage, she slept clad only in her hair because he loved waking beside the silken warmth of her skin. It was a pleasure he had not known before.

Now she opened her eyes. "How bad was the dream this time, love?" she asked softly.

He had been so relieved when the buzzing on his brain from the blow he had taken at Manzikert had ceased, when he could sleep again, when no horrors had waked him. When, shortly after their marriage, his dreams had turned . . . lively again, or the need to rise and prowl about, as if guarding his new home, drew him out of bed, his old fears of madness returned to humiliate him before his wife. "You're better off without me," he had told Asherah. She had welcomed him with all her heart, shared herself and her family's treasures with him; and he was only a burden.

"Don't be foolish," she retorted. It was the closest she ever came to snapping at him. And then she had drawn him into her arms and showed him another reason for wanting to go on living.

If Leo hadn't enough to do helping to fit into his new home and protect it, he really thought he could make a career out of being wrong and learning better. Asherah knew—she *would* know—what it was like to wake screaming from a dream. She believed that lives might depend on understanding what his dreams prophesied, and she was skilled in reading them. She knew, too, that dreams could mean the growth of further, and unwanted, powers. After that first nightmare, when all Leo could do was shiver with reaction and shame in her arms, he confessed his fears of madness to her. He had even told her about the hag, the earthquake, the storm. Then, the miracle had occurred: she had not thought he was insane.

Asherah stirred. Leo shut his eyes. She had worked long and hard that day. Perhaps he could convince her he was sleeping before she came fully awake. He should have known better than that.

"Leo," her voice coaxed him, drawing out his name. She stretched out slim, bare arms, drawing him to rest against her breast.

"I'm sorry I woke you. But this time, it wasn't a dream," he admitted. "I think one of the guards threw a rock at a cat. Or some other beast."

Asherah's body shifted in his hold as she turned toward the covered window. Moonlight filtered in through the silks.

"We had best hope it was only a cat. The moon is still full."

Leo shuddered. With the full moon came Nordbriht's change from man into beast. This time, he knew, the former Varangian had taken himself off. Scouting, he told people. Leo and Asherah knew better. When Nordbriht ran on four legs, he hunted.

"Beasts kill no more than they need," Asherah reminded him.

"Natural creatures." What if, instead of raiding some poor man's flocks, Nordbriht stalked the man himself, or malignant instinct drove him to attack a war band of Turks?

Asherah sighed. They would have to pray that Nordbriht returned when the moon waned. "Did you sense him?" she asked.

Leo shook his head, his lips brushing her skin, turning touch into kiss.

"Did you?"

"I dreamed of the moon. Pagan dreams I should not have had, you would say. Still, I first had them when we first loved each other."

"Then you have had these dreams for years," Leo said. His arms tightened around her as he remembered.

The night of their marriage, he had been escorted to her rooms—their rooms now—by men who left him there, hardly knowing whether to congratulate a groom or regret that their master's daughter married a Christian. He had found the woman made so suddenly his wife waiting for him. He assumed she had been put to bed earlier by her women, but she had risen from the flower-strewn bed and stood alone, wrapped in a gleaming robe. Her hair had flowed bewitchingly over shoulders whose bare smoothness he remembered kissing, and her eyes were huge.

She was as much out of her depth as he, he realized. More so, being virgin. But she had looked up at him, finding the courage somewhere to trust him again. As he had in the underground ways, he reached out and took her shoulders in his hands, leaned forward, and brushed her mouth with his own.

"Now," he said, his voice breaking, "we finish what we began. . . ." Her lips opened, and she pressed against him. It had been three weeks since their wedding night, which had transfigured his life.

Now, Asherah, who seemed to know his thoughts even better than she knew his body, ruffled his hair. "Since we first . . . since our wedding night. I dreamt shining women smiled at me and welcomed me. We could guess what that means, yes, love?"

Leo sighed and relaxed against her. *Oh yes.*

Her breast was soft, fragrant with attar of roses or some other, female scent he was sure belonged to Asherah alone. She was so small, but her body was surprisingly lush, and her response to his touch . . . Leo smiled to himself. So self-controlled a woman, and yet, in his arms, so quick to abandon herself and her habitual modesty.

That first night, how she had flushed and looked away as he pushed back from her shoulders the silk robe that was all her women had allowed her to wear while awaiting him. She had shivered when he looked frankly at her, but when he touched her—just as she had in the caves below, she had blossomed into desire and welcome.

Between husband and wife, her people taught, this was no sin, but a joy. Heterodox in many of her people's ways, Asherah professed orthodoxy in this. If all the faith of the Jews were thus, he would be their most ardent convert and wonder why there weren't more.

He really had stumbled into one of the ballads in which the Ducas lord married a princess of another people: a blend of romance, terror, and outrageous luxury. ("We put out a robe for you," Asherah had whispered on their wedding night. It had lain on the bed, a brocaded thing of Persian splendor, almost purple. "They told me, 'don't let him wear it long.' ")

In the morning, Leo would shut the door on this secret, perfumed refuge, leaving it for the waking world of watches, scouts, raids, and preparations for a war they all knew they dared not fight and could not win.

The men who had escorted Meletios back to his hermitage had returned, those few who survived. The exhausted old priest had protected them on the trip back to his home: returning to Hagios Prokopios, they had stopped to try to defend a village, scarcely more than a tumble of houses—a tumble now fire-blackened—against raiders. No soldiers could be spared to search for the missing villagers.

Leo hardly knew which was stranger, that his army knowledge, sufficient in his past life only to make him the butt of his uncle's humor and his catspaw at Manzikert, had proved so valuable here that an entire town relied upon him and the veterans here nodded respect at him when they passed, or that he had won a lady about whom songs might well had been written. Perhaps the ballad into which he had stumbled was the Song of Songs.

Behold, thou art fair, my love.

Strangest of all, he thought, was how quickly Asherah had become his wife, their hands joined by the old hermit; and how the core of his life had been changed so greatly that he sometimes forgot he should be afraid unto despair. He had despaired, he had been afraid for so long before he came to this blessed, deadly place which he must save if he hoped to save his wife.

There still seemed something almost illicit about their union, from the suddenness with which Meletios had joined their hands, to Father Demetrios' dismay, to the haste with which Joachim found and coerced one of the Jews' own priests . . . in a moment, Leo would remember what they were called. No doubt the man, who bore the look of one badly worsted in a bargain, would recover from whatever persuasions Joachim had inflicted. There was even something illicit about the joy he took in it, though he was prepared to admit that that was his stupidity.

Leo had expected strangeness in their wedding, but found it oddly simple. The strangeness came later, and would no doubt last for years, as he threaded his way through the customs of an older people race than his, one that had, against more cautious judgment, accepted him. He learned to rest in the peace of this household's Sabbath, during which these people prayed in the very tongues that Christ learned at his Mother's knee or in which he had preached at the Mount of Olives, bringing holiness almost close enough for him to touch. He grew able to accept Asherah's regular withdrawals into cleansing meditation. The other members of the household learned to glance aside if Leo bowed his head at the sound of bells or felt the need to visit the church in Hagios Prokopios.

The slight adjustments eased his way into the household. Its care, its loyalty, and its warmth washed over him and warmed him. Oh, his wife's people would have taken in any man Asherah married, but he thought the sly sideways smiles, the gifts—a fine knife, an ivory, a length of fur—pressed into his hands despite his protests, the insistence that he must eat, he must get his rest, were meant for Leo himself, not just the man Asherah had so inexplicably married. And some scar in Leo's heart that he had scarcely known was there healed when Joachim had welcomed him as a son.

"He probably is praying she's not with child already," Leo heard Tzipporah telling a friend with what Leo considered appalling relish. (Leo shut his eyes. That first night, he had slipped his wife's robe from her shoulders and run his hand over her flat belly. Asherah had clung to him until he picked her up and laid her on their bed, so soft, but not as soft as she, welcoming him. So slender she was, except for where her breasts and hips curved outward. A moment more, but if Asherah did not wake . . . he was on fire for her.)

"Maybe he's hoping that she *is*. The old man probably never thought he'd have a grandson," her friend had replied, equally gleeful.

He knew that Asherah's maid had always favored him. He was a soldier, a Ducas son, and therefore something out of a ballad, or out of her most farfetched dreams of a prince for the girl she had helped raise. He had rescued her nurseling from a barrenness that could only reproach her, no matter what else she had achieved. And, his adoration of Asherah, the way he struggled not to look at her or touch her until Tzipporah beamed and announced that she knew they would far, far rather be alone and bustled out made her beam with pride. She would be glad of a child to care for.

When she finally heard Tzipporah's frank comments, Asherah covered her face with her hands; when Leo pulled them away, he saw her cheeks were stained with tears of laughter.

Was that why Joachim had hastened the match? Hopes for a grandson, an heir to bulwark the family against the coming storm, part of his resolve that life must go on, and his family with it?

"You don't *mind?*" he breathed, appalled, to his wife and his father-in-law one evening when Asherah had made them both laugh by telling them women's gossip she had no doubt been meant to overhear.

Joachim shrugged. "My people can count the moons as well as anyone else. Otherwise, they would not have thrived as they do. In time, they will know their stories are untrue." Leo thought his father-in-law looked somewhat wistful.

"Ever since I was a child, people have gossiped about Joachim's witchy daughter," Asherah said. "This would be news to relish. They enjoyed considering us less than orthodox and point that out every time they can. Frankly, I think they like being shocked by us. By that logic, my dearest, you are simply more grist for their mills. Probably, they will think my father arranged our wedding to win some relief from taxes. Or for politics. With me married to a Christian . . ."

"They don't know how bad my position is in the City." Leo had written his parents about his marriage. Communications were bad now: he didn't know if he should expect a response from them or dread it.

Asherah smiled up at him, her shining eyes removing any possible doubt about why she was glad her wedding was quick, rather than elaborate.

From the first time Leo had entered their house, Joachim had treated him well. From anyone else, Leo would have said that he had been encouraged to think of himself as kin. Now that he had married into Joachim's household, Leo saw a side of the merchant, of all of them, that he had not imagined: zest, humor, color, and a ferocious love of life such as he had not imagined. It made his wish to die after Manzikert seem like a child's tantrum.

Why hadn't he known this before? The answer was simple. Before, they had restrained themselves before their Christian friend. Fond of him as they might be, but he had been an outsider. Now he was loved; now Leo knew what a rich life lay beneath the sober, even apologetic visages of the Jews he had seen.

What were the others like? What was life like, say, in the Jewish quarter of the City, or along the trade routes? Would they still send him away if he went to them in the Bazaar and introduced himself as Joachim's son-in-law?

God grant he lived long enough to learn.

He would gladly have spent all his waking hours finding out, best yet, with Asherah, whose touch as well as her voice continued to enthrall him. But she had duties of her own and, unfortunately for him, life was tense enough here that Leo dared not dally in Joachim's house, much less in the rooms he shared with his wife.

Home—where was Nordbriht? If he did not return within a couple of days, Leo would have to seek him out. Nordbriht had quarters somewhere in the house, too; and it was a noisier place now that he ran tame there, or as tame as Nordbriht could ever run. From the gleeful complaints of the gossip he overheard, Leo suspected that Nordbriht, vastly untidy and happy to eat even the immense quantities of food offered him, was a popular—please God, not too popular—addition to the household, at least when the moon was not full. It was only Nordbriht's presence that convinced the other men in Hagios Prokopios to allow Leo to keep his Turkish prisoner with him.

Leo learned to respond to jokes about "the bridegroom" with a foolish smile, an abstracted look, or even a yawn that brought more jokes down upon his head. Curiously enough, it united him to the town more than anything else he could have done. Marriage gave him roots here. Marriage to Asherah—she laughed when he told her he thought every man in the Empire must envy him.

Evenings, though: on trying days, the house was infested by guests, some local, some strangers to him, but connected to Joachim by blood kinship and years of trade or scholarship. On better days, he could look forward to a waiting bath, followed by dinner and talk with Asherah and her father.

Time alone with his wife came later. Sometimes, all Leo wished to do was sleep. Not often, though. Quickly, Asherah adapted to his ways, and he to hers. She tolerated, but was never quite at ease with his need for steel close at hand, while he still blinked in some confusion at servants who considered themselves distant cousins, to say the least, entitled to comment on every possible decision and event, until Asherah, sometimes laughing, sometimes absurdly enraged, drove them away and closed the door.

Meanwhile, his thirst to learn the languages the others moved in and out of as effortlessly as they might walk from one room into the next, to learn what he might of Joachim's holdings in order to protect them as well as this land that had become his home won their approval. For these people, scholarship was not alms or bribe, doled out by a politician with an eye to the future. It was a birthright. Even more than that: it was a commandment.

He had met and come to love a woman whose restraint and dignity had won his respect. Beneath her quiet face, veiled too often in public for his liking, he had found the richness of the Orient. Her bed might have delighted a princess in Babylon or Susa. And as for Asherah herself . . .

She stirred now in her sleep, and he held her even closer. His touch roused her in more ways than one. Delicately, her fingers smoothed his hair, traced his ear, stroked his neck in a way that soothed him now, but that he knew would become a major distraction in a few moments more. He had only to reach up and kiss her, and she would respond ardently to anything either of them might desire of the other.

He fondled her, delighted at how quickly she, too, kindled into the fire that had dazzled him the first time he took her in his arms.

"We might have been making love like this for years," he whispered to her. "So knowing you are. No, don't laugh at me, or . . ."

Now, he did kiss her, opening her mouth with his lips, kissing her more deeply until he felt her tremble.

She pressed her hand where it cupped her breast. "You know I was virgin when we married," she murmured against his lips and tongue. "But no one has ever called me reluctant to learn."

"Thank God for scholarship." Now, he laughed. His body ached for her.

"Shall I tell you how I learned to please you so quickly?"

"My skill, perhaps, and my fine city ways? Or some magic of the East?"

Asherah's voice began to deepen, as it did as she became eager for him. "When we lived in Susa, we had Persian friends, the wives and daughters of merchants. I would sit with the Persian ladies as they talked. I might have nothing to add, but I could at least listen."

Leo ran his hands over her body, feeling her arch and shift beneath them as he caressed her.

"Did they talk about their husbands?" he asked. It was a terrible thought. "Perhaps even compare them?"

Asherah's laughter was mischievous now. "They are very eloquent, those ladies. Very specific."

"And now, as a married lady yourself, and of such vast experience, would you . . . ?"

"It would be selfish of me not to share," Asherah said. "Especially where you are of another people, so very different, as it would seem. If we lived near them, Stateira and Marsinah would weep with disappointment."

Leo thanked God Susa lay nowhere within a month's traveling time. Never mind those women. He bent to kiss Asherah's throat. "Do you know, you purr when I kiss you?"

She laughed, and he felt it as vibration against his lips.

"Do you wish to hear what I would tell my old friends, Leo? You know how Kemal calls you 'Lion's Cub'? My husband, I would say, is no cub, but the lion himself: strong, valiant—and tireless."

He tightened his arms about her.

"Tireless, indeed," she whispered against his mouth. Now, her hips moved against his. At his touch, her thighs parted and she arched her back. Leo reveled in the surprising strength of her embrace. His head was spinning, but her words enticed him almost as much as the fragrance of her skin. Still, before passion robbed him of speech, he had to ask one more question.

"And after you told them this, what would they say to you?"

He pulled away from her lips, which murmured a faint protest. Sight and smell told him how ready she was.

She smiled wickedly. "What would they tell me? To watch what the great cats do, and do it ourselves!"

"Next time," he promised. The heat of her body felt like homecoming after a long absence. She cried out in welcome and held him close, as she had since their first night together.

Afterward, he watched her again. Her skin glowed in the lamplight, though it was flickering now toward extinction. He touched her belly, trailing one finger down to caress her the way, long ago, he had traced the secret curves of an ancient statue so much like Asherah herself. How had she described her dreams? "Shining women, welcoming me."

"Keep doing that, and neither of us will ever sleep," she murmured. Even now, she moved her hips in the oldest dance of all, to delight him further with the sight of her pleasure. "And you will have to bear more jokes about yawning bridegrooms."

"What about you?"

"Tzipporah is always following me about, telling me to lie down and rest or eat something, just in case."

Let there be a child, he hoped, and soon. It was more than he had ever hoped to have, more than he had ever dreamed.

Leo chuckled and drew her closer, breathing in the fragrance of her hair. Perhaps he really had strayed into the Song of Songs. King Solomon had survived a battle or two, hadn't he?

Asherah's breathing grew softer, sleepier as he stroked her hair. After awhile, she slept again. Holding her in his arms, Leo watched the moon set.

The lamp guttered and went out. An earth tremor ruffled some of the hangings on the walls. Leo tried to steady his breathing, to sink his awareness into the land itself. He had, after all, been able to protect her from this one thing. His dreams had not showed him Nordbriht nor any trace of him. He could not hear him. And, more than he wanted to admit to Asherah, who wrestled with demons of her own, that troubled him.

32

They rose in the grey time before dawn. There was no time to linger, or even to yawn, before their work began. Asherah had house, warehouses, and accounts to maintain. The house itself was walled and guarded; she had even finally yielded to her father's and her husband's demand that she not slip out alone.

Leo and Joachim went armed, absurd as Joachim claimed to feel carrying steel, even if it was the finest Damascus. No doubt, in Byzantium, they would hold up their hands in horror: Jews in arms; Jews (other than the Emperor's physician) on horseback at need. It had been lawful to turn one harmless Jew into a torturer! Leo thought, with a stab of the old anguish over Romanus. At least, this time, Jews would defend themselves and Romanus' old land. It seemed only fitting.

Guards accompanied the family, doubled in Nordbriht's absence. Among them, to the horror of all the women in the house, was Kemal.

"He and his sultan treated me as a guest, though I was a prisoner. Can I do less?" Leo had demanded.

It just might be that Kemal would see assassins where an eye more familiar with the local gentry might not. All were equally strange, equally hostile to him. Leo, as Asherah was quick to point out (in private, thank God), entertained hopes of recruiting Kemal to his service.

"You hire mercenaries like a prince now, do you, Leo?" she had commented just that morning. "I warn you, I have no ambition to be Basilissa."

The lad was feckless, unhappy among the Turkmen, Leo started to explain. Turks had settled in the Empire before—admittedly, not all that many, but given the right sponsors and land and herds, he might eke out a decent living for himself. And if not, he could always guard the lion's cub (thanks to Asherah, Leo might never hear that nickname now without a rush of heat) he valued. Each other's lives were the coin they exchanged.

Her laughter at the horror in his face had been the only merriment of that morning.

Thus, when Leo walked out with Joachim to meet the caravan guards and help load those few families who wished to flee Cappadocia for whatever safer place they fancied horses and Bactrians could reach, Kemal went with him.

By the time he could stop to take a breath, Leo would have said that the time for songs had forever ceased—unless they were ballads about hopeless causes, complicated by panic. He had never seen so many amulets on any men as he had on the men who rode with the caravans; the fear among the refugees was so palpable that it frightened their mounts, giving the drovers extra work calming them. Kemal, who understood herds better than he knew human beings, cast an appreciative eye over the caravan. The bells that helped camels and wagons keep from straying had all been put away. This caravan would flee in silence, if it could flee at all.

"Would you want to go with it?" Leo asked in an undertone.

"Cub, they would cut my throat the instant I turned my back. But it is a fine caravan, a rich one." He grinned admiration at Leo's improved fortunes, much of which the caravan would bear away to some safer place, if any existed.

"It would help," Leo said in an undertone to Kemal, "if you knew where your kinsmen rode and could tell us so these poor people could get through."

"Poor?" Kemal shouted with laughter. The other guards bristled.

"I am concerned that the Turks, like many nomads, regard the caravans as gifts falling into their hands. Happily, I would halt them here; but my kin would read that as a counsel of despair. And that we dare not do."

"If it is written that they fall into the hands of my brothers, it is written," Kemal shrugged. "Travel for you would be safer in winter, when only the storms are your enemies. We fight men, not storms."

"This caravan must leave now," Joachim muttered. "Life goes on,

and trade with it. Even your prophet Mohammed worked the caravans."
Leo raised an eyebrow, and Kemal stopped in his tracks.

"I did not know that about Mohammed," Leo admitted.

"The Prophet married his master's widow," Kemal said. He bowed
respect at Joachim.

"We too are people of the Book," the merchant reminded him.

Leo flushed. "Do not expect *me* to start a new religion," he said.

Joachim turned to stare at him. He shook his head. "I meant no
comparison, of course, my son." He smiled, and Leo breathed more easily. It was never simple for a poor man to marry an heiress and retain
his self-respect.

After a noon meal that was more a council of war than a time to
relax, they faced other tasks.

After the meal, Asherah planned to ride, now under guard, to the
underground city that she had helped equip. She monitored the progress
there as flocks were driven far from the villages and the caves filled with
provisions. One thing, at least, was going well, if not to her complete
reassurance: her marriage to Leo ensured, at the very least, the secure
place in that refuge that all her gold and even the nuns' inexplicable
favor might not have gained for her household.

"If there is any trouble," Leo warned her, "you stay where you are
safe." He doubted that she would heed him.

He knew the caves were almost fully provisioned now, food laid in,
bedding laid out, bins filled, and the gear attached to the millstones that
would bar the entrance tested so that even a strong child could secure
them at need. There were arms within the caves, as well. They might
be cities principally of women, but Asherah had her guards, the lean
dark nuns were stubborn and would make good fighters, while any
woman defending her children would fight like a fury as long as life remained.

If it were up to Leo, he would send Asherah and her women to the
caves to stay now. He knew better than to try.

"I am safest at your side," she had insisted. "I will see you tonight."

He saw her to her horse. He helped her mount and, for a moment
more, in case this was the last time, he held her hand. Joachim looked
aside. Kemal suppressed a chuckle.

And then she was gone, riding as easily in her flowing garments as
the men who guarded her.

Leo indulged himself for a moment, watching her graceful figure
grow smaller and smaller as the dust puffed up about the riders. The
ground seemed to echo their hoofbeats.

"Son," Joachim said softly. "Do not forget what other guards ride with her."

In Joachim's presence, Leo could not politely sign himself.

"May they protect her," he muttered.

Joachim returned to his house. Even though he now went armed, Leo's father-in-law was a man of words, not swords. He could best serve by doing what he knew best: preserving the fragile nets of trade and rumor that linked the Empire with the East.

Leo turned toward the officers of what Hagios Prokopios called, with rather more hope than accuracy, its guard. They walked about the town. It was quieter now. Many of the merchants had left, leaving vacancy where their stalls had stood. Many townsfolk retired to the land. Those men who remained often lived in near-empty houses, having sent their wives and children to what they considered safer places.

Ioannes rode up on a dusty horse, dismounting quickly when he saw the other men. With him came a small troop of mounted men, farmers of whom he sought hard not to be overly aware. In better times, this would have been his first command, and he might even have been smiled at if he preened somewhat. But these were hard times, and especially hard on Ioannes. Not only had he lost a father who had been a popular landowner, he had to mourn the man, and play his part as a fighting man. He raised a hand in an awkward almost-salute to Leo, but was instantly surrounded by a group of older men, his father's friends.

Leo gestured at Salomon, an older man whom Joachim trusted and who had refused to leave Hagios Prokopios when he had sent others of his household further north.

"I have heard his life is hard," Leo hinted, nodding at Ioannes. "He might not refuse a sack or two of food, slung across his saddle when it was time for him to ride home."

As son-in-law, not son, and a Christian at that, Leo tried not to order where he could suggest. He had his reward in Salomon's willing nod.

"I have heard. He is a good lad," said Salomon. "My cousin Tzipporah said your wife told her she had heard from a woman in the town"—he smiled mirthlessly at the roundabout nature, as characteristic of Jews as it was of the *Rhomaioi*, of the news—"that he has younger brothers, tended only by a nurse."

"Asherah offered to take them in, but he refused," Leo recalled. Then, more hastily, lest the older man imagine insult, "I do not think . . ."

Salomon shook his head. "That was pride. We are all proud when we are young. When we are older, we learn that others may protect our own better than we ourselves."

Was that why Salomon treated Leo with such consideration? Because he could do more for his master and his master's daughter than he himself? Leo stood very straight. *I pray your trust is not misplaced.*

Salomon regarded him levelly. "Just so. If you can get him out to the house, I shall have Tzipporah see that the young man does not ride home empty-handed."

Ioannes escaped from the men attempting to console him. Under the dust and his ill-fitting harness, he looked thinner and worn. For him, the time of ballads had ceased before it began. Knowing that even sympathy would be another burden now, Leo greeted him only with, "What news?"

"The widow Charis's farm is gone," Ioannes said. "She and her people escaped. One of them told me her mistress would take refuge with the nuns until it is time to . . ."

Kemal came up to stand at Leo's shoulder. Ioannes bared his teeth at him in what might have passed for greeting, or a snarl. Kemal flourished a salute at the youth who had held his life in his bloodied, angry hands.

"We both serve the same master now, young falcon," he said. Leo watched the man and the youth face off.

"Some of us don't change our loyalties with our coats," Ioannes muttered.

"Some of us have only one coat—if we are fortunate enough to have even that. You have land, young lord. Be happy you have friends who have vowed to help you keep it."

Ioannes glared at him. "And if you had land . . ."

"My Sultan had grand plans for you. The men with whom I rode covet your lands. As for me, had I been born with what you own, I would never have left it."

But he might have lost it, Leo thought, as he lost all else. Perhaps, if Kemal's loyalty became truly his, one of the abandoned farms might be given him. Or, given Kemal's propensity for letting gold fall through his hands, perhaps Leo should buy it—should ask Joachim to buy it— and let Kemal run it. He would be a strong defender—assuming the people Leo wanted him to defend did not stab him in the back.

Aware he was being baited, Ioannes shrugged.

"I saw your lady on the way," he said. "She called out to me to tell you she saw the last of the herds led off. From my own land"—the boy's head came up with pride—"I provisioned three teams of scouts: two pair will stay on watch for as long as they can hold out; the third pair will serve as messengers, as you ordered."

Good lad, Leo stopped himself from saying that or from remarking that Asherah, now dignified with "your lady," was probably someone Ioannes might have sneered at for her faith.

"Well done," Leo told him. Ioannes straightened even further. "Your scouts know whom else to speak to if they can't find you?" *If you are killed,* he meant, but best not to say it. Ioannes probably still believed he was immortal.

Once again, they inspected the defenses of Hagios Prokopios. Kemal made some suggestions about the placement of spears that *might* deflect horse-archers, if they were very, very fortunate.

"The Maccabees got beneath the elephants of Antiochus and stabbed upward with their spears," Salomon offered.

"Hard on your Maccabees, wasn't it?" asked Kemal, scandalizing Christians and Jews alike. "You do want to come out of this alive."

The defenses were better than Leo had hoped. But they were not enough: if the storm crashed over them with the force Father Meletios had foreseen, not even the full force of the Tagmata would hold it back.

Father Demetrios emerged from behind his church. He was covered with grit, and Leo wondered if he had been burying those few treasures that belonged to it, preferring to entrust them to the earth rather than to the people, Christian and Jew and maybe even Turk, who would flee into the caves. Behind him walked a man Leo had not seen before. He was dressed for riding, though he lacked the arms of a noble. He could not be a messenger, could he? Any messenger was rare, but a messenger from the City, humbly dressed so he could ride without hindrance, bringing news of troops and supplies heading toward them, would be a miracle.

You're dreaming, Leo. You know that all your true dreams wake you screaming. As well wish to turn the tide at Manzikert. The age of miracles is past.

Demetrios hurried up to them, gesturing to the man to follow.

"This holy man," he began, "has seen a vision."

Not a messenger, then. Well, any news from Byzantium was likely to be bad, cut off as they were here from Imperial aid. Or perhaps Leo's parents had finally decided that they had tolerated all they could from their wayward son and cast him off. Or been ordered to.

Leo shrugged, observing how quickly Ioannes mastered his more obvious disappointment. The older men gathered around, while Salomon stood aloof. He was not yet used to the closer bonds that Leo tried to forge among the different peoples in the town, nor did he trust them.

"I would be glad to hear it," Leo said. "Where are you from, holy sir?"

"You are Leo Ducas?" The man's accent bore the impress of the City.

Leo inclined his head. Even if he had forgotten the pauses required for rank and ceremony in his old home, how they had slowed matters of importance, the man had granted him no title, and that disquieted him. He had *not* forgotten the need for constant suspicion, even more so than the physical fear with which he walked these days. Perhaps there *were* letters. The old fear of having somehow transgressed began to coil in his belly.

"You are he who abandoned his own kin to follow a false Emperor . . ."

Now *that* was too much. The headmen and minor nobles with whom Leo had forged an alliance and a guard here began to mutter. Many of them had served Romanus at one time or another.

". . . who ran blasphemously mad in the Great Church of the Holy Wisdom and fled here . . ."

"Holy sir," Leo held up his left hand, paltry shield though it might be, as if he really expected to halt the man in midflow. His eyes glazed over, and he began to tremble. *I was my uncle's cat's-paw. Whose pawn are you?*

". . . abandoning the cause of holiness for an evil marriage with a cursed *Jew!* It is *you* who bring the storm upon us, *you* who will cause the mountains to erupt, the earth to crack and swallow men of good will, *you* whom God has set as a scourge upon our backs—the enemy within, and the Turks without! We will be taken and crushed as rats in a trap, unless we repent . . . !"

His voice trailed up into madness, real or drugged, Leo did not care. The man was a messenger, but no *angelos.* What had sent him was magic, hellbent upon Leo's death!

Leo was prepared for the man's rush at him, the dagger that he drew, but not for its speed or the deadly strength with which he grappled him. *I thought I was mad, but I never had a grip like this!* was Leo's last coherent thought. They were down now, and wrestling, struggling for their lives. Leo had jerked the man's knife-arm so that his elbow struck the sunbaked earth and his knife fell. From the corner of his eye, he saw someone retrieve it.

He had all he could do keeping the madman's hands from his throat. Strong as his attacker was, he might try to snap Leo's neck, and if he

failed at that, there was always throttling. Leo stiffened his fingers, trying to poke up at the hate-filled eyes of the madman, but he lay beneath,
badly balanced, and lacked his enemy's insane strength. He felt the
other flinch, but red lights were exploding behind his eyes, bells were
ringing. . . .

Suddenly, he could breathe again. He broke free and levered himself up to his elbows as Kemal and Salomon pulled the madman off him.

He scrambled to his feet. "Don't tell Asherah," he gasped to Salomon. He could try to shield her, but she would know. She always did
know, but at least, she could hear it from him.

"Now what?" he snapped at Father Demetrios, who was wringing
his hands. "You housed me, fed me when I first came here. Can you truly
believe what this . . . this offal says because he lards it with false words
about God the Father?"

The priest fell to his knees. "On my head be the judgment as well
as his."

"*Christ!*" Leo stamped on the ground. Salomon would not like that
oath. Too bad; even if the man had helped save his life.

Kemal jerked his chin at Leo. *Kill him now?* It would be the matter
of a few moments to slit the false messenger's throat and dump him in
a shallow grave.

"Well, my friends?" he began.

The madman began to chant. A hymn, Leo thought. How long had
it been since he had heard holy music, apart from the chants of the men
who shared Joachim's house? It was like an ache at heart, an ache in
the center of his chest, stabbing down his left arm. As when the madman tried to strangle him, Leo felt as if he could not get enough air.

He pressed a hand to his chest. What had he eaten to gripe him
like this?

The chant rose louder and more triumphant.

The ground started to slide sideways. Leo flung out an arm. It was
caught and held by Ioannes, whose face was slick with fear.

Now, the air seemed to thin and twist about him, as it had when
Father Meletios chanted. *Oh, Leo,* he thought. *You fool.*

The "monk" had flung Leo's collapse in Hagia Sophia at him. Only
one man knew who caused that. *Do you really think I want your puppet
Empire?*

Maybe Leo could wrest enough air out of this attack to save his life.

"Gag him!" Leo gasped and sagged against Ioannes. The younger
man bore him up with surprising strength.

"Kill him now?" Kemal asked. Salomon nodded solemn agreement.

Wonderful: a Turk and a Jew saving his life, then agreeing on the death of a Christian monk.

Leo stood rubbing his throat, fighting to spit out words of judgment.

"It isn't safe to return him to Father Demetrios," Ioannes spoke over his shoulder. "Or any other monks. They don't know . . . oh, Christ. . . . The Jews and the Turk here are our allies, just like the Northerner. You won't get people here to understand that, not if he keeps praying at them. God knows who else his hymns could hurt."

"Find out . . ." Leo gasped. "Find out who sent him."

They must all be mad in Byzantium by now. He knew that Emperor Michael was weak, but was he truly so weak that his masters would send assassins this far south to take out a man who had made it perfectly clear he wanted no part of Empire?

But who? And how? Those were the problems with which Ioannes now wrestled, and he had not the experience to deal with them.

"Kemal," Leo gestured. "Take him. Question him. Don't kill him." He released his clutch on Ioannes' arm and pointed to three of the older men, a farmer, a Christian merchant, and a landowner of about Ioannes' rank. "You go with Kemal. Keep them *both* alive."

Kemal might be safe by virtue, if you could call it that, of his unfaith. But the others? "Do you have wax?" Leo asked the merchant. "Wax balls . . . in your ears, if he starts up again."

Odysseus, patron saint of desperate Byzantines, help us now, Leo blasphemed silently. He waved away an offer of watered wine: no telling who had touched it first. He scowled at the idea that he should return to his house and rest. He was building his house right here, building it of men and women washed up like potsherds on this shoal of Empire, ground together, mortared one to another by blood and fear and need, and used by a desperate craftsman first to patch a wall or two, then to construct an edifice to replace the old and crumbling one.

"We finish," he said and walked on. The older men followed him as if he had been a *strategos* or a prince, not a man under sentence, now, of death. That was a sentence all men shared.

Dust and sour fear mingled foully in his throat. He paid correct attention to each feature of his home's defense. But his eyes strayed to the horizon like a man awaiting execution but hoping for a reprieve.

When they finished, the sun remained in the sky. Well enough: he had enough time to do what he hoped.

"I have to go out to the caves," he said. "Now." His voice was only a rasp. "Who will ride with me?"

Like rats in a trap. The madman's words had troubled him all day.

Let a madman or a traitor—he had been the prey of both—lead the Turks into the cave cities that had been set up as refuges, and his own people would be trapped. He flinched from the waking nightmare: warriors slashing their way downward through the many levels of the underground, missiles, or even fire, hurled down airshafts, monks bleeding out their lives on their own altars, women, their skirts bloodied, or even burning, clutching children, trampling each other, trampling even those who tried to keep some order, as they pushed through the narrow passageways downward, ever downward, to wind up with their backs against a final wall.

But traps could have different users and more than one door. If it were his last act, Leo meant to make sure that this trap would spring only upon the victims of his choice.

33

By the time Leo reached the entrance to Malagobia, his shoulders and throat ached from the day's two attacks. He wanted nothing so much as to be permitted to sit alone in a safe, darkened room until he felt safe enough to emerge, probably at about the same time as the Resurrection.

"My lord!" Leo started, twisting so violently in the saddle that even his tired horse shied, and he was hard-pressed to control it with hands that shook upon the reins. He pressed his fingers together; the brute danced, then stood, trembling almost as severely as he.

It was only the messenger he himself had sent to Joachim to tell him that he would bring Asherah home himself: not a maddened puppet of the fallen City mage, not a werewolf, not even Turks.

Joachim had given the messenger a message for Leo: Nordbriht had still not returned home. Remembering his dead Emperor's rages, Leo hissed in frustration. His throat hurt too much to curse. With luck, he might be able to say what he needed before his voice gave out altogether. At some point, he was going to have to decide whether to search for Nordbriht or to abandon the man who had been his companion since he arrived in Cappadocia.

Slowly, Leo dismounted. Either the ground trembled, or his knees really were that unsteady. No children ran screaming from the entrance to the caves, and the horses stood patiently, waiting to be led away: it must be his knees, then.

In a flurry of dark fabrics, Asherah emerged into the light of day and ran to him.

"I just heard from your father," Leo assured her. "He is well."

Asherah flung her arms about his neck. "Leo, who hurt you? I couldn't breathe, I felt as if someone were crushing me."

Her eyes were wide with horror as she searched his face. Leo wrapped his arms about her. Joachim's "witchy" daughter, she had called herself. Yes, she would know if anything befell him. She had known.

"Asherah," he rasped.

"Your poor voice! And you are bruised, too,"

Now, she touched his neck with far more care than before. When she hurled herself into his arms, her warmth and strength had reached out to encompass him. Now her touch eased the scrapes and bruises left by the madman's grasp.

Carefully, he eased himself away from her. She had always displayed such restraint. He did not want her ashamed, once her initial fears eased, to be caught embracing her husband in public.

Asherah turned and saw Leo's soldiers watching her. Most of them smiled. One or two looked courteously away. Meeting their eyes, she raised her chin, its stubborn set indicating clearly that she felt that, if their women would not run to them and ease their pain, so much the worse for them. Then, she flushed and reached for her veils. Her hands came up empty. Apparently, she had discarded both veils and self-restraint within the caves. She shrugged and turned back to Leo.

"Come with me!" she demanded. Taking him by the land, she led him toward the entry to the caves. The others hung back somewhat, still abashed, then followed. The entry gaped to receive them, then narrowed as if they crept down the throat of some landlocked Jonah's whale.

Still holding Leo's hand, Asherah caught up a torch. Leo glanced backward. Most of his men had never been inside Malagobia; that was for women and children and such men who had been sent to protect them. As the light of day diminished to a circle the size of a coin, then vanished, their eyes showed white. Shadows flickered on the rough-carved stone. Torches fastened to the wall darkened it with long ashen streaks.

Bending almost double, they descended until they came to the first level of common rooms. In the largest of them, women bustled as if in their own kitchens. Children clung to their skirts or huddled solemnly in those storage alcoves that were not stuffed too full to hold them.

One of the black-robed women moved across Asherah's path. "Some madman hurt him, Xenia." Her voice cracked.

"In here," said the older, taller woman. "You want the nard, don't you?"

"Please." Asherah flashed her a worried smile and led Leo into the refectory in the room beyond. When it had been hollowed out, blocks of stone had been left at its center, and a long table and benches had been carved from them. Trenches before each bench showed the impress of feet over the centuries.

She drew him toward the nearer bench. Her hands pushed at his shoulders. "Sit down, Leo. Gentlemen, pardon me. Be seated, please. Thank you, Xenia."

Opening the alabaster box the old nun handed her, Asherah dipped her fingers into it and rubbed the salve into Leo's throat and along the line of his jaw. The salve heated as it sank into his bruised skin, and its fragrance sweetened the dampness of the room. Leo sighed deeply and leaned his head back, resting it against Asherah's breast as she tended him. How odd her smile looked, with her face upside-down above his as she rubbed his neck. If no one else had been there, he knew she would have kissed him.

Fabric brushed against the wall, and Leo came alert.

"Hush, my love," his wife whispered to him, as if he turned to her after a nightmare. "Your men are thirsty. Your own throat must be parched. I think you can try to drink now."

Two or three dark-eyed children toddled ahead of their mothers into the refectory, followed by a young monk (Leo managed—just— not to flinch) and the nuns. Sister Xenia herself carried a cup and pitcher that she set before Leo. Asherah poured for him. Again, the smell of herbs wreathed him.

Asherah nodded. "The others have wine?"

"Watered." The old nun tightened her lips, a severe type of humor that brought a warmer smile from Asherah.

"This will help you, Leo," she held the cup for him as if he were a child. He took it from it and brought it, and her hand as well, to his lips.

She laughed and tugged her fingers free. To his surprise, the nun smiled again. Some of the other women laughed kindly, or (the younger ones) sighed. The men assigned to guard the cave city entered, and the women turned to leave.

"Sit down," Leo husked. "All of you. No, don't go away."

Asherah sat beside him, her hands flicking dust from his harness or

brushing at him as if she were afraid she would be blamed for neglect-
ing him.

Leo drank again, then wiped his mouth, watching the shadowed
faces turned toward his. Some were thinner than they had been; all
looked more careworn. *I never sought to lead. I wish I could make this easier for you.* Only that night, he had thought he had stumbled into a ballad with a Ducas as the hero. If the luxury of Joachim's house, the wealth
that came with winning his wife were his rewards, the burden of these
people's lives was the payment.

"I beg you, do not fear. I did not come here to sound the alarm. In
fact, you have accomplished more in this short time than I would have
believed."

If his words made people straighten their backs and raise their
heads, they were not as empty as they sounded to him. *I never sought
command. Father, let this cup be lifted from me.*

"But I have thought. More can be done to keep you and the children safe.

"You need a line of escape."

Asherah edged closer against his side, and he restrained himself
from drawing her closer yet. So reserved, so shamefast she had always
been; and now? For everyone to see, she made it clear that he was *hers*
and she was proud of him.

The room erupted into questions and demands. A woman with two
children clinging to her rose to leave.

"Please don't go," Leo called after her. "We need you. We need you
to be as brave as you were when you brought those babies into the
world."

Asherah pressed his hand approvingly.

"Are you settled now? Will they be comfortable? Good. Then, listen to me and do not fear." He drank again. The herbs in whatever it
was Xenia had brought eased the rasp in his throat, but only somewhat.

"You know why you are here, in what has always been your refuge.
But this time, we face Turks. Oh, they are human and not demons. I
have lived among them, and a Seljuk man now serves me. But these,
these are Turkmen, wilder than the men I know. Now, we have no
promise that they won't take prisoners, God have mercy on their souls."

The women blessed themselves repeatedly, the men more slowly,
and Asherah, of course, not at all. "Today, I took a prisoner. He is being
questioned. The Turks would do the same. Which means that these
cities might not be sanctuary enough."

He paused to let that sink in and let them exclaim away their initial fear.

"The reason I want you here is that *you*, not armed men, may be your country's last and best guard. Every woman strong enough to lift a jar or shift a sack can protect her home, and every child.

"You know how easy it is to cut or burn yourself in a kitchen. How if you turn those weapons on the Turks?"

Smiles bloomed then. One woman wiped away a tear. A boychild stood before his mother, trying hard to swagger. Asherah laughed softly. Sister Xenia smiled, her white teeth gleaming like a blade beneath the shadowed blades of her high cheekbones.

"We will set up traps. Spears in the bins of grain, hot oil, simmering on the hearths, to pour down the airshafts or set ablaze to cover your retreat. Even the millstones themselves can be poised to fall and crush the men on the other side of them. I need the men among us with strong backs to set up other millstones to seal off passages as you withdraw below."

These were countrywomen, not sheltered ladies, used to fighting only with their wits and subtle poisons. Some had wielded scythes or carried burdens as well as any man: there was no reason they could not give at least some account of them.

"Below!" cried a woman almost as broad as she was tall. "We burrow out like rats, but we will be trapped like rats below, our backs to the wall."

"What does it matter?" a man told her. "If we're pushed that far back, say your prayers. The Earth may indeed shudder and engulf us. At least, we can die fighting."

"Or by our own hands," someone else muttered, but Leo could not quite see who.

"Not that," Asherah said. "Never again, that."

"What other choices do we have?" the first man asked.

Asherah muttered beneath her breath.

"There is one other way, sir," she interrupted. "Even if Turks force our backs to the wall, there is a way through it."

She paused. In the silence, the ground rumbled. A faint spray of dust trickled from the carved ceiling.

"There is a way out," Asherah said. "I found it."

"Where does it lead to?"

Leo could have beat his forehead on the table. That was the problem, wasn't it? They didn't know where it ended.

"As Basil over there has said, if you're driven that far below, what does it matter where it ends? Run as far and fast as you can, and fight when you cannot run. You will not be alone. The rest of us, I pledge you, will be fighting our way down to relieve you."

"A pincers!" Xenia's voice belled like a stooping hawk. "You would fight through to us?"

"By the grace of God," said Leo. His voice broke, and he drank again. "I will take you to see the passageway my wife found in the depths of this city. Who will come with me?"

Ultimately, the nuns pressed in after Leo, crowding out the soldiers and the other women at the head of the line. Their dark robes whispered against the scarred rock of the narrow passageways, tall shadows gliding in an eerie regularity. This far beneath the surface of the earth, they showed no fear.

"Ai," said Xenia, drawing her finger along the stone, "this looks older than the upper ways."

"So I thought," Asherah replied. "It grows older still. Soon you will see the wall paintings."

"Wall paintings survive?" Xenia's eyes glinted, black under black brows.

"As they do in the walls of your churches. I have not seen the ones in the valley from which you were driven out, but my father tells me that some of the figures are marred about the face. These are untouched."

The tall figures bent their heads, whispering to one another. If Nordbriht were here, Leo thought, he would reach for the amulet he no longer carries. Surreptitiously, he blessed himself.

"Let me lead from here," Asherah whispered. Leo nodded and flattened himself against the rock face to allow her to pass. Asherah took the torch she carried, lit it from his, and slipped by him. Smaller than the other women and far more lithe, she slid past the bend in the corridor where, in what seemed like another life, she had hidden tools and torches. Here, the passage expanded almost into a hall; and here the walls had been smoothed to receive the paintings, mention of which caused such excitement among the women.

"Now you can see." Asherah held up her torch well away from the figures on the walls lest its smoke and grime deface them.

"There." She pointed at the wall through which Leo had broken. Subsequently, they had slipped away together and patched it, but only lightly, in case they must break through again—as they would probably do now.

Even in the brighter light, the nuns looked oddly formidable with their dark garb, dark brows, the hollow beneath sharp cheekbones: aging women, angry women, cast out from a cherished home.

They stared at the paintings of marching priests and priestesses—and Leo was far from certain that they did not represent gods every bit as much as the triple-crowned figures he had seen carved into cliffs above ground. One woman bent and traced the figure of a cat. Another followed the twinings of a serpent from the bend in the wall to where the painting broke off. And Xenia stared at the central figure's face with its olive skin, its too-bright eyes, and harsh brows. They resembled each other, save that the painted image possessed a beauty Xenia surely never enjoyed, even in her youth.

Two of the women laughed with joy. "Our mother, our Queen!" The echoes made Leo shudder.

"You found her?" Xenia demanded of Asherah. "You?"

The two women, tall and tiny, faced each other. Asherah did not drop her eyes.

"And said nothing?"

Asherah only shrugged. "It is hardly a thing the likes of me should spread the news of for the good of her kin. Do you understand what you see?"

"How should *she* find the way within?" Sister Phryne demanded in a harsh whisper.

"Is she not a woman? Was she not barred entry to the valley?"

"She *refused* to enter it. Her father is friend to the man who drove us out."

"Her blood is older than ours; perhaps, she too has been called."

"Did I not *tell* you," Sister Xenia interrupted the whispers, "that she is the one chosen to bring what was hidden up again into the light?"

Leo was certain he did not like the sound of that. Nor of the way the nuns' eyes flicked from Asherah to him and back again. The torchlight beat down on his wife's face: symmetrical, serene, but her eyes blazing with the passion for knowledge. She was going away from him, and he had to get her back.

"Revered ladies, if you would condescend to explain . . ."

Xenia let out a sharp bark of laughter that echoed painfully. "We know where this path leads to, or at least one place, and you do not. That galls you, does it? It galls all men when women have secrets. Especially women like us. Strong backs and bowed heads, you see in us; bowed and *empty* heads. But we remember, young sir, we remember and we wait. And ultimately, we come into our own. Do we not, stranger and sister?"

Asherah held out a hand and touched the older woman's sleeve.

"I am sorry," Leo said. He was not answered, nor did he expect to be. In this moment, he knew himself to be necessary, but not central to whatever mystery they shared. It was clear they shared something; but, as the nuns obviously were asking each other, why Asherah?

The nuns gathered, their heads bent close together. Then they fell to their knees. Xenia bent forward and kissed the wall as if she kissed an icon. A second sister wept. "I can die happy now," she whispered.

"Wait, we may come to the innermost shrine," Sister Phryne cautioned.

"No one has seen it for generations!"

"Hush!" Their eyes flickered toward Leo like smoke and fire. They returned to their prayers. Leo could make out most of the words. They sounded like prayers to the Mother of God, but not wholly.

"Can you understand?" he asked his wife. "What do you hear?"

"Heresy," she said. "By any standards but theirs. God pardon me for saying so, but they act as if we have found the Ark of the Covenant."

"May we see what lies within?" Xenia asked. Her voice was subdued and humble, as if she were on pilgrimage and begged entry to a shrine.

Leo sighed. Once again, he would provide the strong back. He reached for the tools he and Asherah had left behind. The women bowed their heads, as if he performed not labor, but a necessary part of some rite.

Once again, Leo swung at the ancient wall.

Dust shrouded them all, making the eldest women cough. Fragments broke free of the roughly assembled wall. Then, as it had before, the wall gave way.

Rising from their knees more rapidly than ladies of their age might be expected to do, the nuns thrust past Leo into the dark corridor. One ventured down it, into the room in which Leo had dared to tell Asherah of his desires, and she had met them. Leo did not like the idea of outsiders entering that room. Surely, some of the sweetness from the first time he embraced his wife must linger there. Heat prickled beneath his tunic lest they sense that. Asherah took his hand.

The woman emerged quickly from that blessed little room. She smiled at Leo, then turned and kissed Asherah's cheek before she headed further down the corridor.

"Do you know what this place is?" Leo demanded. He had brought them here for his reasons—the defense of this trap of an underground city—but they were exclaiming, laughing, and weeping in joy for their own.

"You have found the way within," Phryne said. "For years we have sought it, and now it is found. Praise . . ." again, the word Asherah had told him was purest heresy, even in its grammar. "God," its root meant; and yet its ending was feminine.

"You know the stories," Sister Xenia reminded Leo. "Doubtless you heard how all the cities are joined by roads dug underground. Well, you have happened on such a road. It joins city to city in a vast wheel; and at its hub lies great power and treasure."

At this point, Leo's hands might overflow with gold, but he would want no more than to wash them clean. It was a shrine, he had found, but unlike anything he had ever believed in.

Again, Xenia laughed, hawk-shrill. "Do not worry about this, young *strategos*. We can guide your people to safety. Only see you come quickly; we would not have invaders penetrate the way within."

A voice, changed almost past reckoning by how it echoed down the corridor, made them all shiver.

"He will not fail us, sisters."

The voice belonged to Asherah.

34

Like the song of Damascus steel tested by a swordsman, magic thrummed at the threshold of Asherah's awareness, bringing her up out of a deep sleep. She sat up, away from the warmth of her sleeping husband. He was a distraction even when he slept, and he had been asleep when she came to bed.

They had ridden home from the underground ways. Joachim, who had heard of the attempt on Leo's life, had met them at the gates, flung his arms about Leo in relief, and led him away to the waiting physician. She and her father were both skilled: that Joachim had thought to summon the best physician he knew here was a sign of his fear for the man who had won a piece of his heart too.

"My place is with my husband!" Asherah had protested. She would have thought that those words, so much like those she had heard other women say and have respected, would have won her her way; but her women had taken her in tyrannous charge, crying out at the dust and grit that coated her and the terror she must surely have felt. By the time she had submitted to a bath, to clean clothes, to calming their fears, and to the solace of dinner with her father, the physician had given Leo a potion and put him to bed.

"He will do better sleeping than talking," the physician admonished her in a way that she might have resented had she not been so distressed, "and just you remember he's not in shape for anything else."

She would do better at his side than anywhere else, she retorted, and if her husband had been drugged, it was not as if she could tempt him to any exertion. Clad only in her unbound hair, as Leo loved to see her, she slid into their bed, letting herself rest against him as she always did. He eased against her, and she put her arms about him.

"Did you see?" he muttered, still more than half asleep. "Threw his arms 'round me . . . s'if I were son, his own son . . ."

"He loves you, Leo. I love you. Now hush and go back to sleep." She kissed him softly, then waited till he subsided back into the healing sleep promised by the physician's drugs.

Rising from their bed, she wrapped herself in an absurd lavishness of Ch'in silk it had delighted her father to give her. The casual way in which she wore it had astonished Leo. Both of them had so much, still, to learn about each other. In this moment, though, Leo was hers.

She seated herself beside their bed and looked into his face. Beneath the curling hair that was turning too swiftly grey, his face looked younger: its true age, were he not constantly burdened. Asleep, his face lost the tautness she had noticed about him from the first, when she had looked up through her veil and her tears of rage and terror and seen him. Leo had come to her side, taking yet another risk to protect her. In return, she had been able to give him what, at that moment, he desired most: a last moment in which the man he served could be his Emperor, not a mutilated lump of flesh that would shortly die.

He had saved her life and her father's and their friends. She and her father had returned the favor that first night in Cappadocia. That left them even: but since then, they had knit their lives together. Something there was in the young officer, almost the icon of an alien Empire, that called out to her. It was akin to the life she had lived—keeping on going, trying to build something that would last, starting over and over again. At the very least, she sensed in him the willingness to try again to seek peace, to change from soldier to aspiring priest, and then, finally, to become her husband.

She wished that could have been the end of the story: a newly married couple, the wife about her duties (even if Asherah's extended somewhat anomalously to the care of a trading empire rather than the mere management of a house), the husband learning his father-in-law's work, and, in time, a child or, better yet, children whom everyone could approve. She had part of it, and more than had ever been prophesied for her: she was as absurdly wrapped up in Leo, in the sight and the touch and the care of him, as the most smugly normal woman who had ever been held up to her as an example. And to think she had always considered herself, had been encouraged to consider herself, lacking in that regard. . . .

Still, the thrum of magic quivered at the edge of her senses. Asherah rose from her leather chair and went to the window. The moon was still full, bathing the walled yard, but its glow was subsiding.

A thick wall protected her home. From outside it came a despairing howl. *Yes, it's high,* she thought. *We built it that way on purpose, to keep things like you out!*

It subsided into a whimper. Silence. Asherah's hands had clenched into small fists. When, deliberately, she opened them, the palms were wet. Walls had proved inadequate before. Which would be quicker, she wondered, snatching up the sword Leo kept by their bed to go herself, or waking him?

Now, she heard scratching against the wall, as if some robber sought to gain purchase on it. Her smile was cruel. Let him try to pause at the top of the wall, just let him. It would be a matter of moments to bring the household to full wakefulness, but sounding that alarm brought back such terrible memories that she hesitated.

Again, she heard scrabbling at the wall, higher up, a yowl of almost bestial anguish. Something dropped into the courtyard. Oh God, was the killing about to happen again? Her tears were hot, but the sweat that touched the silk she had tossed about herself was cold with horror.

Not if she could stop it.

Swiftly, Asherah flung a sheepskin over her silk robe and drew Leo's sword from its hiding place beneath the pillows. Drawing a deep breath and strength that felt as if it rose from the center of the earth, she invoked the powers that would ward her, just as she had the night she had insisted that she and Joachim intervene against Leo's assassins—his *first* assassins.

Leaving the refuge of her bedroom, she ventured outside, down the stairs, into the courtyard. For Leo. For her father. For the people who loved her. She would be Deborah. She would be Jael. She only hoped she would be alive when dawn came.

The moon had almost set, and the sky was beginning to pale with the approach of dawn. She heard no more scrabbling or attacks on the walls. Instead, she heard something whine, something exhausted and in pain. Whatever it was, it lay by the wall in shadow.

The thing was big, Asherah saw. She took a firmer grip on the sword, praying that she could get in one lucky blow or scream even once, just in case the thing had strength enough left to pounce. Light pooled on the sword and upon her trembling hand: she was warded, protected. Her hand ceased to shake.

Small, darker shadows pooled beneath the hulk. As she approached, the light warding her revealed what lay beneath the wall: huge, thin, covered with fur, and that fur matted and, in places, torn, exposing the bleeding flesh beneath. It looked like nothing so much as the body of some great wolf that had escaped a particularly vicious hunt.

She thought she could put a name to it. Or, to be more precise, to him.

Nordbriht.

Don't go near him, Leo would warn her. Leo was asleep. Perhaps Nordbriht was too wounded, too exhausted to be deadly, she hoped.

Fool! That's when they're the most likely to attack!

She knew that. She also remembered the other time she had seen Nordbriht with his curse upon him, and he had slunk over to her, his belly brushing the ground, and laid his massive fanged head at her feet.

And she had another reason to intervene. Leo prized his Guardsman, and she knew he had grieved, thinking him lost.

Soon, it would be dawn. When Nordbriht changed from wolf to man, assuming he did not die as his injured body wrenched itself from one substance to another, he would be naked, and the morning was chill. She flung the sheepskin she had worn about her shoulders over him. Now what? If she tried to drag him back to her room where Leo could tend him, wounded as he was, in pain, and in this form, he would have every reason to wake and to savage her.

Asherah glanced up at the sky. There was time until dawn, considerable time for her to be out here clad only in a silk robe that was lavish, concealing in its way, but hardly warm enough. That was no reason to leave poor Nordbriht alone. She sighed and edged herself down a safe distance along the wall where she would be hidden by the wolf's shadow.

Shutting her eyes for a moment, she drew up strength from the earth. It seemed to warm about her bare feet. For now, the earth had ceased the tremors that had been so constant that most people simply ignored them. It was harder to ignore them in the underground cities: but that was what prayer was for. The nuns had made an art of it. They showed no fear at all, and they seemed to think she should be as fearless as they. Why they felt this kinship with her, she could not imagine.

Do not fear. Again, she found herself sustained by the earth beneath her, as if she rested against it, listening to its heartbeat. *Her* heartbeat: the earth was her mother. It cradled her, taught her rhythms of which she had begun to have increased awareness and even a few forlorn hopes.

I had pagan dreams, she had told Leo the night before.

Half-bedazzled now by waking dreams, Asherah waited for dawn.

As the first sunglow touched the wolf in the courtyard, its battered body writhed and spasmed. Nordbriht cried out in the throes of change. His hindquarters lengthened; his forepaws turned into the huge hands that wielded his heavy axe as if it were little more than a toy; and silvery fur melted away from his body, except for glints on arms, legs, and chest where the sheepskin did not cover him, and the tangled masses of his fair hair and beard.

When the change was complete and he lay silent, face against the earth, Asherah dared rise and approach.

"Forgive me," she whispered.

Setting down Leo's sword and seizing Nordbriht by the ankles, she tried to drag him to her room.

He was dead weight. She tried again. She would never drag him across the yard, let alone up the stairs; and even if she could, it would probably hurt him at least as much as he was hurt already. All she accomplished was to trail her silks in the muck of blood and dust left by the wounded creature. Her hair fell about her, tangling almost to her knees. If she bent too far, it too would be filthy. She knotted it carelessly out of the way, muttering a phrase or two she had heard from an Aleppan muleteer.

At any moment, lights would be kindled in the kitchens. The entire household would begin to stir. And when they found Nordbriht . . . and her husband's sword . . .

"I'm not abandoning you," Asherah whispered. "I promise I'll be back."

Picking up the sword, she sped across the courtyard and back up the stairs into her room.

Leo had turned in his sleep so that the light did not brush his face. Asherah rather thought his breathing was less heavy. Good, the drug had worn off, and he would be easier to wake. If this were a ballad, she could kneel at his side, kiss him sweetly awake, and chances were, they wouldn't leave the room until noon. Besides, she had learned that waking Leo required some precautions. Let her simply bend over and kiss him when his body had gotten used to being alone in the bed, and he would probably jump up, alarmed.

She stood at the foot of their bed.

"Leo," she called his name repeatedly. Shouting would wake him only to memories of battles. She would not hurt him in that way; she would not even let him suspect that she knew how those memories made him react.

She saw the stealthy motion of hand toward sword, followed by a thrash when he couldn't find it. He fought toward full alertness.

"I have it." Asherah showed him the sword.

He was up in an instant, tugging on the garments he had arranged within arm's reach. Then he had snatched the sword from her and drawn her into the circle of his other arm. His nostrils flared.

"Blood," he muttered. "Asherah . . ." Sudden, terrible fear for her, for the strange illnesses that men thought women suffered, even grief . . . *and had there been a child so soon that she was losing?*

She brushed her cheek against his shoulder. "Nordbriht came home, Leo. Terribly injured, at least in beast form. I couldn't bring him up here. He was too hurt, too heavy. So I threw a sheepskin over him and sat by him until dawn."

"He'd be better off in his own bed." Sheathing his sword, Leo ran ahead of her down the stairs. By the time Asherah could assemble salves and bandages, he was kneeling by the half-naked guardsman, wishing, no doubt, to call the physician who had tended him yesterday and knowing he dared not wake the man.

"With two of us here, we can shift him," Leo told her. Again, she bent, tossed her hair out of the way, and clasped Nordbriht's ankles. This time, with Leo supporting the big man's shoulders, she was able to help half-carry, half-drag him across the courtyard. Leo kicked open the door, and they laid Nordbriht on the long, fleece-strewn pallet that had been all he would accept in the way of a bed.

"Fetch water," Leo told her. With her husband present, Asherah could move with complete propriety about a guardsman's room— though she would have tended Nordbriht alone if she had been able. If his wounds had taken cold as he lay out on the ground while she was too weak to move him . . . she brought a filled bowl and pitcher and set them down by Leo's side.

"He won't want you here," Leo said.

"Neither do you. But I know more about nursing than you do."

"I'll bathe him. He may wake and jump up and send you flying into the wall. When I'm finished, you can see to him."

Nordbriht moaned as Leo worked on him. The water grew foul and had to be replaced two or three times, and Leo passed her the bowls. Finally, Leo beckoned her back into the room.

Asherah bent to the serious work of tending the injured man. Grazes and scrapes had to be salved. In several places, arrows had gashed him. Thank God for His mercy; Asherah had never yet had to draw an arrow from a wound or had to burn one with a knife. She swallowed bile: Menachem's hand shaking, the iron slipping awry, the Emperor's body bucking despite the shields and kneeling soldiers holding him down.

"Love, if this is making you ill . . ."

She shook her head to clear it and to deny her weakness.

Nordbriht sat bolt upright and spat out words Asherah did not understand. His birth-speech, no doubt, and a demand to know what was going on. Leo grabbed him by the shoulders.

"What did you get into, man? You've been gone for days. Asherah found you, brought you here."

"Lady shouldn't be here," Nordbriht protested. Asherah took a cup and filled it with the last of the water.

"You try telling her."

"Give him the cup," Asherah said. Nordbriht would be ravenous. By now, the kitchen fires would be lit.

Nordbriht tried to speak. His voice husked over. He drank and tried again. "Turks. Turks swarming all over. They attacked the valley, and they'll be coming here. Not Seljuks. Turkmen. I tried to . . . night came, and I . . . I Changed." He grinned, showing huge teeth within the mats of his golden beard. "God, what a hunt. Turks don't fight at night, but they're vengeful as Hela herself. I outran them as if the Wild Hunt breathed down my neck."

Perhaps it had.

It was a miracle Nordbriht was still alive. Asherah glanced down at his feet. He had run them raw, but already, the soles were healing. Apparently, wounds sustained by the man-wolf in one guise healed quickly in the other.

A growl emerged from Nordbriht's belly, not his throat. He flushed practically down to his belly and gestured protest at her presence to Leo.

"Asherah, wake the house," Leo told her. This time, he didn't even try to apologize for commanding her. "Nordbriht's right. We have to move. Get one of the men. . . ."

"Ioannes stayed the night. . . ."

"I couldn't ask for a better messenger. Tell him to get the men assembled. Then, you tell your father and the women who are supposed to hide to get ready."

Leo had turned his back to open Nordbriht's storage chest and hurl whatever garments came first to hand at him. "Send Kemal to me. I suppose he's slept across our threshold again."

For a man who had fled any breath of Imperial power, now, its trappings ensnared him. Asherah stood, waiting for the word that would release her to the errands that would shatter her life.

"I'm going to want him to ride with me. Nordbriht, you're for the caves with my lady."

The Varangian bellowed protest. Already, he was sounding stronger. He hated the caves, Leo knew that. And what if the change came upon him while they were immured underground? Leo would know to fear that, too. Still, if he knew all that and still ordered Nordbriht below . . .

"If Kemal isn't with me, he's meat. And you can't ride with us, not in the shape you're in. We'll have to ride fast, without remounts; and your weight will overstrain the horses. You need to rest up, and I need you with my lady and her father in case the Turks break through or some damned fool among the villagers decides that they can hold out longer if they don't have to share with Jews. Besides, you might—who knows?—even be guarding my heir. . . ."

Asherah froze. That had to be a ploy to make Nordbriht go along with Leo's plans—didn't it? It was much too early for her to know, let alone for any man to sense. And what a time for it! Even now, it was only a hope, just the earliest possible moment to hope, well before she had even thought of sharing it with him. She reached deep within her for body-sense, which had strengthened over the past months—ever since whatever powers lingered beneath the earth had roused her and sent her eagerly into Leo's arms.

"This isn't . . ." She blurted.

"Asherah, get *to* it!"

Asherah started out the door. So her husband thought he could command *her* like that, did he?

Just this once, he could. She ran to rouse her household and prepare it, once again, to fly for its life.

The third time the spare cloak Asherah was trying to roll neatly dropped from her chilled fingers, she tried to take herself, not her packing, in hand.

Outside her room, she could hear women calling to each other, checking off lists of supplies, the sounds of packing: orderly preparations for flight. In the kitchens, she knew, jars were being loaded and carried out. From across the courtyard, where the guards slept and kept their stores, came shouts and clatters as men armed and assembled. The same swift, orderly tumult would be racing through the stables. By now, Joachim must have packed his most secret records and his most treasured books.

Why did she alone fumble at her work? God knows, she had practice enough in fleeing. Just look, she scolded herself, how wealthy they were. They had time to get their property out. They had allies. They even had a place to run to—and a way out.

What more could she possibly want?

Tears overflowed her eyes and spotted the cloak she still held.

She knew what else she wanted. Time to live. Time to live *here* in a place she had made her own: her own home, rather than a rest stop for the caravans or a fortress where she lived on sufferance and the blade's edge. She wanted the land. She wanted her friends. She wanted long, serene days.

And she wanted Leo at her side for all of them.

Their wealth of allies and protection only gave them more to lose. God spare them this time, those whom He could.

Asherah hated to run, hated to cower in a maze beneath the earth. She obeyed—just; and only because she knew and agreed with the reasons for sending her to ground. She was not a fighter, at least not with bow or sword, no more than her father was. *His* chosen battlefields were wisdom and trade; reluctantly, he had conceded that he must be safeguarded for his memories, at least, if not his pride. And Asherah was his heir.

Over and over again, she could give herself good advice. But Leo was riding off. She would see him for the last time, armed among other armed men. It was bad enough that armed men of the Empire had always attacked her and hers before; but now she loved one of them. He would ride off against fighters whose deadly skill she knew almost as well as he.

Against that, her "wealth" was worthless. She rubbed the marks of her tears from her spare cloak and duly stowed it in its proper place.

Known footsteps raced down the inner corridor. Quickly, Asherah busied herself with other tasks. Leo must not see her cry. He ran into the room and wrapped his arms about her, turning her so she could rest her head against his shoulder. The boiled leather of his cuirass—probably, they were loading his mail upon his horse right now—felt hard against her cheek.

They should leave this place. Every instant was precious. *Just one moment more*, Asherah pleaded with herself. *I will be careful. Unselfish. But just let me hold him one moment more.*

More than a moment had passed by the time Leo's words finally worked through the panicked roaring in her ears. "Even now, you had hoped I would command defenses in the caves? Asherah, you should have known better. Surely, you did. They want me as their leader, and I must ride with them. We'll let you know when it's safe to emerge. Or we'll fight through to you. I promise."

"Don't!" She turned her face against his leather-clad shoulder. His arms tightened around her.

"Asherah, listen to me. *I am coming back to you.* I have never wanted to live more in my life."

You may not have the choice. She forced that fear back down into the inmost recesses of her mind, where she kept her panic. Let it rattle around in there all by its dreadful self. It had just lost a companion fear, that all her love and caring had not been enough to pull Leo back from his old yearnings for that cruel Christian God Who might grant him escape from the world into faith or death.

And that was more wealth to fear the loss of. Leo tipped her face up and kissed her eyes, then her mouth. His lips tasted salty from her tears.

"Asherah, why didn't you tell me before?"

"It is still too early to know. Truly it is."

He rocked her, close against him. "If anything . . . I want you to put yourself in your father's care, and Nordbriht's."

She had to stop him from talking about *that*, even if she never heard another word from his lips. She trembled as the familiar dark breath swept over her and possessed her voice. "I want this to be over. I want you to live. I want our child to know his father."

"His?" Leo smiled down at her. She shook her head at him.

"Or hers. *If* there is a child."

A shout from the courtyard. "Ho, Leo! Leo Ducas!"

"We have to go," she whispered.

Deftly, Leo helped her pack the last things she could take. In his way, he had had as much practice fleeing as she.

"I'll come back," he told her. "I know where my heart is."

She had arguments she wanted to blurt out. She did not want to hear about honor. Leo was not a Frank. He was not a Varangian, sworn to follow his lord into death. She wanted to teach him a different kind of honor, the kind that had kept her people alive all these thousands of years. You found it in staying true, in manifesting God's will by keeping His people alive.

One last time, he embraced her, holding her up after his kiss weakened her knees. When she could stand again, he released her.

"Now, Asherah."

She let him go out first. They cheered him, the men who served her father, the men riding in at the gate of what had always been "the Jews' house" before, his own oddly matched servants, the Northerner and the Turks, even her women, their voices rising high and shrill like the cries of women from the desert tribes.

Asherah followed Leo down into the courtyard and out where the horses were waiting.

She stood unveiled as she had before the Emperor. The fire was burning; danger prickled in the air; and honor lay in keeping her back straight and her face composed. She, Joachim's witchy daughter, had actually won herself this tiny interval of love and tenderness and passion. If it were all she was to have, she would devote the rest of her life—which might not be that much longer—to reliving this part of it, its radiant core.

The dawn wind scoured tears as hot as a burning iron from her eyes and cheeks. Leo mounted and rode out. As she knew he would, he turned to glance at her one last time. Asherah smiled like an antique statue. She did not expect to see him again.

══╬ 35 ╠══

One more gift Asherah had made Leo: when he rode off, glancing back for what might be the sight of her he would take into eternity, she stood unveiled and tearless. Smiling for him to see.

A silk thread stitched to his heart seemed to want to pull him back to Asherah's side, never to leave her. It tore at him, gaping wider in his heart the further he rode.

His wife faced, he knew, a quiet battle of her own. At least, Leo could ride. He could fight. Asherah must go into hiding beneath the earth; and if she were forced to fight, it would be only because his men had faltered and he had failed her.

Leaning out over his horse's neck, Leo rode as if—how had Nordbriht described it?—he felt the Wild Hunt's hot breath against his neck. Then, the thread joining him and Asherah snapped. The pain of that parting twinged once more, and shrewdly. Then, it left him free yet oddly disconsolate in the midst of his fear.

Kemal followed, careful to ride at Leo's horse's tail. Leo had no doubt at all that the *gulam* could outride him. But his hope of life depended on Leo's, upon guarding him; and Kemal wanted very much to live. He had always seen reasons for life beyond power and destruction. He had served in the tents of Alp Arslan. In a way, it was as well that the sultan who had befriended Leo and his Emperor had died: he could oppose a Wild Hunt of Turks with body, soul, and will. But the sultan Kemal remembered? He was a better ruler and a better man than the Ducas who kinged it in Byzantium.

The thunder of hooves rumbled out to his left: men joining them. To his right: more men. Such a force had not been seen in Cappadocia since Romanus had stripped it of its best men. They rode.

Heat and clouds shimmered at the horizon. Far off, thunder echoed in the sky above the thunder trampling the earth. It shook, as it had for months, in faint protest. Haze glowed around the sun like the diadems of the storm gods. The morning was very hot for early autumn. The horses would be lathered long before they reached the valley. God send that Turks had not choked the river with corpses. But they would do nothing to ruin the land, Kemal had said. No use ruining what they *wanted* to rule.

They rode out of the field of rock dunes on the outskirts of the town, and more men joined them. Not all: some must be left to reinforce the monks who prayed for their souls and the souls of every man, woman, and child in the Empire. If the monks' prayers proved not to be enough, Leo hoped they would know to snatch up rocks, the swords that it had been most reluctantly decided to place in their hands, or, like Samson, the jawbone of an ass and give some account of themselves before Archangel Michael reviewed them in heaven.

Leo rode now to relieve another such valley. The faces of a blind man and a lame boy flickered in his mind's eye now, mercifully clouding his memories of Asherah. She was as safe now as she could be made: Father Meletios and the souls in his care had no such refuge unless Leo's troop could somehow blunt the Turkmen attack upon their valley and carry them off to safety.

Smoke rose, mixing with the autumn haze. The fields were not gold, as they usually were this time of year. They were charred, burned upon orders lest the Turkmen, raiders who lived off the lands they ravaged, thrive upon the harvest. The ash from the fields the Greeks had burnt and the ash of homes burnt by the Turks: you couldn't tell them apart. All wasted. All wasteland.

A wave of Leo's arm freed a troop from the pathetically small host: attack the attackers; defend the survivors; ride once more. To fight Turks now, they would have to fight like Turks. If Leo lived, he would ache from riding. But his shoulders would not bleed from galls left by the chainmail of the cataphract whom he had been in another life. He had not wanted to be a soldier. Convinced by his uncle's lies, he had thought meanly of his skill. Now, he still did not want to be a soldier, but he was gambling lives on the hope that where Andronicus had lied once to him, he had lied many times.

They urged the horses to settle into a gait that would eat up the miles. Here, the land was dangerously, deceptively peaceful. No one shot arrows at them from ambush or rode out to bar their way.

The men rode quietly now, lulled by the rhythm of the beating hooves, deep in their own thoughts. Leo's musings, as always when he rode, were as haunted as the land through which he rode.

By now, everyone in Peristrema was probably dead. That was a fact Leo had to face. Why, then, was it so important that he find Father Meletios? Already, he had heard rumblings as one soldier argued that such and such a village must be protected above all else, while a friend insisted that another one (usually the debater's home) was of even greater importance or wealth.

I will have things as I will them to be! Leo had ridden close to Romanus long enough to know how quickly the former Emperor could fall into a rage when his will was crossed. Leo knew it was foolishness to draw so large a force away from the towns. It was rash; it was even a provocation to attack. But Meletios' wisdom had saved his sanity. And, by his kindness, he had Asherah to wife earlier than he might otherwise have done—*had her at all*; for who knew if he would survive even the next hour? Beyond what he owed to any holy man, he owed Meletios his soul.

Not my will alone, but Thine. Leo made for the valley with the harsh high wind of prophecy blowing at his back.

In the afternoon, they reached the bend in the road and turned, riding toward the valley carved into the soft rock. The poplars rustled thirstily; and, in the sultry weather, the buzz of insects seemed to rise from the green valley floor.

They paused to send out scouts. From the valley floor, the river's siren music reached them. Leo took off his helmet, letting the air cool him for a moment. He sucked up a few grudging sips of water. He had been this thirsty before, when he had fought or when he had fasted, or when he had hacked out the walls of the hermitage he would never use now, thank God.

A low call brought his head around, and he slung the bottle away.

"What's a Turk doing here?" one of the soldiers muttered and reached for his sword.

"That's no Turk. That's Kemal," Ioannes told him.

"Well, what is he but a Turk?"

"He's *our* Turk. If he hadn't offered to scout the road, one of us would have had to." Probably, Ioannes should not take that tone with an older man, but the weather was hot and the men edgy.

Leo mounted. His horse, reluctant to leave the coarse grass it was cropping, sidled, then reluctantly plodded forward.

He raised an eyebrow at the *gulam*, who served him now.

"Were there ever stables at the head of a great cliff, where stairs lead down into the valley?"

" 'Were there?' " Leo echoed. The news was as bad as he had expected.

"They're gone now. Burnt to embers. They took the horses with them, of course."

Leo shut his eyes. Horses feared flames and screamed as piteously as men if they were trapped in them. Thank God, the Turks were horsemen, whatever else they were.

"What about the monks?" Ioannes demanded. "There were men down there too!"

And his friend Theodoulos, not to mention chapels and hermitages that should not be defiled.

Kemal shook his head, his hand going out in a cutting-off motion.

"It is quiet down there now. I went belly-down on the ground and couldn't see anything move. Except," he added in a lower voice, "the birds. You can see them from here."

The birds looked as if they fled. But they would return, and with them—don't think of that, Leo warned himself. Some monks in the valley may yet be alive.

And I alone escaped to tell you. Leo remembered the stinks of blood and burning and bowels voiding in death. Bowing his head, he shut his eyes in prayer. *Protect them, Lord. What did they ever do but praise you?*

A wind blew up from the valley, ruffling Leo's hair, dank from the helmet he had taken off. He could smell smoke on the wind. A kind of dark exhilaration akin to a compulsion lay upon him. Leo turned toward the valley that he knew was filled with dead men and possible ambushers, and he knew that he was going to climb down into it.

Leo set his helmet back on his head. It might as well have been made of lead. Reaching for his shield, he saw the others copy him. Once more, they rode toward sure destruction.

Beyond the burnt-out stables, Leo stationed guards. Some of the men covered their horses and walked them until they were cool. One or two, those who lacked horror in the face of fire, picked through the rubble. Leo and Ioannes, Kemal, and several others stretched flat out on the lip of the valley, trying to see whether anyone still moved down there.

"You have to go up over that ridge before you get into the center of the place," Ioannes reminded Leo.

He nodded. From here, he could see no bodies, whether monks or servants or their attackers. That meant nothing, least of all that it would be safe to take the usual path downward.

He gestured at it.

"What do you think?" he asked Kemal.

The *gulam* shrugged. "I couldn't be sure of a straight shot," he said. "If it were me, and my fate drove me to clamber down there, it might be safe to try. Or, it might not; and you'd die cleaner simply hurling yourself off the rock, here."

Leo grimaced. Driven as he was by a compulsion with the force of prophecy to find the old priest, he found Kemal's fatalism aggravating, to say the least.

"Would you try?" he asked.

Again, the shrug. "Why not?"

Reckless to a fault and more than a bit of a fool, his Kemal. It explained why he now served a Byzantine rather than reclining at his ease, enjoying an Emperor's ransom, in Persia.

It was folly, too, for Leo to descend into the valley. His men looked to him. Doctrine and his own conscience told him: you have no right to abandon them. The people who loved him had set him free to do as he saw best. In doing so, they had risked their hearts and lives on his judgment, had become hostage to it where now they crouched deep below the earth. It was folly to have trusted him, to have trusted anyone so utterly—as he too had done.

Before God, Leo thought, they must all be fools.

One last time, he leaned out, marking the path he would take downward. There was no Theodoulos to urge him forward, hastening despite his lame leg. There was no Father Meletios to heal his spirit. There was only the compulsion upon him to descend.

He would need both hands for the climb down. Still, he loosened his sword in its sheath and made certain that he could quickly reach the other weapons he wore. Despite the boiled-leather harness he wore, his back ached as if in imminent expectation of an arrow fleshing itself between his shoulderblades.

He began the descent. The others, at a safe distance either from attack or from what they must consider madness, left their fears on the lip of the cliff and descended after him.

Already, the day's heat had brought the reek of a battlefield to what Leo remembered as a sanctuary. As Leo descended, he could see thick, greasy smoke mounting above the ridge that divided the inner from the outer valley. The river ran brown and clean, but blood splashed the rocks that served as a bridge. That trail ended in the body lying half in, half out of the water, washed as clean of sins as of blood.

Ashamed of his relief at not being able to see the monk's face, Leo bent and lifted him out of the water, turning him over to look into the pale face. It was not a face he knew. Death had drained the pain and terror from it. Leo closed its eyes, composed the dead man's limbs upon the warm grass, murmured a prayer for the dead man's soul, and went on.

The battlefield reek grew stronger as Leo neared the cluster of shrines and cells that lay at the valley's heart. Fire blackened the entry to some of the caves. Flies buzzed nearby and above the tumbles of coarse brown and black homespun, quilled with arrows, the unsightly awkward feet halted forever in their flight.

Leo drew his sword as they headed upslope to Father Meletios' cave. He had never expected to draw a weapon in a shrine. Coming here for the first time as a madman and penitent, he had been dumbstruck by the light that poured from the holy man's cave. Blind himself, he had affixed a kind of mirror to the rock wall to provide light for his sighted visitors. But now, no blade of light parried Leo's sword. The mirror had been cast down. The polished metal lay dented on the rough floor, together with shards of broken pottery. Someone had trampled on the statue Leo had admired upon his first visit: he grimaced at the sight of its mutilated body. Such a foolish thing to care about with so many good men killed.

Where was Meletios? Leo had expected to find him crumpled on his pallet or before his icon.

Leo emerged from the cave, waving his arms to signal: no one here! A few butterflies erupted from a bush that had been grubbed only partially up by its roots. The bush, at least, would heal.

He could see hope light his men's faces. Perhaps not all the monks had been slain. Perhaps, survivors would creep out of hiding to help the soldiers bury the dead and pray for them.

The butterflies hovered, then flew upslope toward the church to which Meletios had led Leo on that first visit.

Then Leo heard the hopeless weeping issuing from the darkness.

He shuddered, or the ground trembled: he could not tell which. He pointed at the cave chapel and started toward it. In the rough-cut narthex Leo paused, letting his eyes become accustomed to the dark before he entered. He knew he should not bear arms into a church. There were other things that should not be done there. Judging from the evidence of Leo's eyes and nose, he thought the Turkmen had done all of them. The pictures of tall, formidable ladies in their red and ochre robes had already been defaced. Now they endured further indignity, illiterate obscenities that made Leo grit his teeth. The reek of urine rose from a puddle in a corner. Stone benches had been hacked in a vain attempt to knock them over.

And the weeping, which had drawn Leo, ended in a stifled sob.

Leo thought it came from the direction of the altar. It too had been hacked about, but he was glad to see it had not been desecrated. Then, he saw the hardening pool on which dust had already settled, darkening at the edges.

"*Kyrie eleison,*" he said. How many men had died here?

"*Christe eleison.*" The response came from behind the altar, very faint and broken by a gasp.

"Father Meletios!" Two long strides brought Leo to where the old man lay. One hand touched the altar-stone. The other pressed down on a wound in his breast. Meletios was almost corpse-pale. Bled out. Bled white, despite his long-ago desert weathering.

From the shadows of the apse, presided over by the fierce Theotokos Leo remembered, Theodoulos forced himself to unsteady feet. He smeared a filthy hand across his eyes and nose.

"Nordbriht told me," Leo said. He was down on both knees, fumbling in his pouch for soft cloths, for all the good that would do. No care on earth could staunch that wound, and if God couldn't spare a miracle for Father Meletios, mankind was totally out of them.

Meletios lifted his hand free of the altar. "God sent you, my son. His last mercy to me. I cannot die with this undone . . . unguarded . . . no one to come after me. No one to restrain her."

"Her?" Leo whispered.

"What lies below," Meletios replied. "I drove out the sisters. Oh, I knew, though they lived as nuns, that they only waited to do *her* will. I tried to blot her face from the walls—and from my sight, but . . ."

Meletios tried to rise, shaking with pain and urgency. "Can't you feel it? She rises!" Leo tried to press him back down.

Theodoulos' eyes gleamed, immense in his smeared face. More than ever, he looked like a boy—no, a young man—of the very oldest race to dwell here. Leo gestured over his shoulder for Ioannes to see to his friend, who watched the dying monk with horror.

"Whatever it is, lay the burden down," Leo leaned forward. "I'm here now."

"You . . . you do not reject . . ." Again, the trembling hand came up, trying to compel Leo's belief.

"I tell you, I will see to it."

Meletios smiled and yawned. Bleeding to death could be a sleepy death. Leo half-lifted the bloody hand that had tried to staunch the chest wound, but gave up the attempt at Meletios' convulsive start. Even the glance he got at it told him that the holy man's case was hopeless.

And that was precisely what it should not have been. Meletios' teeth were chattering, his blind eyes distended. Mortally wounded he was, to be sure. Still, a holy man, sure of heaven, should not die in mortal fear.

And he would die soon, too, drifting away on the tide of of his own bloodloss. How much time could he have left? Surely, the Turkmen would not return to put them all to fire and sword if they knelt and said a simple prayer for the good old man's soul. Leo clasped his hand.

"No! No time!" Meletios interrupted. "You have to go back, protect . . . protect."

He had just welcomed Leo, told him that God had sent him.

"They can spare the time to say a few prayers," Leo told him. "I will not leave you this way."

"I cannot be moved."

Leo shook his head, then remembered that Meletios was blind. "You never could."

"We . . ." another jaw-cracking yawn, a foreshadowing of death's rictus . . . "have been comrades, soldiers in this war."

"Yes."

"Then give me . . . what any injured comrade might ask. Don't leave me . . . not for *them*. The mercy-stroke, son of mine. Do it."

"How can you ask me to kill you?" Leo demanded. Meletios was a holy man. He had healed him, had wed him to Asherah.

"You cannot leave me in the dark," Meletios begged him. "Not like this. Not . . ." He tried to raise himself upon his elbow, so frenzied Leo knew that terror would kill him in a few moments.

"Easy there. Steady," whispered Leo.

"Sir," called a man stationed at the entrance to the cluster of caves. "Up above . . . the guard is waving. Horses! They're coming, and they're not ours."

Leo gestured his men into hiding.

"You must flee now. . . ."

"God have mercy," Leo murmured.

"I absolve you of my blood, son. Now . . . quickly." Leo groped for his sword. Meletios, who had braced himself for the blow, raised a hand at the sound of the blade, freed from its scabbard.

"I . . . have not lived by the sword, and I . . . I refuse to perish by it. Use . . . the little knife, the black stone you told me of."

Leo sighed deeply and laid his sword aside. He drew the tiny knife. "Bless me, father," he begged. He blinked his eyes free of tears lest his aim fall awry and the old man die in more pain.

"Blessings . . . now . . . to you and the way below. Below!" He braced one hand against the altar once more and raised his chin.

Leo struck. Blood flowed over his hand and the black knife, soaking in an instant into the altar. Meletios' hand jerked convulsively against the altar. To Leo's astonishment, it toppled. Leo caught a glimpse of a rough sarcophagus, incised with a girlchild's remote, delicate face.

Behind him, Theodoulos sobbed aloud. "The Sisters always said she was *my* sister. And now I am about to join her."

Ioannes hugged the other lad against him. "They'll hear you, they'll hear," he warned.

"So will they . . . below," said Meletios' servant.

A whistle sounded from outside. The Turks must be very close indeed. Anger flashed through Leo, and he felt stronger than he had for weeks. Surely, he had not come all this fruitless way just to kill a priest, then be slaughtered on his body!

He glared up at the defaced Theotokos on the wall. What remained of her eyes glared back at him, drawing his eyes. Beneath her, snakes, leopards . . . *just like the paintings he had seen far below the surface of the earth near where the caves were walled off from—what had the nun called it?*

Sister Xenia had called that path "the way below." So a branch of it led here? The nuns had known of it and guarded it. And then Meletios had driven them out and settled down to guard it in their stead. All these years they had known. Yet Meletios had died in fear. What did lie below the earth, and why was the entry hidden in this shrine?

"Get Theodoulos over here," Leo ordered Ioannes. "Quickly!"

"What is this 'way below'?" Leo grasped the boy by his shoulders. "If there is a bolthole from this place, show it to us so we don't all die like rats in a trap."

And, when Theodoulos hesitated, Leo snapped. "You heard him. He willed it to me. Show me. *Now.*"

Theodoulos stumbled forward. Terror and grief made him more awkward than Leo had ever seen him, and he had to harden his heart against the sight. He thrust forward with the boy's crutch. It wedged in one of the blocks that underlay the fallen altar. He leaned his weight upon it and wrested it up . . . up . . . he was weakening; the stone would fall back; the Turks were coming—Leo hurled himself forward and thrust his shoulder beneath the stone. A draft of air struck him in the face, cooling the blood that had washed him.

Though the pounding of the blood in his heart and temples nearly drowned them out, he could hear footsteps, almost as awkward in their way as Theodoulos. Kemal never walked if he could ride.

The Seljuk raced into the church, ignoring the unfamiliar surroundings and the filth. "Turkmen, lord. I recognize the standard. Probably coming to see if anything's left."

Leo glanced frantically about the church for answers. They came as his eyes met the half-blinded visage of the woman painted on the wall. With one hand she held her Child. The other pointed downward. To the way below.

"Quick," Leo gasped. "Get the men into the cave. Theo, do you keep torches down there?"

Their lives might depend on his answer unless they burnt every scrap they wore.

"He made me . . . made me see to it."

"Down!" Leo ordered.

Into the pit. The men paused.

"Come *on!* The holy father tended it. You think he'd send you down to hell?"

A small farmer from outside Hagios Prokopios knelt. "He might be guarding its gate. Protecting us from the demons below."

"How's this cave any different from where your wife—and mine—took sanctuary? Who knows? Maybe we'll meet up with them. Now," Leo rose and took a step forward. "In, or so help me, I'll send you to the gates of hell myself!"

And God forgive me for saying so.

At Leo's gesture, Theodoulos led the way. "By the time I get down there, I want a torch lit!" Leo ordered.

He shut his eyes. He could feel footsteps in Meletios' valley—which was now his. Alien footsteps, confident of any prey that remained. And beneath him, fear and temptation. Was this the terror Meletios had felt? Or another of Leo's own hauntings? If he didn't hurry, his blood would drown it. His heart swelled, demanding life, more life. He had promised Asherah to return to her. But one man had to remain outside and close the passage.

The last man except for Ioannes and Kemal made it into the pit. There had to be a way out. There had to. Why else set a priest to guard this?

"Quick," Leo pointed to the passageway. "Ioannes, you're next. Then you, Kemal."

"You can't leave the rock like that," Kemal gestured at the hole beneath the altar. "They'll see the good old man down there, decide he was guarding treasure, and follow you."

"Right. I have to rejoin the troop anyhow," Leo said. "So I'll tip the rock back over and take my chances. It worked for you, after all. When you surface—make that 'when' and not 'if,'—look for me."

"Sir . . ."

Leo gestured with the point of his sword at Ioannes.

"Now, you . . ."

Had the Turk gone mad? He stripped off his tunic, tore his other clothing, then slashed his own flesh as if in the barbarous mourning of the steppes. He smeared blood over his face and chest, and grinned at Leo like something from the Pit.

"I'm the poor foolish *gulam*, remember? Pissed away an emperor's ransom, and never had a day's luck after. So stupid that even monks can knock me on the head. And when I wake up, they're gone. I'm no kin of theirs. They even stole my horse, I'll say. Now, get moving."

He laughed at the look on Ioannes' face.

"You gave me life, lad, like the master there. He took me in. Now he doesn't stand a chance. You don't stand a chance. But *I* do. If it is written, we shall meet again. And do you think I won't like gulling those . . ." he trailed off into his native tongue. "How I'll laugh at that, even if the Turkmen do tie me to their horses and whip them to the four corners of the earth!"

Leo started forward to plead with Kemal. "Friend," he began.

The Turk gestured. "Move!" he snarled. "Does it take a vow of silence to keep you Christians quiet?"

Leo raised his arms, then felt them seized. *Ioannes, you Judas!*

"Forgive me, prince," said Kemal. "But even a fool of a *gulam* knows you cannot be spared. Speak to your sons of me."

White light and red pain exploded in Leo's skull, and he fell forward into the pit.

Leo flinched from an explosion of red-gold and hot above his head. One of the familiar sick headaches he had suffered after Manzikert pounded in his skull.

A young voice, self-consciously brave and dignified, caught his attention.

"Yea, though I walk through the valley of the shadow of death, I will fear no evil . . ."

Carefully, Leo turned his head. He really thought he might live now.

He attended to the words of the psalm. Even Ioannes knelt, listening to Theodoulos pray. The sobs were gone from his voice. So was its youthful reediness; and that, no less than all the others, was a loss. Fire-shadows washed over them all and danced on the walls.

All of the figures depicted upon them had their eyes scratched out. *If thy right eye offend thee, pluck it out.*

Leo shut his eyes once more. Meletios had been a blind guardian of the underground ways. What did they contain that he feared to see, so that he had ordered the faces of the women—the goddesses—on the walls to be scratched out? That is, if they had not been scratched out earlier by someone equally orthodox, equally fearful, and equally blind.

His head spun. If he moved, he would spew out anything in his stomach. The air was warm. His men were safe. His wife was safe in hiding. God grant Kemal proved more clever than he had boasted.

The warm air took on a spicy scent. *He and Asherah entered the maze, the first—what? trespassers? worshippers?—to do so for God knows how long. The air turned warm and spicy. His mouth grew dry with longing, and he had turned to her and seen the same desire in her eyes. The caves had brought him new life.*

A saint like his namesake, Meletios was—almost. But saints could cast out fear, and Meletios had feared this way so much that he had died rather than escape into it. Year ago, he had even sacrificed his sight lest he see and be tempted. By what?

An answer struck Leo like a blow to the back of the head: whatever power lay beneath the surface of the earth had to be female. Why else would Meletios cast out the old nuns? Why else would the valley teem with female idols? Why else would the faces of the women painted on the stone be scratched out?

Why else would it have drawn Asherah, and drawn him to her?

The power had to be female. And he had sworn to protect the way within to it.

Leo groaned. Instantly, his men, half of them only boys, clustered about him.

"Hold off, you men," Ioannes commanded. "Let my lord breathe."

Gently, Theodoulos ran his fingers over the back of Leo's skull. "Not broken," he murmured. "The Turk knew what he was doing."

Ioannes blessed himself. "I hope so."

Leo grimaced. That hurt too.

Theodoulos held a water-bottle to his lips. It smelled of goat, but the water could have come out of an Emperor's goblet, so welcome was it. He gulped avidly, then forced himself to stop.

"How much do we have left?" he asked.

Theodoulos shrugged and put away the bottle. Might as well let him guard it. "You needed it, sir. We'll find more."

"Keep it down," Leo cautioned. "They may still be up there. And there might be some way they can hear what's going on."

Ioannes shook his head. "I made them move further down." He gestured into the darkness of the unlit tunnel that stretched behind them and before like the belly of some great serpent. "I was afraid of the noise. So I stayed behind to find out. You can hear from below. You can see, too."

Kemal? No matter how cunningly he had struck, Leo thought he would have heard Kemal scream if the Turks tortured him.

Ioannes grinned, his teeth bright in his dusty face. "I heard scratching and banging on the church's walls. Kemal let them see him, and they all laughed. Then they all rode off."

So Kemal had been spared! That gave Leo a little more hope.

Bracing himself against Theodoulos, Leo struggled to sit up. The cave whirled about him, then steadied. So did his stomach. Good.

He glanced at the torch. Now, he could bear its light. His head wasn't broken. He remembered how it felt from last time.

As he made it to his feet, supported by both youths, he could hear his men gasp in relief. One or two muttered prayers that echoed in the passageway. It was dusty here: warm, not dank.

And it had to lead to somewhere.

"Let's go," he ordered.

Ioannes moved to Leo's side, holding aloft the torch. Their feet scuffed up ancient dust as they walked. Not knowing where they went, his soldiers marched. Each bore fresh torches. Almost none of them had water. The passageway widened into a tunnel and ran from there into what seemed like forever.

 36

Hours ago, they drank the last of their water. Now they had to fight not to think of the thirst that teased at their awareness and that would soon fight to rule them. They trudged down the endless dry passage, without even a gurgle of water in the stone beside them to torment them with the hope of drink. They would bless Malagobia now, with its deep wells, but where did it lie, and how could they find it?

Leo had one hope: this underground path, cutting below rocks and hills that a surface road would have to circle, shorten the distances between town and town.

That hope had better prove true. Thirst, unlike bleeding, was a very painful death.

Speak to the rock; strike the rock; and find water in a desert? Meletios had been the holy man, and Meletios would have died in terror had Leo not released him.

The tunnel sloped downward, running at that lower level in what felt like a straight track for a long time. Here were no wall-paintings, only the unevenness of rock hewn by hand and hardened by fire. From time to time, the earth trembled.

Hours ago, they had given up looking at the cave's ceiling as if their eyes could harden the stone and bear it up, should the incalculable weight of rock above take a fancy to crash down upon them.

Kemal had had the right of it after all. What was written was written. And Theodoulos too was right when he prayed for peace in the valley of the shadow of death.

Abruptly, a gust of wind blew across their faces. The guttering torch that Ioannes had been nursing, since who knew how long their supply would have to last, flared up, then out, in a gout of stinking smoke. That left them in the dark. Ioannes cursed once, fumbling for flint and steel and one of their supply of torches. Someone else laughed a little hollowly into the darkness.

A small farmer named Petros dropped his spear, fell to his knees, and cowered, covering his face. Theodoulos limped back and laid his arm over the older man's shoulders, easing him back up onto his feet. The boy was doing surprisingly well down here. Leo would almost have thought it were his native earth. Meletios had probably had him crawling through these tunnels from the time he was old enough to walk . . . no . . . limp . . . no, forget that. His limp was less of a weakness than the other man's fear.

The others stopped, blinking somewhat. One or two leaned against the rock wall, pressing their brows to the damp stone as if that might assuage their growing thirst.

They had reached not just a bend in the tunnel, but an actual fork in the road. And it surprised them that this underworld could hold any direction but straight ahead.

Now, which way should they go? One path, the one on which they had been marching for what felt like forever led downward, the other along the way they had come. In the instant before the light blew out, Leo had even fancied he saw it turn slightly upward.

Downward: Leo remembered the old stories, that linking the underground cities was a maze of tunnels, all of which, ultimately, met in a central treasury. Desire flared in him to know the truth, to explore, to see.

The upward path was the obvious choice. If he were building this maze, he would construct it with blinds and false turns, to trap the overconfident and the merely unlucky.

But above them, under the sun, the Turks invaded with fire and sword, and time was wasting. Time was wasting down here, too. One could not drink gold or jewels, or eat them. If too much time passed as they wandered in the entrails of the earth, they would lie here until they died. Leo shut his eyes.

It was not prayer that he called upon, but instinct. The land had spoken to him before, the land and its hauntings. Now, he had taken over the guardianship of the ways from Meletios. In obedience, he had killed the good old man, whose blood had splashed upon the altar guarding the ways as well as upon Leo's hands. That all ought to count for something, he told himself. Shouldn't it?

If he could only *see!* If only, he could see the land above him as clearly as he could see the folds and chisel marks of the tunnel's roof!

He heard Ioannes mutter satisfaction. The torch caught. Light again flickered in a protective circle around Leo and his troop.

He tried to remember how the roads ran. As above; so below. But, outside the realm of philosophy, matters were never that simple. If only he had some map, or some way of retracing his steps! He wanted to be able to sit down and think it out, perhaps send out a scout or two. Someone coughed. Leo's tongue swelled in his mouth. They would only become hungrier and thirstier, until thirst crowded out hunger, crowded out sanity, crowded out life.

Finally, because no choice was a choice only to die hard where they stood, Leo pointed toward the tunnel leading upward. "Perhaps it will bring us to the way out," he croaked. His mouth felt as if he had licked the cave walls clean. His throat seemed to shut.

They turned and climbed. After an hour or so longer, the way grew steeper. The stillness that had oppressed them since they began their march seemed to fade somewhat. Now, not only Leo's head hurt, but his ears.

"We're still climbing," Theodoulos whispered.

"Tell me what I *don't* know," his friend grumbled back.

"The air's different," Theodoulos said. "I can feel it."

The passage narrowed. Soon, they would walk only two abreast, then, one at a time; and then, they would have to edge sideways.

Ioannes put out a hand to steady himself as well as his friend. "I just found a torch-holder."

So this place had been known, prepared. Please God, it wasn't a blind.

That reassurance came just in time. Now the footing grew even more difficult. The passageway became an uneven stair, with the steps cut at long intervals. They breathed in gasps and took turns boosting Theodoulos up each step. The boy's leg must ache like fire, but they had no time to rest and rub the aches out for him. A mist hung over their eyes, and the blood pounded in their temples from the effort.

The air grew cool, then moist. A gust of wind, heavy with blessed dampness, swept over them. Quickly, Ioannes shielded his torch against his body.

He set it down, propped against a rock wall, and turned to give a hand to the next man up.

"We're through," he muttered. "Theo, do you have any idea *where* we are?"

Theodoulos, chest heaving, head down, paused for a moment before the others boosted him upward. He crouched on the ground, hands rubbing at his weak leg. "There . . . should be some sort of peep-hole. . . ." he gasped.

Blind Meletios had been, but he had thought to teach his servant how to spy out the underground ways. What else had he taught him?

When Leo pressed, Theodoulos recoiled. "That's all I can remember now." He shuddered. "Sometimes, he made me walk in the dark. If I called him, he would not come. He said I had to learn how to find my way, just as he did."

Leo ran his hands over the rough walls. A fissure in the stone, yes. He leaned close and found himself peering upward into an enclosure little different from the tunnel in which they stood. An empty enclosure.

"Hide the torch," he ordered. They would not dare to clamber blind into the upper air. And when he emerged from the underground ways into the kind of cell he had been cutting for himself out of living stone before Asherah changed his world for him, it was with sword in hand.

They had emerged into one of the rock pipes that played such weird music when the wind blew across the plain. The dark distant horizon alarmed Leo. Meletios' blood and the flight beneath the earth must have worked some spell: Leo did not belong out here, he thought. He ought to retreat back to the ways below. He had been sealed to them, he belonged to them, not to this frightening horizon.

No wonder Meletios hated to leave the valley and feared to leave the entrance to the paths of which he had been the guard. He had passed his tasks—and his fears—on to Leo.

So, it was Leo's turn to defend his charge. And he must defend Asherah, who, even at this moment, could be found if he only knew how to search for her in the underground ways.

Whatever he must do, he would need water and food if he were to live long enough to do it. And light to traverse the ways beneath the earth.

Leo made himself step to the entrance and glanced out over the plain. It was full night here, as it was in the ways below. That much of a reassurance he had. He squinted. The sky was dark, the horizon even darker: dark of the moon, thank God for the people in the caves huddled anywhere near Nordbriht. In one or two places, he could see light. How strange to see light that was not torches: the lamps of a farmhouse accounted for one spots of light; the uncontrollable brightness further down what had to be a road was, most likely, a fire set by raiders. Even as he watched, the flames seemed to sink, a beast that had killed, crouching to feed.

Where there were raiders, there was likely to be plunder. Something might even be left over from that farm's destruction. And there would be water.

In silent accord, they set out across the surface of the world. Leo went last of all, almost frightened by the wide land. *What coward am I?* he demanded of himself and forced himself to his proper place at the front of the tiny group.

The house they found was in ruins, the stable even worse. The horses, of course, were gone. But an outbuilding held supplies. Petros, wise in the ways of farmers, kicked through a charred wall.

"Almost always works with tax-collectors," he muttered with satisfaction. It had worked with the Turks too. In this hiding place, they found hardened bread that had gone unnoticed, even a skin of wine. They would be able to eat now, with enough to take away into the caves. What the Turks had not taken, Leo and his men did. Perhaps hearing the sounds of men, a goat wandered back. One of the farmers milked her, a taste of incredible luxury after so long beneath the earth. Best of all, outside, they found a well. Scraps of wood to make torches were, unfortunately, all too easy to find. Leo took careful note of the house and its location. God send that one day, Leo could repay these people for their involuntary kindness.

Ioannes flung out an arm, indicating the trackless night and the vast horizon ahead of them. Even the snow capping Mount Argaeus seemed blackened. Leo glanced back at the rock chimney from which they had emerged. He wanted to return, to climb back down into the safe channels beneath the earth. Venturing out on that plain, he would feel like a bug upon a stone table: how pathetically easy to squash them, petty and visible as they were.

He should not abandon his charge—and the paltry army he had made from farmers, nobles, veterans, and merchants was clearly his charge. Equally so were the cave passageways. What to do, what to do? Oh God, his head would split.

Prudence rescued him. One man might cross the plains, or perhaps two—say a man and a boy, almost turned man. A troop, however, on foot or on horse, would draw the Turks' attention—and they were not Kemal, to crave it as a ruse.

There would be other exits from the passageways in this land. And it might be—temptation swept over Leo like a dark tide—that he would even find the road that led to Asherah's sanctuary.

"I promised the old father I would guard these ways," Leo began hesitantly. "Somehow I feel as if I'd be breaking my word if I left them right now. If we all go, we'll be too conspicuous once dawn comes up. Theodoulos proved it once—Turks sometimes don't bother with one or two men who look poor and helpless enough. It's a calculated risk, however. . . ."

You give your orders; you don't ask. He could hear his uncle Andronicus' voice, imperious, if not Imperial. His uncle had enjoyed telling him that he was no sort of soldier. But he was soldier enough to worry about his men, not betray them. So he would ask, rather than command, in a place where he could not lead.

Theodoulos' mouth opened to volunteer. Leo shook his head. "You, I need. If your master ever gave you any hint how to navigate that maze, I want to hear it. You sit and try to remember."

"I can't." Theodoulos' voice cracked. "I'm not fit. The sisters found me when I was a baby. Even then, I was crippled—maybe that's why my . . . my parents threw me out. Father Meletios was a priest before he lost his eyes, but me? You could dream of it, but I, brought up in the valley, couldn't even try to be a priest. I'm not *whole.* And now, you want to depend on *me* . . . I just can't."

Ioannes knelt beside Theodoulos, who sat and shook. *Make it right,* his gaze demanded.

Leo knelt too and took the lame boy's shoulders between his hands. Theodoulos flinched, as if expecting to be shaken.

"The stone that the builders rejected," Leo quoted. "Remember that. You must be our cornerstone now. I will not let you fail."

The boy sagged against Leo's shoulder. He tried to make his grip sustaining, tried to make himself look strong. He was making it up as he went along, and he only hoped it was good enough.

Theodoulos pushed free and sat up. Good enough for the moment, then. Leo could turn to the next problem. His eyes met those of Ioannes. So young the boy was. Had Leo been that young, even before Manzikert? He didn't think so. It must have been exposure to the City. Ioannes was older in years than Leo's friend Alexius; but it was easier to think of Alexius as a man and an equal than Ioannes, whose courage and endurance Leo had tested.

I hate to ask, he thought.

But Ioannes offered.

One of the men from his land spoke up too. Ioannes jerked his head around. Petros' offer violated generations of farmers' instincts to keep their heads down and let wars and the demands of soldiers sweep by them whenever they could.

Leo nodded.

"Take Petros with you."

"He does know the land better than I," Ioannes admitted, the desire for help, companionship warring with his evident desire to protect one of his own. Let the boy see that taking Petros with him would save the man another journey underground. Every step that Petros took beneath the earth was a soul-deep battle: if Leo could spare him that, even open battle might be a better fate for a man as frightened as Petros of the ways below.

"I'll try to rejoin the troop," Ioannes spoke up. "I'll tell them that you are circling about and will join up as soon as you can. And I'll warn them of the double game Kemal is playing. God forbid he pay with his life for saving ours."

Leo clapped him on the shoulder before he and his man went out into the dark. Good lad. What an officer he would have made. There was no time or strength to waste precious moments blaming himself for not going with them. The dark was calling him back. It might even be that he could travel faster and more quietly under the earth.

Leo insisted Ioannes and Petros take the best of the supplies, repeated his instructions, and clapped both of them on the shoulder. Then he and the men who would accompany him back into the dark saluted Ioannes and Petros. For a long moment, they watched the two trudge down from the rock onto the plain until rocks and darkness hid them.

Then they turned back toward the steep passageway to the road below. The path was straight and steep. One turn, then another to make certain that any glimmer of light did not pierce the spy-hole Leo had used; and they lit torches and proceeded through the darkness, silent except for their own footsteps.

How long had they wandered beneath the earth? Leo wondered.

It was not that the travel was so arduous. Any one of them, even Theo, had climbed steeper slopes, had wriggled through narrower passages (including the passage through which each one of them had struggled to be born), had borne heavier loads.

It was the weight that oppressed them: the weight of the rock not that far from their stooped backs; the weight of knowing that their families hid in similar caves; the weight of knowing that even as they wandered below ground, their brothers-in-arms fought and their families feared. And if that was not enough, they sensed the darkness outside the circle cast by the torches they carried and kindled, waiting ever so grudgingly, for the light to fail.

Leo kept Theodoulos at his side: the boy's wits were as quick as his leg was halt. What would this boy have become, assuming he had been exposed to more than doting former nuns and a blind priest? If Leo lived, Theodoulos would never want for a thing.

Once Leo told Theodoulos how many thousands of paces comprised a day's march, they could work out a system for telling the time. They knew from Leo's own experience how long it took to walk however many thousands of paces. They measured that against the length of time it took to burn a torch down to a bluish, smoky stub that scorched the hand. And they knew distances between places in the upper air.

So now they could measure time and distance in torches. For a longer interval than a torch, they had the times between meals. And then, there were the times between sleeps, which could be measured and double-checked by the guard who tended the torches.

In the first sleep, Theodoulos woke screaming. His cries brought Leo up out of dreams of his own in which storm gods doused the fires that he was certain engulfed the land above them, firestorms piping the music of the damned across the rock pipes as the Turks rode, treasure-laden, into safety to await the destruction of all that dwelt there. Leo grabbed his sword and cast a quick glance at the torch. Mid-watch: struggling to keep up with them, given the weakness of his leg, Theodoulos ought to be sleeping like the dead, not shrieking like the damned.

The pupils of his eyes were surrounded by white, like those of a horse led from a burning stall just before its roof crashed inward, sending flames skyward.

"It hurts," he whispered to Leo.

"What hurts?" Had he strained his leg or broken some small bone in his foot?

Theo shuddered. "I was asleep in the dark. So warm, it was. And then, the ground shuddered. I had nothing to grasp, nothing! And I was cast out, and I fell on my leg. . . ."

"Sir, he didn't move, not even to turn over, till he started screaming."

Leo fumbled at the task of examining Theodoulos's withered leg. "It doesn't look any different," he said. "See?"

"My leg? Oh, that's as right as it ever gets." Theodoulos sighed. "I was a whole lot smaller in the dream. And I remembered something else.

"You want a way up? You look for torch holders. They expected people to hide their lights when they left the caves."

That much Leo had guessed. He fought a temptation to order Theo curtly back to sleep.

"What about the downward tunnels?"

Theodoulos shut his eyes. Then he shuddered. "Father always told me to avoid them. He said you could tell that they were the really oldest ways by the feel of the rock. It was smoother, see? I took a torch down a time or so, and I always saw paintings there. That was another way to tell."

"Mostly of women?"

"Snakes, too. And people wearing high crowns. Father said they were pagan and to not look. 'If thy right eye offend thee . . .' He kept telling me that at some point, they ought to be scratched over, but there was never time. . . ."

"No," Leo said gently, "there never really is time, is there? But you might have time to sleep now, if you were quick about it."

He arranged himself between Theodoulos and the torchlight. Half a torch. Soon they would be on the move again, bound for . . . *do you have a purpose, Leo? Or do you just skulk below because you are afraid?*

It was not fear. He had lived through fear, lived with it more closely than he had lived with Asherah (no stranger to it herself), and he knew it intimately too. Theo, so much younger than he, however; Theo might be afraid. Leo sat with him until he drifted off to sleep. His own head tilted to one side, and he jolted abruptly awake.

"Didn't mean to wake you," he muttered at Theodoulos, who had taken his hand. "I didn't want to sleep. We're moving on at the next torch."

"You didn't wake me," said Theodoulos. "The earth shook again. Didn't you feel it?"

Leo had felt nothing.

The next tremor came just as they changed torches. The light flickered toward extinction as the fresh torch was kindled. Eyes flared. No one said anything. But Leo noticed how the men studied the walls, seeking the torch holders that led to the outer air.

Paths upward to the light usually opened into a cave or rock chimney through which the wind piped laments for the wasting of their land. Once or twice, as Leo's men emerged, they smelled smoke. Another time, they heard the cries and clash of battle not too far off. A third time, they emerged almost out in the open and had to fight their way down beneath the surface once again, leaving a blood trail that could mean their deaths. They would have to remain below ground until their wounds ceased to bleed, Leo decided: they were too easy to track.

But their blood seeped into the stone, and the stone, he sensed, welcomed it as it had welcomed the blood of Meletios. It was no longer just Leo who was bound to these ways: it was all of them, for as long as they lived.

And, every half torch or so, the tremors kept quivering through the rock, almost as if it were thick mud that had somehow just not settled during all these centuries.

When they again spared time to sleep, Theodoulos dreamed again. He jerked upright just as the earth trembled. This time, the tremor woke Leo as well, and he half-staggered, half-crawled to the lame boy's side.

"Sir, look at his *eyes*," whispered one of the men.

Leo would not have been surprised to see them filmed over. But they were clear: they simply did not focus when he waved a hand before them.

Had the youth gone blind in the flicker of a torch? It seemed inconceivable.

And it was proved false in the next moment, as Theodoulos reached out to snatch a chunk of rock.

"Should I put him out?" asked the soldier.

"He's out already," Leo said. "Hit him, and we may have a madman on our hands." *Or a lad who never wakes up.*

Curious, Leo leaned forward, just as Theodoulos scrawled a crude grid upon the wall. From time to time, he would pause, shake his head, and look away, still with that glazed stare, as if attempting to remember details. Finally, once the scrawl had been completed to his liking, he sank back into normal sleep and did not wake until the changing of one torch for another—they were running low—meant that it was time for them to be on the move.

All had straightened themselves and their fragments of equipment as best they could: like the men, the caves were in Leo's charge; and he would have order in his domain. Only Theo still sat, staring at the grid, as if he had never seen it before.

"Do you remember?" Leo asked. "You woke, drew that, and went back to sleep."

Theodoulos shook his head. Then, he picked up the rock that had served him as a chisel before. "The valley," he muttered, "is here. Was here." He scraped a mark on the cave wall. Red powder drifted from the wall.

"That would mean Hagios Prokopios is *there*." Another red mark, some distance away.

Leo tried to calculate it in paces and torches, but quickly gave up.

"It's a straight track," he said. "Look, here is the cave city."

He had two cities now to think about. Hagios Prokopios was the town. The City was always and forever would be Byzantium. And then, of course, there was the underground city that was never far from Leo's thoughts and prayers, Malagobia where Asherah waited for him and his men to lift their siege.

Gently, he set down the stone. Theodoulos' eyes had the same tranced stare that they had had when he had risen from a sound sleep to scribble upon the cave wall.

"We can get through!" he whispered.

One of the guards leaned forward, holding the torch.

"We may not even have to leave the caves. But this way we can get through and warn our families."

Leo shut his eyes in brief thanksgiving. *I can get word to Asherah, maybe even see her again, hold her, know she is well.*

She had Nordbriht to protect her, and he was a better fighter than Leo could ever be. Still, the thought that he too could add his sword to her defense warmed him.

"No! It hurts, it hurts!" Theodoulos wailed.

"What hurts, son?" Leo asked. He bent to peer at Theo's withered leg.

Theodoulos uttered a choked cry and coiled in upon himself, twitching. As they reached to steady him, their torch dropped onto their meager supply of food. It burned through the water and wine bottles and charred the stale flat breads beyond use.

The tremor in the earth brought dust sifting down from the ceiling of the cave. A hunk of rock broke loose and toppled onto the floor.

37

The ground heaved underfoot. Leo imagined ripples across the ceiling of the tunnel, as if it were indeed a giant serpent that prepared to twist in upon itself, coil upon belly coil, and crush them. Someone whimpered.

"Move!" Leo commanded. In a minute, they'd all be screaming. He'd have to get them moving, forward and up toward the outer air.

The grid that Theodoulos had scratched onto the wall and then embellished seemed to glitter before his eyes, shifting into a maze, drawing him in.

This time, they heard the ground rumble. A shower of pebbles stung down.

"Black . . . dark . . ."

Scraping and draggings along the rock told Leo that two men had picked up Theodoulos. He wanted to stay beside the boy, but his place was in front. He flung out one arm against the rock wall at the level at which he expected to find a torch holder. Let the tunnel twist. Let it twist *now*.

Upward. Thank God. They'd reached a bend.

"Run for it, lads," he gasped. They probably wouldn't make it, but at the seat of Judgment, someone would at least know they had tried. The footing grew rougher. Leo's legs ached as he forced himself to longer and longer steps upslope. His heart tried to pound its way out of his mouth, and every breath seemed to lance through his chest. What the men who carried Theodoulos must be feeling was probably a foretaste of hell. Please God, it was the only hell they would ever feel.

The next spasm threw him onto his face. Just when he thought he might have won through. They weren't going to escape, were they? At least, they wouldn't have to worry about Christian burial. But Asherah would never know for certain what had become of them, except that her dreams would probably darken for all time.

No! The thought and Theodoulos' scream erupted simultaneously.

Leo forced himself back to his feet. Why bother to wipe the blood from his mouth and nose? He'd be dead in another instant or so. Shaking all over, he braced himself with a bloody hand against the wall. The stone trembled. More dust and pebbles sifted down. He felt through his boots how the vibrations in the rock subsided, then, finally, died. For now, the land rested.

He dared to unclench his fingers, spread his hand out over the rock. It closed about cold metal.

"We've found our way out, lads," Leo rasped. Now that the ground had ceased to shake, his knees were turning to water, and his bowels might not be far behind. He allowed himself the luxury of sagging against the wall for an instant. If his men were that fearful, they could climb over him.

No. That wasn't right. He knew it. Once again, he forced himself up. Someone behind him fumbled out flint and steel to kindle another torch—they had managed to preserve at least one, then: good.

Already, it was growing lighter. Perhaps it was actually day in the upper world.

But how would light pierce through here from a spyhole? If the one here was like any other, it was tiny, well-hidden.

Leo glanced about. His eyesight had somehow sharpened. Here, in what should be the blackness of a living crypt, it seemed no darker to him than twilight. He could pick out the roughnesses on the corridor walls, the rocks underfoot, even individual blows of hammer or pick. He rubbed his hand across his face. Before, when he had steadied himself, his blood had seeped into the stone, as Meletios' blood had before him. He was bound, just as Meletios had been. But with one important difference. Meletios had feared to see. Leo dared to try.

Hissing for silence, he edged up to the spyhole. Sensitive as his eyes now were, he would have to take care when he gazed out, lest the sunlight strike him temporarily as blind as the old dead guardian of these ways.

Again, Leo heard shouts, jostling, and the scream of a man in an agony of pain and mortal terror. Leo looked through the spyhole. There they were: Turkmen, their horses, and a man, half-clad except for blood and bruises, stretched out before them. They had built a fire. One or two squatted beside it, roasting chunks of meat. The smoke teased at Leo, making his mouth water with the fragrance of lamb, and burning his throat with the rasp of ash.

From time to time, one of the invaders leaned forward and did something Leo hated to watch to their victim with a knife. He screamed and writhed, and they laughed.

Leo's men pressed at his back, eager to leap out and save a man who, all unseen, they had accepted as their brother.

Leo held up a hand. *Wait.* The way the Turkmen spoke was different from the language Kemal had used, but he could understand it. The Turkmen weren't just torturing for the love of it; they were questioning their victim. And, in their own fashion, combining tactics with amusement.

Question after question they asked about troops, treasure, cities, and defense. And then, "I have heard you can find caves here, a vast honeycomb of caves leading to treasure here."

The man flinched, then tried to conceal his new fear.

"You cannot conceal that there are caves. What will you win by hiding what else you know? Only more pain and a slower death. Tell us about the caves."

Again, a frantic negative, followed by a scream and an attempt to lunge free so frantic that the man's face came into view.

It was Petros. Had Ioannes been killed, then? Had they already failed so completely?

Those deaths would weigh on his soul for however long his life might last.

Petros, he turned to mouth at his men. Rage swept over him and into them; that must be how Nordbriht felt whenever the madness touched him. But Leo was not a madman, not a beast. He fought for self-control and prayed that watching a comrade's agony might be forgiven him. Petros knew the underground ways, had walked them. For the sake of everyone in this land, they must know what he had already surrendered.

"Stupid man, turning to fight while your friend got away," said the raider. "Maybe we should hunt him down and cut the truth out of him. He's just a boy, only a boy. Think he can sing?"

Petros jerked his head, *no,* then tensed. A shrewd touch with a blade, and Petros screamed. It was a wonder he had any voice left.

"You out there! Bring in the . . ." the word was unintelligible to Leo; and he was certain he didn't want to know.

"Coming!" More words Leo could not understand; he took them for curses as the man outside the cave finished whatever unholy work he had been set to, and stomped, bearing what he had been commanded to bring.

It was Kemal. And he was carrying hot irons.

Blood seemed to flood Leo's vision, and fire harsher than what would shortly sear poor Petros made him feel strong enough to punch through the stone himself, kill Petros' torturers, and escape, single-handedly. He didn't even need to wish for Nordbriht.

Not again. Never again would he watch a man tortured by hot iron. They were out of time.

"*Now!*" Leo ordered. He drew his sword and brought his torch down for the charge.

Screaming, they erupted from the hidden cleft in the rock and leapt upon the Turkmen. Lolling at their ease, intent on their food and their sport, they lost a precious instant to surprise. Just enough for their attackers to leap upon them. Leo cut down the man leaning over Petros with a knife he had heated in the fire. Georgios behind him thrust his torch into the face of the man who lunged forward over the first Turk's body. The stink of flesh brought bile to Leo's mouth. He spit it out—fortunately right at the next man he faced—before, more by luck than skill, he hacked through his sword-arm.

A third man flung himself beside Petros and began to cut him free.

"No," Petros whimpered. "I can't walk . . . can't . . ." again, that soul-destroying shriek, this time caused by one of their own.

Kemal paused, frozen only for an instant as he took in the situation. Then he darted forward, a knife appearing almost by magic in his hand and cut Petros' throat, giving him the gifts that the others had not the heart to provide: silence and release.

"Traitor! Greek-lover!" One of the surviving Turks leapt upon his back, bringing up his blade to slit Kemal's throat. Leo shoved forward to try to stop him. But Kemal erupted to his feet, hurling the man off his back, and into the fire. Frantically, he rolled free, only to watch, his eyes rolling in terror, as Kemal brought an iron down shrewdly on his head. The last Turkmen turned from Georgios to attack Kemal. Leo stepped in, and helped him finish the man off.

Byzantine and Seljuk faced each other over the bodies of their dead kindred. "Lion's cub!" Kemal cried.

In his narrow-eyed, blood-stained face, his welcoming grin was horrible. If they had the time, Leo would have embraced him.

Leo bent to bless Petros. The man had feared the caves so much— and death was what his fear had bought him. At least, he had died swiftly, granted mercy by what had to be one of the strangest allies the Empire had ever known.

Kemal looked aside. "I didn't want to kill him. But he was dead already. His body just didn't know it."

"I know," Leo said. "His death is on my soul. He isn't the first I've had to release."

"Horses—they're coming!"

Leo grabbed at Kemal's arm. "You're coming back with us, and so is he. Get him."

Kemal bent forward and scooped up the dead man. His head lolled against the Seljuk's battered armor. No one protested that it was the Turk who bore their comrade home.

"Quick!"

They flung themselves back toward the slit in the rocks, the last man disappearing just as the first of the Turkish reinforcements stuck his head into the cave and shouted in rage.

"Wedge it!" Leo gasped.

Frantically, they heaped up rocks, trying to bar the way within. But there was precious little hope of that: once the Turks found any evidence that such a way existed, Leo knew that they would batter through the rock until they found it. They could only hurry and trust in. . . .

The land shuddered as two men laid Petros out with what hasty decorum they could muster. Theodoulos gabbled prayers.

Georgios flourished the torch he had used to dispatch an enemy. Fire brightened the narrow passageway as he led his comrades down. Leo followed, shoving Kemal ahead of him.

What difference did it make now if the earth caved in? Turks gnawed at their backs.

They ran. Someone flung his arm about Theodoulos when he flattened himself against the rock, determined not to hold the others back, forcing him along at a stumbling run quicker than he could have managed on his own.

"Damn you, Turk!" Leo heard him gasp. Kemal managed to spare enough breath to laugh.

Down they ran, stumbling and picking themselves up, and praying that no one snapped a leg as they fled. Back down to the bend in the tunnel, further down and to the straight track they had traveled for so long, and along it, then even further into the tunnels that Leo had noticed angling off at a gentle descent. Down, and always downward. When they could go no further, they flung themselves panting upon the trembling stone.

Here the rock was reddish, warmer. How far had they descended? Leo rested his cheek against the rough stone. Was that really water he could hear dripping? They said that thirst produced hallucinations before you died. He had not realized he was so very thirsty. There was so much he had not realized. The warm stone seemed to rock him. The torchlight swirled about him.

And then the world went dark.

The trickle of water woke Leo. He was lying, face down, upon warm rock. Once again, he had the sense of having abandoned himself that he had felt on Prote, when he stretched out like a faithful hound on the stone floor before his Emperor's tomb, and an Empress had ordered him back to the world.

An Empress: so many women in his life who had the power to command him. He remembered what he had thought about the rocks. There was power in this land, power in the earth below it. And that power was female.

He swallowed. If he judged by how dry his throat was, half of the rockfalls he had lived through seemed to have lodged in his throat.

"Here." Kemal handed him water in a helmet—had he dipped it in the stream or pool or trickle they could hear? Best not think of how clean it might or might not be. Leo sipped, then drank avidly. He passed the helmet back to Kemal. The man was covered in grit: not just the dust that anyone inevitably collected down in these ways, but greyish powder and even a few shining wisps that adhered to his armor.

Leo gestured at him. "What happened?"

"I didn't see it. Ismail swore he saw smoke rising from that cone-shaped mountain. Snow's melting on it, they say."

Would Mount Argaeus erupt like Etna, then? In Joachim's house, Leo had heard merchants speak of such things. Snow melted on such mountains' peaks, and they spat molten rock and hot ash, while the land beneath them rumbled and shifted.

Tilting his helm, Kemal finished the water. He looked down, then away, then in any direction but Leo's. Courage, however, was one thing he had never lacked. "Why'd you bring me back with you?" he finally asked.

"You saw what I had to do with Father Meletios. How can I fault you for following my example?" Leo said. "You're *ours*, Kemal. Or the land's, I don't know which. You've proved that."

Kemal leaned back on his heels, almost satisfied.

"This whole warren of caves may collapse on our heads," Leo reminded him. "So don't think I've done you any favors."

It became his turn to pause.

"You want to tell me what happened? What Petros said before he died?"

Kemal grimaced, *no*, then went on. "A raiding party picked me up in the valley. Some of your men may have heard it. I played the fool, and they gave me a pretty rough time of it. Then they gave me a horse and took me along, partly to do the hard work, partly because they liked laughing at me. They . . . we . . . happened on Ioannes and Petros as they were coming *back*. They must have got through, sent a message down into the caves, or something. Anyhow, they had gotten themselves horses. Fast ones.

"Petros hit Ioannes's horse across the rump with his sword, and it took off, leaving him to fight it out with the lot of us. Give Ioannes credit: he tried to turn and come back, but he's not that good a rider."

"Petros looked to Ioannes. Local nobility," Leo murmured.

"Probably, he thought he knew less, so if it came to that, better him than the boy."

Leo bowed his head and murmured a prayer for the man's soul. He would lie forever in the caves that he had feared—finally beyond all fear.

"From what they let me hear—you can imagine how little they trusted me . . ."

"It's a problem you have," Leo interrupted.

Kemal grinned and went on, "Some of the Turkmen have your cave city under guard. Siege, you'd call it."

"Have they got provisions to last out a siege?" Leo demanded. They might not. But if they could bring in reinforcements and a supply train, it wouldn't matter. In that case, they'd be starving in the caves. The best thing would be to evacuate them . . . but to where this time? He could hear Joachim's voice and Asherah's, saying that, sooner or later, there was no place to hide and you had to take a stand.

Kemal gestured to recapture Leo's attention. "Now, if it were me—and remember, I *know* how your mind works—I'd have had riders coming up from behind and people come pouring out of the caves. Come to think of it, that's what you planned, wasn't it?"

"Purely by mistake," Leo murmured. "I meant to keep it quiet, but I couldn't let Petros be burnt. I couldn't."

Kemal nodded, grave for once. After all, he had captured Romanus and set this entire caravan of the damned into motion.

They had been trained, the people who had withdrawn into the underground city. They had even turned their retreat into something that could be used as a weapon. If need arose, as it seemed it might, they would withdraw further, past the wall that Asherah had discovered and into the innermost ways that led down, always down. Asherah and the redoubtable Sister Xenia would lead. A Jew and a heretic nun leading an exodus of farm wives. *Christe eleison.* It made almost as much sense as a Byzantine patrician who trusted his life to a Turkish turncoat.

Leo raised his head and met the Seljuk's dark eyes.

"You think we have a chance?"

The ground beneath them shook. Leo suppressed the impulse to grab hold of anything for safety. If the land buried them, it buried them; if it spat them up into the open air, it was a miracle. They had no chance to choose.

"We?"

"You're ours now," Leo said. "You've killed for us, bled for us. If you want to be one of us, you've paid for it."

"If these quakes keep up, I'll leave my bones here, that's for certain," Kemal said. "What is written, is written."

"This isn't written," Theodoulos interrupted. "It isn't."

Byzantine and Turk rounded on him simultaneously.

"How do you *know?*"

"I know," Theo persisted. "I *saw.*"

"You had the falling sickness," Leo practically accused him. "Like Caesar. Did you have a vision while your mind wandered?"

Your old men will dream dreams. Your young men will see visions. Or however the saying went. It wasn't as if Leo hadn't collapsed into a few prophetic fits himself.

"Look at this place," said Theodoulos. "See how the rock glows in the torchlight. It welcomes us."

"Like a serpent lures its prey," Kemal muttered.

Almost predictably, came another tremor.

"We've been feeling about five of those in every torch," Georgios said. "They're getting more frequent. You know, I honestly think I'd rather be killed in an honest fight with the Turks, if you'll excuse me saying so, Kemal, than be swallowed by my own land."

Leo found his men watching him. "Do we go and get them out, sir? There might be time to save at least a few."

We would see them before the end. We would have that.

It was a terrible thing when temptation and need ran in harness. Leo nodded. "We'll go there and help as best we can. Assuming we can make it. Theo, I take it we'll have to climb, won't we?"

Theodoulos shut his eyes. His fingers moved as if he scrawled the grid Leo remembered in midair. Finally, he nodded.

"You said this place welcomed us!" Georgios shouted. Theodoulos cried out shrilly, then toppled as his weak leg failed to maintain its balance.

The next tremor, which hurled them all onto the cave floor, was the worst yet.

The rock lurched and shuddered for at least an eternity, jerking the projections that they clung to all but jerked from their grasp. The tremors buffeted them, sent them rolling from side to side, caroming into one another. Beneath the crash, the rumble, and the clatter of rockfalls some distance way, the very bedrock seemed to groan in its own anguish. A wide crack gaped not five feet from Theodoulos, opened further, and then grew no wider.

God help us! and *Allah!* were choked off by the dust. For a while, they lay coughing, their arms raised over their heads to protect them.

Inexplicably, they had been spared. God only knew what else had fallen; for all they knew, the entire region might have sunk as if swallowed up for its wickedness. They were not in an age of miracles; it was too much to expect the earth to engulf invaders, as it had swallowed up Abiram and Dathan during the Exodus. Someone whimpered, then choked it off.

There was silence in the cave as the last grumbles and clatters of rockfall subsided for the moment, except for Theodoulos, who never ceased whispering prayers, and Kemal, who was probably cursing his luck. He didn't know how good his luck was, then. Hadn't he survived? How many of the Turkmen could say that?

Probably, Leo thought, too many. He would have been glad to fall asleep where he lay, but now a new urgency was on him. What had become of the refugees in the underground city? He staggered up. "We have to go now," he choked.

If any of the men had hesitated, he knew, he would have drawn his sword and whipped them with the flat of it until they obeyed. Though they looked as if they had lived through Armageddon (and would no doubt look worse before that battle actually ensued), they staggered up, one leaning mistrustfully against the wall. Kemal and Georgios bent to raise Theodoulos.

Groping for handholds, staggering as if on the deck of a ship pitching in a storm, Leo led the way toward the upward paths. Or up as far as they could go. Boulders blocked the tunnel leading to the upward passageways.

He should have expected that!

The same red tide that had thrust him, screaming, out to avenge Petros flooded his eyes, and he attacked the stone, trying to pitch huge boulders aside. The dust sifted out from the broken rock, seeping into his lungs. He hacked and spat as he tossed debris out of his way.

"You said this place welcomed us," he reproached Theodoulos.

"It does," Theo said. He sat up gingerly and rubbed his weak leg. "But . . ."

Leo turned away, snorting in disgust. A few more boulders, or whatever you called this . . . this stuff, no better than cheese, and they would be able to move upward toward the passageways that might, if Theo's grid and his map were at all accurate, lead them where they wanted to be. That is, if the path was clear beyond this obstruction. Damn it, why did he have to lift all the rocks himself?

Sweat stung in his eyes and mixed with the rock dust that had filtered through his clothing. He felt encased in a sort of bubble of fear fury, and pain. And he must stink like a sewer. Christ, this was *worse* than battle.

Somehow, he would make it all come out right. Somehow.

Again, the ground shuddered. They had been lucky so far, if you could call this luck. Another shower of pebbles spattered down from up above, followed by the crash of what had to be a large chunk of rock. Even if they cleared a path through to the upper tunnel, it might be even less safe than where they were.

Wind sounded in the tunnel, still partially blocked by the earlier rockfalls. Leo could practically see it, so heavily it was loaded with dust and grit. Just as he opened his mouth to shout for the men to help him, the gust struck, catching him in the face.

He fell to his knees and bent over, coughing, almost retching from the dust he had swallowed and scrubbing frantically at his eyes. Lights exploded behind them, like glowing metal approaching his eyes. He would have screamed if he had enough breath left.

Instead, he doubled over, twisting away from the hands that sought to steady him or move him to a safer place. There *was* no safer place. Not his eyes. Dear God, not his eyes.

After a time (and another tremor), the racking spasms of coughing subsided. Leo raised himself on trembling hands and leaned against the fallen rock. A faint dank odor lingered in the air, the remnants of that gust of wind that had almost smothered him. He rested his aching head against the stone.

Stand back, he had told Asherah, in what felt like another life, before he broke open the seal to the deeper ways within the rock. The air might be bad. Perhaps the air was bad here, too, and it would madden him or cast him into sleep.

But the air was so soothing now, and the rock had turned warm, as warm as in the tunnel below. Almost, as Theo had said, welcoming. He let himself absorb whatever comfort the warmth might give him before he moved on. Then he noticed how the dust itself had changed. No longer did it hold that faint musty odor, a combination of crypts and a kind of wasteland. Now, it seemed tinged with cinnamon. No, not cinnamon, incense.

He remembered that scent. He and Asherah had broken through the wall separating her current refuge from the deeper passageways when they had first noticed it. Once again, Leo's heart pounded with excitement and fear. It had intoxicated him, had given him the courage to go over and embrace Asherah. Since then, her response had transformed his life. They had both had the sense that some power had swept them up in its embrace, that some power wanted them as much as they realized they wanted each other.

Whatever it was, it was a power that could not be forced, no more than Asherah itself. Perhaps, it could be coaxed. Perhaps it could be persuaded. Leo raised his head and looked into the darkness of the half-blocked passageway. His eyes were still blurred and sore. A soft wind blew, easing them. The incense scent intensified, wafting out toward him, and the darkness was transformed from enemy into a type of comfort.

Not here. This way, instead; as if the woman he loved took his hand and showed him how she wanted him to touch her.

Leo shook his head. Dreaming dreams and seeing visions, indeed! This was hardly the time for the type of vision he stopped himself from having. But the voice that had teased at his awareness spoke again. *This way. Down this road.*

He turned his back on the rockfall and all his labor there.

"You were right, Theo. We can't go that way. It won't let us."

"It? Won't let?" If he didn't say something quickly, he might have a panic on his hands; and the idea of a band of armed, panicked men running about beneath the earth was not one he liked—or one that he thought that this power would approve, any more than any great lady would approve of mice scurrying about her skirts.

"The sun will not strike thee by day, nor the moon by night," Theodoulos recited a line from the reassuring old psalm.

"He will keep Thy soul," Georgios joined in.

Or *something* will, Leo thought.

"You know, Father Meletios said I was sealed to these stones," he told his men. Cold comfort to him, however reassuring they seemed to find it. "You know there's something odd about them, something odd. . . ."

To his astonishment he saw Georgios nod. "It's the land," he said. "Petros—God rest his soul, he was a better Christian than I, and he didn't hold with whatever it was. Said it was heathenish and smashed any of the long-ago things he would find when he was plowing. The rest of us, though . . ."

"Wouldn't have thought you'd feel it. Being from the City and half-royal, you might say."

Who better than a king to sense the power in the land?

He was not a king. He was only Ducas, and dishonored of his line. But that sense of the land, that response to power, maybe even the ability to focus it through his own senses, were all strong in him. They had almost led to his destruction, as men who would do anything to retain their grasp on the throne sought to take him out of a game he had never wanted to play.

They had cast him out, and here was where he had come to land. Precisely where he could listen and respond. Leo found himself smiling through the blood and dust that caked his face. Sometimes, the powers were sly. The fates, you might call them. The pit in his stomach hollowed as he recalled that, to the pagans, the fates were female.

Kemal trudged back down the corridor. "If I can't wash, I can't pray. I could wash in the dust, I suppose." He spat. "Allah will have to take my intention for the deed."

He prostrated himself and prayed. The others looked away. One or two muttered what might have passed for holy words and blessed themselves. Leo bowed his head. "Into Thy hands," he began; but into whose hands was he commending them? They had come to a place where even prayer was of less use than blind faith.

At the brink of a rotten death, Romanus had trusted. Could Leo do any less?

"Let's go," he said simply. "This time, we let ourselves be guided."

He was sealed to this place. Let it and the power within it guide him. He had no other choice. The torch guttered, but the scent of the incense flared up more strongly.

They would have to make the torches last as long as they could. And then they would go on in the dark. The drip within the rock occupied his attention.

Will you see that we have water before . . . before whatever is supposed to happen to us does? Leo implored whatever guided him now. The scent of cinnamon embraced him again. He felt a vast calm, as if he had been lost and suddenly spied a known landmark.

The path turned downward, switched back, and turned again. Then it evened out, wider even than the road within that Asherah had discovered. The walls of the tunnel had been painstakingly smoothed. Into them, at regular intervals, were set torch holders, bronze, heavy, infinitely reassuring.

"Keep your eyes open," Leo ordered, then broke off, as if shy of speaking in a place where no words had been heard for countless years. The sloping walls seemed to drink in his words; no, he could not think of drinking in words, or anything else, thirsty as he was.

"Look for side chambers," he said more softly. The unknown builders had placed torch holders of bronze upon the walls they had planed with such care. Perhaps they had left torches behind, too.

Half a torch, and four tremors later, they found side chambers. In one of them, they found ancient wood, dressed and stacked and terribly dry. Perhaps it had been intended to shore up a side tunnel. But, no, it was too finely planed. Still, it would serve to make torches.

It would have been good to rest here, but the same compulsions that had drawn them into the tunnels, that had forced them to march on and on drew them forward.

Another torch later, they came upon another side chamber. Weapons dulled with the years were mounted upon the walls. Why would the builders leave an armory down here? Leo stepped close to the walls, examining the weapons. Ancient, they were; crude, perhaps; and wrought of bronze or flint of—he blew the dust away—black volcanic stone; but deadly for all of that. Georgios paused to test the temper of a bronze blade. Leo laid finger to a knife as like the tiny one he carried as a final weapon as if the same man had chipped them out of one chunk of glossy black rock from the fire's heart.

Kemal laid finger to a bow. After this many years of hanging idle, its string had perished.

"Take what you need," Leo ordered. "They will not begrudge us."

Taking the weapons stored here for so long felt like robbing a shrine. At the same time, he hated to leave anything behind lest it be used against them.

His men obeyed. Even Theodoulos took a dagger shaped like a deadly leaf. Now, they moved as if in a procession of dreamers. Did some alchemy of the underground taint the air with some drug that would first control them, then make them mad, and then, when it had stripped all vestige of their manhood from them, slay them?

If their deaths had been required, they would have happened already, Leo told himself. Death? If it were like sleep, it might even be welcome. His tongue felt huge in his mouth, but at least now the gurgle of the water running deep within the rock no longer tormented him.

"Look at the paintings," Theodoulos whispered. "They make the ones in the valley look like a blind man's scrawl." In among designs of vines, great cats, and serpents, came astonishingly lifelike representations of what had once, surely, been people who had posed for their portraits before the underground ways were sealed.

Priestesses, perhaps, wearing the regalia of their office and, in some cases, little else over bare breasts, the nipples painted in such a way that they glistened as if heavy with milk. Godlings, wearing the triple crowns that Leo had seen incised onto cliff walls in the upper air. Warriors and kings, marching in procession alongside him and his men.

Georgios blessed himself. "When I was a boy, they would tell me of the road that joined city to city beneath the earth. We all thought it was just a story we wanted to believe."

"The sisters told me, too," Theodoulos said. "They would tell me of a great city in the center of an underground plain, how it held all the treasures of the ages." He swallowed. "How my mother waited for me there. And then they would feed me honeycake. I was the only son they had, cripple as I was."

Kemal's belly growled. Someone else chuckled ruefully. Once or twice, as they had marched, someone had fallen out briefly, or leaned against a wall, faint for an instant with hunger that would be assuaged when they won through to their goal or not at all. For now, their bodies' weaknesses were enemies to be kept at bay, too.

"I hear something," Theodoulos broke the silence of their march.

Leo paused. Alive to every shift now in the air currents below the earth, he did not yet hear "something," but he sensed a shift in the currents of air as they flowed through the great tunnels, forever refreshed from some unknown source. He shut his eyes, listening so intently that his head spun.

No, nothing yet. He signaled the men forward, but cautiously, regretting even the scraping their boots made on the stone.

The underground corridor widened yet further. Now it smoothed out almost into a road that expanded into a cavern vaster even than the halls within the underground city toward which they journeyed.

Now, the walls of the tunnel glistened with more than bronze or red and blue and green paints. Now, the walls shimmered in the circle of their torchlight with mosaics: purples and golds and silvers assembled with art and meticulous care, then abandoned.

Kemal ran a hand over the mosaics. "Seeing this could make someone believe that treasure city beneath the earth is more than a dream. I am afraid my kinsmen probably heard just enough that they decided to try to find their way down here themselves."

Leo nodded. That was another of the many things he feared.

Again, the land quivered. Almost automatically now, he adjusted his pace to compensate.

Theodoulos waved them to a stop. "Don't you hear it yet?" He pointed. "Look up ahead."

Ahead of the circle of light cast by their torched loomed complex shadows. Here several tunnels fed into the main highway, their entries arching in wide curves, as if this rich gathering of bronze and mosaics were a crossroads beneath the earth.

The shadows flickered and danced.

"Hide the torch!" Leo hissed. They dared not douse it.

The dance grew more intricate as another source of light beamed from a branching tunnel and quested at the shadows that they cast, even with their own torch hidden. Leo drew a deep breath, then held it, willing himself not to breath until he found the source of that light.

In the silence, he heard the pad-pad-pad of footsteps. And, from far behind it came a clash and a roaring that Leo had prayed never to hear again. Somehow, the Turks must have broken into the underground ways. They would be battering down the millstones and the walls; they would be slaughtering women and children, if the men left to guard them had failed utterly in their mission—and perhaps they had already done so and had spread out, determined to trace the legend of a queen city among the caves to its source and wrest what treasure they might from the earth.

Best to deal first with the enemy at hand, if they were to try to add their futile swords to the battle they heard.

Leo strained to filter the sound of footsteps from the clamor of far-off battle. This crossing-point deep within the earth was like a whispering gallery, bringing far sounds deceptively near.

There it was again, the soft, rhythmic pad of footsteps. Did a ghost, a demon, or a godling make noises when it walked? It was drawing closer.

For that matter, did a beast? Leo nodded, hoping his men would see. As they had done when they found Kemal, they drew their swords as soundlessly as they could. Leo's temples pounded. In a moment, he would have to breathe, and the unknown person approaching them would hear the sound.

Leo flattened himself against the wall, thinking a brief prayer of thanks to the ancient builders who had slanted the walls so that he could see, but the unknown approaching them could not.

The bobbing light paused, as if whoever bore it hesitated. Abruptly, it died.

They heard a lull in the far-off battle, as if two armies poised before hurling themselves forward again. Now, they could hear breathing. It was coming very close. There was only one person: one enemy, perhaps, or one demon—assuming demons breathed.

The cave trembled: well, they might have expected that. But the person up ahead came on more warily now. A few more steps and whoever it was would advance into the crossing. They could leap out with light of their own and dazzle him.

The footsteps paused. Then light kindled and bloomed, a gleaming sphere, white at its top and shading down the rainbow into all the colors of earth and sky. As it advanced into the center of the cave seemed to shake, as if whoever bore it were uncertain of what lay ahead or as if the lightbearer fought for endurance. Or courage.

A gust of wind, scented with the complex incense that stirred Leo's senses, made the torch that Georgios bore flare up. At the same time, the torch coming at them from that side tunnel also flared up, just as its bearer stepped into plain sight.

It was Asherah.

His own blood roared in Leo's ears. Only the cord securing his sword about his wrist saved him from dropping it with a clatter that might have made all their hearts burst. He started forward.

"Don't go, lord!" Georgios dropped to his knees. He tried to hurl himself forward to restrain Leo, but Kemal cuffed him back.

Leo ignored them. *What* did Asherah think she was doing here? Hadn't he found her the safest place that he could? And where was her father, or, for that matter, Nordbriht, whom he had primed with nobly sentimental stories about guarding his heir until it was a wonder if the big man hadn't tried to sleep at her feet.

He was glad to know that she had had the sense to douse her torch, but those shimmering wards—he had seen her cast them once or twice before, but never so brightly. They might safeguard her, but she might as well also kindle a beacon that would tell any man or demon for miles around: *here I am, abrim with power . . . and with no damned brains at all.*

She gasped and turned toward his footsteps. The light of her protective warding ran down the short blades she held in either hand, rippling down the markings of fine Damascus until her knives gleamed like icicles in the sun.

"Asherah!"

The knives clattered on the rock as she staggered back. The break in her control extinguished the sphere of light warding her. As the light faded, he saw her face: that of a sleepwalker waked from some dream. He had seen Theodoulos look just as moonstruck in the grip of some fantasy.

Insane coincidences happened in battle; and this was battle. But there was more to it: Asherah had walked as if she were in the grip of some power. Leo would have to wager his soul on that power's being the same one that sought to control him.

Her awareness of the world restored, Asherah drew breath to scream.

"Asherah, what are *you* doing here?"

Recognizing him at last, she cried out his name, then ran forward to hurl herself into his arms.

No one had ever terrified Leo that much. How had she dared?

"I tried to keep you safe, and I find you wandering down here," he told her. He wrapped his arms about her as if he could shield her with his own body and the strength of his embrace. His hands smoothed frantically up and down her back—what was that bundle on it? Some sort of pack? At least she had not simply wandered off without preparation.

He heard himself chanting her name in welcome and reproof.

"It's all right, Leo, I was sent, I'm all right. . . ." Once he was convinced she would not vanish out of his arms, he would have time to listen to what she said. But for now, it was more important to hold her and let her feel his relief, his fear, and his anger at finding her here. His tears ran into her hair, still fragrant with attar of roses.

Asherah flung her arms around him to brace herself as Leo shook her. She pressed her face against his shoulder until his passion of rage and fear abated. She was so little, and she had such strength. Her arms around him were the best thing he had ever felt. Leo let his fury subside in the comfort of her embrace, as if seeing her here below the earth was no different than waking at her side in the aftershock of a nightmare. The ground trembled underfoot, paused, then trembled again like a heartbeat. For the moment, that did not matter.

She raised her face, and he kissed her, feeling how cracked and dry his lips were as they pressed thirstily against hers. Her tears touched his mouth, and her welcome assuaged a fear Leo hadn't even known that he had: that only some lure or compulsion of the power beneath the earth had thrust her into his arms the first time. He knew the look of a woman who had given herself for fear or power, had seen it on his mother's face. But it was not the look he saw now. She wept, but with joy at the sight of him.

Reluctantly, he freed his mouth from hers and looked down into her eyes.

"I tried to protect you," he told her. "I thought I could at least give you that. Why couldn't you stay where I had you safe?"

"I'm safer where you are, Leo. Wherever you are."

Again, he hugged her close and again kissed her, this time even harder than before. He felt the resistance leave her body and her knees buckle, and he swept her up for a long moment of welcome.

When he finally set her down, his men had edged out of the tunnel in which they had hidden. Kemal, of course, was grinning. Theodoulos had limped out to stand almost at her side.

Asherah turned in Leo's arms. "Your lips were parched," she whispered to him. "Are you all so thirsty?"

Reaching for the pack she carried, she produced a leather bottle and handed it to him. "Here. Did you think I would just wander off? You should know I could not be so foolish!"

Her eyes glinted at him in what would have been anger if they had time for the luxury.

Theodoulos slipped to his knees, his hands going out to her. Hastily, Leo pressed the bottle into his hands. He drank, passed the bottle on, and tried to collect himself.

Leo's shaking ceased. For now. Keeping an arm about his wife as if to ensure that she would not slip away from him too, he drew her back toward his soldiers. If anyone snickered, Leo would not have to wait for the Turks to kill him: he might, or he might simply turn the wretch over to his wife.

"How did you come here, love?"

Asherah edged in against Leo's side, magnificently casting away the reserve she had always maintained in public.

"Were you down here for the earthquake?"

Leo's arm tightened about her shoulders. "The place rang like a bell," he said. "I don't know how we were spared."

It must have been hell up in the underground city, with women and children screaming, all crammed into such close quarters, supplies falling. A horrible thought struck him. "Your father . . . Nordbriht. . . ."

"You should have seen him, love. A millstone toppled, and he got his shoulder under it and held it long enough for the rest of us to shore it up and retreat. He managed to grab his axe and follow us. My father says he strained something, but Nordbriht swore he could fight. 'Go now,' Sister Xenia told me, and I went. She knew I had to find you."

"Retreat?" Leo knew retreats, knew the terror and confusion that could slay almost as surely as swords or arrows. It would be bladework beneath the earth.

"The quake shocked open one of the entryways," she told him. "All our work, and they got in anyhow."

He pulled her close and held her, temporary reassurance, but one that he knew was as precious to her as to him.

"Did Ioannes' message reach you?"

She nodded against his shoulder. "And then the earth seemed to try to turn itself inside out."

If they lived, Leo knew that he would not be the only one to wake screaming from nightmares, to shiver in fear of the dark.

The shouts from levels high above them intensified, carried to them by the uncanny architecture of this place. The mosaics, half in shadow, seemed to quiver with the shocks and aftershocks that resonated through the earth. Asherah flinched.

"Let's get her someplace quieter," said Leo. *Safer*, he meant; but safety had long since been forgotten.

"Begging your pardon, sir," said Georgios, "but those are our families up above there." He paused, clearly uncertain of how to address a woman who was his commander's wife, but also a stranger and a Jew. The struggle showed clearly on his face. Leo gave him no help.

"Lady," Georgios ducked his head as he might before any woman of high birth. "I beg you forgive me, but I have a wife and three children up there, and one on the way. . . ."

Asherah turned to smile at him. "We sent all the women with young children to safety. Sister Xenia led them. She wanted to stay and fight, and she is almost as strong as any man, but we told her that if she didn't go, my father would stay too. And he can*not* fight, you know that."

Frankly, Leo knew nothing of the sort. In a final battle, Joachim would fight until his heart gave way.

Georgios grunted, clearly skeptical.

"Remember the Exodus," Asherah told him. "A desert wanderer who had been a prince, a priest, and a prophetess led an army of slaves. Could we do less?"

My heart, you shame us all. Leo smoothed back her hair from her forehead. As usual, she had lost her veils or discarded them.

"We did as you told us," she looked up at Leo, all compliance now. "We withdrew, those of us who were told we must not fight. Nordbriht and the others said they would cover our retreat and join us." Her voice broke. "Join us if they could."

"Please God they can," Theodoulos said. He leaned against the wall, drooping visibly. Asherah watched him, clearly concerned.

He should rest, her lips formed the words for Leo to see.

When Leo shook his head so slightly that only she could see it, she reached for her pack again. "I have wine here, food, drugs, even. We will need them to keep going."

Leo shook her very gently, to stop her. "Where do you think we must go?" That was one question he had to ask. And the next one followed naturally. "And why are you here, and not with Sister Xenia and the others?"

Asherah pulled free of Leo. "For the same reason that you are here. I was *guided*. You remember, how when we first discovered the way below, something called out to us? Well, when I stayed in the caverns, I had no peace from it. The Sisters understood; they've heard the same call. My husband, you are not the only person who has a land and people to defend."

She glanced down, and Leo's eyes followed hers: if she were with child, it did not yet show. "Nor are you the only defender of this land to act on dreams. And faith."

"How did they let you go?"

It was a pity that she had been separated from Nordbriht, who would have slung her over his shoulder to keep her out of danger, if he had had to.

"I would have slipped away," Asherah admitted. "I thought of it. No one knows those ways as well as I, except perhaps Xenia. I am so much smaller than she, however, that I was certain I could elude her. But she came to me, said I was the one chosen, and that if the call came . . ."

"The call?"

Asherah gave him an exasperated look, then softened it by taking his hand. "If you hadn't felt it, you wouldn't be here either. God only knows why *I* should feel it—maybe what I've always studied."

Asherah, surrounded by bright lights and prayers; Asherah's eyes widening at the sight of the Woman in the caves; Asherah lying in his arms as music piped inside his head and blood and memories of long-ago rites fired their blood.

"You saw those pictures painted on the walls," she said. "Pagan, all of them. Pagan dreams I said I had, and I was right. It was *something* reaching out to us.

"She's here with us, you know. And God forgive me, I can't see her as the blasphemy I know I should.

"At any rate, Xenia said I was chosen. So I gathered a few supplies, as much as I thought I could take without depriving the others . . . and then I thought again.

"And I went to my father and to Sister Xenia, and I told them honestly, that I had had a vision and must act upon it."

"And they let you go?" Leo cried. *"They let you go?"*

Asherah shrugged. "For my own soul's sake, they had to. And possibly for my sanity. Nordbriht?" Despite himself, Leo smiled, knowing how his wife must have calculated her chances of eluding her guardian. "The vision gave me no rest. So . . ." She swallowed hard and blinked away tears. ". . . my father gave me his blessing and his own knives . . ."

"She dropped them. Theo, see to them." Theodoulos limped out into the darkness beyond the charmed circle of torchlight.

"And I left. Oh God, it was hard," she sighed into Leo's shoulder. "I left. And when I was safely out of reach, I prayed, and I was *answered* and guided. I don't know how long I wandered, but then I heard footsteps, and I heard voices. I doused my light and cast my wardings . . . and there you were!"

She reached up and kissed him very lightly on the side of the jaw.

"Lady, lady, the battle . . ." Georgios practically danced in an agony of suspense. He had not even paid heed how casually she had spoken of visions or wardings that, in a time long lost and better so, might have put her life and the lives of all her kin in jeopardy.

Leo eyed him, then silently counted off the others. "Asherah, can you find Sister Xenia and the other women again? I want you to take Theo and Kemal to them. And, Kemal, Theo, I want you to protect my wife with your very souls."

"No!" Their instant protest overpowered the earth tremor that rumbled through the caves.

"I won't be sent away again," Asherah declared.

"My place is with you," Kemal told him.

Saddest of all, Theodoulos just *looked.* "Protect my wife" was a kindly lie to save his pride, and he knew it. She had foiled stronger protectors already. But if Theo fought, Leo feared his first battle would be his last.

"Leo," Asherah spoke quickly, "he has to have something. Take us with you. Theo, you had better keep the knives."

"Not you . . ." She was too precious to risk.

Not you either!

Another quake, much stronger than the rhythmic tremors to which he had almost become inured, hurled him off balance. He staggered forward, just as the ceiling cracked and a chunk of rock dropped where he had been standing, followed by a shower of smaller stones. Flinging out his arms, he tried to protect Asherah and Theodoulos with his own body, while Kemal tried to push all of them into a safer place.

Safer? Now there was a joke.

When the dust subsided, and they could almost see and breathe easily again, Leo gazed hopelessly at the mass of stone separating him from his force . . . from the rest of his force.

"Take it as a sign," Asherah murmured.

He looked beyond her. One or two of his men blessed themselves. Clearly, they had already interpreted this latest rockfall as a warning.

"You are *sealed* to this land. Chosen, Xenia told me, just as I am. It will not release you. Let the others go. . . ."

Leo stretched out his hand to Georgios. "As you see . . ."

"You are not just a soldier anymore," the farmer said. "I shall pray for you as I fight, because you have chosen the harder part."

Or it has chosen me.

Leo let his hand drop. "Go, then, if you think you can help. All of you. And the Lord of Battles be with you."

"With all of us, sir."

They bent to divide the torches.

"Take them all," Asherah said softly. Her voice sounded distant, hollow, and Georgios gasped, recognizing the tones of impending prophecy. "We will not be needing them where we go."

They would have saluted him before they left. Leo tried to fling out his hand, to clasp their arms, but too much stone divided them. With no other choice before him, he stiffened to the salute himself until the curve in the tunnel hid them from sight.

He sighed deeply and turned back toward his wife.

"Now where do we go, Asherah?"

39

Shocks trembled underfoot every few moments now. Drafts seemed to pant from the tunnel. Leo had the sense, too, of intense concentration: perhaps not upon them, but upon some task that required them.

He cast one longing glance back at the way his men had gone. It seemed so much simpler, so much safer, simply to draw sword, scream *Nobiscum!* and charge, to live or die as God willed.

If he had wanted simplicity, he should have been born into a different family and definitely married into a different one altogether. He had duty. And now he had prophecy and necessity.

"This way," whispered Asherah, and touched his arm. Theodoulos followed without comment and, Leo thought, without surprise. Kemal came last, muttering prayers.

Their way wound down and down from the crossroads beneath the earth, where the slightest whisper echoed forever. They had entered a maze. They wound through it, Asherah leading surely, though Leo would have put his hand on burning iron—don't think of that!—and sworn she had never seen this place before.

Except in her dreams, of course, or in the prophecies that had come to haunt them both, sleeping and waking, devouring their lives and seeking now to eat their souls.

No! Leo thought.

Asherah beckoned them onward. He was guardian of these ways, or so Meletios' blood had sealed him. That did not reassure him.

The tiny quakes seemed to come almost without let now, and gusts of air rustled by like troops of ghosts, or some bellows from the mouth of hell.

"Hurry, oh do!" she pleaded with them. "The sisters told me that when the earth shakes . . ." To Leo's horror, when she turned to urge them on, her eyes were huge with tears.

The tunnel widened into a more perfect arch than any Leo had seen down here. Guarding it on either side were huge stone lions such as the ancient dwellers in this land had once carved. They were incised with what could have been vandals' blows, but with what Leo suspected were words of power in a language long vanished beneath the earth with those who spoke it. Asherah reached out and touched the glyphs, then beckoned them onward.

Theodoulos' torch sputtered and went out. Asherah's voice hummed softly. Moments later, a soft golden light bathed her as if she had been transformed into some icon herself. She led the way down the deep, smooth passageway. Here the walls glistened not with mosaics, but with glazed bricks of gold and turquoise. On them ramped or stalked bulls, lions, and the immense twisting coils of a kind of dragon.

"It is," Asherah whispered, "the sirrush. They say Nebuchadnezzar and Nimrod hunted such creatures. But then . . ."

Any absurd scholarly observations she might have made were interrupted by a sharper tremor than before.

"Quickly!" Asherah's voice was urgent though she did not dare to raise it.

Leo bent close to her. "Did they tell you *what* you run toward?" he asked.

Asherah shook her head. "The secret at the center of all this maze. I don't know which is worse, what they told me or that I believe them, or will when I see. But I *must* see!"

Now all the years-long terror of the child who feared she was mad quivered in her voice. Leo nodded at her and stepped up the pace. They passed by the bulls and the lions and the dragons as old as Babylon without more comment. Gradually, the glazed brick gave way, to be replaced by processions of men and women—more women than men—wearing crowns like those of the storm gods who had shadowed Leo's life and dreams since Manzikert.

Was that what he heard and felt: wind and thunder underneath the earth? Again, the ground shook. As above, so below.

"They're coming closer together," whispered Asherah again.

They hastened, Leo bracing himself against the slope of the tunnel's floor. He spared a glance for Theodoulos. To his astonishment, the boy easily kept pace. They hastened, joining the procession of ancient storm gods and goddesses toward some unimaginable rite.

After a time, the figures gave way to bare stone—the tufa that had once been spat from the molten depths of the earth, carved, and then hardened by a breath of fire. Now, carved, daubed in red here where the rock was scorched were symbols, some elaborate, some so simple and worn that Leo could barely detect them: the triangles and bars that they had told him in the town were butterflies; the figures that the most ancient pagans meant to be goddesses, horned skulls, and felines.

Even in the glow of the wards Asherah had cast, the painted symbols danced and flickered in the shadows that the wind, rushing through the tunnel, seemed to shred from off the ancient walls. All the chimerae that had besieged him, waking and sleeping, since Manzikert joined in a kind of hunt: not a waking dream, but a waking nightmare.

Pain stitched itself down his chest, lancing into his left arm. Leo forced himself to ignore it and to hurry after Asherah, whose pace had taken on a kind of urgency. Behind him, Theodoulos urged on Kemal.

The corridor made one last turn, then opened into a central cavern that might, at its widest, rival the Hippodrome. And facing him, painted in red upon the wall, was a face Leo had seen before, the woman from what seemed to be the beginning of time, with her harsh eyes and her cruel smile.

"The Gorgon!" he whispered. He had seen her face in the cistern and then collapsed. All of the hauntings leapt out as one to oppress him, and he sank gasping to the ground.

Now the creature's face was savage, scornful.

"No, Leo, no!" Asherah knelt at his side, her arms about him, her chin up as she faced that unbelievably ancient, alien woman. How could she withstand her? The creature was older by far than his Empire or her people or any civilization he had ever heard of. And, if her expression were any evidence, she despised them all, especially the people of the upper air, who had fled for refuge beneath the earth and into her realm.

He should *not* be ascribing power to pagan deities: that was for certain. So, even as he tried to steady his breathing, to slow the wild heartbeats that made his temples throb in sympathy—and so much like the tremors that rippled through the rock—he tried to pray.

And failed wretchedly. They were in no place where any prayers that *he* knew had any validity: except, perhaps, appeals to the woman whose face now confronted Leo. She had been waiting for him. She had always been waiting for him. And if he dared go on, no doubt, she would stop him and wither him as, indubitably, she had withered Father Meletios.

Meletios was a saint, or almost a saint, but he had recoiled in terror from this underground mystery, so unlike the kindly Mother of God whom he venerated. He had driven out the women, then set himself, lifelong, to guard the underground ways, lest this creature penned for so long in the darkness dare to rise again into the light. And he had even survived, after a fashion.

Not being a saint, Leo would probably not survive. And what sort of afterlife could he, married to a Jew, expect if he were slain, his soul devoured by this creature—goddess or demon?

He shut his eyes, winning a respite from the presence before him. Asherah's arms sustained him: a precious luxury he dare not allow for much longer. Once terror and this creature's gaze stopped his heart, she would need all her strength. Like the nuns, she was not just drawn here, she had some protection from what laired here—and perhaps even some sympathy, deep in blood and soul, with it.

At least, now he knew why so many of the men who ventured to seek out the deepest underground ways and the treasure that legend heaped them with never returned to the light of day. Only Theodoulos, who was a boy and crippled. And Meletios, who had been a blind man.

He had been a blinded *man,* the thought intruded into Leo's consciousness.

But Leo had cowered here long enough. He forced himself, despite
the pain that stabbed into him with every breath he took, to stand erect.

Overpowering relief swept over Asherah like a gale: I am *not* mad.
Strong compulsions ripped at her defenses, commanding her forward.
The nuns had had their traditions, their prayers, and their faith. She
had her own faith, as much at odds as it was with this hidden cult, whose
core was female. It was pagan, it was hostile—and it was a part of herself. She would advance into the valley of the shadow . . . she heard
herself reciting the Psalm. The ground did not crack, and no rock
shower punished her.

She spared one glance back at her husband, the crippled boy, and
the warrior who huddled beside him. Could they manage as they were?
As long as Leo had even one person he thought he must protect, he
would force himself to endure. She could best protect him by going forward.

With a fragment of her consciousness, she noted that she heard
water rippling somewhere in the cave. Then, she was aware of nothing
but a raging demand to *know*—curiosity in the guise of a storm wind—
impelling her forward, coupled with a kind of triumph. Now, finally,
she was aware that she would find answers to all of her questions.
Whether she would live beyond the moment of revelation, she didn't
know: but she would learn.

To her astonishment, she sensed her own curiosity met by an equal
demand to know, plus a sense of relief—a relief that swiftly vanished
as the earth shuddered underfoot and seemed to groan.

No: something else actually was groaning. Some *one* else. The sisters had not been lying. Their Mother, they told her, needed aid. But
they were all pledged virgins, while she, she was a wife who might, even
now, bear renewed life: she was chosen for the task they could not do.

She looked down. Before her, flowed the trickle of water she had
heard. She would have to cross it if she were to go any further. Abruptly,
stepping across that stream assumed heroic proportions.

Go on, *fool. You want to know, don't you?*

Asherah had always thought she had. Now, she feared; but she still
wanted to know. So, she took the step that put her, irrevocably, beyond her husband's reach. She entered the great cavern and started toward its center.

Eons ago, some great bubble rising up out of the molten rock had formed it. When the builders of the underground ways had found it, they had smoothed its walls, then left it much as it was.

Now, however, the walls were pitted once more, as if with long use. Shadows seemed to crouch like a wounded animal in the center of the room, watching her. The menace that had brought Leo to his knees was only quiescent. Leo still swayed behind her. Theodoulos wavered at his shoulder. And Kemal sank down in awe, his forehead pressed against the rock as if he prayed, even if he had no idea here before the shadows where East might lie.

Blasphemous as the idea was, here and not in Jerusalem, lay the Omphalos, the navel of the world. Blasphemous as the idea was, what crouched in a recess at the far side of the room was as far beyond blasphemy as the stars were above her head.

The shadows dissipated. A faint glow rose from the living rock, a brighter one from the triangles and circles, the woman-symbols daubed so long ago upon the walls.

Asherah had entered a birthing chamber.

Here, beneath the fire and snow of Mount Argaeus and the changing cliffs and towers of the volcanic rock, here, beneath a thousand years of Christianity and thousands more years of her own faith and those of other gods, she had found the deepest mystery of this ancient land. And, despite all the wisdom that had been taught, all the lessons dinned into easily frightened children, and, on too many occasions in all those years, enforced by fire and sword, the mystery here was one of and for women. She should have known: look at the statues. Look at the symbols on the pottery. And—perhaps the greatest proof of all—look at the prohibitions that burdened women, not least of which had expelled holy women like Xenia from their ancient home.

The valley was old, true. But the mystery itself was older. It was old when Bathsheba, wife of Uriah the Hittite, ensnared a king as she reclined, dreaming in her bath. It was older still: it had watched dances such as the temple whores of Canaan danced at harvest festivals, luring men away from the women of the tribes of Israel. And it had laughed in joy.

It was older than her own faith, her own people, though they knew it, and feared it, and ripped down its holy places when they could find them.

And here it crouched in monumental labor before her.

She was sealed to this creature by no more than their common womanhood. What promise did she have that this power would not blast her?

Only that she too was female.

A gust of pain rushed out and engulfed her. She swayed, but did not fall. If it had meant to destroy her, it could have reduced her to less than dust in that instant. She sensed its caution and its need.

It was female and in long travail. Here stood a woman. How foolish to destroy her out of pain and fury.

In the recess within the great cavern, as if what crouched before Asherah had retreated long ago to the safest, most secluded place, she saw what looked like a statue. It was huge, and so old that its features, even in this protected chamber beneath the earth, had worn away: faceless, nameless, and indubitably female. She sat between weathered, inimical beasts: leopards, perhaps, or lions, or some other hunting creatures. It was difficult to see, more difficult yet to concentrate, because Asherah's attention was riveted by the statue, larger by far than the largest of living women, her arms out, grasping her guardians for support.

She was huge and totally naked. Immense breasts dangled almost to her massive haunches, as if she had nursed many children already. Her throne was little more than a birthing stool, her legs splayed to support her immense belly, which seemed to cast a glow upon the figure's deepest privacy, now exposed past shame in the extremity of a labor that had surely gone on as long as these hills stood.

The belly across which each contraction rippled seemed to be a huge violet gem that pulsed with each pang of the colossal labor. Was it a statue Asherah saw in travail, or a goddess?

Before she could stop herself, Asherah backed away. Surely, this was a demon, an image, perhaps, of Lilith or even the fiend herself, who abandoned Adam. Or perhaps it was some other form of the Mother/Whore who had been the enemy of her people since before the coming of the Hittites.

Whatever else it was, there was no doubt that it was a *graven image*. As a daughter in Israel, Asherah should not be in the presence of such a thing, much less an image of a goddess, and less altogether an image of such obscenity. And—this was worse yet—here she was, actually looking at such a naked thing in the presence of her Christian husband, an innocent boy, and a Turk!

Again, the statue's belly rippled, the gem lighting, then turning dark again. Again, the earth groaned.

The goddess was carved as if in the act of giving birth: but was *that* obscene? Without willing it, Asherah realized that her dusty, scratched hands had come out to rest over her own belly. It was still too early to

be certain, but she looked down, imagining herself swollen to that immense, laboring girth.

Imagining herself holding her own child. Nursing it. Showing her
child to Leo.

How could she consider that obscene? All her life, she had heard
about birth and children. Long after she had known that the women
of her household had lost all hope that they would ever attend her in
labor of her own, she had continued to listen and to learn and to assist
in childbirths.

She was a woman, a woman who might bear fruit not that long from
now. What squatted before her on this birthing stool beneath the earth
was a representation of all women.

Her labor had gone on so very long. She must be so very tired.
Asherah sensed her anger. Perhaps she was afraid, too. And so alone,
here in the dark with only beasts as midwives.

Poor thing. Poor sister. Or, perhaps, poor mother.

*This is what your mother endured to give you life. Look upon it. Look
upon it well, and learn.*

Asherah started forward.

"Lady, my lady!" Theodoulos' voice cracked as he limped hastily toward her.

With the next tremor, the cave rocked so violently that he toppled,
half-in, half-out of the water.

*My son, mine to me! My daughter died and was buried in the earth above
me; but my son, my son! Men took him, stole him from his nurses. Give him
back!*

Dust and grit sifted from a web of cracks that formed in the ceiling,
smelling like an ancient grave.

Once again, the great violet gem in the image's belly flashed: blinding light, followed by darkness filled with dancing sparks.

Who are these intruders? And why should I not destroy them?

Stunned by the force of the thoughts that had been thrust into her
mind, Asherah reeled. She held to consciousness—and to logic—with
the last remnants of her strength.

Her son? What did she mean: Her son?

Asherah reeled before the frenzy of unleashed emotion and fought
for composure as she had fought for physical balance only moments before. Think, Asherah. Think. Here is a creature: well enough, call it a
woman. She shook her head in frustration at her own cowardice.

Call her a goddess.

Here she was, alone in the dark, except for her guardian beasts, about to give birth, and not for the first time. She had had a daughter, who died. And she had had a son, born lame because no help could come, and taken into the upper air to live as best he could among her enemies. And he had even, inexplicably, come to love them.

This land had been sealed. It is safe; behold, we give you guardians. And they steal my son, they ride over my fields, and they leave me alone in the dark!

Oh God, Asherah thought. The meanest beggarwoman should not have to labor naked and alone as long as she was there to help. Asherah began to piece together the story.

Years ago, when the figure before her had given birth, a girlchild had died and been buried. Another child had lived and been taken into the outer world, nursed by women whom the goddess trusted—Xenia? Again, Asherah tried not to faint from the shock of her realizations. And then, the child was snatched from them.

The crippled child who now staggered forward and whom his inhuman mother had greeted with such a fury of possessiveness: Theodoulos.

Leo struggled across the few steps it took to bring him to her side.

"All these years," he murmured. He looked at the goddess, then away; and she could sense how his fingers must itch to bless himself in the way that Christians used, but that was so alien to her, or to the laboring goddess. A mother, and her child: what Leo made of that, given the theology in which he had been brought up, might even hold some weird fascination for her some other time—assuming that she survived to contemplate it. Then, again, if she started laughing at it, she might never stop.

"Back and forth," she murmured. "People after people, back and back again over the land. Invader after invader, ramping across her realm, destroying it, raping . . ."

The goddess was in pain, furious, and frightened. Why should she not allow the warring spirits in this land to tear it asunder? Why should the storm gods not dance, and the mountains not belch fire before the land cracked asunder and let in the long-vanished sea?

Why indeed?

"It was Meletios," Leo whispered.

"He was Theo's father?" Asherah blinked. For a moment, Leo trembled on the verge of laughter that could drive him over the edge into madness. Then he controlled himself.

"Not Theo's father. The discoverer of this place."

Asherah met her husband's eyes and smiled. They were much of a mind, had always been so. And now they assembled the last piece of this puzzle. In his youth, a boy here in Cappadocia, Meletios had wandered far beneath the earth. Who knows? Perhaps he had been searching for the way between the underground cities and the treasure that was supposed to be found there.

Instead, he had found the way within; and he had found, not a treasure of gold and silver, but this. Perhaps even that long ago, the goddess labored. Perhaps the mere sight of her to a thoughtful boy, torn between the raptures of his mind and the urgings of his growing body, had been enough to drive him from his home. Perhaps, too, after seeing what lay beneath the earth and the power of that darkness, he could *never* find enough light: even in the deserts of Egypt, where he sacrificed his vision.

He had been left blighted by this place: that was for certain. But he had also been rendered profoundly sensitive to manifestations of the power that dwelt within. And that awareness was something that another person, similarly akin to power, could detect. Thus it must have been that Saint Meletios, his namesake and mentor in Egypt, sent him back to Cappadocia, to seal and to guard the shrine lest anyone else see it.

After all, a blind guardian would be the hardest of all to tempt.

"He must have found the boy. . . ." Leo whispered. "Much, much later."

Asherah looked down at Theodoulos, who crouched beside her. Perhaps the goddess had indeed given birth, she thought: some attempt to reconcile herself and her land with the invaders who had come to it. If so, she had failed, partially, and sent the boy, who had been born less than perfect, up into the light of day to be cared for by the women who served her.

She had thought herself—and her child—to be protected by them. But, by then, Meletios had cast them out. Thus, it was he who found the lame infant and who cared for him as if Meletios had been his own father or grandfather.

My son! My son! He hid him from me and hid me from the light of day as if I were some demon. . . .

"Be at peace," Asherah ventured to say. "Possibly, just possibly, he protected you from the sight of those who might have considered you just such a demon."

Again, the statue seemed to writhe with the effort of giving birth. The ground shuddered.

Theodoulos flinched, then drew a shuddering breath.

"Mother?" his voice quavered upward in pitch, then broke. "Are you truly my mother?"

Blasphemy that this was the mother of them all trembled on Asherah's lips, to be overpowered by waves of emotion that forced her to her knees.

Theodoulos rose, as if strengthened by it. He started slowly toward the seated figure, favoring his weak leg as he always did, but moving faster and faster until he had flung himself at her feet. Another tremor racked her, and the violet gem in her belly pulsed, great spasms of light and darkness. Theodoulos cried out as if her pain had become his.

At his cry, the goddess removed her arms from about the necks of her beast-midwives. She raised his face, illumined now and shadowed by the gem's light, in her hands and kissed him on the forehead. Brighter lights gleamed upon his cheeks: were they Theodoulos' tears—or hers? Then, with a gesture that looked like a farewell, she took her hands away.

Go back.

It was not, Asherah thought, rejection. It was, pure and simple, that this was a birthing chamber and no place for the man that Theodoulos was rapidly becoming.

Take care of him.

Theodoulos ran to Leo, who caught him in a hug.

"He didn't limp," Leo marveled to Asherah. "Did you see that? She healed him. Just a touch."

He held Theodoulos off at arm's length. "Walk for me, son. Walk for me."

His eyes brimmed, and he turned to Asherah to share his joy. *Out,* she mouthed. *Now. While it's safe for the boy to go.*

For her part, she knew what she had to do: see the creature who crouched before her through her ordeal and bring her child into the light.

"You're coming with me," Leo demanded. Asherah's heart sank. Now, of all times, was precisely the worst for such a display.

He started forward, but a blast of rage halted his footsteps and, from the way he staggered, might have stopped his heart for good.

Who are you? the goddess demanded of Asherah. *And this . . . this man with you . . . do you claim him?*

In the upper air, the magic of Psellus' envoy had struck at Leo's heart and throat. But Leo had resisted Psellus and his servant: he had always been able—at a cost—to resist them.

This assault was worse by far, as if a deft, but gentle hand passed through his chest, cupped around his heart, and gave it a cautionary squeeze. Let that vastly powerful hand crush into a fist, perhaps by instinct during a particularly harsh birth-pain; and he knew he would die before he had a chance to scream.

Theodoulos lunged forward—on *two* good legs, praise God—to catch him, but Leo swerved.

Asherah extended her hand to him.

Let her pour her rage out on me! Leo wanted to command her. But he had no breath to shout. He still gasped and swayed from the folly of his last command, and he had never commanded Asherah when he could try to persuade.

He had never let any appeal she might make to him go unheeded, either. He clasped her outstretched hand.

"Oh yes," said Asherah, her voice as tremulous as it had been before Father Meletios, "I claim him."

Why have you come here, you and this man you claim?

Asherah awarded the goddess a level glance. "You drew me. You know you have always drawn me. You know you lured us to the underground ways and made certain we knew we belonged together."

The pressure in Leo's mind lessened. The light in the great belly of the laboring statue quivered with each labor pain.

"Besides," Asherah finished, her voice shaking, "your servants said you needed help."

Even in the pulsating light of the huge amethyst in the statue's belly, Leo could see Asherah glance slightly downward. So *this* was what had inspired them when Leo had walked over to her and taken her shoulders in his hands, had kissed and caressed her until they had ached to possess each other right then—but the torches had burnt out, driving them back to the surface.

Why have you not fled now? Helpless as I am now, I can scarcely compel your presence.

"Can you not?" asked Asherah, her voice edged. "I did not come here for dread or pity. I came here for love. Love of the man beside me, care for the boy—but now that I see you, I will not leave you, not as you are."

Leo shut his eyes. Kemal, prostrate beside him, pressed his brow against the rock.

Asherah's words did not particularly surprise Leo. So short a time they had had together, but he knew her so well. The goddess' grip tightened within his chest. How long could a man live with the heart cut out of him? Asherah, he knew, would insist on staying here to bring this birth to whatever monstrous conclusion it could be brought. Very likely, she would insist on sending him away—men had no place in a birthing chamber, women always said—and boys like Theodoulos even less. The ground no long seemed to shake at ever-shorter intervals: it trembled constantly, as if he trod on living flesh that occasionally twinged in a sharper spasm of anguish. Worse still, he could hear shouts and echoes, clashes of battle from far above.

The people were falling back before the Turks into the maze far below the cities.

He would be dismissed, and he would go and fight. It was his duty. But duty alone was very bleak, and, if he lived, all the years of his life would be even bleaker without Asherah. He could no more sweep his wife up and away from here—assuming that the tunnels did not collapse, crushing them all—than he could demand that she break the promise she had just made.

For a moment, the goddess paused. Leo thought the rage that she had used to threaten him abated somewhat, to be replaced in the brief intervals between labor pangs with tenderness. The Mother had seen her son. She had been offered the nursing service of a woman, and one of no mean strength, to aid her until she gave birth. Dark amusement filtered through the statue's pain. What more could she ask?

Love? It has been long, long since anyone—besides the usual beautiful doomed men—has dared to love me. Be welcome, daughter. In the shadows, it seemed as if her head, its features all but rubbed away, came up and deep pits of eyes regarded him. *And you, oh man, be worthy of her.* Those eyes regarded him. *She is very like . . . very like the girls who decked me with flowers when I lived in the sunlight.*

Leo bowed his head. He could see those girls, dark-eyed, glowing with youth and health, flashing-eyed, and garlanded with flowers. Then the goddess had withdrawn beneath the earth. A different faith had ruled, its Father stern, its Mother stripped of power, though still beloved.

Now, instead of all those worshippers, all the old goddess had to tend her was his wife, even if Asherah was infinitely more powerful and beloved than any pagan girls that this maddened creature might pull from its ancient memory.

The goddess' entire body clenched. Something akin to lightning flashed in the gem glowing below pendulous breasts, and the stocky legs strained against the rock of the cave floor. The rock trembled: Leo balanced as if on shipboard. The stream that flowed across the floor widened, as if life fluids gushed forth to feed it. Leo thought he could smell blood. Had the battle in the upper levels drawn this close already?

And there was silence in hell for the space of half an hour?

Less than that. As the goddess' attention turned inward again, Leo could hear the clamor of mortal combat in the ways above. It was nearing them. The Turkmen must have interpreted retreat as defeat, pure and simple. How astonished they would be when their victims simply vanished into the subterranean byways that so many villagers had explored since childhood. But they would rush down here, seeking treasure—and find only two men, a boy, a woman, and a laboring statue.

It is well, the goddess' voice cut into his thoughts. As gently as it had entered, the touch that had menaced his heart was withdrawn. *This is my daughter. Even reared as she has been in the faith of her fathers, with no mother to guide her, she remembers: the child follows the mother. You too, oh man: you look strong enough, and you have sense enough to fear me. You are stronger than the last one; see that you foster my daughter well.*

Sunlight, not the light of the amethyst, filled Leo's thoughts. If they were spared, he and Asherah would leave this place with *two* of this creature's offspring: Theodoulos, and whatever infant slipped from between those immense thighs. It would be a strong child, a healthy one. Leo was not certain he could bear the thought.

Dust and grit cascaded from the cracks in the ceiling. This time it was not the earth and stone above them that groaned: it was the laboring figure herself. Asherah swayed and fell to the ground, her body writhing as if sharing the statue's birth spasms. A reek of blood and iron filled the cavern.

The great gem in its belly darkened, then flared into a greater light than it had shown before. The light increased in intensity until it quivered like the purplish white heart of a flame. Then, abruptly, it fluttered toward extinction, shot up, then visibly trembled: light/dark, light/dark, light/dark, like two sides of a butterfly's wings. If the light faded, the "child" would die, and with it, its mother, the land, and any hope anyone in it had ever cherished.

The roar of battle neared. Definitely, the Turkmen had found the inner ways. Who knew when they would reach this shrine?

Again, the great cave resonated with the goddess' birth anguish and rage. After all these thousands of years, the power that lived below the earth would be extinguished, along with what it struggled to bring to light. If she were to die, why allow any of these puny creatures to live? Perhaps the land itself *should* die in fire, quake, and molten rock, as better lands had died, and then lie covered by the sea.

Leo drew his sword. At the very least, he and Kemal could guard the door of this birthing chamber and trade their lives for a chance at a healthy child.

He stole one last look at Asherah. Somehow, she had struggled back onto her feet. Her eyes met his. They held fear, but a blazing determination as powerful, in its way, as the fire in the amethyst's core as it struggled to break free.

"You can't do it alone, you know," she spoke to the goddess. "In all these years, haven't you learned that yet? You need a human focus. And you need a midwife. I am here."

The goddess and Leo cried out as one. Asherah picked her way back to him, stood so close that he might have embraced her, might have carried her away to safety, had a dream like safety existed.

"Leo," she whispered. Her breath warmed his cheek. "My Leo. Look at her. See what pain she has lived with. I have a chance to heal that. How dare I not try?"

Now, he did embrace her. The upright, curving body in his arms made him ache. "God, I shall miss you," he whispered. The words turned into one sob before he imposed ruthless control upon himself. "All the long years . . ."

She had healed him: would he begrudge her attempt to heal what labored before him? Still, he feared the immensity of the pain he would face for the rest of his life if she failed.

"Leo," she told him, her head against his shoulder as it had rested during the weeks they had had together, "it is my choice. My will and that of my mother. Tell my father . . ." She managed a shaky laugh. ". . . that like Deborah and Judith and Esther, I risk my life to save a people. Now, let me go."

His arms opened as if he had no power over them.

"Leo." That beloved, inexorable voice. This time he was certain his heart *was* being ripped out.

"I must have your knife. To cut the cord, you know, when the baby comes."

Theodoulos had her father's daggers, and she would not ask for them back. Leo offered her the sword he would have no heart to use, but she shook her head.

"That is your weapon. A man's blade. Give me . . ."

He knew her mind. From within his garments, he drew the obsidian blade that she wanted. He bowed as he presented it.

"Thank you, my love." Asherah turned away quickly. Too quickly. Did her courage waver too? She advanced upon the laboring goddess, deliberately as matter-of-fact as a midwife in the upper world. "Now, you and the other men must leave."

Once again, he thought, he stood before a general and faced certain defeat.

"Get up," he told Kemal.

"Lion's cub . . ." the Seljuk grasped his arm and clambered back to his feet.

Leo shook his head. He did not want pity. What he wanted, he could not have. He would take what he could get. Death stalked the corridors, no doubt eager to collect the debt Leo owed.

"It is Manzikert again," he told Kemal. "Only, this time, we fight on the same side."

Then, Leo saluted his wife and her mistress and marched out of the birthing chamber toward his war.

$$=\!\!=\!\!\Vdash 41 \Vdash\!\!=\!\!=$$

K emal's sword rasped out of its sheath, a partner to his, as they stationed themselves outside the door.

"If I told you to flee, would you obey me?" Leo asked Theodoulos. He had two sound legs now: he might get quite a way before he was brought down.

"Not a chance," said Theo. Out came the daggers he had fetched for Asherah, but not returned to her. Joachim's daggers: a man could spend a lifetime as a soldier and not see steel as fine. Theo might fall fighting, but not because his tools betrayed him.

"Stay behind us," Leo ordered.

At least, Asherah would not have to see him finish what he should have done at Manzikert. Still, if he had died then, he never would have known her. Don't think about it, Leo. You have no time to think.

The clamor of battle, the reek of blood and voided bowels, bodies falling against rock, rolling, and taking other victims with them, the steady clatter and crash of rock falling from above drew nearer. He advanced some way to meet it, feeling as if he walked upon the most treacherous of seabeds. The further they went, the better their chances of deflecting invaders from the shrine. Perhaps, if they could make it to the whispering galley where so many tunnels met . . .

Torches sparked and swung, used as often as weapons as they were to provide reddish tongues of light. The stink of burnt flesh mixed with the iron tang of blood, the hot reek of excrement, polluting the ancient cleanliness of the ways beneath. This was not even battle as strategists described it. They were down to swords, and if the blades snapped, doubtless, they would continue fighting with whatever rocks they could snatch up. This was not war—the massing of wings of riders, the positioning of archers, the game of wits pitted against enemy wits. This was sheer, brutal hacking, as old as the eldest primal curse.

Torchlight glinted off the blade of an axe used as deftly as farmers might use a scythe. Nordbriht fought, standing at bay, swinging his axe, surrounded not just by Turkmen, but by a host of shadows that snarled and pounced like maddened wolves.

A scream of pain echoed through the long, long corridor, drowning out all other noises. Was that a battle cry, or the scream of a woman in torment?

Triumph, of course, was as past praying for as Leo was done hoping. Despair keened in his blood as shrilly as the battle cry of a Varangian who had seen his lord die on the field.

Two Turkmen rushed up to him, and Leo stepped forward, ready to meet them.

The ground *buckled*, hurling Leo against the cave wall. As he fought back onto his feet, his sword out before him to ward off attackers, a leopard rushed past him, pouncing into the fray, followed by another.

The ground quaked one final time, and then stilled itself. The torches, those not quenched in bloody wounds, flickered. Their fire changed color and form. Flames of a spectral white twined out, creating a half-light to illuminate an unholy resurrection.

Now, allies fought at his side. Some wore arms and armor such as the land had not seen for thousands of years. Some of that gear could have been issued by Alexander's officers as his troops marched through Gordion. Some of it was new when Uriah the Hittite paid his respects to David the King in Jerusalem. And some . . . the men shambled forth in skins, swinging clubs in which deadly shards of flint or wickedly edged obsidian had been embedded. He could not touch those men, could scarcely bear to look upon them; but their eyes were alight, glowing with a terrible eagerness.

Where they struck, Turkmen fell. Where they struck, enemies and unwilling allies gave way in horror. Swords and spears passed through their bodies, but still they advanced. Turkmen and villagers, monks, farmers, and aristocrats gave way before these fighters who had appeared out of the bowels of the earth.

When it seemed as if no more men could possibly emerge from the caves behind Leo and Kemal, the screaming reached such a pitch that Leo's hearing mercifully blanked. Now, as though protected, Leo watched men fight and fall. The leopards reemerged from their battles, to be joined by great, blocky lions such as he had seen carved of living stone, by maddened bulls, even by serpents hissing as they tangled warriors' ankles and brought them down before raising wedge-shaped heads and lunging at their throats.

The terror was gone now, replaced by utter despair and the last desire of fighting men: to give as good an account of themselves as possible before the strength fled their hands, the light from their eyes, and the blood from their bodies.

That scream of pain again, prolonged unto madness. This time, Leo was certain he could not have imagined the note of triumph in it. He shivered as if plunging into a mountain stream at dawn. Then he recovered just in time to slash the sword hand from a man who had leapt for him, rather than for what safety he might contrive. He knew he was going to die. He had never felt more alive.

The scream arched upward into exultation, to be met by shrieks of pure panic.

The land was no longer defended by men from all the years of this land's settlement, no longer beasts that menaced the land's invaders. Now, butterflies poured upward, legion upon legion of fragile, beautiful creatures. Their wings glowed and glittered as they darted past toppled bodies, flew in circles about flaring torches and blades awash in blood. Clouds and clouds of gleaming winged things poured out of the caves, from the very cracks in the walls that had split asunder in the terrible series of earthquakes and aftershocks that had all but turned solid rock into heaving mud.

Then, the butterflies attacked in their own fashion, flying at the faces of soldiers who tried to thrust them away with weapons, or who dropped their swords to swing at the tiny creatures with their hands.

They seized upon one warrior, alighting on his head, clustering about his eyes. He screamed, dropping his sword, his hands tearing the butterflies away from his face. His fingers came away red.

Like a wing of cavalry, butterflies attacked a man who stood astride a wounded man, choosing his moment to plunge his sword down into his throat. They flew into his mouth, open in a grin of triumph. Eyes bulging, he toppled upon his victim.

The very strangeness of this apparition created a panic as bad as the rout at Manzikert. Turkmen and townsmen alike pressed against the walls, huddled on the floor. They pitched from side to side, staggering up, crawling if they could not rise. The winged fighters were herding them, driving them upward like killer moths to the light of day, if they could reach it.

A roaring sounded in Leo's ears. The mad tide of panicked rage drove him toward his enemies, sword in hand, screaming. Dimly, he was aware that Kemal and Theodoulos had survived to follow him, but his sword was flashing, blood was sluicing off it—

Now, he could hear himself screaming. The blood that spattered his hands and face, his harness, and his now-notched sword steamed and glistened in the setting sun.

He had won through to the outer air. As he watched, other men and some women emerged from cracks and pits in the tumbled earth. Some wept. Some staggered. Some measured their lengths in the grit and just shook.

The wind wrapped around him, and his sweat made him shiver. He fell silent, his throat burning from his screams. No enemies were in sight, except the plain itself, under which the network of caves ran. The land rumbled. Dust puffed upward. And then the land collapsed inward upon itself, burying the living with the dead—those freshly dead as well as those who should never have risen at all. Beasts, butterflies, and ancient fighting men had all disappeared.

One final crack; one last rumble; and the land went silent. A few rocks toppled down the new slopes. Then all was still. The sense of the land that he had gained when Father Meletios' blood splashed him ached in the stillness, ached with the losses that his domain had sustained. Malagobia would no longer be difficult to subsist in: it would be impossible.

Keening, Leo dropped to his knees, then collapsed, gagging, if there had been anything in his belly to heave up. The anguish of his true, lasting loss hit him like a belly wound. He hid his face upon the troubled land and wished the light would go away.

42

T he sunlight had darkened from deep gold to glowing crimson
by the time Leo's breathing steadied.

"Sir? Leo?" It was Theodoulos' voice.

The word you want is "father," isn't it? Leo thought. The boy—no,
anyone who had survived what Theodoulos had, including a miracle,
could never be a boy again—knelt beside Leo, earnestly trying to raise
him.

He had survived. If he had survived, others had survived. If others
had survived, he had no right to wallow in his personal sorrow. An Empress had told him that as he mourned—good dog, Leo, good fellow!—
before the tomb of his old master.

He would, as he vowed, take Theodoulos in charge. Sooner or later,
they must return to the valley, bury whatever dead the land's collapse
(assuming it stretched as far as the valley) had not dealt with, then come
back to the world.

The wind blew, tugging at his matted hair, cooling his temples. He
shuddered at the faint whistling sound it made.

Was all truly lost?

Closing his eyes, he felt for the awareness that he had tested like a
rotten tooth, resented with all his heart, and, at the last, come to rely
upon. Vertigo seized him at the thought that he might never again
reach that union he had known.

Not lost. Not now, or ever. But for now, the door was shut.

In the future, it would fall to his lot to see that no foolish boys in
search of adventure, treasure, or any other false tokens of manhood ventured within the caves. For months, perhaps years, he would have to
guard them against aftershocks, further rockfalls, and pits opening even
in familiar passages. He and Theodoulos, probably, would have to inspect the underground cities, see if enough was left of them to reclaim.
For now, the underground ways must remain shut.

He laid his arm across Theodoulos' shoulder, whether to give support or get it, he did not know.

"Sir? Sir?"

They were approaching, they were circling, they were waiting on
his attention. The boldest of the villagers had dared to pluck him by
the filthy sleeve, penetrating the sphere of silence that had somehow

surrounded him ever since he had had to abandon his wife to serve as midwife to a goddess.

Leo turned to stare blearily at them. A cut, scabbing over messily, marred one man's cheek, but he would have recognized that face on the shores of the Styx.

"Georgios!" he cried. "Did you . . ."

"My wife and children live!" the man exclaimed. He threw himself to his knees, took Leo's bloody hand, and carried it to his cheek. "This holy Sister and the old Jewish merchant led them all to safety."

Georgios pointed to a knot of women and half-grown boys, surrounding children too young and adults too feeble to fight. They were blood-stained, and their eyes still seemed distended with horror as if they had gazed into the Pit. Reassured by the light and air, they laid aside their weapons and, as if robbed of the last of their fighting strength, sank to their knees.

Sister Xenia stalked forward, her robes pale with dust, but otherwise unmarred. Leo would have known that footstep, that glower before the throne of God. She held a scythe she had not yet cleaned. Seeing Leo's eyes upon it, she gestured for a lad to come and take it away.

"We followed your plan," she said. "It worked. Just about."

And that, Leo knew, was all that he would ever get from her.

He bowed his head. "I saw Her," he told the woman.

Her eyes lit, then closed in sorrow.

"I tried. I failed. And now the earth covers them both. Your lady. And . . ." his throat closed, but he had to force the name out or damn himself forever as a coward. ". . . my Asherah."

"Death is not an end, but a beginning," said Sister Xenia. "The earth restores itself."

But she forgot herself to the extent of smearing a hand across her face. It left a clean swathe. Then she, too, remembered what she would far rather forget. "Your wife's father stayed with us. It was either that, or that monster with the axe you sent us would have staged a one-man riot." She tried to smile, but failed. "He must be told."

And it was Leo's duty, not hers, to bring him word. Joachim was a good man, a kind man; and God knows he did not keep the Persian custom of killing the messenger. Still, Leo was certain that he would far rather die than tell Asherah's father she had not escaped.

Leo followed Sister Xenia across the plain, littered now with the figures of survivors and the few motionless bodies that were the only ones that they could carry to the surface.

"Lion's cub!" It was Kemal hailing him. He strode toward Leo, wobbling somewhat from side to side. Truly, to the end of his life, Kemal would prefer horseback. His face bled from parallel slashes. Those wounds, Leo realized, were self-inflicted. Out of grief? He knew Kemal might never say.

A rumble sounded from behind him. Nordbriht. The ends of the big man's braids were stiff with blood. One was half a foot shorter than the others. He did not so much walk as limp across the plain, and he favored one side. Like Leo's sword, his axe was notched. But he had already wiped it clean of the worst stains and was burnishing its blades with a piece of leather he had found somewhere Leo was sure he preferred not to identify. No, one could not doubt that Nordbriht had been in the thick of the battle beneath the earth. But the shadowing that marked his face every time he fought, every time he changed shape was gone, leached away by what he had just survived. Exhausted as he was, he moved lightly, a man who has shed some terrible burden and has not yet had time to rest.

"Where are the Turks?" Leo asked Nordbriht. Stupid question. The earth had swallowed the Turkmen who had penetrated into the underground; and the defenses of the land itself and those who loved it had driven the others off.

For now. They would be back. Some would leave their bones in this land, and some would escape it; and none of them, Greek, Turk, Jew, or Northerner, would ever be the same again.

There would have to be a memorial here, he thought. Were he a great one in Byzantium, a church could rise, dedicated to the Holy Bearer of God. It would be a church, however, in which Maria bore the face of a Jewish woman who had loved him. Just as well he had no aspirations to greatness. He could imagine the howls of "blasphemy" if he had such a church built.

Some sort of memorial there would be. Perhaps Joachim would help him plan it.

His father-in-law had not lost flesh in the time he had spent sequestered in the underground ways. But now, it seemed to hang upon him like the folds of his heavy robes. So short a time, yet Joachim, the dominant, brilliant merchant and thinker, had withered into an old man.

A broken heart could do that to you. Leo's hair had started to grey practically overnight when Romanus was blinded. By that indication, it should be the color of snow now.

If he did not cut it and, this time, withdraw from the world for good, to contemplate his losses.

Joachim turned toward Leo. His face lit. He would have run to meet him if Leo had not run to him first. Joachim caught him in a hard embrace, a father's embrace, as if in holding Leo, he could embrace the daughter who was lost.

"I tried, I tried . . ."

Apologies and laments tried to gabble themselves out of Leo's throat, burdening the poor old man, who now had only an unworthy son-in-law to love him. He had lost his wife and sons in days gone by. And now, he had lost a daughter worthy to compare with the mothers in Israel or the greatest ladies of Byzantium. Leo forced himself not to increase Joachim's grief by burdening him with his own heartbreak.

Deliberately, then, Joachim released him. He backed off one step, then looked up into Leo's face.

What will you do now?

He could hide forever in a monastery, he knew that. Leaving Joachim without an heir, and, worse than that, alone.

The distance between them grew intolerable.

"Let me *be* your son, not merely your son-in-law," Leo offered. "Adopt me. I will become a Jew, and one day . . ."

He would convert, undergo whatever rituals it was they whispered about and inflicted on boy babies on the eighth day, if that was what it took. However fearsome they might be. More fearsome by far was the sacrifice that, ultimately, he must make if his offer were to bear fruit: ultimately, he would have to marry and produce grandchildren to comfort Joachim and ease his final years. Would any other woman have him? And could he bear to take any other wife?

"You have living parents, my son. It is a sorrow to lose a child. I would not have them endure what I do. But stay with me. Stay, as long as you wish."

Joachim reached up to put an arm around Leo, who allowed himself, for just this short time, to relax into the luxury. They stood, watching the sun set. Banners flared behind it, crimson and the purple of Empire: no, the purple of the gem that had flashed in the goddess' belly and had cost both men far more than any gem was worth.

"I should wash," said Joachim. "Sundown brings the Sabbath. Asherah always used to . . ."

"I know. I know."

An aftershock distracted Leo from that unwelcome knowledge. After the quakes he had endured, he balanced easily.

"They will want to sleep out-of-doors," Joachim said. "I confess, I may find it hard to sleep inside after this."

It was astonishing: the old man kept his voice from trembling. But Leo saw how his hands shook.

And could Leo ever go back to the rooms he had shared with Asherah? The ache of something missing began to grow in him: a sense of the land, would he call it? He had been sealed to it by blood and loss, and now by a triumph that was so dearly bought that he might well have called it a defeat—save that Asherah would never have understood how he could scorn her sacrifice. The ache of loss, filtering up from the land through the soles of his boots, should have been stronger, he thought. Like the really bad wounds: you didn't feel the agony till afterward.

He could wait for it, lifelong. He wouldn't have that chance.

"I may join you. I have the need to pray." Leo forced a smile. It came out sharp-edged, and the men who were watching him too closely flinched when they saw it. They would be clustering around him soon enough for orders and for comfort, and their families with them.

"You men! Careful how you dig. You don't know what sort of land-slide you could set off, and we've already lost too many!"

"They're idiots!" he hissed at Joachim. "Let a few of them try to re-trieve . . ." He flinched from the idea of what they might need to ex-hume from the caves. ". . . and we'll have bigger idiots trying to dig for treasure until they bring the whole place down about us once again."

Or lure yet another blood tide of invaders.

They had won time. They had not won the war forever; only for their own time, if they were lucky and very watchful. God grant it.

Grumbling, Leo broke away from Joachim and started down toward the laboring men. The sisters were ahead of him, pausing to tell each worker of his kin, occasionally helping shift a rock or steady a man who stumbled. Every muscle in Leo's body had begun to ache. His father-in-law followed, somewhat more cautiously.

Again, an aftershock, stronger, this time, and followed this time by a sustained rockfall, some of it clattering into a tunnel that must still be partially clear. A child's thin cry wailed up, then subsided. *Used to it, are you?* Leo thought.

They would have to put up barricades. Tomorrow.

A beam from the crimson sun struck light from the toppled rock. The light flared and shifted. It paused, then moved again as if it climbed out toward the freedom of the air. It grew as it moved, as a torch's flame strengthens when it is taken out of foul air into an open cavern. And when it had put the scattered rock behind it, it stopped. Again, the sun-set haloed it until those who watched had to look away.

But the light was fading fast. Leo turned back to see what had emerged from the rock.

A cloud of butterflies like those that had flown out of the caverns and helped panic an invading army swirled upward from the ground and circled the source of light, then withdrew.

"Leo?" The barriers Leo had put up so hastily to protect him against his loss crumbled at the sound of that beloved, not-to-be-believed voice. Please God, this was real, and not madness, come to claim him irrevocably.

Asherah stood there, watching him. Smiling for him alone.

She was swathed in fabrics so stiff with gold thread that they had not rotted away in all the years they must have been stored in the caves. Butterflies, but creatures wrought of gold and jewels, clung to her hair, distinguishable from the living creatures only by the fact that they did not fly away with the others. And in her arms, swaddled in glinting fabric, she held a child.

Sister Xenia sank to her knees at the apparition. The faces of the woman and child were so bright she had to avert her eyes. If they were not careful, Leo thought, they could have a religious panic as well as the aftermath of war and earthquake to deal with—assuming bandits, the remnants of this wave of Turkmen, and treasure hunters were not more than enough to fill one day. Oh God, that was his wife down there. Not crushed beneath the rock, but alive and smiling at him.

He didn't care how many tremors might occur. Half-blind, he raced down and drew Asherah into his arms, carefully, for the sake of the infant she held.

She put up her face to be kissed. Her tears wet his lips—or was it he who wept?

"What happened?" he demanded, sweeping his arm about her and urging her upward toward her father. "Come, come quickly. I thought your father would have died for grief at losing you. I thought that I . . . oh, God, Asherah, I saw the rest of my life stretching out without you, and I didn't want it."

She smiled. Her tears ran down her cheeks and fell onto the infant's face. It turned and looked at Leo. Immense eyes opened, violet and unfathomable, the color of the gem he remembered from the cave.

"Her child?" Leo stammered. "Yours?"

"Our daughter," Asherah told him, serenely confident that he would welcome the child. He held out a trembling finger to the baby who took it and smiled. Not for the first time that day, Leo's heart turned over from sheer adoration.

Then he reached out to catch and steady Joachim. Of course, he could not wait for his daughter to climb up the slope to him. He would have to try to run down; and naturally, he tripped and pitched forward, practically into Leo's arms, blind with tears of joy.

Leo had his family in his arms, then, all but Theodoulos, who had spotted his friend Ioannes with his arm in a sling. He bore himself with a flourish that would have done credit to a youth in one of the Tagmata regiments. At some point, Leo would have to deal with that, too. Then, Joachim, trying to hold his daughter as close as he could, jostled the baby Asherah had brought from beneath the earth. The child squirmed and set up a wail that made the people digging out of the rubble or trying to figure out how and what they would eat, and where they would sleep tonight pause and smile.

"Asherah," Joachim brushed his daughter's hair away from her forehead. His fingers glanced over one of the butterflies gleaming in the dark curls, then over the cloth of gold she wore. "What is this?"

She smiled. "I will explain it all. First, this is my daughter. Mine and Leo's."

Joachim raised his eyebrows.

"I rescued her from beneath the earth."

"She must have people, child. You cannot simply claim a child, a Christian child at that. Why . . ."

"Leo can," Asherah pointed out, impeccably logical. "But . . . Father, you know those statues. Those and the dishes with the women symbols on them, the ones that the monks tell people to break? For that matter, you've seen the icons they have in the churches, the ones with the women's faces scratched out?"

Joachim nodded. Even in the darkness, Leo could see that his eyes were glazing. Too many shocks, already. How would Joachim deal with what he was about to hear?

"There was a reason for it all. You knew, as I did, that there was power here. I found it in the ways beneath the cities. They are joined; or they were."

"You found them!" Joachim said. His eyes lit, flicking over the butterflies she wore in her hair.

"Oh, there was treasure there. This is some of it. But there was also . . . you would call it a statue, only it was alive. Theophany: goddess made manifest, and a goddess, at that, about to give birth and very angry at the intrusion of invaders, wave after wave, year after year, over her land. So I helped her."

"You," said Joachim to Leo. "You let her?"

"You were the one who warned me that Asherah was no puppet of mine or anyone else's. When she offered to serve as midwife and sent me away, saying that a birthing chamber was no place for men, I went." He chose his words carefully, trying to shield Joachim from the terror and despair he had felt in those last hideous moments before the beasts and the Wild Hunt leapt out from the birthing chamber to drive the Turkmen from their domain. "I judged I could best serve everyone by fighting."

"The Mother *drove* him away, Father. She might have killed him, only she saw we had chosen each other and spared us. I think she wanted parents for her child, too." She held up the infant to her father.

"My dearest," he recoiled. "I am hardly in a position to be a Spartan father—or grandfather—to expose a child, or a man of Canaan to sacrifice a first-born. I thought I had lost you! Now, beyond hope, you return, and you say this is your daughter, yours and Leo's? She is welcome, she and those who will follow her." He touched the infant's forehead. She opened her eyes and smiled at him. It was not the smile of a newborn, but a much older, wiser child.

Joachim's wrinkled face seemed to ease, wax smoothing beneath the sun of his granddaughter's healing regard.

"Would you . . ." Leo had never heard his father-in-law so hesitant. ". . . would you call her Binah?"

"Mother's name!" Asherah nodded happily. "I was hoping you would suggest that. The right name, a name of power . . ."

"Like your own, child, like your own."

Asherah leaned her head against Leo's shoulder, pressing in to stand as close to him as she might. Leo was not at all certain that he wanted to share her just yet with a child, much less with a newborn and with Theodoulos, who would still need attention before he entered fully into manhood. Then he recalled: Tzipporah and the other women of the household, assuming they survived, would be ecstatic at having a child to care for. He would have what he longed for: a bath, a meal, and time alone to reassure himself that Asherah would always be by his side.

Except, of course, when she chose otherwise.

Then the child caught him in the gaze of those remarkable violet eyes, and he was lost. No, his guardianship was not at an end.

"Let me tell you, Leo. After a long time,—" She opened her mouth, considered, closed it again, and started over. Leo had the distinct sense that she was censoring details of midwifery that she considered unfit for masculine ears, "I caught the child. Caught it as it was born, and then the world seemed to turn upside down. It exploded about me—

light and sound, and the terrible, terrible shaking of the earthquakes. I heard the land crack wide open, the goddess' guardian beasts run by; and I told myself, 'you will never see the light of day.'

"Then the shaking stopped. I found myself lying on my face, dressed as I am now. When *I* stopped shaking and could focus my eyes, I saw the statue. It had toppled, and the gem in its belly had shattered into thousands of tiny shards, each one glowing, each vanishing when I put out a hand to touch it. I leaned forward and saw Binah—" She did not so much smile as let her eyes glow at her father. "—lying there, unhurt, and swaddled. Just as you see her.

"I picked her up, and then, oh Leo, a flight of butterflies just erupted from the cracks in the walls. They swirled around me and the baby as if they were trying to hide us. It was dark in the cave, and a great cat, like one of the statues beside the goddess, walked beside me, leading me out into the light."

It was a ballad that they lived in, a ballad that bled and feared and rejoiced past the ability of any one singer. One last question remained.

"What happened to the other lion?" Perhaps it was a foolish question; but he wanted to know, if he could, and thus knot up the edges on this exceedingly complex tapestry.

"Don't you understand yet?" Asherah laid a hand upon his arm. The child stirred and opened its astonishing, too-wise eyes.

"Leo, it was you!"

Behind him, Leo could hear Joachim muttering prayers. Sensing his attention, his father-in-law smiled. "I thank God, son, not just for keeping us alive, but letting us live until *now.*"

They stood, not speaking, letting the shouts and clatter of a people returning to life wash over them.

"I'm afraid you won't have much of a Sabbath, sir," Leo commented. The work to come would be backbreakingly hard, leaving Joachim little time for prayer and contemplation, probably for years to come.

"I couldn't ask for better." Joachim raised an admonishing eyebrow at Leo: don't keep people waiting.

They stood outside the charmed circle that good fortune and a now-buried statue of an ancient goddess had cast for them, waiting on Leo's pleasure.

Nordbriht, worn out, but oddly relaxed, came over to stand behind him, a small boy clinging to his leg. "I've been helping families locate their men."

It was laughter that Leo heard, then, laughter and sobs of joy, mingled with the grief for losses only now being discovered.

Leo nodded approval at the Northerner. The wolfishness was gone from his grin—almost. "Now, just you look at them, brother—I mean, prince. They know who saved their lives. Say the word, and you could be Emperor. And I would serve you more faithfully than my kinsman Haraldr served all the Jarls of Miklagard gone by."

He made as if to lay his axe at Leo's feet or raise it in salute, whichever he might prefer. Leo forestalled him.

He looked from Kemal, whose gaze darted before and behind him as if he expected imminent attack. Something must be done for him in the way of lands, perhaps, or herds. Ioannes stood among the landowners, drawn, but determined to press beyond battle-courage and achieve the endurance of his elders. Fanning out behind them, suffering occasional demands from Sister Xenia and her companions for messengers to fetch food, blankets, wine, or anything else from their lands or warehouses, were the farmers, merchants, and aristocrats who had eyed Leo askance when he had first arrived, a cloud on his name and his soul.

"Ducas," one of the nobles hailed him. "Well done."

The heat that had made that name dangerous to bear here was gone. A Ducas might have betrayed Romanus, Cappadocia's son. Another Ducas had helped preserve his old land. Noble to noble, was it? What did the man want?

"We have our work cut out for us now," Leo said, gesturing at the effort to bring order out of earthquake.

"Whatever you decide. *Whatever.*"

Leo suppressed a shiver. He had not missed the undertones in that reply. A moment longer, and they would be cheering him, riding yet another whirlwind.

Perhaps *that* was what the man wanted, what they all might be led to want: for another man to rise from Cappadocia at the head of an army. A man, say, who had the backing of all people in the region; who had Imperial connections and experience with the ways, more treacherous than any underground roadway, of Byzantium; who could point to a Varangian and that very Seljuk who had taken an Emperor prisoner as a sign of the men who would follow him; and who had contacts among the richest trading caravans in the East and a wily, courageous wife. On the whole, it was easier when Leo had only had to worry about assassins.

Him. The Basileus Leo Ducas. Leo Digenis—twice-bred; twice-born. If he had a sufficient share of his family's ambition and ruthlessness, he might even manage it. There could even be fulfillment in replacing an incompetent with a capable administrator.

Could he withstand Psellus? He was sealed to *this* land with blood, not made Emperor in the Church, the bridge between Asia and Europe, the intermediary between God and earth. Any power that he had was something other, something of the earth. Even now, he could feel it appealing to him: so many ravaged homes, torn-up fields, plundered flocks; so much in shards or ashes. The appeals made him want to set to work right now, not hasten into battle or to the nearest palace.

There might indeed be treasure to be found here, if they spared time from rebuilding to dig for it. It might even prove useful in repairing an empire.

But why bother, either to dig or to scheme? Such treasure could attract only more enemies and more traitors. That belonged to the world that he had left behind, the world in which he and Kemal would have been enemies, and Joachim only a resource to be exploited and despised. As for Asherah . . .

Glistening in the gold and jewels that had been her midwife's fee, she came over to stand by him. The wily, courageous wife that an aspirant to Empire would need: absolutely. He could just see her in Purple, as elegant as any lady in Byzantium and as deadly.

His mother had hoped for grandchildren, and now she had at least two he would never dare to bring to her.

Asherah leaned her head against his arm. As always, she knew his mind.

"I have told you," she said, "that I have no ambition to be Basilissa. The days of Queen Esther are gone for good. And can you imagine it? A Jewish Basilissa with a goddess-child in the Great Palace? The Bosphorus would rise and drown the city!"

Leo laughed helplessly at the irony. "I have all the Empire a man could want. Right here."

Psellus and his puppets had drawn their line in the earth, forbidding their enemies to cross it. To protect what little they clutched, much though it seemed to them, they had abandoned all that lay beyond it—a far greater share.

They had thrown *this* land away. Leo would take up its care and cherish it. He would not be an Emperor. Instead, he would rule here by influence and example, first among equals. Had he not thought that he had strayed into a ballad? Henceforward, ballads might be written about him.

"Then," said Asherah, "I suggest we get as many people as we can under cover of some kind. We will, naturally, open our courtyards to those who have no home, if they will consent. . . ."

To take bread from the hands of Jews? They had never refused before. If Asherah would not be Basilissa, she would be this land's provider, giving of herself and her wealth without stint. *And she laugheth at the time to come.* He was her husband; it was right for him to use such words to praise her. In days to come, he suspected the people watching her would take them up.

They all were shards, all these people, washed up upon this shore, powerless by themselves, but capable of combining into a pattern that spelled life for as long as they could keep it.

"We need to get Binah home."

At the sound of her name, the infant laughed and raised a hand to the golden butterflies that gleamed in Asherah's hair.

Leo also put out a hand, pulling one of the ornaments free. His wife widened her eyes at him: this was hardly the place for such a liberty. At home, perhaps, in the luxurious quiet of their bedroom, but here?

"These could cause too much wonder," he said quietly. Perhaps they should save out a few as part of Binah's dowry, if, indeed, her mother meant her to live as a human child. But the rest of them were too-visible reminders of the ancient treasure that still lay below, however hidden, and that might lure people out to test the goodwill of a goddess whose temper, as always, was uncertain.

"Quickly," Joachim urged them. "We can tell anyone who thinks he saw them that it was just a trick of the light."

Asherah took the butterfly he held from him. "There is no need," she agreed, "to bury them in the earth again. Or hide them in a strong-box."

She showed the ornament to her daughter, who laughed again and waved her hand. Then, she raised it to her lips. It trembled on her fingertips, then rose into the air, followed by the others, as, one by one, she kissed them back into life. Like a living halo, they circled mother and child once, then rose into the sky, just as the last of the sunlight faded.

Again, Joachim's voice rose, his daughter's echoing it in translation. ". . . who kept us alive, sustained us, and permitted us to reach this joyous festival."

Joy? It would do to start with, Leo thought. Tonight, he would offer thanks and see that his people were fed. Tomorrow, there was work to be done.

Drawing his family with him, Leo climbed out of the pit and stepped forward into the rest of his life.

Author's Note

Shards of Empire was inspired by my 1990 trip to Turkey. That, in turn, was inspired by a long-time fascination with the Near East that has, at various times, provoked me into studying the Arab Revolt (I carefully did *not* mention T. E. Lawrence during my stay in Turkey, however), writing a fantasy trilogy set in an alternative Egypto-Byzantine universe (*Byzantium's Crown*, *The Woman of Flowers*, *Queensblade*), and setting out—so far, more's the pity, only in research and writing—from Byzantium along the ancient Silk Roads (*Silk Roads and Shadows*) into Central Asia, the site of several others of my books and collaborations (*Imperial Lady* and *Empire of the Eagle*, written with Andre Norton).

While in Cappadocia, I examined the millstones closing off the caves from the upper world, leaned backward out an air conduit, examined the depth of a grain bin, then asked my guide, "How would you attack one of these places?"

He had only himself to blame for such a question from the "lady novelist" placed in his care by the American Embassy, after all: he should never have told me the story of how the underground cities are allegedly joined by tunnels and connected to an as-yet-undiscovered central city—but I'm glad he did.

"I do hope," said Dr. Toni Cross, a classicist who is married to a Turkish economist and who directs American Research in Turkey (ARIT) in Ankara, "that this isn't going to be one of those books about the terrible Turks." All I can say is that it would be a very poor return on their hospitality if I did that. As John Keegan says, it is difficult to share a border with the steppe because you must confront wave after wave of predatory horsepeople.

But if horsepeople took away wealth, I took away memories of an unforgettable trip, my pictures of the caves, and this story. I even have my own physical shards: a chunk of fool's gold I picked up on the mound at Gordion that's commonly referred to as Midas's tomb, and a sharp-edged fragment of obsidian I grubbed out of an earth road across from the Salt Lake.

In keeping with Clausewitz's aphorism about the "fog of war," a great deal of dispute still exists over the August 1071 battle of Manzikert in Eastern Turkey. Most contemporary European scholars accept August 19 as the date, while almost all modern Turkish scholars conclude that it occurred on August 26. As was the case at the time, people still debate the abilities before, during, and after the battle of Romanus IV Diogenes, yet another in the procession of imperial military husbands who propped up a throne that had deteriorated rather markedly since the glory days (about 1025) of Basil the Bulgar-Slayer, the role played by Romanus's Norman mercenaries, who withdrew to sit the battle out, the family factions in Constantinople, chiefly those of Caesar John Ducas, his son Andronicus Ducas, who withdrew at the worst possible moment at Manzikert, and the role played by historian, politician, and (to this more-than-skeptical critic) time-server Michael Psellus.

Since I am not, by any stretch of even the most charitable imagination, a Byzantine scholar, I shall simply refer readers to standard works on the period, such as those by Vryonis and Ostrogorsky, and restrict myself to creating story, rather than popular history. I must express my gratitude to Harvard University's Center for Byzantine Studies at Dumbarton Oaks, in Washington, D.C., for its hospitality and forbearance, especially Dr. Irene Vaslev and Mark Zapatka.

In its day, the battle of Manzikert was regarded as crucial. Not only was it, as has been said in another context, a day that would live in infamy, it was the "dreadful day" from which Byzantium never recovered. An Emperor of the Romans had been taken, for the first time since the emperor Valerian surrendered to Shapur I of Persia in 270. Manzikert was even more of a debacle for Byzantium than the battle of Adrianople in 378, in which Valens, emperor in the East, died fighting the Goths (shortly after the death in 363 of Julian the Apostate while on campaign in Persia).

Runciman points out in his *History of the Crusades* that "the Byzantines themselves had no illusions about it. . . . Again and again their historians refer to that dreadful day." Because of the vulnerability of Asia Minor now to the *Dar al-Islam*, a balance of power in that area was shattered. With Byzantium now more vulnerable than ever to the forces of Islam, western rulers—and clerics—saw opportunity and provocation for the Crusades, which received further impetus when Michael VII, Romanus IV's immediate successor, appealed to Rome for help. *La Chanson de Roland,* with its ferocious opposition between pagan and Christian, jihad versus Church Militant, also dates from about this time.

The first of the Crusades reached Constantinople, by then under the rule of the capable and wily Alexius Comnenus, who figures briefly, but notably in this story as well. He was able to withstand and circumvent the Westerners (as readers will see in a subsequent book of mine): other Emperors were far from that fortunate; and ultimately, even before the Turks took it in 1453, Constantinople was sacked by the forces of the Christian West.

What I hope in this explanation to do is convey some sense of the overlays of history in the area. Now, as then, Turkey is a gateway through which many peoples have passed and which many nations have fought to hold. Take, for example, the city of Amasya. It is a pretty town, used in the Ottoman Empire to house dissident nobles. Romanus passed through it in his attempts to regain his Empire. And it was old then. A visitor to this town can see the layers upon layers of history: an Ottoman house stands by a railroad and tunnel that could probably date from the time of Ataturk. Above the tunnel, Pontic tombs stare out blankly as a muezzin—not a tape—calls today's Faithful to prayer.

I quite recognize that the task is as presumptuous as it was exciting, and I would like, for the benefit of readers whom I hope may be as fascinated by the Near East as I, to cite some of the sources I used.

For the reader who simply wants a "scorecard," Alfred Friendly's popularization, *That Dreadful Day: The Battle of Manzikert, 1071* (Hutchinson, London, 1981), will provide a start and some useful bibliographical material.

Thereafter, matters grow more complicated. First, the primary texts from the period. Chief among them for me were *Fourteen Byzantine Rulers: The Chronographia of Michael Psellus,* translated and with an introduction by E. R. A. Sewter, Penguin Books, and Anna Comnena's *Alexiad,* translated by A. S. Daws as well as by Professor Sewter. Dr. Harry Turtledove was kind enough to allow me to use his manuscript translation of Michael Attaleiates, a partisan of Romanus who wrote an eyewitness account and whose will provides interesting insights into Byzantine private life. I have made him a friend to Leo Ducas, and I hope he would not have minded too much breaking in an aristocratic recruit.

Helping to explain the players, who are every bit as complicated as the Julio-Claudians in the West, is Demetrios Polemis' *The Doukai: A Contribution to Byzantine Prosopography* (University of London, 1968). Thereafter, I follow the histories, chief among them Speros Vyronis' magisterial *The Decline of Medieval Hellenism in Asia Minor and the Process of Islamization from the Eleventh through the Fifteenth Century* (Berkeley/Los Angeles/London, 1971). Much of his research on the period, on Turks, and on Manzikert in particular appear in the following: "Nomadization and Islamization in Asia Minor," Dumbarton Oaks Papers 29, 1975, and "The Internal History of Byzantium During the Time of Troubles, 1057–81," which is drawn from Professor Vyronis' doctoral dissertation at Harvard University.

In regard to the people and their actual history, I apologize for grafting Leo and his parents onto the already turbulent Ducas family. I make no excuse for Andronicus Ducas' conduct. I also admit that I've mishandled Michael Psellus. He is a superb writer and chronicler of the times, but nevertheless a self-satisfied and ambitious man for whom I conceived an extreme dislike; and his letter to the blinded Romanus is nothing short of vicious.

Also alive at the time of Manzikert was Alexius Comnenus, who would become emperor in his own right. As pragmatic as he was able, he married Irene, daughter of Andronicus Ducas. Among his children was Anna Comnena, the historian and rebel who chronicled the coming of the western knights in the First Crusade. Even allowing for his daughter's adoration, Alexius was a remarkably capable and skilled ruler. As a sidenote, I learned that Alexius befriended the sons of Romanus IV Diogenes. One—and I discovered this after naming my own characters—was named Leo.

For information on the Turkish tribes, there is the monumental work by Maenchen-Helfen, *The World of the Huns*, which cites Ammianus Marcellinus on the Huns. I also used Rene Grousset's *A History of Central Asia* (Rutgers University Press) and S. R. Turnbull's *The Mongols* in the invaluable Osprey Men at Arms series, which also provided me with a volume on Byzantine armies. The story of the *gulam* who captured the Byzantine emperor is true. What happened next to him is my invention.

For archeological materials, I am indebted to my visits to the Ethnological Museum of Ankara, which contains treasures from the excavations of Catal Höyük, one of the oldest human habitations on earth, numerous carved Hittite *arslans*, and many goddess images, from stately figures of Cybele to the tremendously beautiful figures of the Mother

Goddess such as we are more familiar with from the Willendorf Venus. In this context, I found Marija Gimbutas' *The Goddesses and Gods of Old Europe 6500–3500 B.C.: Myths and Cult Images* (University of California Press, 1982), as fascinating as it is controversial. I consider *Hagia Sophia* (Turizm Yayinlari Ltd., 1985) by Erdem Yucel, director of the museum of Hagia Sophia very helpful. Unfortunately, I lost a companion pamphlet about the cistern of Justinian and have only my own photographs and the account of Ms. Marta Grabien to remind me of the existence of the Medusa at the base of the pillar.

Judaica plays a great role in *Shards of Empire*. From the medieval period, I drew *The Itinerary of Benjamin of Tudela*, and also found helpful Elizabeth Revel Nehen's *The Image of the Jew in Byzantine Art* (Pergamon Press). Most helpful to me was Joshua Starr's 1935 book, *The Jews in the Byzantine Empire* (Texte und Forschungen zur Byzantinisch-Neugraekischen Philologie). As an example of the kind of sidenote that occurs in the type of research one does for novels like *Shards of Empire*, I discovered that Starr was a student of Gershom Scholem, the Cabbalist scholar.

Also helpful were *The World History of the Jewish People* (Medieval Period, Vol. II, London 1966) edited by Cecil Roth, et al., and Robert S. Lopez's seminal 1945 article, "The Silk Industry and Byzantine Europe" (*Speculum*), which documents the role of the Jews in the silk trade. Scholars at the Metropolitan Museum of Fine Arts in New York have assured me that I can safely push back the rug trade, which is still active in Cappadocia, into the late eleventh century. For a more recent history of the rugs that are called "Turkish," I used *Contemporary Hand-Made Turkish Carpets*, by Ugur Ayyildiz (Turistik Yayinlari, Istanbul). Cappadocia, in particular Ürgup (Hagios Prokopios) and Göreme, is still a center for the rug trade, and I have the bills to prove it.

Jewish trading families were well documented, both in the Empire and along the trade routes as far as Ch'ang-an, and a Jewish marriage contract from the second decade of the eleventh century survives. (See *A History of Private Life*, edited by Philippe Ariès and Georges Duby, Evelyne Patlagean's "Byzantium in the Tenth and Eleventh Centuries.")

Cappadocia has long been a site of Christian habitation and prayer. St. Paul passed through it in his third journey, and, in the fourth century, it was associated with famous theologians such as St. Basil, "light of the Cappadocians, or rather of the world," along with Gregory of Nyssa and Gregory of Nazianzus. Leo the Deacon mentions the cave dwellings in Cappadocia as being commonplace in the tenth century. Until relatively recently, the caves were inaccessible to the West. Paul Lucas, traveling at the orders of the Sun King, was the first European traveler to reach Cappadocia. In 1718, he published a highly colored account of his journey. Missionaries ventured into it in the nineteenth century, occasionally dying of exhaustion. The scholar Hans Rott visited the site in 1906, and Fr. Guillaume de Jerphanion, whose impressive work on the valleys, *Une nouvelle province de l'art byzantin* (Paris, 1925–1942), is still a classic, in 1907.

Among the books I consulted on this fascinating and formerly inaccessible area were *Caves of God: Cappadocia and Its Churches*, by Spiro Kostof (Oxford Univ. Press, 1989); Lynn Rodley's *Cave Monasteries of Byzantine Cappadocia* (Cambridge, 1985); Rowland J. Manston's 1958 typescript of "Notes on Rock-Cut Churches of Cappadocia" (preserved in the Center for Byzantine Studies at Dumbarton Oaks); *Tenth-Century Metropolitan Art in Byzantine Cappadocia*, by Ann Wharton Epstein (Dumbarton Oaks, 1986); and Fatih Cimok's *Cappadocia* (Istanbul).

For the underground cities, I relied upon my own experience (the caves have been partially electrified, but exploration of them is incomplete) and on Omer Demir's *Cappadocia, Cradle of History* (Ankara, 1990). This is a charmingly quirky volume, which assigns to rooms in Derinkuyu an insane asylum, a church, and places for tying up prisoners. Demir speaks of the tunnels between cities and mentions the graves in the underground cities. He also mentions the discovery of the mummified body of a young girl in Ihlara Valley (Peristrema), one of the most remote of the Cappadocian monastic communities and cut by the Melendiz River to the depth of 150 meters, which is where I placed Father Meletios and his friends. The tunnel joining Ihlara with the underground cities is, of course, a figment of my imagination.

I have taken considerable liberty with distances between Ihlara and the underground cities, the underground cities and Hagios Prokopios. It's known that a Turkish mount could cover 40 miles in a day and perhaps 60. The Cappadocian horses were good, but the Greeks rode, by and large, heavier than the Turks. Still, if you work on the assumption that Leo and his people rode flat out and the shortest way possible—and that it was a *very* hard ride (though hardly impossible for people like Asherah and her father, who were hardened by travel along the caravan routes), you can about make the distances work. Demir makes the correspondences between Derinkuyu ("deep well") and Malagobia ("difficult subsistence") and identifies Kaymakli with Enegobi. I was delighted to read Allen Varney's "Turkey's Underground Cities" (*Dragon*, #201, January 1994, pp. 16–23), and am indebted to John Bunnell, Barbara Young, and Dr. Esther Friesner for pointing it out to me. I should add that the city I chose to use in *Shards of Empire* was Derinkuyu.

From either Ürgup or Ihlara, you can see mountain peaks from far off. In May 1990, they were snow-capped. Hasan Dagi is probably the more visible from Ihlara, but I chose to refer to Mt. Argaeus (Erciyas Dugi) to the East since it is the tallest in the region and I had a contemporary name for it, as I did not for Hasan Dagi.

Any work with Manzikert or Byzantium, in my opinion, demands some research into Byzantine military history. The Byzantines were among the best military administrators, paymasters, and spymasters of the medieval world. I began with Ian Heath's *Byzantine Armies, 886–1118* in the Osprey Series, and matters grew substantially more complex from there. While at Dumbarton Oaks, I was delighted to meet (and, in the immemorial fashion of armchair *strategoi*, to deploy pens, pencils, and pieces of paper to represent the various forces at Manzikert) Fr. George Dennis, S.J., translator of *Three Byzantine Military Treatises* (Dumbarton Oaks Press, 1985), including "On Guerrilla Warfare" attributed to Nicephorus Phocas, and *The Strategikon of Maurice* (University of Pennsylvania, 1984). Also useful were two unpublished doctoral dissertations: "Aspects of Byzantine Military Administration: The Elite Corps, the Opsikion, and the Imperial Tagmata from the Sixth to the Ninth Century," J. F. Haldon, Ph.D., University of Birmingham, 1975; and J. S. Howard-Johnston's "Studies in the Organization of the Byzantine Army in the Tenth and Eleventh Centuries," Oxford University, June 4, 1971.

You may regard all of these references as shards, as carefully pieced together as I could, into a mosaic that is definitely *not* the pattern of history, but that I hope you will find as much pleasure in reading as I found in assembling.

Susan Shwartz
December 1995